DISCARDED
Huron Public Library

PRAISE FOR

Blood Wyne

"Readers are in for an action-packed ride that is sexy to the max!"
—*Romantic Times Book Reviews*

"The Otherworld novels are always fun, sexy, and magical, and *Blood Wyne* is no different."
—*Fresh Fiction*

"*Blood Wyne* has action, sizzling romance, and some majorly startling discoveries that will cost dearly . . . This series just gets better and better!"
—*The Bibliophilic Book Blog*

Harvest Hunting

"Fast-paced and filled with action, this series continues to capture the reader and keep them on their toes . . . Ms. Galenorn delivers a fantastic adventure that leaves the reader satisfied and yet wanting more."
—*Night Owl Paranormal*

"Yasmine Galenorn just keeps upping the intensity in the Otherworld series with each successive book. Don't miss a single page."
—*A Romance Review*

"Heartbreaking and enlightening with twists and turns that will surprise all of us who are fans of the series—and leave us eager for the next book. A five-star read!"
—*Fresh Fiction*

Bone Magic

"Erotic and darkly bewitching, *Bone Magic* turns up the heat on the D'Artigo sisters. Galenorn writes another winner in the Otherworld series, a mix of magic and passion sure to captivate readers."
—Jeaniene Frost, *New York Times* bestselling author

"Quite simply A-M-A-Z-I-N-G!"
—*Sidhe Vicious Reviews*

continued . . .

Demon Mistress

"As always, [Galenorn] delivers intriguing characters, intricate plot layers, and kick-butt action." —*Romantic Times* (four stars)

"*Demon Mistress* is just as exciting as the last episode in the Otherworld series." —*The Romance Readers Connection*

"The tense fights, frights, and demon-bashing take front and center in this book, and I love that . . . All in all, *Demon Mistress* certainly makes for enjoyable summertime reading!"
—*Errant Dreams Reviews*

Night Huntress

"Yasmine Galenorn is a hot new star in the world of urban fantasy. The Otherworld series is wonderfully entertaining."
—Jayne Ann Krentz,
New York Times bestselling author

"Yasmine Galenorn is a powerhouse author; a master of the craft who is taking the industry by storm, and for good reason!"
—Maggie Shayne,
New York Times bestselling author

"Yasmine Galenorn hits the stars with *Night Huntress*. Urban fantasy at its best!" —Stella Cameron,
New York Times bestselling author

"Fascinating and eminently enjoyable from the first page to the last . . . *Night Huntress* rocks! Don't miss it!"
—*Romance Reviews Today*

"Love and betrayal play large roles in *Night Huntress*, and as the story unfolds, the action will sweep fans along for this fast-moving ride." —*Darque Reviews*

Dragon Wytch

"Action and sexy sensuality make this book hot to the touch."
—*Romantic Times* (four stars)

"Ms. Galenorn has a great gift for spinning a compelling story. The supernatural action is a great blend of both fresh and familiar, the characters are each charming in their own way, the heroine's love life is scorching, and the worlds they all live in are well-defined."
—*Darque Reviews*

"This is the kind of series that even those who do not care for the supernatural will find a very good read."
—*Affaire de Coeur*

"If you're looking for an out-of-this-world enchanting tale of magic and passion, *Dragon Wytch* is the story for you. I will be recommending this wickedly bewitching tale to everyone I know!"
—*Dark Angel Reviews*

Darkling

"The most fulfilling journey of self-discovery to date in the Otherworld series . . . An eclectic blend that works well."
—*Booklist*

"Galenorn does a remarkable job of delving into the psyches and fears of her characters. As this series matures, so do her heroines. The sex sizzles and the danger fascinates."
—*Romantic Times*

"The story is nonstop action and has deep, dark plots that kept me up reading long past my bedtime. Here be dark fantasy with a unique twist. YES!"
—*Huntress Book Reviews*

continued . . .

Changeling

"The second in Galenorn's D'Artigo Sisters series ratchets up the danger and romantic entanglements. Along with the quirky humor and characters readers have come to expect is a moving tale of a woman more comfortable in her cat skin than in her human form, looking to find her place in the world." —*Booklist*

"Galenorn's thrilling supernatural series is gritty and dangerous, but it's the tumultuous relationships between all the various characters that give it depth and heart. Vivid, sexy, and mesmerizing, Galenorn's novel hits the paranormal sweet spot."
—*Romantic Times*

"I absolutely loved it!" —*Fresh Fiction*

"Yasmine Galenorn has created another winner . . . *Changeling* is a can't-miss read destined to hold a special place on your keeper shelf." —*Romance Reviews Today*

Witchling

"Reminiscent of Laurell K. Hamilton with a lighter touch . . . a delightful new series that simmers with fun and magic."
—Mary Jo Putney, *New York Times* bestselling author

"The first in an engrossing new series . . . a whimsical reminder of fantasy's importance in everyday life." —*Publishers Weekly*

"*Witchling* is pure delight . . . a great heroine, designer gear, dead guys, and Seattle precipitation!"
—MaryJanice Davidson, *New York Times* bestselling author

"*Witchling* is one sexy, fantastic paranormal-mystery-romantic read." —Terese Ramin, author of *Shotgun Honeymoon*

"Galenorn's kick-butt Fae ramp up the action in a wyrd world gone awry . . . I loved it!"
—Patricia Rice, *New York Times* bestselling author

"A fun read, filled with surprise and enchantment."
—Linda Winstead Jones, author of *Last of the Ravens*

Titles by Yasmine Galenorn

The Otherworld Series

WITCHLING
CHANGELING
DARKLING
DRAGON WYTCH
NIGHT HUNTRESS
DEMON MISTRESS
BONE MAGIC
HARVEST HUNTING
BLOOD WYNE
COURTING DARKNESS

The Indigo Court Series

NIGHT MYST
NIGHT VEIL

Anthologies

INKED
NEVER AFTER
HEXED

Berkley Prime Crime titles by Yasmine Galenorn

GHOST OF A CHANCE
LEGEND OF THE JADE DRAGON
MURDER UNDER A MYSTIC MOON
A HARVEST OF BONES
ONE HEX OF A WEDDING

* * *

Yasmine Galenorn writing as India Ink

SCENT TO HER GRAVE
A BLUSH WITH DEATH
GLOSSED AND FOUND

Courting Darkness

An Otherworld Novel

YASMINE GALENORN

JOVE BOOKS, NEW YORK

THE BERKLEY PUBLISHING GROUP
Published by the Penguin Group
Penguin Group (USA) Inc.
375 Hudson Street, New York, New York 10014, USA
Penguin Group (Canada), 90 Eglinton Avenue East, Suite 700, Toronto, Ontario M4P 2Y3, Canada
(a division of Pearson Penguin Canada Inc.)
Penguin Books Ltd., 80 Strand, London WC2R 0RL, England
Penguin Group Ireland, 25 St. Stephen's Green, Dublin 2, Ireland (a division of Penguin Books Ltd.)
Penguin Group (Australia), 250 Camberwell Road, Camberwell, Victoria 3124, Australia
(a division of Pearson Australia Group Pty. Ltd.)
Penguin Books India Pvt. Ltd., 11 Community Centre, Panchsheel Park, New Delhi—110 017, India
Penguin Group (NZ), 67 Apollo Drive, Rosedale, Auckland 0632, New Zealand
(a division of Pearson New Zealand Ltd.)
Penguin Books (South Africa) (Pty.) Ltd., 24 Sturdee Avenue, Rosebank, Johannesburg 2196,
South Africa

Penguin Books Ltd., Registered Offices: 80 Strand, London WC2R 0RL, England

COURTING DARKNESS

A Jove Book / published by arrangement with the author

PRINTING HISTORY
Jove mass-market edition / November 2011

Copyright © 2011 by Yasmine Galenorn.
Excerpt from *Shaded Vision* copyright © by Yasmine Galenorn.
Cover art by Tony Mauro.
Cover design by Rita Frangie.

ISBN: 978-0-515-15007-0

JOVE®
Jove Books are published by The Berkley Publishing Group,
a division of Penguin Group (USA) Inc.,
375 Hudson Street, New York, New York 10014.
JOVE® is a registered trademark of Penguin Group (USA) Inc.
The "J" design is a trademark of Penguin Group (USA) Inc.

PRINTED IN THE UNITED STATES OF AMERICA

10 9 8 7 6 5 4 3 2 1

Dedicated to
all the musicians who inspire me . . .
Music feeds my soul.

ACKNOWLEDGMENTS

Thank you to my beloved Samwise—my biggest, strongest, and cutest fan.

And my gratitude to my agent, Meredith Bernstein, and to my editor, Kate Seaver—thank you both for helping me stretch my wings and fly. A salute to Tony Mauro, cover artist extraordinaire. To my furry little "Galenorn Gurlz," LOLcats in their own right. Most reverent devotion to Ukko, Rauni, Mielikki, and Tapio, my spiritual guardians.

And the biggest thank-you of all—to my readers, both old and new. Your support helps keep the series going. You can find me on the Internet at Galenorn En/Visions: www.galenorn.com. For links to social networking sites where you can find me, see my website. I'm on Twitter and Facebook.

If you write to me snail mail (see my website for the address or write via my publisher), please enclose a self-addressed stamped envelope with your letter if you would like a reply. Promo goodies are available—see my site for info.

The Painted Panther
Yasmine Galenorn

Revenge does not long remain unavenged.

—GERMAN PROVERB

The most dangerous creation of any society is the man who has nothing to lose.

—JAMES A. BALDWIN

Chapter 1

Home.

There it was—waiting for us. Home, with smoke drifting from the chimney and an array of multicolored sparkling lights surrounding the porch. From the driveway, the three-story Victorian shimmered like a beacon, both on the physical and on the astral. Flares of energy shot up like sunspots. I leaned back in the car, smiling. *Home.* Our haven against the demons.

A dragon built from snow guarded the lawn and driveway, rising stark and white out of the banks piled high around the yard. My herb garden hid under the creature, nestled under mulch until spring. Winter had claimed the land, full force, and we were getting hit hard. La Niña held sway, and we were all her toys. At least it wasn't Loki this time. The Norse giant had brought unnatural amounts of ice and snow with him a year ago, until we'd dispatched his servant, a vampire named Dredge.

But as cold as it was, this was nothing compared to the Northlands, from where I'd just returned. There, in the high reaches near the top of the world, the winds had raged starkly through the winter woodland, shaking the timbers and sending avalanches down the mountainsides.

Up in the Northlands, life was harsh and often short, and fire became a lifeline. The Northmen were as stoic as they sounded, and they partied hearty—there might not be another day to live, facing the dangers they faced.

As Smoky, Iris, Rozurial, and I had struggled through the woods, ranging higher and higher toward the lair of Howl, the Elemental Wolf Lord of the snow, more than once I thought sure we'd end up as Popsicles, frozen to the rocks.

But the trip had been worth it. Iris had come to terms with her past and forged a future for herself. She stood clear and free, able to marry the man she loved. But she'd been through hell, and now she, like me, faced a path that promised to swallow her up, to force her into a position she wasn't sure she was ready to shoulder. And to mark the changes, she was now sporting spiffy—well, beautiful—indigo tattoos that spiraled their way across her forehead, down her cheeks, and across her back. Her goddess had marked her, and marked her in the most ornate manner. The gods seemed to like to brand us with divine ink.

The car slowed to a stop and Delilah turned off the engine. The weariness of the past few months welled up in my throat as I pushed open the door. So much had happened, and yet so much still lay before us. We were barely a week from midwinter, and I was facing initiation into Aeval's Court, where I would willingly hand myself over to the Dark Queen to learn her magic and the ways of a priestess.

As I let out a long breath and climbed out of the Jeep, a crisp wind swept through the night and I pulled the elfin robe tighter around me. I was wearing the cloak of the Black Beast beneath that, but even with both, they couldn't fend off the chill that had lodged itself in my bones and I wondered if I'd ever manage to shake it off and feel the warmth again.

"You okay?" Delilah wrapped her arm around my shoulders. She'd picked us up at Grandmother Coyote's portal and now all I wanted was a hot bath, a soft bed, and a lot of sleep.

As Smoky hopped out of her Jeep, then helped Iris to the ground, Roz slowly hoisted himself out the other side.

"You're a good sister," I said, leaning against her arm. "I'm just tired. The journey was harder than I thought it would be. It was cold—so cold. And there were ice spiders—"

"Yuck." She wrinkled her nose. "How'd it go? Did Iris . . ."

I just shook my head. "It's her place to tell you about it, but, yes. She's still with us, and Vikkommin is dead for good. She survived and broke the curse. But the Northlands are terrifying. I'd hate to be trapped there. It's not a vacation home in the tropics, that's for sure. I don't know if I'd have the strength to face the raw elements without a lot of help. All I know is that I don't want to visit again for a long, long time."

We headed toward the house just as Menolly came racing out, the beads in her braids clicking in the chill night. She was carrying my purse.

"Finally! I've been waiting at the door for you. I just got a call from Derrick. We've got problems. Turn right around and head for the cars. Sorry to do this to you, Camille, but you need to be there." She motioned toward my Lexus. "Hurry up."

"I don't want to hurry *anywhere*. What the hell is going on?" My heart sank. I was tired. I didn't want to fight goblins or ghosts.

"Demon in the bar, demanding to talk to you. He's already mowed down an elf and Derrick's got him in a standoff. Iris, you, Roz, and Vanzir stay with Morio and Maggie. Shade and Trillian are on their way—there they are!"

Shade, Delilah's new love, and Trillian—my alpha husband—rushed out of the house and clambered down the steps. Shade was part dragon, part Stradolan—a shadow walker. Trillian was Svartan: one of the dark and Charming Fae. They both wore jeans and heavy jackets, and Trillian was carrying a serrated-edged sword with which he'd recently taken up training.

"Demon? Asking for *me*? How delightful. *Not*." I didn't bother asking if they knew why he wanted me. I'd find out soon enough, and probably—knowing my luck—I'd find out the hard way.

Menolly whipped around, barking out orders. "Delilah— you and Shade take your Jeep." She tossed me my purse and keys. "Camille, here you go. You drive Smoky and Trillian. I'll go in alone."

And once again, we moved to our respective cars, off and running. There was no more downtime, anymore. Everything had taken on an immediacy. With that thought, I put the Lexus in gear and—as Smoky and Trillian jumped in— hit the gas and plowed out of the driveway.

Holiday shoppers abounded and I groaned, looking for a parking space as people rushed by with bags and boxes, shiny paper and bows glimmering under the streetlamps. The Wayfarer Bar & Grill wasn't exactly located in an area that promised shopping Nirvana, but there were plenty of small boutiques ready to cater to the odd and unusual. Like Hot 'n Bothered, the sex shop that had gone in next door. On one hand, it had proved to be a bonanza of new clients for Menolly. On the other, a lot of seedy guys came in, trolling for "dates."

We pulled into a parking place that miraculously opened up in front of the Wayfarer. With a quick nod to the parking goddess, I forced myself out of the driver's seat. Holiday season? Open parking spot on one of Seattle's city streets? Insanely hard to find at best. But I seemed to have a knack for locating them, and I embraced my luck. Hell, considering the rest of my track record when it came to serendipity, I considered the smallest good fortune cause for celebration.

As Trillian opened the door for me, I paused to give him a long kiss. "I missed you," I whispered, getting some tongue action in while I could. He felt warm in my arms, and smelled of apples and cinnamon. "I missed you a lot."

"Tonight, we'll see about wiping away those longings." He brushed my hair back from my face. "I never spend an hour without thinking about you."

Smoky grunted. "There's time enough for that later. Come.

We have a situation to take care of. And Trillian, I assure you, I took pains to make sure our wife didn't miss you *or* the fox too terribly." He arched his eyebrows in a knowing way, and two tendrils of his hair rose to wrap themselves around my shoulders, tickling me as Trillian glowered.

I bit back a retort. My three husbands were constantly zinging each other, each one striving for the top place in my heart, but I knew that beneath all the bluster and insults, they'd developed a healthy respect for one another. None of them would ever admit it, but I suspected they even liked each other—at least a little. On more than one occasion I'd caught Smoky and Trillian playing chess, or Morio helping Smoky carry in firewood without being asked.

From the outside, the bar looked normal, but I could hear the commotion from the inside. We trailed behind Menolly as she slammed her way through the doors. She owned the Wayfarer Bar & Grill, and it was a hangout for Supes from all backgrounds, as well as the first stop on the journey for a number of Otherworld visitors. And now, the Wayfarer also sported seven rooms, a makeshift bed and breakfast.

It had proved extremely popular and was full up almost every night. Menolly had hired a maid just to keep up with the cleaning, and a second cook for the grill.

As we hit the polished wood floors, I skidded to a halt, catching my breath. The bar patrons were crowded against the back wall, huddled together, looking terrified. Some were trying to edge toward a side exit, but for the most part, they clung together in a little clump, afraid to move. I turned to see what was holding them hostage.

At the front of the bar, a demon watched them, his head bobbing back and forth like a cobra in front of a snake charmer. There was no passing for any generic Supe with this creature. He looked like the full-fledged demon of nightmares—with smoky skin, and coiled horns rising high over his head. His skin, leathery and taut, shimmered across muscle hard enough to beat a sledgehammer against. He towered seven feet high on cloven hooves, and his hands bore long, razor-sharp nails.

And he was standing over one very dead body.

"Sure enough, that's a demon all right . . . I think." For some reason, he didn't seem to have quite the same energy as most of the demons I'd met, but they weren't all alike, I reminded myself. And besides . . . if it looks like a demon, and it fights like a demon . . . then it's probably not a duck.

Derrick, the werebadger bartender, had wedged himself between the patrons and the demon, a sawed-off shotgun aimed at the creature. I bit my tongue. That gun had a better chance of tickling the hell spawn than it did of hurting him.

Menolly gazed at the body on the floor and let out a low whistle. "Yeah, that's one dead elf, all right."

I nodded. "And one freaky-assed demon."

We were too late to help the elf, but with a little luck, we might be able to prevent wholesale carnage. We spread out, motioning for Derrick to move to one side. He waited for Menolly's okay, then nodded and stepped out of the way. As I turned toward the creature, I wondered just what kind it was. There were as many types of demons as there were spiders, it seemed. Unfortunately, we'd become familiar enough with some to name them on sight, but this one . . . I was clueless as to what we were dealing with.

Vanzir could have told us what we were facing, but I really didn't feel comfortable having him and Smoky in the same room just yet. Smoky still didn't know what had happened between us, and I intended to keep it that way, at least until I could ensure he wouldn't go wholesale whomp-ass on Vanzir.

Menolly snarled. "What the fuck are you doing in my bar? Get your ass back to the Sub-Realms, and tell Shadow Wing we said hello." She strode forward, but the demon raised his head and his gaze caught her full on. She let out a squeak and dropped to the floor.

I rushed over to help her, but before I could get there, she scrambled back up and shook her head, looking stunned. "What the hell . . ."

Damn, this was not the time for Morio to be laid up. Our death magic was far more powerful than my Moon magic, and we might be able to corral the demon with a spell. But he still had a long ways to go before he was healed up and would be out of commission for at least three or four more weeks. The hungry ghosts from our last skirmish had siphoned a dangerous amount of life force off him and left him bedridden for now.

"Stand your ground." The creature spoke. "I bring you a message from Trytian."

Trytian? Holy crap, this thing wasn't a demon—it was a *daemon!* No wonder we hadn't been able to tell what it was. Daemons and demons tended to be enemies, and the daemons were not thrilled with Shadow Wing moving in on their territory. They had formed an underground resistance movement, along with some of the unhappier demons, and were working against Shadow Wing the way we were, both down in the Subterranean Realms and here, Earthside.

Well, they weren't *exactly* following our model. Not so much. We tried to avoid collateral damage. They didn't give a fuck.

"What does he want?" I didn't trust Trytian. Not only was he a daemon, but he'd tried to blow us up when we were fighting Stacia Bonecrusher, a lamia/demon general/necromancer Shadow Wing had sent to destroy us. She'd turned rogue, but that hadn't meant she'd played things our way. Trytian had joined forces with her till we squashed her flat. Now he and his forces weren't exactly on the best of speaking terms with us, but we'd reached a rudimentary truce.

"You are the one named Camille?"

I nodded.

"I speak with you. Alone."

Alone? No way in freaking hell was I cozying up with this creature alone.

"Um. Can I just say, *no* and *are you out of your mind?* Trytian has to know better than that. Whatever you have to say, you can say it in front of the others."

I backed up, motioning for Delilah to get out of the way. If he could knock a vampire off her feet with just a look, I didn't want to see what he could do against someone who was still alive.

"You wish me to speak freely in front of all of these patrons? You really want them to know about Shadow—"

"Stop!" I glanced back at Menolly, and she read my expression.

We couldn't let him talk about Shadow Wing. No one in the general public knew that Earth was on the verge of a demonic war. *Yet*. And we were inclined to keep it that way in order to stave off panic. We were slowly gathering our allies, but no way in hell were we prepared to fight any sort of a demon army at this point.

"You can't seriously be thinking about talking to him in private? He's already killed one person." Menolly pointed toward the dead elf. "Just what are we going to tell Queen Asteria? Oh, she'll believe us, but do you think she's going to be thrilled?"

"You have a point." The Elfin Queen loved her people. In fact, she'd always been fair and just, if not totally aboveboard, with us, too. "But Menolly, I have to do what he wants." I lowered my voice so nobody but the nearest Supes could hear me. "Can you imagine the chaos if any one of those Faerie Maids over there huddled against the wall finds out there's a full-fledged daemon in the house? Demon, daemon, devil, they're not going to care. It's just going to mean panic. Right now, they still think this is some kind of Supe with a bad case of the grumps. We need to keep it that way."

Smoky glowered. "My wife is not going to snuggle up in a room alone with you, beast. I insist that someone else be present, and I claim the right."

The daemon looked at him, sniffing. "Dragon. Silver dragon—and white. A *mix*. The world is full of half-breeds tonight, it seems." He looked at Shade. "Half dragon, half shadow." Then, to my sisters and me, "And three human-Fae girls. Interbreeding weakens the strains, you know."

"Irrelevant." Smoky let out a loud *hrmph*.

The daemon cocked his head. "Now you, dragon, you are a lord among your kind, half-breed or not. And I do not play toad to royalty. There are reasons you will not be present, my own skin being one of them." His voice was harsh, like the vocal cords had been burned long ago, and he kept moving his head in a sinuous dance, as if he couldn't keep it still.

"Then my wife will not attend you."

"Actually, your wife *will* attend him." I glanced at Smoky. "I have to—we *can't* discuss these matters in public." Turning back to the daemon, I added, "We'll have our chat alone, but in a place of my choice."

It occurred to me that if we went to the safe room in the basement of the Wayfarer, the daemon wouldn't be able to (a) teleport out with me, (b) shoot magic at me, or (c) bathe me in fire. He could still break me in half, but if he'd wanted to do that, he already would have.

I pointed toward the floor. "Menolly, we need to use the room *downstairs*."

She frowned, then her eyes lit up. "Oh, *that* room. All right. Come, follow me. Don't hurt anybody and don't destroy anything, either of you. Daemon, I hold you on pain of death that you won't hurt my sister."

"As Trytian would say, big fucking whoop." The daemon grunted. Then, with a suspicious look, he followed Menolly, shaking the floor with each meaty step. I swung in behind. Smoky, Trillian, and Shade followed, leaving Delilah and the staff to take care of the dead elf and the frightened patrons.

Just what they were going to tell them, I wasn't sure, but I couldn't wait to hear the story they concocted. As it was, we were already in for a lot of damage control just from the daemon's appearance in the bar. Word would leak out, no matter what we did, and we didn't have cool blue flashy-flashy things like the *Men in Black* did. We were lacking somewhat in the mind-control department, and our glamour wouldn't work on a daemon.

Downstairs, we came to the safe room. No magic could enter here, nor any creature teleport in or out. All natural abilities were muted within the room. If a nuclear blast hit this bar, the safe room would stand.

I gazed at the door, swallowing my fear. The thought of being shut up alone with the daemon was daunting. Not so much fun. Not so safe. But because the alternative was worse, I gathered my courage and motioned for him to enter the room and, with a scowl, he ducked his head so that his horns cleared the archway. As I followed behind him, Menolly touched me on the arm.

"One peep and we're coming in. Don't get near him. He can't work his magic, but he could tear you apart."

"I know. Believe me, I know." And, reluctantly, I shut the door and turned to face the daemon, crossing my arms. The best defense was to show no fear. "Trytian has a message for me? Deliver it and then scram, hell spawn." I didn't bother asking for his name—chances were he wouldn't give it to me.

The daemon looked around. "A no-magic zone? Not stupid—not so stupid as some." A dark grimace crossed his face. "I would relish a fight with you, girl. And your friends. But this is not my battle to wage."

I decided to let that one pass. No need to press my luck. Letting out a long sigh, I asked, "What do you want? Why did you kill the elf upstairs?"

"He got in the way. He had to be eliminated." He said it nonchalantly. *Dare to interfere with the daemon? Poof— you die.*

"Again, I ask: What do you want?"

"I bear a warning from Trytian."

I rolled my eyes. "Why would he warn us about anything? He tried to kill us, for the sake of the gods." Not only that, but Trytian was rude. *Very rude.*

"I bring only the warning. I have no other answers for you."

Hmm . . . I played out the reasoning in my mind. The only reason Trytian would offer us a warning was if he anticipated needing our help in the future, which meant we would have a bargaining chip. Unless he'd suddenly sprouted wings and become a cute little cherub. I sincerely doubted the latter.

"Okay, I'm listening. What's so important that Trytian sent you over here to stir the pot? And why you—why not someone who can pass out on the streets?"

I leaned against the small bistro table that was pushed against one wall. The room showed signs of occupation—Erin, the daughter Menolly had sired into the vampiric life, was staying down here during the day, sleeping in safety until her room at the new Vampires Anonymous Shelter was ready. The bed was piled high with comfy blankets; there were cards and books on the table, and an empty bottle that had held blood.

"I was the only one available to send at the moment. Trust me, I do not enjoy playing messenger boy. But Trytian is my leader and I obey. Here." He handed me a letter. "You will understand why I did not want to be in the same room with your husband when you read it."

Oh hell. Something to do with Smoky. I couldn't imagine the daemon being that afraid of Trillian, and Morio was at home.

Gingerly, I took the paper and opened it. The writing was tight, neat, and precisely printed in red ink—at least I *hoped* it was ink, considering the color. As I began to read, I started to sink toward the floor, but one grunt from the daemon and I straightened back up again. No dropping my guard, not when we were alone together. No use asking for trouble.

I glanced up at the creature. "Wait here, please." Before he could say a word, I slipped out of the room and slammed the door, locking it behind me. He could hammer all he wanted on it, he was locked in there till doomsday if we wanted.

"What's going on? Are you all right?" Smoky leaned over me, looking for signs that the daemon had laid hands on me.

"I'm fine . . . at least physically. He gave me a letter from Trytian. If it's true, then you and I are fucked. Just plain and simple."

"Read it." Shade was staring at me, concern creasing his face.

I cleared my throat and held up the paper.

Rumors are running rife through the grapevine, but I assure you, this is no wives' tale. A white dragon was recently seen in the halls of the Demon Underground, hanging out with a

*snow monkey. He is not welcome here, but no one dares tell
a dragon to leave.*

   *Camille: Scuttlebutt is that he'll be marching in your
direction soon. He's made it known that you and your
husband are on his hit list. And frankly, though you and I
disagree on the method, all allies against Shadow Wing are
valuable at this point, and I may need to call on your aid at
some point. So be cautious and don't get yourself killed.*

Trytian

I shuddered, letting out a long breath as the world crowded
in too closely around me. *Hyto* was in the area.

Hyto had thrown a fit when he found out Smoky had married me. It had driven the already dangerous dragon over the
edge, and now he had a vendetta going against us.

And now, he was on the rampage. A dragon as lecherous
and deadly as any demon ever could be, he'd tried to kill
Smoky's mother for denying him. He'd decided *I* was to
blame for his being thrown out of the Dragon Reaches and
turned pariah. And now, Hyto wanted both Smoky and me
dead—*worse than dead*. Hyto wanted revenge.

Smoky's pleasant demeanor drained away and his eyes
began to swirl. Very softly, very slowly, he spoke. "My father
has just signed his death warrant."

"Crap." Menolly leaned against the wall. "He's here, in
Seattle? Not the news we needed right now."

I fingered the paper. "What's a snow monkey? Why
would he have an ape with him?"

"Trytian's not talking about an animal," Shade said. "A
snow monkey is slang for a monk from one of the upper
monasteries in the Northlands. Usually, snow monkeys are
rogues—having been either kicked out of their order or leaving of their own accord. They're most often mad as a hornet,
and they don't give a damn about anybody but themselves.
It's not hard to buy one of them off. And if one's taken up
with Smoky's father, then he's bound to have been offered
plenty of money. They're dangerous." He gave me a sad
smile. "I'd start watching my back if I were you."

"Like we haven't been already." Sighing, I leaned against the wall, letting them talk around me.

Mad monks were bad enough, but the thought of Hyto being so close—the thought of him actually being in the city—made me want to run screaming home to Otherworld. But I couldn't do that, either. My father had exiled me from Y'Elestrial. Oh, I could go back to OW, but I couldn't go home again.

Smoky's father . . . Hyto *hated* me. He hated my breath, my life, my very existence. He had nothing to lose. He'd been cast out of the Dragon Reaches, denied by his wife, disowned by his children. And he blamed it all on *me*. The memory of his hands on me the one time we'd had the misfortune to meet still gave me the creeps.

My cell phone rang, and I flipped it open. Caller ID told me it was Chase Johnson. I punched Talk and answered.

"Camille—I was hoping you were back. I need you down here. We've got a problem in Tangleroot Park, and I am pretty sure it's magical in nature. In fact, I almost pissed my pants when I saw it. There's some really funky energy running around lately. I've got my guys blocking it off for now, but I'm scared to try anything before you come have a look-see."

"*It?* What are you talking about? A monster or something?"

"I don't think so. Honestly? I'll bet you my paycheck it's a portal of some sort. And I can hear singing through it. The voices call to me, Camille. I hate to say it, but I'm afraid. I get near and all I want to do is run through it."

My blood ran cold. Hyto was my big worry right now, but he wasn't standing here in front of me. First, if Chase was right and there was a portal opening up in Tangleroot Park, we could be in for big trouble of a different sort. Because the random portals that had started showing themselves around the city were rogue, and could lead anywhere—and could have anybody on the other side, waiting to come through. Second, if it was calling loud enough that Chase could hear it, who else might sense its presence?

"We'll get our asses over there right now. Meanwhile,

don't let anybody touch it or go near it." As I shut my phone, it occurred to me that my life was quickly coming to resemble a roller coaster, and right now, we felt at the peak, poised to take a long, dark ride down the tracks.

Chapter 2

Smoky was all for killing the daemon, but I shook my head. "Better to keep Trytian on our side. After all, he did warn us about your father. And if we kill the thing, Trytian will be in our face about it. Right now, we don't need that."

"We can't just let it run around the streets loose. What will people say?" Shade stared at me for a moment, then burst into a peal of laughter. "I can't believe I just said that, considering some of what you've told me about your exploits, but still . . . a daemon?"

Menolly held up her hand. "Let me attend to it." She disappeared inside the room, and a moment later she came out, the daemon in hand. He flashed her a guilty look, then cleared his throat.

"I'll cause no more trouble. Any return message for Trytian?"

I blinked. What the fuck had she said to him? Oh well, whatever it was, it seemed to have worked. "Tell him we'll be on the lookout and do our best to stop the dragon. Tell him . . . thank him for the information. He didn't have to tell me."

The daemon nodded, then started to head for the stairs.

"Wait!" I called out. He turned around. "Let me cast a cloaking spell over you. You simply can't go wandering around the streets looking like you do."

A sly smile stole across his face. "You want to try, girl?"

I nodded, even though Trillian and Menolly were both frantically shaking their heads. Motioning for them to stand aside, I began to work up the magic that I knew for cloaking spells—if I could just get him to pass for human, that would solve the problem of people on the streets. Then we'd just have to explain to the folks up in the bar that they'd seen a crazed lunatic wearing a costume who had a thing against elves.

"Sweetheart, I don't think this is wise—" Trillian began to say, and Smoky, for once, chimed in on his side, but I brushed away their fears, too.

"My magic has grown stronger since I've been working with Morio. And there's no other way to avoid incurring questions that we do not want."

Disguise spells, or cloaking spells, weren't all that hard—at least not for the average Moon Witch. Given my background, there was always the chance I'd muck it up, but I was ever the optimist, and besides, I was the only one here who could even try to cast a spell.

Without further ado, I focused on the daemon and summoned the Moon Mother's power into my hands, willing it to flow into the creature's aura. With a tingle raging through my fingers, like pins and needles pricking a thousand nerves, I began to rearrange the shape of his energy field, focusing on smoothing out the bumps and modifying the color.

Even if we could get him to pass for a Supe of unknown variety, chances were the *Seattle Tattler* wouldn't be getting calls about some hellish creature rampaging through the streets. Maybe a weredog or something . . .

With one last shove to set the energy, I blinked and stood back. The daemon began to shift form. We all waited with pent breath, and then as the spell settled into his aura, I let out a gurgle and face-palmed my forehead. *Not* quite what I'd been going for.

The daemon stood there, on all four feet, tail wagging, staring up at me. "What did you do to me, woman? I didn't think you'd actually be able to do anything. I heard you were a bumbling idiot! How long am I going to look like this? *A poodle?* Are you *serious?*"

He took a threatening step toward me and nipped at my ankles, but Smoky leaned over and scooped up the daemon.

"Do not threaten my wife, even if it is with rabies."

"I don't have rabies, you idiot! I'm not actually a dog!"

"Um, I hate to differ with you," Menolly said, "but you are for now. And it could last ten minutes or it could last ten days, knowing my sister. I advise you get back to the Demon Underground before the dogcatcher sees you."

The string of obscenities that issued forth made even my ears hurt. Apparently, my mind hadn't been as focused as I'd thought, because he was nowhere human or Were looking. In fact, he was a very ornate white poodle, clipped in the typical powder-puff stereotype. With two glaring exceptions: both his eyes and his toenails were brilliant red.

"You look like some sort of wacked-out hellhound," Trillian said. "I'm sorry, dude. My wife tends to fritz out on her magic a lot, but it does work, contrary to what Trytian seems to have told you."

"Put me down, you lunatic, and let me out of here now!" The daemon dog snapped again, and Smoky promptly curled his thumb and index finger together and gave him a *thunk* on the muzzle. Not hard enough to hurt, but hard enough to humiliate.

"Mind your manners." He rolled his eyes and headed toward the door. "I'm going to go release this one outside so he can go home. Camille, my love, think twice next time. We could have simply given him a cloak to wear."

I snorted. "Whatever. It's not going to hurt him. But hurry it up because Chase needs us in Tangleroot Park."

As Smoky carried the struggling mutt up the stairs, I turned to Menolly. "What are you going to tell your patrons up there? They have to have some plausible explanation."

She frowned. "Fire troll?"

"There's no such thing."

"Most of them won't know that. Tonight it's mainly a bunch of Earthside Supes and Faerie Maids up there. I could tell them that dragons turn into pixies and they might believe me."

I chewed on the inside of my lip. "You're probably right. Tell them we subdued him. But we're going to have to tell Queen Asteria the truth. That poor elf has a family somewhere and you can bet, ten to one, they're back in Otherworld. I don't think he's going to willingly oblige us by being homeless, without next of kin."

Menolly chewed on her lip. "Yeah, I know. Let's go. I'll have Derrick bring the body down here until we can identify him. You guys go on ahead. Call if you need me."

As we threaded our way out of the bar, it occurred to me that with our luck, Santa would come riding into town with a sawed-off shotgun. Considering that I'd met the Holly King when I was a young girl, it wouldn't surprise me a bit. He was a terrifying figure and it never failed to awe me just whom the FBHs would invite down their chimneys without asking for references.

Leaving Menolly to tackle the damage control at the bar, we headed over to Tangleroot Park. The snow was falling lightly, and the soft swish of my windshield wipers kept up a lively rhythm. Trillian was riding shotgun, Smoky sprawled in the back.

I glanced at Smoky through the rearview mirror, wondering whether it was a good time to discuss what the daemon had told us, but decided to wait. We already knew Hyto had it in for us. Mentioning it would only set Smoky off, and I really didn't want a pissed-off dragon in the backseat. Even one whom I loved.

As the asphalt sped by, I thought about the past year. So much had happened. When my sisters and I were first sent over from Otherworld, we didn't have a clue as to what waited in store for us. We learned the hard way, all too fast.

* * *

I'm Camille D'Artigo—that's Dee-Ar-tee-go. At home I'm known as Camille Sepharial te Maria, because in Otherworld, Fae take their mother's first name as a surname. When we came Earthside, we just started using our mother's last name.

Either way you slice it, I'm half-human, half-Fae, and all trouble, at least according to my husbands and my sisters. I'm married to a dragon, a youkai-kitsune, and one of the dark, Charming Fae. *Simultaneously.* That doesn't go over well with some of the Earthside community who call me a slut and a whore, but I don't give a fuck what they think. My mores are my own, and if loving three men is a crime, I'll happily play criminal.

By heart, soul, and trade, I'm a witch, recently promoted to priestess. The Moon Mother rode me on one hell of a rough trial, but I walked through the shadow and—like Ishtar—came out of the Underworld triumphant. In the wake of destruction, a new path opened, upon which I am preparing to embark.

My sister Delilah—a two-faced Were by nature and a Death Maiden by calling—is second born. Until recently, I worried that her naïveté would be her downfall, but she's toughened up and come to accept herself for who she is. She seems much happier now, less angsty. Delilah had a twin who died at birth. Arial watches over her, in leopard form, and the two have met in the astral realm.

And then there's Menolly, who was a *jian-tu*—a spy/acrobat—until she was tortured and turned into a vampire back in Otherworld. Last winter, we managed to dust her sire, one of the most vicious pieces of filth that ever walked the Earth. Menolly runs a fine line, controlling her predator nature but accepting who she is. But even in death, she's my baby sister.

Together with our lovers and friends, we're fighting a demonic war, alone except with scattered help from the elves and a few other Supes we can trust. We're on the trail of the spirit seals—nine artifacts broken from a single treasure

formed by the Elemental Lords and the ancient Fae Lords
when Otherworld split off from Earth during the Great
Divide. We've managed to find several of them, but Shadow
Wing snagged one, which makes the danger more precari-
ous. The rest are up for grabs, and we're trying to prevent
him from getting hold of any more. Every spirit seal the
demon lord possesses brings him one step closer to the day
he manages to break through the portals, to raze both Earth
and Otherworld to the ground.

And we're the only ones standing in his way.

Tangleroot State Park was ostensibly closed for the night,
but Chase was waiting near the front gates for us. A day
park, the 400-acre sprawl was a maze of picnic tables and
jungle gyms, huge maple trees and conifers. The maples
were bare-branched, naked to the sky, but the firs and cedars
towered dark and brooding over the area. Snow clung to
both naked limb and needled bough, creating a surreal,
cloaked feel to the park.

As we drove through the gates and parked, I quietly slid
out of the car and stood, gazing up at the giant sentinels that
guarded the grounds.

Something about woodlands and glades, parks and forests during winter muffled my thoughts, sent me into a qui-
etude that I seldom found except within my magic and
meditation. They reminded me of my days spent in study
back home, when I first became a witch under the Moon
Mother's watchful eyes.

Chase smiled tightly, raising his hand. His eyes glimmered with magic. The Nectar of Life was taking full hold
of him. Just where he'd end up was a mystery none of us
could fathom, but watching his journey was fascinating, and
I hoped to hell it ended well for him. He'd helped us so much
and, although I'd started out wanting to smack him every
time he stared at my boobs, over the months I'd come to
respect and even like the detective.

As Delilah and Shade pulled in, a flicker of regret skittered across his face but disappeared so rapidly I thought

I might be imagining it. Chase was dating Sharah now—the elfin medic at the FH-CSI—the Faerie Human Crime Scene Investigation unit. They seemed casually happy together.

"Thanks for coming," he said. "I know you must be tired from your trip." He searched my face. "How's Iris?"

I shrugged. "Better than when we left. But it was hard—it was rough on her. It was difficult on all of us. The Northlands are a terrifying and harsh place. And I kept worrying that we might run into Hyto. Speaking of which . . ." Chase had to know. Hyto could wreak havoc on the city. "Chase, Hyto's hanging around here."

Chase gave me a sharp look. "Smoky's father? Here? In Seattle?" A faint look of bewilderment skittered across his face. Or perhaps it was denial. "You've got to be kidding."

"I wish I were. Apparently, he's stirring up trouble. And we know he's out to get Smoky and me. We just got the word tonight. I don't mind telling you, Chase, I'm scared spitless. Dragons are dangerous—all of them. Even Smoky. And Shade, who's only half dragon. But a dragon with a grudge . . . Hyto threatened me when we met. I know he's more than capable of carrying out those threats."

Shuddering, I let it drop. There was nothing more to say. Chase couldn't do anything except keep a lookout. If he tried to go up against Hyto, he'd be charcoal. Or worse. The memory of Hyto's hands on me, of his whispered threats, ran through me like ice water, and I tried to shake it off.

"What have you got for us?" I asked, before Chase could say anything else.

He paused for a moment, our eyes meeting. A flare of magic whirled in those dark orbs, and for a moment, I felt pulled toward him—as if there were a connection that resonated through both of us. It wasn't sexual, but a deeper link, one born of magic, of the dark of night.

"Camille," he whispered. "What . . ." And then, as quickly as the mind-touch flared, it vanished, and we were standing among the others as if nothing had happened.

I shook my head at him and mouthed, *Later*.

"You were going to show us what you think is a portal?" I didn't want anybody else noticing what had happened.

Chase was going through so many transformations that a bunch of nosy questions weren't going to help him. But I decided to privately have a long talk with the detective. We needed to test him, find out just what sort of magical talents were emerging.

He stood there for a moment, pensive, then nodded and motioned for us to follow him. "Yeah, this way."

As we fell in behind him, he explained how he found it. "I got a call on the tip line, of all things, telling me there was something in the park that wasn't right."

"Male or female?"

"I honestly don't know. But I sent Shamas and Yugi out here and they found this . . . thing. It reminds me of Grandmother Coyote's portal. But it's . . . different. It doesn't have the same *feel*, if that makes sense." He frowned. "Like when you see an impersonator. Maybe he looks like the real thing, but there's something off . . ."

I pressed my lips together. There were so many things in our world that were "just a little bit off" that the normality of life had taken a backseat. "Yeah, I know. Show us, please."

We scuffed through the snow, along the ice-covered sidewalks into the heart of the park. Tangleroot Park gave me the creeps, to be honest. I usually loved the outdoors, but some woods are too dark, some places too wild for comfort. Especially over here, Earthside.

The home of massive cedar and fir trees, Tangleroot Park also housed a couple of ancient yew trees. The tree of death, the tree of rebirth. A dark soul in a bright night, the yew was one of the most holy of trees, and yet it calved off into a hundred trunks, a hundred roots, all twisting in on the heart of the trunk. The spirit of the yew belonged to the winter, to the barren and fallow season, to the Underworld.

And the minute we began to walk toward the center of the park, I could feel the yews watching us. Watching *me*. They were curious, and their curiosity came creeping out, feelers reaching for my energy.

Death priestess . . . dark moon priestess . . . we feel you pass by.

Startled, I jerked my head up, but even though I glanced

around, I knew that no one walking on two feet had said that. It was the forest. The yews.

I tried to keep my thoughts to myself, tried to rein in my aura. Lately it had become a challenge not to blast it wide. The more Morio and I worked together on our death magic, the stronger I was becoming.

And when I backfired, the backlashes were more intense, and more dangerous. As I cloaked up, warding myself against prying eyes, we turned off on a side path, silently filing through the snow-laden trees. A faint mist ran through the park, sparkling and electric. Mist didn't usually crackle; something had to be infusing it for it to shimmer so much.

I glanced up at Smoky. "Something is feeding the mist."

He gave me a faint nod. "I feel it, too. This is unnatural."

Delilah slipped up beside us. "Shade just told me that he senses Netherworld energy here, but there's something more. Something far removed from the spirit realm."

Shit. What were we dealing with? As we wandered farther into the flurry of white steam rolling along the ground, my ankles began to tingle, and then the tingling moved up my legs and before I knew it, I was shaking like a leaf.

"What's wrong?" Smoky reached down and cupped my elbow. "You're trembling. Are you thinking about my father?"

"Yes, but that's not what's making me shiver." I stopped long enough to tell everyone what was happening. "Anybody else feel it?"

Shade nodded. "I do, but it's not affecting me as bad as it appears to be hitting you."

Chase let out a short sigh. "I feel something—a discomfort, like a prickling—but I thought it might be the cold."

"Hold on for a moment and let me suss it out."

We had stopped near a bench. Trillian swept the snow off, and I gratefully slid onto the seat. I pulled my cloak tighter around me, then lowered myself into a trance.

"Just what's out there? Who's creeping around in the fog?" The mesmerizing strands of energy clouded my focus, and I shook them off.

Peel back layer after layer of sparkling mist cloaking the reality behind the magic. Dig into its core, seek the central thread. And there it is... a cold thread, a dark thread, steeped in the energy of peat bogs and old forests and bonfires deep in the grove at midnight.

Touching the strand, I sucked in a deep breath as it sang to me, reverberated through me like an electric fiddle, ripping out an ancient, keening reel. Like a live wire scorching the inside of my eyelids. I caught a glimpse of sentinel fir trees dripping with moss, and toadstools growing off downed snags. Silhouettes flittered here and there—sparkling with energy and yet the sparkles were shrouded in darkness.

Evil? Not really... and yet, not good.

Red eyes glimmered at me from the forest. An ancient entity, male, old beyond reckoning, he waited in the shrouded night.

Come, join my dance. You know you must, sooner or later. The Huntress must dance with the Hunter as the moon kisses the sun. Come, join me in a frenzied ring. You, guardian of the Dark Moon.

I shook out of the web being woven around me and realized that while I'd been in trance, I'd been warm—warm as a summer's night under the stars. I could still smell rich roses, and honey wine, and the fragrant loam of the earth. The winter snow around me glared, stark and unyielding, and I longed to join the summons.

Clearing the catch out of my throat, I stifled the impulse to run toward the energy. As foreboding as it was, I still longed to reach out, to touch it, to embrace the entity waiting in the dark.

"What is it?" Delilah asked.

I shook my head. "I don't know, but it's Fae in origin. There are several beings waiting down this path. Something dark and hungry—all scuttle and cunning. And the Hunter, I think. He's old and crafty, waiting in the dark of the night. I want to shed my cloak and go running toward it." I turned to Chase. "Show us the portal, please."

Another five minutes of ever-increasing energy and we were standing in front of a shimmering blue field between two trees, off the sidewalk, to our left. Chase had been right—the thing looked just like a portal, only it had a distinctly different feel from the ones we were used to. Which meant it was either a different kind, or a mimic.

I motioned for Shade to join me. He was the most versed in magic now that Morio was laid up, and he'd have a better chance of helping me if some Big Bad came tumbling through.

He leaned down and whispered, "This portal stems from the ancient forests. Be cautious, Camille. Powerful beings inhabit the woodlands of Earth."

Smoky cleared his throat, eyeing Shade as his lips neared my ear. I rolled my eyes. Dragons didn't do all that well in the same territory; even a half dragon like Shade had territorial issues, but mix him with Smoky—whose full-blood dragon testosterone put most alpha males to shame—and we'd been breaking up sputtering matches for several weeks. As polite as Shade could be, he was still, beneath it all, part dragon, and that side had risen to the challenges Smoky had pushed forward.

I took a slow step away from him to calm Smoky down. Shade cracked a faint smile, and I realized he'd stirred the cauldron on purpose.

"A real jokester, huh?" I mumbled, then turned back to the others. "We can't just walk through—we have no idea where it might lead. This has the energy of the Fae Queens written all over it, but I sincerely doubt they conjured it up. They'd summon it to their Sovereignty if they summoned it at all."

"That makes sense." Trillian stroked his chin. With his glistening obsidian skin, he was almost lost in the dim light. "But they might know what it is. What do you think about asking them?"

Delilah and I glanced at each other. The idea of asking the Triple Threat to come out here to help us wasn't an easy decision. As much as I respected Aeval and Titania, I equally distrusted Morgaine. She might be our distant cousin, but she was out for pure power—her own—and I wouldn't put anything past her in her attempts to claim what she could.

I slowly shook my head. "I don't know, but—"

"Do you hear that?" Chase interrupted me, blanching as he turned toward the portal.

"Hear what?" I listened but couldn't catch anything different from the energy I'd already been feeling. But Chase looked like he'd seen a ghost. He wavered, his eyes taking on a glassy look, then began to bolt toward the portal.

"She's calling my name . . ."

I jumped to grab his arm, but he shook me off, like he might shake off a leaf. I knew damned well that Chase didn't have the strength to do that.

I whirled to Smoky. "Catch him—don't let him get through that portal!"

Both Smoky and Shade rushed past me, but Smoky suddenly stopped, bouncing back as if he'd hit an invisible barrier. Shade was struggling, his steps sluggish and forced.

"I can't move." Smoky's hair lashed out at whatever the force field was, sparks flying every time the whips hit the invisible barrier.

"I can barely slog through it," Shade said, his voice strained.

"Fuck! Come on!" I motioned to Delilah. We began to run. It felt like I was running through mud, but at least I could move. So could she.

Trillian was on our heels, and he passed us by, faster than we were. "Elder Fae energy—pure, crystal Elder Fae energy," he shouted over his shoulder.

And then, the siren song enveloped me, a beckoning dance that promised to last forever if I'd just embrace the energy. I gasped, reeling from the desire to shed caution to the wind. The wave of passion rolled over me like the scent of peaches, ripe on the vine. Beside me, Delilah let out a choking sound and dropped in her tracks, grasping at her throat.

Chase was almost to the portal. I paused, torn between going after the detective and helping my sister. But Trillian was within arm shot of Chase, and Delilah was struggling for breath.

Making my decision, I grabbed her wrists and began to drag her away from the mist that now encompassed us like a sparkling fog. The siren song still lodged in my head, I did my best to block it out as I pulled her to safety. Shade loped in our direction, while Smoky was still trying to break through the barrier.

Delilah sat up, wheezing. "I couldn't breathe—it felt like I was breathing water. Chase—what's happening to Chase?"

Turning, I saw that Trillian was struggling to control the detective, but Chase broke away, pushing him back. With a wild, panicked look, the detective plunged into the portal, screaming. The gateway exploded with a brilliant light, and then—in the snow-filled night—it vanished, taking him with it.

Chapter 3

"Chase! Chase!" Delilah scrambled to her feet, still breathing heavily.

I let go of her, seeing that she was all right, and ran over to Trillian's side. He was staring at the last sparkles of the portal as they faded slowly. Magic still reverberated through the air, but the pull—the siren song—was gone.

And so was Chase.

"Chase! Chase! Where the hell are you? Chase?" I called for him, not really expecting an answer. Finally, I turned back to stare bleakly at where the portal had been. "What happened?"

"I had hold of him, but something from the other side was stronger—while we didn't see any hands, I guarantee you, there was something holding on to him. We played tug-of-war, but then he slipped out of my grasp. He didn't run through that portal on his own—he was yanked in. He might have been drawn to it, but he didn't go willingly."

Chase's scream echoed in my ears. "Great Mother, what took him?"

Trillian shook his head. "I don't know. But whatever it

was, it was big and mean and felt old as the world itself." He gave me a long look. "I tried to hold him, Camille. I tried." A broken look crossed his face. Trillian held no real love for Chase, but he would never have willingly let go.

"I know." I pressed my hand to his cheek and kissed him softly. "We have to find out what this thing is . . . was. And why it opened up here."

Delilah stared at the sparkles as they scattered, dissipating. Tears streamed down her face. "Oh, Chase . . . is he . . . do you think he's dead?"

I swallowed the rising bitterness that rolled in my stomach. "I don't know. We can only pray he's okay."

Smoky and Shade stared somberly at the spot.

Smoky let out a soft growl. "What next? How do we even hope to find him?"

I bit my lip. "Delilah's right. We bring in Aeval. Ask her to suss out the energy. She's our only hope. I'm to pledge to her Court in less than a week. And remember: She owes me a favor for breaking her free from the crystal in the cave. I'll call in my marker, ask her to help us with this."

"That's a big marker to give up." Smoky slid his arm around my shoulders. "Are you sure you want to do that?"

"We can't just let Chase get swallowed up by . . . whatever that is. *Was.* Yeah, I think we have to get the Triple Threat involved."

Delilah nodded. "When will you go talk to them?"

The urgency in her voice made me wonder—could she still have feelings for the detective? But I knew the answer. Of course she did, and always would. But her love for him was different now—that of a dearly beloved friend, a brother. He was no longer her lover. And I felt the same way. Chase was part of our extended family. And family wasn't disposable, contrary to what my father thought.

"Tonight. I'm exhausted, but this can't wait. Don't wait up for me. I'll go alone. The Triple Threat have no love for Smoky, and I don't think they want a stranger on their land, Shade."

"I'll come with you." Delilah glanced at me, her eyes flashing. "Don't even say no."

"All right. Trillian, can you drive Smoky and Shade home in the Jeep? We'll take my Lexus."

"As you wish, my sweet." Trillian motioned to the two dragons, and they turned to go. Delilah tossed him the keys, and then we watched as they vanished into the snowbound night. I'd been surprised when I found out he'd quietly gone off and gotten his license with no problem. Trillian was an excellent driver, but he had a thirst for speed.

I turned back to the area around where the portal had been. "You okay, Kitten?" A glance at her showed she was still crying.

"Yeah, I'm okay, but Chase . . . did it kill him?" She closed her eyes and I could tell she was searching, hoping to find some sense that he was still around. I lightly touched her on the arm.

"Let's go. We can't help him by just standing here." Reluctantly, I turned and she followed me, her head down. As we jogged back to the car, I kept thinking that if Chase hadn't drunk the Nectar of Life, he might not be in this predicament.

Yes, but he'd be dead, a voice inside whispered. *And would that be any better?*

"Perhaps," I whispered beneath my breath. Because what I'd sensed on the other side of the portal was old beyond reckoning, and the elder forces of the Earth could be terribly fierce. "Just perhaps."

The drive out to the compound took us half an hour in the blowing snow, and I gave a breath of thanks that Morio had insisted I get snow tires on the Lexus. The thought of him home, still hurting, rankled. But he was healing up and would be good to go within a couple of months. The attack from the hungry ghosts had left him weakened, and regaining life force was a lot harder than just regaining physical health. Hungry ghosts sucked out life energy, and there was no quick fix for regaining *that*.

Keeping him and Menolly apart had been a chore in itself. They'd bonded when Sharah used some of Menolly's blood to keep Morio from dying, and like it or not, the two had a *thing* for each other now. Both had been very conscientious about not staying in the same room alone together, but I feared it would only get worse once Morio grew stronger. The tension when they were together drove me nuts. It wasn't that I was terribly jealous—if they ended up sleeping together, fine. I could handle that even though I'd prefer they didn't. But I had to admit to myself, I didn't want him in *love* with her. And right now, I wasn't sure just what he felt beyond the lust.

And I—I had my own secrets. Secrets that could lead Smoky to murder. I'd had no choice at the time—or rather, the only other option I'd had was worse than the fate I'd chosen. However you sliced it, this Solstice promised to be less than merry at our house.

As I navigated the ice and snow, Delilah stared out the window. "So tell me about Iris. What happened? And don't give me any bull. Of course she needs to tell me herself, but you were there. What went on?"

I bit my lip. We'd been gone only a few days, but it seemed like a lifetime. "She found Vikkommin. Or rather, what was left of him. Apparently . . . it's a long story, Delilah, and I don't feel like talking about it. But she proved . . . she won back her right to have children. She *was* responsible, but there were extenuating circumstances."

Delilah let out a long sigh. "She's powerful, our Iris."

"More powerful than you know, and the powers they stripped away from her are returning. Everyone thinks of house sprites as cute, winsome little creatures who exist to be cleaning machines, but they're so very wrong. Iris could probably level the three of us if she were mad enough. I don't ever want to see her have to use her powers the way she did against Vikkommin. It nearly destroyed her the first time."

"But she's free now? To marry Bruce?"

"Yes, and to have children. I'm not sure that will be enough for her, though." I paused at a red light, then turned onto the freeway entrance, gaining speed as I pushed the car into higher gear. The traffic was light this time of night, and it was cold enough that the snow was sticking to the road. By morning, it would be another solid sheet of black ice. "This weather's crazy. We need a break. Have they said when it's going to stop snowing and go back to rain?"

"We're in an Arctic cold snap—it's supposed to last another week or two and then gradually warm back up. And what do you mean, you're not sure that will be enough?" Kitten fidgeted, tugging on the seat belt.

"Something happened out there on the ice fields, and before you ask, no—I don't know what. But Iris returned, both happy and pensive. Something's in the works with her. But you know how close-lipped she is. Until she's ready, she's not going to dish."

I sped up, matching the speed of the oncoming cars, and darted left into the next lane, then left again so we'd be away from the upcoming exit-only lanes. As I eased into the speed—we weren't going that fast, considering the weather—I let out a sigh and relaxed.

"So what about you? Sharah cleared you for combat?"

Delilah grinned. "Yeah, and boy am I ready for it. I hate being on bed rest. But I need to work out. Eight weeks of sitting around the house has turned my body to jelly, and she warned me the first few weeks are going to hurt when I start using my muscles again. She's had me on some physical therapy, but the muscles are tight and they're going to pull." She sobered then. "What do you think happened to Chase?"

I shrugged. "I have no idea, Kitten, but what I sensed on the other side of that portal wasn't altogether friendly. You . . . you aren't having second thoughts, are you?"

She looked startled. "You mean about Shade and Chase? No—not at all. But I still love Chase, dearly. He was my first love, and you don't just blow that off, not unless the person hurt you. I adore Shade; he's good for me. But Chase . . . he's our detective, you know?"

I smiled softly. "Yes, I know. He's our detective. He's family."

As we sped along the road, an easy silence fell between us then, one born of being who we were. None of the three of us needed constant chatter, though Delilah liked to keep the TV on for background noise. Both Menolly and I were content with silence or background music.

"Do you ever think about the future?" she asked after a little while.

"What do you mean? Are you talking about Shadow Wing?"

"Yes . . . No. Maybe? I mean, if we do manage to stop him, what then? Are we going home to Otherworld? You're married to Smoky, Morio, and Trillian. I'm with Shade and bound to the Autumn Lord. Menolly is in love with Nerissa, who's an Earthside Were. Our lives are bound up on both sides. And you . . ." She stopped suddenly. "Never mind."

"No," I whispered. "Go ahead and say it. I can't go home to Y'Elestrial because Father disowned me."

"If Queen Tanaquar lifts the ban, would you?"

"Would I go back? Maybe. But I don't know now . . . even if Father comes around, I'll always remember that he cut me off. I don't think I'll ever be able to forgive him for that. And Y'Elestrial is all bound up with memories of our childhood. I don't know if I could go home again. At least not to there. Maybe Dahnsburg—Feddrah Dahns and his father like me."

As I thought of the unicorns, I smiled. I'd recently received a missive from King Uppala-Dahns exonerating me of killing the Black Unicorn. In fact, I'd become somewhat of a folk hero there, for freeing the Black Beast to reincarnate as per legend. But I hadn't told my sisters about it. For one thing, it sounded a little like bragging. For another, I hadn't had time to fully process the whole situation.

"Now there's a thought," Delilah said, giggling. "The unicorn city. I still haven't seen it—and I'd like to."

"Maybe we'll get a chance to go there. Next time we need a break, let's take a vacation—we can skip Y'Elestrial and go via the Elqaneve Barrows. We should check in with Queen Asteria, anyway." Ever since my father had disowned me, my sisters and I had quit the Otherworld Intelligence Agency and gone to work for the Elfin Queen.

"There—there's our turn," I said, veering back into the right lane as I checked over my shoulder to make sure we were clear. The night sky was silvery as the snow continued to fall, and the exit ramp was slippery—we skidded slightly as I slowed, but I managed to keep us from fishtailing, and then we turned east and headed toward the compound.

The Triple Threat—as I'd dubbed the Court of the Three Queens—owned a thousand-acre compound northeast of Seattle, buttressed in the foothills of the Cascade Mountain Range.

Earlier in the year, the government had set the Earthside Fae Queens a limit—they could buy up and hold five thousand acres of land for now, with the possibility of expansion in the future. This land would be considered a Sovereign nation, and a treaty had been ironed out with the understanding that it would stand only if no threats were made against the government or the people of the United States by the Earthside Fae who signed up on the rolls.

Titania, the Queen of Light and Morning, and Aeval, the Queen of Shadow and Night, had agreed. And they'd forced Morgaine, the half-Fae Queen of Dusk and Twilight by default, to agree to the terms. Although I had the feeling Morgaine hadn't been asked for her opinion, the three Queens had agreed to name their nation Talamh Lonrach Oll—loosely translated as the Land of Brilliant Apples.

As we wound through the foothills toward the Fae Nation, I began to feel the energy a good five miles before we were there. In the darkness, the trees glowed and sparkles skittered across the road, making me smile. I loved the magic out here—especially at night, for Aeval and Morgaine were both connected with the Moon Mother, as was I.

We eased onto the road leading to the towering silver-plated gates that had been erected across the driveway leading in.

I wasn't due to show up until the Solstice. The guards seemed surprised to see us, but they waved us through once they realized who we were. As we pulled in, the road veered to the left, toward a major parking lot. Cars weren't permitted beyond this point. It was either walk or take a horse-drawn cart or a bicycle.

Easing into a parking space, I turned off the ignition and opened my window. The sound of magic filled the air. Not everyone could hear it, not even all of the Fae, though the average person might get a humming that irritated them or a headache from a buzzing in the ears, but I could. Soft and on the wind, like a thousand dancing chimes.

Delilah scratched her neck. "I feel like ants are crawling on me."

"That's magic," I said softly. "Come on, you'll get used to it after a little bit and won't notice it so much."

We climbed out of the car and locked it. No use taking chances—our father's people generally weren't trustworthy unless they'd given their word of honor, and even then, I was cautious.

"Over there." I pointed to the stalls where we could borrow a horse and cart. I had no intention of walking all the way to the palace barrows. I was tired from the trip with Iris and felt like I'd never warm up, though compared to the Northlands this storm was a spring breeze.

The woman who was manning the stables gave us the once-over, then broke out in a smile. "Welcome, Otherworld Sisters. You have need of a cart?" Her voice was clipped, and I realized she wasn't used to speaking English. She must have recently come out of the forests.

There were still enough wild places that some of the Fae remained relatively untouched by society, but that was dwindling and pretty soon I feared there would be a struggle between the FBHs and the Earthside Fae over territory.

Andy Gambit, tabloid reporter for the *Seattle Tattler* who did his best to make our lives a spectacle, was afraid of those of us from Otherworld, but the fact was, he'd better keep a watch in his own backyard first. We were far less of a threat than the Earthside Fae who had quietly absorbed the shock of deforestation and development for the past hundred and fifty years.

"Thank you." I accepted the reins to the covered cart. It was a two-seater, with one horse to guide it. As Delilah and I settled ourselves inside, I realized that although the buggy would protect us from the majority of the snow, it wouldn't do much against the cold. Delightful.

"Do you remember how to drive one of these things?" Delilah glanced at me, then at the horse. "It's been a while."

"Not that long." I paused, testing the reins. Truthfully, it had been a good two years or so since I'd sat behind the reins of a buggy, but I'd spent a hell of a lot more time than that driving one when I lived in Otherworld. And, after one mistake of reaching for the gas pedal, the feel of the leather in my hands came back and I *tsked* to the horse, keeping a steady hold on the reins.

A thousand acres is a surprisingly large area when you're cold, and snow is blowing in your face. I blinked against the flakes as they landed on my eyelashes, grateful for waterproof mascara, and guided the horse through the middle of the cobblestone street. The stones were covered with packed snow and ice, and more than once I was actually relieved we were in a buggy and not the car. The Triple Threat seemed averse to shoveling snow, and the horse was now plowing us through a good ten inches of the white stuff. Up here in the Cascade foothills, it snowed more often, and with more depth than in the lowlands or the sea-level cities.

By now, the only visibility came from the silver-dark sky and the lights shining to the sides in barrow houses, where the Earthside Fae—those who had been accepted into Talamh Lonrach Oll as actual inhabitants—lived.

The member rolls were far greater than the inhabitants. *So far.* What the government would think when they saw how many Fae there really were, was yet to be seen. Although FBHs had accepted—some more reluctantly than others—that they were not the only beings on the planet, I had a feeling they weren't going to be comfortable when they knew the full extent of just how many Fae there really were in the world. Or vampires. Or Weres. Or Cryptos, for that matter. The fairy-tale stories had opened up and come to life. The monsters had come out from under the bed, and we were among them.

"Would you want to live here?" Delilah asked, gazing at the lights that shimmered by the sides of the road.

I gave her a faint smile. "I don't think so. I doubt if they'd accept Smoky into their hearts . . . or even Morio. Trillian, maybe—even though he's a Svartan and they're actually part of the elven line. And Svartans and elves don't mix well."

"Svartans and Fae don't mix well." She blushed. "I'm sorry Menolly and I gave you such a hard time about him all these years. Now that we've gotten to really know him—"

"You mean, now that you've been forced to live with him?"

"That, too." She ducked her head, grinning. "He's really a pretty good guy. I still think he's arrogant as hell, but that's just his nature. He loves you, he dotes on you, he helps out with the household, and he adores Maggie."

"Well, thank you for finally noticing." I reached over and bopped her on the nose.

"Anyway, you were saying?"

"What? Oh, would I want to live here?" I let out a long sigh. "Don't get me wrong—I think what Titania and Aeval are doing is a good thing. And it is beautiful. The magic sings to me. But it's cold, Kitten. The magic leaves me cold and feeling alone. Like starlight—it's brilliant, but it's so far from anything you can touch or feel that it's almost . . . empty."

The horse's quiet clipping of hooves on snow-covered cobblestones soothed my nerves as we wound our way through the maze of paths and trails. A lot of construction was going on, and it looked like houses and barrow mounds were springing up all over the place.

None of the houses were over a single story, though—and all were cottagelike in structure. No electricity lines crossed through the land, nor would they. I knew that Titania and Aeval had insisted on that—the power to fuel these homes would come from magic, and solar and geothermal energy. From the wind and from sun and from steam.

Eye catchers glimmered along the paths, marking each new street. It seemed odd to see the shimmering lights over here, Earthside, but I had a feeling that more than a little crossover was happening. Otherworld was borrowing some of Earthside's technology, and the Earthside Fae were latching onto some of the wonders back in Otherworld. It rang odd, like the two worlds were reuniting, in their own way . . . roots long torn apart winding back together again.

With so many of the portals that connected the realms going rogue, and the veil separating Otherworld from Earthside tearing in places, I wondered how long it would be before everything imploded and the two worlds spiraled in on each other again.

When Otherworld had split off during the Great Divide,

the yawning chasm in the astral plane had eventually created an unnatural tension that kept stretching, pulling at the edges of the veil. But the spirit seals had kept everything neat and tidy and divided. Until now.

"What do you think will happen if the worlds come back together again? From what Aeval has told me, it was a cataclysm when they split—earthquakes, volcanoes erupting, unnatural weather in the areas least hit by the ripping of the fabric of space and time." I glanced over at Delilah. "I think I'm scared that it's already happening, and if it's inevitable, if the spirit seals fail, then what does the future hold for both of our worlds? There are so many more people now. Thousands could die."

She pressed her lips together and stared at the window. "I don't know," she said after a moment. "We can speculate all we want and we won't know if we come up with the real answer. I guess . . . we won't know until it happens. *If* it happens. Earthside is already crowded . . . can you imagine the mess if all the people back home were dumped into this space? And what will happen to the landscape? I just can't imagine it."

I clucked and lightly pulled on the reins to slow the horse down. We were almost there. "You're right, of course. How can we possibly envision what it would be like? We can guess, but too much thinking about it is going to drive me nuts. Anyway, here we are . . . the Court Barrows."

The palace was beautiful, but less ostentatious than anything back in Otherworld. Nestled beneath a giant barrow mound, the palace held three courts—one for Aeval, one for Titania, and one for Morgaine. The grass over the mounds was rich and green under the snow, and the towering firs around the palace stood sentinel, watching over the land.

During the spring, the barrow mound would abound with flower gardens of all kinds, and huge, sweeping ferns, and at the center of each barrow—atop the central point—stood an oak tree. They were growing faster than any normal oak, fed by magic and the strength of Faerie.

As we pulled up close to the guards stationed in front of the Court of Darkness, I sucked in a deep breath. Within a week, I'd be pledged to this land, pledged to Aeval. And my father would forever disown me.

"I have no choice," I whispered to the trailing flakes that lightly kissed my collar as I slipped out of the buggy. "The Moon Mother wills it . . . and I am her daughter."

"What?" Delilah glanced over at me. "Camille, are you okay?"

I shivered, pulling my cape closer around me. "I don't know. Things are changing for me, Kitten. I'm worried I won't be up to the challenge."

"Well, worry about that when it comes. Because if I can face my training as a Death Maiden, you can face it as a priestess. Even though it means you're going to have to cozy up to our cousin Morgaine."

And with a grin, she shot a snowball at me.

The snow hit me square in the face and broke me out of my reflection. I snorted, then dashed it away and headed for the entryway. She was right. We had work to do. Now. Chase was depending on us. And that was as close to wallowing in depression as I was going to let myself get.

"Come on, Kitten. Let's go have tea with a Fae Queen." I motioned to her and she fell in beside me as we entered the Court of the Three Queens.

Chapter 4

❦

The inner halls of the palace were earthy, reminding me of Queen Asteria's palace, with tree roots winding their way through the walls and sparkling crystals jutting through the soil. The dirt was so compact and smoothed over that it looked like Venetian plaster, and the chambers were lit by a glimmering luminescence, a pale light that might have been green, might have been white, filled with sparkles that danced like electric synapses.

Members of the court—probably servants—quietly passed by, some carrying bowls of fruit or trays of bread, others carrying notebooks and clipboards. One, in an odd juxtaposition, rushed by, a short sword in one hand, a netbook in the other. I wondered just how they were powering it and if it had Wi-Fi. But everything all fit, somehow, this new emergence of the Earthside Fae into human society.

I motioned to one of the guards. "We need to speak with Queen Aeval."

He raised his eyebrows, but kinked his finger and motioned for us to follow him. "I assume you don't have an appointment?"

"No, but she's going to want to hear what we have to say. I'm Camille D'Artigo and this is my sister Delilah. If you could announce us . . ."

We followed him down the hall, turned left, and entered a small chamber, where the smell of earth mingled with the scent of white roses and bayberry and wintergreen. A small potted tree sat in the corner, covered with miniature eye catchers that shimmered in pink, blue, green, and yellow.

A true Yule tree, I thought, as magical as the origin of the tradition. We took our seats on an upholstered bench covered in a swirling paisley. A print of a Monet hung on the wall over our heads, and on the opposite wall, a tribal mask that looked dryadic in origin.

"Wait here," the guard said, and disappeared through the door to the left. I stood up and took a closer look at the mask while waiting. The base was wood, with crystals and dried flowers adorning it. Beautiful, almost ephemeral in nature, but yet the energy was so grounded I could imagine the mask lasting a thousand years. My fingers itched and I realized it had been a good two or three years since I'd thought about the hobbies I'd left at home. Menolly was the singer of the family; Delilah had her stable of animals at home. I'd spent hours in the gardens—first by necessity and then out of love—pottering around with plants, communing with their spirits and the energy of the ground itself.

To be a Moon Witch meant you had to come to a connection with the Great Mother first—for the Earth and Moon were sisters and connected.

"I envy Iris," I said, turning to Delilah. "I miss having the time to spend in the gardens, to walk through the forest and listen to the trees. I miss Otherworld, where the energy practically jumps off the branches and limbs. Here the forests are either unpredictable and dark, or gently asleep, waiting to wake up again."

Delilah gave me a half smile. "We need to make more time to get out in the woods around our house. I go running a lot—I know you aren't into that, but we could take a walk every day together. Maybe in the evenings, after Menolly wakes up, the three of us could just make it a habit to go for a stroll."

The thought of a quiet walk down to Birchwater Pond sounded like heaven. "As long as we're not dragged away to fight demons. I'm so tired, I think I'm going to fall asleep right here if they don't come get us."

"It's eight thirty now," Delilah said, glancing at her watch. "I'm still good, I can drive us home."

I leaned against her shoulder, letting my eyes close. "I'm so tired," I whispered. "The Northlands were so cold . . . and then having to immediately deal with the daemon and then Chase vanishing . . . I can barely keep my eyes open." Inhaling slowly, I could feel sleep stealing up on me, but I started as the sound of the doorknob turning woke me up.

The guard nodded. "You can go in now. Aeval will see you."

We headed through the door, not knowing what to expect. The Summer Solstice ritual where the land was officially dedicated had taken place in an outdoor venue, and none of the three of us had ever been inside any of the finished palaces. As I led Delilah into the throne room, I caught my breath.

Whereas the main structure was more utilitarian, Aeval's throne room was brilliant and beautiful. The domed roof sparkled with silver filigree, etched across a jeweled pebble surface. Like cobblestones, except the arched ceiling glowed with scattered gems of polished obsidian and onyx, moonstone, and a cobalt blue stone with which I wasn't familiar. Inset into the stonework were mosaics of the moon and stars, of Aeval herself, rising against the night sky, standing in front of a silver ocean, with breakers crashing on the darkened shore.

The throne room itself was swathed in a landscape of silver and indigo and blue. Aeval's colors—the colors of night. Mist floated along the floor, and a pale ice blue light emanated from beneath the wisps of fog that floated up to curl softly around my wrists. Scattered banquettes buttressed the walls, all in shades of gray and navy with silver scallops embroidered across the seats.

The sheer beauty of the austere hall caught in my throat, and I raised my fingers to my mouth, in awe of the work that had been done and the magical threads running through that work. Beside me, Delilah gave a short gasp.

And in the center, a silver-clad throne. The seat and back were hewn of yew and elder boughs; silver embellishments wound their way through the arms and along the back. The throne was more wild than regal, primal like the night, sprawling across the back of the barrow.

And on the throne sat Aeval, tall and frozen, like a statue carved from ice. Her hair was dark as the night and her skin, alabaster and porcelain. She wore a gossamer dress woven of silver threads, and as she stood, it made a shifting sound like soft metal chain clinking gently against itself.

I knelt at the base of her throne, and Delilah curtsied.

"Camille, you are not summoned to report until the Solstice. What brings you to my feet this night?" Her voice echoed in the chamber as she made her way down the steps of the throne. "Has something gone amiss?"

"Actually, yes," I said, finding my tongue. Titania made me so nervous I had trouble talking to her—she'd gone from drunken and downfallen Fae Queen to regaining her powers and shining like the sun. Morgaine was my cousin, but I no longer trusted her and every word out of her mouth was a riddle, fraught with ulterior motives. But Aeval—Aeval I could talk with, once I overcame the immediate fan-girl factor. I hadn't mentioned it to anybody, but if I had to pledge myself to *any* of the Triple Threat's courts—I was relieved it was her.

"Then by all means, tell me." Aeval motioned to a pair of banquettes that sat near the throne. "Please, take rest, and eat with me." She clapped her hands, and a serving girl appeared from out of the mist, bearing a tray with fruits and cheese, sliced venison, and sugar-sprinkled cookies.

I eagerly accepted a plate—the chill of the Northlands had increased my appetite, as had the exhaustion. Delilah also accepted a plate, but I knew her mind was only on the cookies. My sister was the original junk food junkie, and I worried about what all that crap would do to her system after a while. And if we *did* go home to Otherworld, there weren't any Cheetos over there, nor were there a lot of candy stands. Cookies—yes, but a Snickers bar? Not so much.

Protocol dictated that we eat a few bites before diving into our business. Even with Chase's life on the line, the

Triple Threat took protocol and manners seriously, and if we broke with tradition, we'd be looking at no help at all.

After a few moments, I set my plate down on the seat next to me and turned to Aeval.

"I have come for help. And I've come to redeem the favor you promised me." The words stuck in my throat, but I managed to get them out. Having a marker like that was big business, and having to spend it meant I would be back at a disadvantage. But Chase was worth it.

Aeval inclined her head. "The matter must be grave indeed, for you to approach me. What is it that only the Queen of Night can help you with?"·

I quickly ran through the incident at Tangleroot Park. "And whatever it was sucked Chase right in. We need your help. Whatever it was felt heavily Fae to me. I don't know how—or, even if—we can reopen the portal. I doubt Chase can get out on his own. We need help rescuing him."

Aeval rested her hands on her knees. She gazed into my eyes. "You would use your marker to save your friend?"

"Yes, but there's more to it than that. This portal—we need to know where it leads, because I have the feeling that isn't the last we've seen of it. So far, we don't know if anything came through, but I have a nasty premonition that next time it opens up, something might enter this world. And whatever it is, I have a feeling we're dealing with a Big Bad here."

"Really? As in . . . demonic?"

I thought about it for a moment. My sense wasn't that we were dealing with demons with this portal, but something else. "No, I don't think it's a demon. But the siren song . . . the sense of heavy Fae energy—it made me nervous."

"You really think there's something that big back there?" Aeval never fidgeted, but I could tell I'd piqued her interest. "Elder Fae?"

"Perhaps. I wouldn't be surprised. Aeval, Chase is one of our closest friends. And he's one of the best allies the OW Fae can claim. We have to save him." I let out a slow sigh. "Are you willing to help?"

I waited. Aeval would help or not as she chose. Making

one last plea, I held out my hands. "For some reason, I think you're the only one who can aid us with this."

Another moment passed, and then the Queen of Night gave me a slight nod. "I will come with you and examine the energy signature. But we will go there my way. It won't take as long. I sense you are tired, Camille. You smell like the Northlands and your aura is diminished this evening."

She rose and called for her guard. With five stalwart Fae attending us—all as dark and pale as their queen—we left the palace and walked across the snow-covered square to a twin pair of oak trees. A portal—similar to the one we'd seen in the park—shimmered between them, and the crackle of energy woke me up.

Just as silently, we entered the portal one by one, following the Queen, and the world ripped into a million pieces as we went singing through space and time.

We ended up, not in Tangleroot Park, but in a portal two streets over, in the backyard of what looked like an abandoned house. But on closer inspection, I realized the house was inhabited.

"Who lives here?" I pointed to the faint light that emanated from the windows.

Aeval smiled faintly. "We have our spies and guards. This is a safe house, should there ever come need of it."

I didn't press. Her tone told me that wasn't an option. But I memorized the address—24132 Westerwood Lane—in case we ever needed it.

I glanced over at Delilah, who was examining the yard. There were overgrown ferns and towering firs everywhere, and the lot must have been a good half acre in size—unusual in the city. But we followed Aeval and her guards, setting off for the park on foot. The sidewalks were icy, but one of the guards offered his arm to me and I gratefully accepted, too tired to see straight.

We reached the park within a few minutes and led Aeval to where the portal had been. As we neared the place, Delilah and I looked in vain for any sign of Chase, but he was nowhere in sight. The energy still hung thick in the air, and I could catch glimpses of it here and there—sparkling like a shadow that was there one moment, then gone the next.

Aeval silently approached the place where the portal had been. She held out her hands and closed her eyes, her fingers divining the energy. I could see her aura—the more tired I got, the better my Sight was for such things—and she looked lit up like a Yule tree on steroids.

Wearily, I saw a bench a few yards away and trudged over, sitting down, not caring if the snow was freezing my ass off. Delilah joined me, though she brushed the snow off her side of the bench first.

We said nothing—there was nothing left to say until Aeval was done and had figured out whatever she could. But Delilah took my hand and I curled my fingers around hers. I knew she was hurting. Even though she and Chase were just friends now, they would always care for one another. And I cared, too.

"I never thought to sense this again, not here, not in this day and age." Aeval was suddenly in front of us, staring down at us with a horrified look on her face. Holy hell. Not good. Not good for a Fae Queen to be afraid—that could only mean trouble on the horizon.

"What is it?" I asked, my voice barely audible in the dark of the night.

"Several things, all from the Elder Fae. First, a dark energy—one I do not recognize except that it's female, and hungry. Second, Stollen Kom Lightly." She said the name so abruptly that at first I didn't understand her. But then it registered, and I slowly raised my gaze to hers.

"The Bog Eater."

She nodded.

The Bog Eater . . . I closed my eyes. "No . . . he can't still be alive after all these years. I thought he was killed by one of the gods."

"So it was rumored, but apparently the gossip mill was wrong in this case. Come, we must discuss this before taking any action. There is much to be lost if we aren't careful, including your detective's life."

Aeval motioned for us to stand, and we began to walk back toward the safehouse, to the portal leading to the barrow.

"Stollen Kom Lightly was thought long lost in the haunts of time. Legend goes he was killed by Lugh the Long Handed, but apparently that was only a rumor, probably started by Lugh's followers."

I began to tune out a little. I knew where she was going with this and really didn't want to follow it through to the logical conclusion. Wishing Smoky were here, or Trillian, I pulled closer to Delilah and she wrapped her arm around my waist.

"Who is the Bog Eater?" Delilah asked. "I don't recognize the name."

Aeval glanced at the sky. "Cold tonight, and colder still tomorrow. A bad time for grim tales, but perhaps there is no right time." After another pause, she said, "There was once a goblin who was so terribly vicious that he was noticed by Jac-O HorseTail. Jac-O was known as the scourge of the Western Wastelands before the Great Divide."

The Fae Queen inhaled deeply, slowly letting out her breath in a white stream. "Jac-O HorseTail was the son of one of the Long-Cutter Gray Sisters—the webweavers who spin out confusion and hatred into the world. The three hags are not members of the Hags of Fate, but they *are* from the Elemental world, and it's thought they have some relation to Fae."

She paused as we crossed the street, skirting a car slowly edging along the icy path. The driver slammed on the brakes and jumped out to gawk at us, but Aeval waved her hand and whispered "Heed us not," and he just as quickly slipped back into his car and drove on.

When we were standing by the portal leading back to Talamh Lonrach Oll, I stopped her. "How is this portal guarded? What if some kid comes up and decides to explore the pretty sparkles?"

She laughed then. "You see this because it is of your heritage—Fae magic. But mortals do not see the portal, nor will they sense it unless they are gifted with the Sight like your detective. And even if they sense it, they cannot pass without the activation words. Yes," she added with an impish grin that suddenly made her look all too young and playful, "we password-protect our portals."

Aeval whispered the keyword (taking pains to keep it out of earshot), the portal opened, and we slipped back through to the barrow palace. She led us back into the throne room and bade us sit, while calling for cups of hot cider.

"As I was saying, Jac-O HorseTail was the son of one of the Long-Cutter Gray Sisters, and he was a loner. Even in the darker realms of the Unseelie, there are outcasts and misfits. He was a vicious and evil creature, but he was lonely. The goblin befriended him—perhaps he anticipated a reward, or perhaps he truly found a friendship with the creature. Either way, Jac-O's mother was so grateful that she did what many mothers do. She gave the goblin a gift. She changed him, made him far more powerful than he could have ever hoped to become as a regular goblin. And so Stollen Kom Lightly was born—the Bog Eater."

"He's considered one of the Elder Fae, isn't he?" I was running through my memory, trying to dredge up what I'd been taught about him.

"Yes. And his first act was to kill and eat Jac-O Horse-Tail. That, of course, did not sit well with Jac-O's mother or her sisters, and so they laid a curse on him to wander through bog and marsh, ever hungry, never able to sufficiently fill his belly. They could not kill him—Jac-O's mother had made him almost invincible—but they could curse him with a miserable existence."

Delilah cleared her throat. "I vaguely remember mention of that story in childhood but didn't remember the names."

"The Bog Eater will forever starve, no matter how much he eats. He's always hungry, and he hates all who are happy and filled with life. It was thought Lugh the Long Handed killed him in battle before the Great Divide, but apparently we were wrong. The energy I sensed through that portal was dark and boggy, and the smell of peat rang thick. I know the Bog Eater is in there, somewhere. But behind him stands an even stronger shadow—the female energy I sensed. And that shadow—*that* is where your detective has gone. I do not think the shadow is for good, but I cannot tell for sure." She fell silent.

I didn't want to ask the question but had to. I especially didn't want to ask it with Delilah around. "Do you think Chase is still alive, considering that the Bog Eater is hiding there?"

Delilah cringed, but Aeval didn't pay any attention.

"Your detective has gone into the shadow behind the Bog Eater. Whether he is alive, I do not know. But the Bog Eater did not gobble him up—that I can tell. Chase's signature still trails, so my best guess is that yes, he is alive."

Delilah breathed a sigh of relief at the same time I did, although I didn't want to think about what might be happening to him. That would be too much to deal with, so I focused on the next order of business.

"How can we get in there to save him?" The thought of getting past the Bog Eater—an Elder Fae—was terrifying, but if Menolly could deal with the Maiden of Karask, we could cope with the Bog Eater.

Aeval crooked her head to the side, a faint smile on her face. "I can rip open their portal, but I will not go in with you. I've better things to do with my time. But you should go soon—tomorrow at the latest."

Leaning back, I closed my eyes. This was all too much. To come home to the news about Hyto and now—this? I wanted to scream.

"Tomorrow then? Day or night?"

"Day. I am no vampire; I can walk abroad during the daylight hours. The two of you—no more—be here by noonsong, and bring your weapons. You will need them. Remember: The full-blooded Fae love silver. A silver blade will be of use, but not as much as cold steel." She looked at me. "Or iron. You know of what I speak."

And with that, she dismissed us.

We headed out to the cart, and Delilah took the reins, guiding the horse back to the parking lot. She tucked me in the passenger seat of the Lexus and I dozed all the way home, unable to even verbalize my thoughts.

* * *

By the time we reached home, I'd caught a little bit of a second wind, but it wouldn't last long. The three-story Victorian had never seemed so welcoming, and I wearily pulled myself up the porch steps. Once we were inside, we found everybody still up, waiting to hear what had happened. We ran down the gist of what had happened at Talamh Lonrach Oll, and then, before anybody could say a word, I raised my hand for silence.

"Somebody call Menolly at the bar and fill her in. I need to go to bed." I stood up, all too aware of the aching in my body that cried out for peace and relief from the chill.

Smoky stood. "She's correct. We were hard pressed in the Northlands. Iris, you need your rest also. We can discuss this over breakfast." He swept me into his arms, and—followed by Trillian—carried me up the stairs.

I leaned against him; the scent of cool wind and snow clung to his shirt, and his ankle-length silver hair reached around to caress my arm. We stopped in Morio's room first—he had been set up in my study, in a hospital bed. Although he was allowed to sit up and even walk a bit, my youkai-kitsune needed every ounce of energy he could conserve in order to heal.

His topaz eyes flashed with a smile as the three of us entered the room. Trillian checked to make sure Morio had plenty of water and snacks, and Smoky deposited me in the chair next to the hospital bed. I leaned against the mattress and reached out to take Morio's hand.

He had dark hair, long enough to trail down his back, and he was of Japanese descent, lean and wiry, strong as a demon—which, in essence, he was. In his fox form, he could dart rings around Delilah, and in his demonic form, he towered over everyone, eight feet of fighting machine.

Now he just looked a little tired, but the color was returning to his cheeks and he seemed in good spirits.

"Are you feeling better, my love?" I leaned over and kissed his lips.

"Only a few weeks till I'm allowed back on my feet. I'm

still tired, but I can tell my health is returning." He brushed back my hair and trailed his hand down my cheek. "I'm so glad you're home safe. They told me you made it back but that you were immediately called out. How's Iris? Did she accomplish her mission?"

"She did. I'll let Smoky tell you about our trip. Meanwhile, I just want to rest and sleep."

Trillian took my hand, guiding me up. He turned to Smoky. "Camille's weary. We can take away her fatigue." The corners of his lips turned up in a faint smile.

Smoky frowned. He was possessive—all dragons were—but he'd learned to share. I seldom went to bed without at least two of my husbands with me.

"I'll be in after I tell Morio what happened. Don't start without me." He kissed me deeply, his tongue flashing in and out of my mouth as tendrils of his hair slowly caressed my shoulders, stirring me even through my exhaustion. I leaned down and gave Morio a goodnight kiss, and he returned it.

"I promise you," he whispered, "Menolly and I kept apart during your absence."

"I'm not worried," I whispered back.

I allowed Trillian to guide me back to the bedroom. As tired as I was, I knew that sex would rejuvenate me and help me sleep. I enjoyed the thrill of my husbands' hands trailing down my sides, of their bodies filling me full in every way. I realized Trillian was right. I needed sex, I needed to release all the tension that had built up, but my energy was so low that I could do little in the way of initiating anything.

Trillian shut the door behind us, turning to me. "My Camille," he whispered, and began to undress me, one piece of clothing at a time. I held out my arms and closed my eyes, almost shy.

"Make me forget," I said softly. "Make me forget everything except your touch and smell and taste."

With a crafty laugh, Trillian reached for me.

Chapter 5
❦

Trillian stood in back of me, wrapping one arm around my waist, and with the other he ran his hand along my skin, fingers long and narrow, making me shiver. I let out a long breath and leaned my head back against his chest, drifting at the feel of his touch.

I could sense him—I could sense all my men, thanks to the Soul Symbiont ritual. We'd bound ourselves into a quartet, forever and always, beyond time, beyond death. But Trillian was my alpha; he'd been the first man I'd ever truly loved—not the first one I'd fucked, but the first one I'd loved. Magnets we were, from the very beginning, and we'd defied family and custom to be together.

He blew in my ear, a gentle stream, tickling me until I laughed and reached up to swish him away.

"Stop." It came out as a whisper, but the force behind his voice cut through and I dropped my hand. "I want to possess you tonight. I want to be your master."

"You are my alpha." I acquiesced, my own voice low and sultry, caught in the rising passion that filtered through my system as if I'd drunk sweet wine or a fiery brandy. My tiredness gave way as the desire began to build, and the combination made for a delicious sensation as I gave myself over to Trillian.

"Dance for me, my beloved." He slowly let go of me and crossed to the bed, sitting on it, crossing one leg over the other as he leaned back on his palms, watching me.

I flicked on the music, as my heart rose to match the heavy beat. Slowly, I began to sway my hips to the drums, sliding my hands up my body to cup my breasts. And then the music took over and I immersed myself in the song, my skirt swirling as I turned, trailing my fingers along my sides, over my breasts, up to greet the stars.

Swaying lightly, I gently rolled my head to let my hair trail down my back. As I fell into the music, the beat became a rhythm mirrored by my body, carrying me away down a dark path, fraught with bloodred roses and night-blooming jasmine. And then, just like that, I was topless and my breasts bounced gently as I freed them.

Trillian let out a short gasp and I caught his gaze, drawn to him like a moth to flame.

"I want to fuck you hard and fast," he whispered. "I want to feel my cock in your mouth. I want to eat you out, hear you scream, rub my face against your breasts." His words, raw but not coarse, sent a shiver up my spine. I loved hearing my men tell me what they wanted to do to me.

Just then, the door opened, and Smoky entered the room. I whirled, so ready to be played, like a harp, like the drums, like an instrument of joy.

He glanced at Trillian, then back at me as his hair rose up to grasp my wrists, the silken strands coiling around my skin, their grip so strong I couldn't break it even if I wanted to. A faint smile broke through his lips, turning them up just enough at the corners to remind me that he might look like a man, but he was all dragon, hungry and possessive.

His hair stretched my arms wide as the strands brought my hands up to slide them behind my head and hold them there firmly. My hips shifted in sync with the slow pulse that echoed through the room.

The music picked up, switching songs, and I was in a

woodland glade as the threads of Smoky's hair swirled me
out, twirling on my toes. And then, I was free again, the music
playing a trail of bread crumbs for me to follow. The room
darkened as Smoky lit candles and turned off the lights.

At some point, I unzipped my skirt, letting it drop to the
ground. Eyes closed, naked I danced, leaving care behind,
leaving worry behind, letting the music cleanse and purify
me as it burned through my body.

And then an arm snaked around me, and my eyes flew
open to meet Trillian's; he was holding me by the waist as he
circled with me, both of us caught in the web of music. We
circled the room, the music growing darker, and he let out a
low growl, ripping off his shirt.

His jet black skin glistened under the light. I gasped, once
again mesmerized by his beautiful body. Slender but well
built, he had the perfect V-waist. A thin sheen of perspiration glistened over his muscles, and I snaked toward him,
pressing my tongue to his neck, and slowly—ever slowly—I
slid down his body, drinking in the salty taste of his skin, the
drops of water melting in my mouth as I approached his belt.

I knelt in front of him and reached for his buckle, and—
with precise movements—opened it and slowly drew the
belt out of the loops and tossed it away. He reached down
and unzipped his pants, and I slid them down his legs, facing
his erection, thick and pulsing.

From behind me, I felt Smoky step up to press against my
back, and I turned to him. He had undressed and now his hair
fluttered, ankle length, around him as if a wind had caught it
up and was tousling it. The silver strands whipped this way
and that, dancing to the music. Caught between fire and ice, I
reached up and grasped Smoky's cock in my hands, leaned
over and trailed a line of kisses along its length.

He moaned, his head dropping back as his hair went
snapping into the air. Holding him firm in my hand, I turned
to Trillian and slid my lips over the head of his penis, the
salty taste of his pre-cum tickling my tongue. I knew them,
intimately—my men—inside and out. I reveled in the taste
of their bodies, the feel of their skin against mine, their girth

inside me, filling me full, spreading me wide, taking me out of my head when the demons played too loudly against my thoughts.

As my lips formed suction around the tip of his penis, Trillian shuddered. I began to slowly lower myself onto my hands and knees, facing him, snaking my tongue down his length, slightly widening my mouth so I could take more of him in. Quarter inch by quarter inch, I swallowed him down. Breathing through my nose, I matched my breathing to the rhythm of the music, slow and pulsing, as Trillian began to pump ever so gently into my mouth, sliding in and out between my lips.

And then Smoky was kneeling behind me, his fingers reaching around my waist, down to finger my clit, tweaking me, caressing me, driving me higher as my desire grew on dragon wings. I let out a muffled moan as my pale knight thrust himself inside me, sliding through the folds of my pussy, pulsating with hunger and life.

As Smoky began to drive deeper into me, the music shifted and we were riding a breezy riff, a flute leading us like the proverbial piper, and I closed my eyes, my tongue flickering along the length of Trillian's cock, the shining darkness of his skin in sharp contrast to my own paleness.

A flash of light flared on one of Trillian's thighs and for the briefest of seconds, I saw one of the spiraling tattoos that had buried itself within him—and within me—during our initial bonding. The silver spiral shimmered through the depths of his skin and then was gone, but I knew it had merely faded from sight. The bond we'd forged that night in the temple would never break—not only were we bound by the Soul Symbiont ritual, but by the Ritual of Eleshinar.

Smoky's hands found my waist and held tight as his hair took over. The silky threads found their way to curl around my nipples, and one strand began tickling my clit, stroking lightly across it, vibrating to the music, driving me further into my sex haze.

All fatigue was forgotten as the three of us moved, one beast, one creature joined together, rhythmically twisting and writhing to the music, a bright aura forming around us as our passion magnified.

Trillian pulled gently out of my mouth and lay down on the floor, and I began to rub against him, as even more of Smoky's hair reached out and held my breasts tight, a firm passage for Trillian's cock. My nipples slipped over his skin as I trailed up and down against him, with Smoky still driving me onward, a musky odor filtering through the room from our passion.

Beads of perspiration began to glisten against my skin, dropping in a line to splash against Trillian's stomach. The music heightened, as did the mood of our union. I closed my eyes, my breath deepening into ragged pants as the feel of Smoky inside me, the tickling of his hair intensified. The friction of Trillian's cock sliding between my breasts settled into a lathered drumbeat as I pressed against him. A low mist began to rise from the floor, the icy chill from Smoky mixing with my moonbeams and Trillian's dark fire.

And then, missing Morio, I reached out with my mind—with the bond that connected all of us—and felt him there, on the edge of our union. He heard me and responded, his energy swirling into play with mine. I coiled around him, touching his essence, stroking his aura. We spiraled together, and then Smoky and Trillian were there, supporting us both, helping keep Morio on track.

Here we could see how tired he was, how much energy had been drained off him. And the change that Menolly's vampire blood had wrought was apparent, too. His youkai side—his inner demon—was afire, stronger in spirit.

Together, Smoky, Trillian, and I poured our focus into bringing Morio into our midst, entwining him in our web of passion. I could feel him catch his breath, could feel him gasp as I coiled around him, merging with his being, and then, as I started to come, soaring ever higher, I grasped all of my men and we bolted, like a group of stallions and their queen.

Sweat glistened on my body. With Smoky's driving thrusts, and Trillian's musky gliding between my breasts, I held tight to the spirits of all three of my husbands and went diving over the edge, spiraling into that black void that is *la petite mort*, the little death of orgasm.

I slept like the dead that night—at least the dead that Morio and I weren't scaring out of their graves. When I woke, Smoky and Trillian were already up and my nightgown and bathrobe had been laid out on the bottom of my bed, three red roses gently placed atop the silk. I smiled; they often did things like that—bought me flowers or perfume—and I felt truly loved.

Slipping out of bed, I took a long, leisurely shower, still unable to warm up, then dressed in a warm rayon skirt, a hunter green jacquard bustier, and a light silk see-through shirt over the top as a nod to the weather. I slipped into stilettos and brushed my hair. Placing the roses in a bud vase next to the bed and adding water, I gave them another deep sniff, inhaling the warm scent, before peeking in on Morio.

He was asleep, so I tiptoed back out of the room and headed downstairs.

Delilah and Iris were at the table. I glanced around. "Where's everybody else?" Menolly, of course, would be asleep, but the house seemed unusually quiet.

"Smoky and Trillian are out patching a hole on the roof. Morio's asleep—he seems to be resting deeply today. It's good for his healing." Iris handed me a plate of waffles, bacon, and scrambled eggs.

"He's still asleep. I checked on him before coming down." I took a seat and doused the waffles with syrup, wiping the drip with my finger and then licking off the sweet maple. "What about Shade? Roz?" After a pause, I added, "Vanzir?"

Delilah cleared her throat. "Shade's off . . . I don't know where he is, to be honest. He took off early this morning."

"Rozurial is outside playing with Maggie in the snow." Iris bit her lip. "Apparently, Vanzir has decided to spend some time hanging around down in the Demon Underground, looking for news of the remaining spirit seals." She gave me a long look. "You're going to have to deal with the fallout eventually. When are you going to talk to your men about what happened?"

"How about never?" I mumbled. That was the *last* conversation I wanted to have. Trillian and Morio would manage, but Smoky—no way in hell could I keep him from going after Vanzir.

Vanzir was a dream-chaser demon, and during our last crisis, he'd ended up feeding on my life force. There had been no choice; he was trapped by his nature, and though he tried to break off the attack, he couldn't.

The only option I'd had to stop him was to fuck him—it put a stop to his feeding on me. Although it was the last thing I'd planned on, it was better than him siphoning off my energy, which was terribly painful and a much more invasive violation.

But try telling Smoky that and making him understand. I knew he wouldn't take his anger out on me, but I wasn't so sure he'd leave Vanzir alive. The Moon Mother had already punished the demon—she'd stripped away his powers. She had also stripped away the soul binder that kept him our slave. So he was now a free agent, but without any protection, which was more punishment than I would have come down on him with.

I finally pushed back my plate. "I'll talk to them in a day or so. But first, we have to meet Aeval and check out what's going on with that portal." I stared at my half-eaten waffle, then stabbed at it with my fork. "I'm really hungry this morning. May I have another waffle, please?"

Iris laughed, but slid one onto my plate, along with another egg.

As I dug in with appetite, the phone rang. Delilah answered and when she hung up, she motioned to me.

"That was one of Aeval's assistants. Hurry up and finish that. She got impatient and is already waiting for us in the park. We're to meet her there instead of heading out to Talamh Lonrach Oll. What should we take? Will you bring the staff she gave you?"

I shook my head. "It's more for ritual, or journey. I still

don't know how to use it, so I'd best leave it here. No, she made it clear to me last night. We take iron rather than silver. I've got some of my old paraphernalia around here."

When I'd been younger, a new member of the OIA—although at that time we'd been in the YIA, the Y'Elestrial Intelligence Agency—I'd often used iron. It had been considered illegal by government officials. Or rather *immoral*. But I didn't care. It got the job done.

I'd worn heavy leather gloves to protect my hands and done what was necessary to apprehend our suspects. Nobody but one supervisor ever made an issue out of it, and he—Lathe—had been determined to fuck my brains out. I kept refusing him, so he made my life hell during his time there.

Delilah blinked. "Iron? You still have that stuff?"

"Yeah, but even if I didn't, we'd have a much easier time here than back home getting hold of it." I shrugged as she stared at me. "I never could follow the rules, and hey—it saved me from Roche."

Roche had been a savage serial killer I'd caught back in Otherworld. Actually, truth was, Trillian had played a big part in his capture. I owed him my life, and he'd won my heart. The chemistry had been instantaneous; we'd ignited like gasoline and a match. But nobody else knew the full story. And they never would. The truth would stay between my alpha love and me. I'd wanted to give him credit, but finally, he convinced me it was best to keep the details of Roche's capture quiet.

"Yeah, that's true," she said. Delilah still tended to bend to authority, although she'd grown out of a lot of her naïveté over the past year and was becoming a strong, vibrant woman in her own right. I was proud of how far she'd come. "We'd better get moving, so if you want to grab your torture instruments, let's get moving." Her nose wrinkled, but she grinned at me.

I shrugged. "We don't have a choice anymore. We have to fight dirty. We do whatever we need to win. Because winning is the only acceptable option."

"It seems that's what our life has become. I need to

change into my boots before we go. You'd better get out of those stilettos if we're going through that portal. You said you smelled peat and that means bog marsh."

I glanced at her. She was dressed in heavy jeans and a sweatshirt with a gray tabby cat on the front, but she was wearing canvas Mary Janes. Her hair was short and spiky, an edgy cut that fit her new found confidence.

Delilah was tall, six one, and lean. Menolly was lean also, but short—five one—and petite. I was somewhere in between—at five-seven, I outclassed Marilyn Monroe in the hips and breasts department by a long shot, with an hourglass figure from a porno king's fantasy. My boobs and hips could move men to weep.

Which meant wearing a lot of separates so clothes fit me right. But that was okay with me. My closet could have furnished a fetish bar, considering my love of leather, lace, bustiers, and chiffon skirts.

We headed up to the study, careful not to wake Morio. My family trunk was sitting in the corner, and I quietly grasped one handle on it while Delilah took hold of the other. Together, we carried it to my bedroom. Our mother had commissioned hope chests for each of us when we were little girls, and mine was made out of the starblazer tree—a black wood similar to ebony that resonated with strong magic, only found back in Otherworld.

I opened the lid for the first time since we'd arrived here. A scattering of treasures—mostly sentimental—filled the trunk. I picked up an old photograph of our mother. She'd had it taken while still a student in Spain, and I held it up, looking silently at the beautiful blond woman who stared back at me. Delilah draped her arm around my neck, gazing at her with me.

"She was beautiful," I whispered. "You look so much like her. Only a lot taller."

"I miss her. It's hard to remember her, though. I was still pretty young when she died and you took over. But I always remember she smelled like something . . . I don't know what, but it was good."

I smiled then. "I know what." As I pulled a bottle from the

trunk and opened it, the fragrance filled the room. Chanel No. 5. "You should buy some. They still make it, you know."

With a wistful look, Delilah shook her head. "That smells so much like Mother. I remember that scent. But I don't think I could wear it the way she did. I might get some, though, just to keep on my dresser, for when I miss her."

Slowly, I capped the bottle again and kissed it gently, a wave of homesickness rolling off me. With Mother gone, I'd clung to Father, and now I'd lost him, too. At least Menolly and Delilah still had his love. Shaking off the sense of loss, I put the bottle back in the trunk, along with her picture, and then pulled out a bag and gingerly opened it.

A spider came crawling out, and I automatically squashed it. Ever since our encounter with the werespiders of Kyoka, we'd left none standing inside the house, still worried that the remnants of his cult might have spies around.

I shook out the contents onto the floor, and we stared at the booty. Two pairs of iron handcuffs. An iron-bladed dagger with an antler hilt that I'd managed to procure. And Trillian's gift to me—a silver flail with nine thin iron chains. They were long enough to snap back on me, so I needed to aim carefully, but they'd give a world of hurt to any Fae who dared to stand up to me.

"Sometimes I miss the days when we were looking for common criminals, don't you?" I stared up at Delilah, feeling bleak. Life was a lot harder now, and the stakes a lot higher.

"Yeah, I know what you mean." She sighed and knelt beside me. "You really want to take this stuff with us?"

I nodded. "Considering the Bog Eater's hanging out in there, as well as who knows what, you want to chance not being able to rescue him? Something like this flail could turn the tide. Your dagger is silver, and as aware as the blade is, Lysanthra can't stand up to one of the Elder Fae."

"I see your point. Okay then. We take it. I just . . . fighting dirty has never set well with me." She scrounged around looking for gloves for the two of us. "Here, these are thin but will give us enough protection to handle the iron."

Iron burned us—not quite so bad as full-blooded Fae, but

enough to leave marks. If we didn't get the metal off our skin, it could eventually kill us, eating through our flesh like acid.

"Dirty or not, when dealing with the insane, the murderous, and the freaks, I'm all about anything that gives me an edge." I slid on the gloves and gingerly picked up a pair of handcuffs. "I can't decide whether to bring the Black Unicorn horn or not. We're going after Fae, and I have my qualms about whether it would help our enemies or hurt them."

"Bring it. Please. We might need it and you can't know how it will affect the Elder Fae until you try."

"True enough." I pocketed the handcuffs and flail as Delilah picked up the other set of handcuffs along with the iron dagger. "Let me grab it and then we're off." As she headed downstairs to get her coat, I went into my room and changed shoes, then withdrew the horn from the hiding place I'd fashioned in a small space under a trapdoor and throw rug.

I held up the glistening horn. Crystal, with threads of gold and silver running through it, the horn of the Black Unicorn was only one of nine known to exist. Each had been shed as he reincarnated.

And with this horn I'd brought down the Black Beast, sent him into his next incarnation. He was running free now, a young stallion, set for another thousand years. And I—bloody and battered—had earned my spot as a priestess for the Moon Mother by being the conduit for his sacrifice.

I was still leery of using it—each time, it felt like the horn vied for some power over me, though I hadn't mentioned it to anyone else. At the core of the horn lived Eriskel, the jindasel through whom the Elementals of the horn channeled their energy. And through Eriskel, their magic channeled to me.

Putting the horn in the deep pocket of my skirt, I closed the hidden Velcro fastener. I'd had Iris retrofit most of my skirts to carry the horn safely, so that even if I wasn't wearing the Black Beast's cloak—fashioned out of his hide—I'd be able to carry it with me.

As I put on a warm black microfiber jacket and made sure my boots were tied securely, I wondered just what we were getting into. I cinched my jacket with a silver chain belt, then tied the bag with the handcuffs and iron flail to it. Delilah was waiting for me outside by my car. We were going together, and my Lexus had snow tires and handled the snow better than her Jeep.

As we silently belted ourselves in and I started the car, I breathed a short but sweet prayer for protection. I just hoped the Moon Mother was listening.

Chapter 6

Aeval was standing in the snow, waiting for us. She did not look amused. I curtsied deeply, after elbowing Delilah in the side. She hastily gave a low bow.

"Enough. You are late. It will not happen again, Camille, especially when you join my Court. And now, you are sure you wish to cash in your marker? On a mere mortal?" Her gaze held mine. She was gossamer and silk, she was dark sparkling fire and the hazy mist of the winter night.

"My Lady, I will not disappoint you. And yes, I am sure." I pressed my fingers to my forehead, in an ancient salute. "What do we need to do?"

Aeval, surrounded by a guard party of five, walked over to where the portal had been. "It is here—I can see the signature. Camille, come."

Obediently, I stepped up to her. She placed her hands on my shoulders and stood behind me, then with a little gasp leaned close. "I feel iron in your presence. You are crafty. You will make a formidable acolyte. But for now, look with your soul, look with your magic. Look through the Moon Mother's eyes."

I unfocused my vision and let my mind drift, gazing at the spot through a hazy blur. And then, I caught it—there it was, a sparkling signature. The portal we'd seen the day before hadn't disappeared at all. It was there, unseen to mortal eyes, unseen to the Fae not looking for it. The blue vortex crackled and snapped, and behind us, I heard Delilah gasp.

"I can see it," she said.

"Your sister and I brought it to the forefront." Aeval patted me on the back. "Good job. You have much power—though I can feel where some of the synapses are skewed. You can never fix them, you were born that way, but there are ways to work around the misfires. As time goes on, you will learn, my daughter. You will learn."

Her voice was still cool and aloof, but beneath the icy exterior I heard the soft opening of a door. I turned to her, smiling, and for the first time she truly smiled back. Her eyes were dark, spinning orbs of power and glamour, and in their reflection, I saw myself. Half human, but also half-Fae. Even though my father had disowned me, I was his daughter, and there was no denying his heritage.

"Now what?"

Aeval motioned for me to join Delilah. "I will open the portal so you can venture inside. I will give Camille the charm to reopen it when you need to—when you're ready to return. Hopefully you will find your friend. And with hope, you will survive what lies within. The powers there are deep and dark; they are ancient moss on still older trees. They are powers that can match the Black Beast. Be cautious, girls, for you do not know half what you think you do, and snares and traps are sown deep within the heart of the Elder Fae."

As we stepped aside, she held out her hands toward the portal. The vortex shimmered and, like an iris door off some science fiction show, slowly swirled open. I could feel the warm scent of summer and peat bogs and once again, the feeling of red eyes gazing at me latched hold and I couldn't shake it off.

I glanced at Delilah. "Should we do this alone?" But Aeval had bid us come alone, and we had a chance now. "I guess that's a moot question."

"Chase is in there. Let's go. We can always come back for reinforcements if we can't handle what's in there." She sucked in a deep breath. "We owe Chase a lot."

"Yes, we do." I turned to Aeval. "You said you'd teach me the charm?"

She nodded and for the first time looked hesitant. "I do not want to lose you, Camille. Be cautious. Be wary. Do not trust our kind—you grew up among the full-blooded Fae. You, yourself, are half-Fae. You know what we are capable of doing if we allow ourselves to." Leaning close, she whispered in my ear. "The charm to return is *Akan v'la'the*. It will work on either side. When you incant the spell you must be within sight of the portal, and you must use your energy to twist the charm—you know how to do that."

I did. There was a certain inner force that witches applied to the charms. Someone who wasn't a witch, who hadn't been trained, could sing all the charms and spells they wanted and nothing would happen. But with training, the words became weapons, became keys, became tangible power to be manipulated.

"Akan v'la'the," I whispered slowly, my tongue testing the pronunciation. A small shiver ran through me, and I realized I'd found the magical signature of the charm. I inhaled deeply and let my breath out in a slow stream. "I'm ready."

"Then go and may the gods be with you." Aeval nodded to us.

I turned to Delilah. "Let me take the front. I can suss out the energy better than you can." And without a second thought, we stepped through the portal, into the deep. Into the dark. Into the wild.

The aperture closed behind us and we were alone amid a jungle of foliage. The temperature here was chill but not icy, humid and cool and filled with mist. The scent of tangy earth echoed up, along with sour peat and old rotting wood.

We paused to take stock of our surroundings. As I turned, I realized the portal appeared to have vanished, but when I closed my eyes and searched for its signature, there it was—right where it should be.

"I can find the portal now, no matter whether it's visible or not." I didn't want Delilah panicking. "And I can open it, whether over Earthside or here. Wherever *here* is."

She nodded. "Good. Speaking of which . . . what *is* this place? Did Aeval say?"

Slowly shaking my head, I gazed at the thick ferns that grew nearly at eye level. Old oaks towered over us, their limbs bare and wet. The ground was frosty and I realized that although there was no snow here, we were definitely in the midst of winter. The ferns were gray, their fronds drooping and dormant. The brambles that interspersed the undergrowth were leafless, their thorns showing through in thick, profuse abundance.

"I think . . . We're in a subset—one of the Faerie dimensions. And from what Aeval says, the Elder Fae roam here. This is not Otherworld, but neither is it fully Earthside. I've never heard of this place before. Perhaps it was created by the Elder Fae, or the Elfin Lords . . . or perhaps by the Elemental Lords. Whatever, I doubt if many humans have ever come here."

"Or if they have, they never escaped."

"Yeah."

Delilah muttered something under her breath.

"What did you say? I didn't catch it."

She turned to me. "I don't like the energy here. It feels . . . hungry. Like it's waiting for something to walk into a snare. Not like most predators, though. There's a craftiness to it that unsettles me."

I let out a shaky sigh. I'd been feeling the same thing. "I keep thinking about Aeval's story about the Bog Eater. Here we have peat and we have dark hunger . . . and I can smell rats." I pointed up to a nearby tree. On the boughs perched vultures. "Scavengers of the dead."

Falling silent, I prayed they hadn't been feasting on Chase's remains. We had to find him, and the faster the better. There was no real path, but the grass seemed trampled in one direction.

I pointed. "There, we follow that trail."

Delilah turned to me. "If I change into my panther self, I might be able to catch his scent and lead us."

"Please, if it will help." I hadn't thought about that, but it made sense. And she knew Chase's scent.

As I watched, my sister began to shimmer and shift. It looked terribly painful, but she always insisted it wasn't, as long as she didn't rush through the shifting. And then, as hands and feet and arms and legs lengthened into paws and furred legs, as her body stretched and transformed, and her beautiful face became heavy with dark fur, I could only marvel again at how different the three of us were. Well, four—if you counted Arial, Delilah's twin who had died at birth.

Within a couple of minutes, a large black panther stood there, a jeweled collar around her neck. Those were her clothes, I knew, plus being the marker that claimed her as belonging to the Autumn Lord.

"Can you catch his scent?" I asked, petting her head. I loved cats, and whether she was tabby or panther, I always cuddled my sister when she was in cat form.

She let out a low rumbling purr as I scratched behind her ears, and, impulsively, I leaned over and kissed her head. She looked up, her glowing emerald eyes gazing into my face, and with a loud slurp she licked my cheek and gave a happy growl. I laughed, then let out a long sigh.

"Find Chase, Delilah." It wasn't always easy to keep her on track when she was in cat form, but I loved her anyway.

Delilah glanced from side to side, then raised her head to the air and inhaled deeply. She sniffed, her nose twitching, and then, with a low huff, she swung her head at me and set off at a light run. I ran along behind, and we headed into the mists that rumbled through the glen. Up ahead, I could make out two large rock faces, one on either side, that opened into a narrow channel. A ravine between two cliffs.

We loped along, she watching her speed so I could keep up, and I pacing myself. I had far more stamina than any FBH, but I couldn't match her speed when she was in panther form, that was for certain.

As we entered the ravine, I glanced around nervously.

Trees lined the top of the ravine on either side and I couldn't pierce the veil of vegetation. And with the mist rolling along the ground, spiraling up in columns, I couldn't even see the ground. Luckily the ravine was short, soon opening up ahead. It looked like it led into deep woods, and I slowed, calling to Delilah to return to my side. I paused, examining the energy.

Holy hell.

We were entering the realm of a dark god. Not evil, but wild—some ancient forest entity. The masculine energy was overwhelming, and it rode me like a horse, rode me like a beckoning partner. Herne . . . the wild one. Herne, the lord of the forest. Herne, with his antlers rising to the sky. We were entering his realm, and here we would have to be cautious. The gods were not always pleasant, and we were two women in male territory.

"Is Chase in here? Did he come this way?"

Delilah huffed again, nodding. She sniffed the air, then motioned toward a side path. I followed her into the wood, onto the path, wondering what we were getting ourselves into.

The woodland here was dark and ancient. Older than Darkynwyrd, back in Otherworld. Older than Thistlewyd Deep. This was the ancient forest that had sprung up from the loins of the gods. This was primal forest, primal energy.

The silence was deafening, with only the steady sound of water dripping from bough to ground to mark our passing. The sky vanished—the overhanging trees thick with needles and cones, branches entwining across the path to blot out the sky. Everywhere I turned, I smelled moss and mushrooms, tree pitch, and the sweet tang of freshly turned earth.

And peat. Again, I smelled the bog.

The Bog Eater. It had to be him; he had to be near.

Delilah paused, then moved away from my side. A shimmer surrounded her as she began to change, and I realized she was turning back into her two-footed shape. Something must have caught her attention that she needed to tell me about. Or perhaps she just felt more secure.

As she shifted back, I gave her a moment to catch her breath, then asked, "What is it? Did you sense something?"

She nodded, and in a low voice whispered, "We're being followed. There's something behind us."

I slowly turned, cautious, my hand reaching for the unicorn horn. Behind us, I could only see the undergrowth through which we'd come, thick and unmoving. But when I let out a slow stream of breath and lowered myself into trance, I could sense someone out there. Someone old. Someone powerful. Someone not a god, but more powerful than we were.

I glanced at Delilah, trying to figure out what to do. Confront them? If they meant no harm, why weren't they out in the open? Unless they were nervous about what we wanted. If they were going to attack us, would we be able to throw them off their guard by calling them out?

Delilah waited, ready to follow my lead. I readied a spell, calling on the energy of the Moon Mother to channel through my body. Her presence was heavy here, too, and I realized that anywhere the wild reigned, I would find her.

After the lightning filtered down into my body, I sucked in another deep breath and stepped forward. "Show yourself. We know you're there."

Delilah readied her iron knife, wrinkling her nose.

A moment later, the bushes parted and out stepped a thin boy. He was full Fae, that was obvious, and glorious in his beauty, but he was like no Fae I'd seen before. He might stand on two feet, with two arms and one head, but he was far from human looking. Antlers rose from his forehead—a small rack with three tines on each side. His eyes were slanted, with the faintest of lids, and wide set to the point of making his face look top heavy. His hair flowed to his butt, rich brown, and he wore what looked like torn jeans, cut off at the knees, and no shirt. His abs were defined and he was buff, but not heavily muscled.

"Who are you?" I gazed into his face and realized he was far, far older than we were, but he still seemed like a boy.

He let out a garbled cry, then leaped toward us, landing in a crouch at my feet. He reached out to touch my feet, and I cautiously let him, trying to avoid being poked by the tips of his antlers. Delilah poised to put a stop to him if he attacked.

"Aeval—Aeval . . ." His voice was guttural, and I could

barely understand what he was saying, but I knew he'd called me by the Dark Queen's name.

"No. I am not Aeval," I started to say, but stopped as Delilah fervently shook her head. I paused, realizing he hadn't understood me. Or if he had, he showed no sign of it.

"Aeval . . . *Q'n da dir.*" And then he snorted, like an animal, and stood to face me, his eyes luminous and glimmering and crafty. He reached out and placed his hand on my wrist, and slowly began to slide his fingers up my arm.

Nervous now, not sure what he was getting at, I glanced over at Delilah. He might seem young, but that was illusion. And he looked far stronger than me. As I waited, poised to go on the defense, he leaned close and sniffed long and hard at my neck. As he neared my skin, I reared back; I could feel the gnashing of his teeth right behind those closed, full lips.

His eyes turned bloodred, and he let out a loud screech and began to dance around me. I jumped over to Delilah's side.

"What the fuck?" She held up her knife and he stopped, sniffing in the blade's general direction. With a snarl, he shifted from one foot to the other.

"I don't know. I told you, the things in here are not human. The Elder Fae are as far from our people as we are from . . . well . . . the people of Aladril. Who knows what thousands of years has done to them?"

Antler-Boy was gnashing his teeth now, dancing from foot to foot, glaring at the knife. He knew what iron was, that much was obvious, and it didn't make him happy.

"I have no clue what he wants," I said, trying to keep my voice even.

Delilah lunged forward, waving the blade at him. He dodged to the side, quick as a cat. She countered, and he took another couple steps back. "I sense Chase is in the general area, but I don't know quite where. We can't just leave."

"This one would follow us anyway. It's obvious he's latched onto us for some reason. And I don't trust him. He may have the antlers of a deer or elk, but he's got something behind that mouth—I keep sensing nasty teeth waiting to rip me to shreds."

I gazed into his eyes and once again fell into his beauty.

Beauty? *No*, it was more of a glamour. "He's trying to charm me." I turned on my own, lowering my masks so my Fae heritage shone forth.

He blinked, rearing back. *"Aeval?* Heh . . ." And then the shifting movements began again, as if he were dancing to a hidden beat, or—like a shark—couldn't stay still.

"He seems to be fixated on you as Aeval," Delilah said, cocking her head to one side. "As if he thinks only Aeval could have glamour?"

"Maybe Aeval is the only woman he's seen?" I motioned to her. "Let down your glamour. See what he does."

And so Delilah unmasked herself, too. And Antler-Boy gazed from her face to mine, back to hers, looking disconcerted. He backed away another step, looking less certain.

Growing weary of this, I decided we should teach him a lesson. I had no reason to kill him, but maybe a light thrashing would take care of matters. I shook off some of the Moon Mother's energy, shifting what was left into a pale ball between my fingers. Antler-Boy watched, suspiciously, as I gazed up into his eyes, slowly smiled, then sent the spell spinning at him.

I didn't aim it to kill, but merely to glance off one shoulder.

He watched it approach, without trying to duck. When it lashed into his arm, striking with a force strong enough to knock him down but—I hoped—not leave lasting damage, he let out a scream and scrambled to his feet.

I motioned away, like I was shooing a cat. "Go—get out of here. Leave us alone!"

But at that moment, a loud rumble echoed through the woods. I jumped back, ignoring the odd Fae.

Through the forest, from deep in the dark wilds, the sound of thunder echoed with each footstep. Something huge was coming our way. Something ancient, older than time, was striding through the woods like we might walk through a garden. The scent of musk washed through the air—of primal male energy, strong and erect and dark.

We began to back away, but there was nowhere to run.

I glanced at Antler-Boy. A smug look crossed his face and he stuck his tongue out at me. I did not return the taunt but instead focused on keeping my wits about me. Whatever was coming our way was nothing to mess with.

And then, in a crash of lightning and the scent of heavy forest rain, out stepped a being who towered over the trees. Tall he was, with skin the color of moss. Spiraling horns rose into the sky, black as night, and his chest was matted with thick hair. His legs were shaggy and goatlike. A satyr, with hooves sparking fire every step they took. His arms were muscled and his face lined, and his cock and balls hung so heavy that they might be boulders in their own right.

"Herne." I whispered his name as I fell to my knees, unable to wrest my gaze away.

Herne . . . Lord of the Woodland. Herne. Lord of the Rut. Lord of the Vine. King Stag of the World. Lord of the Wild.

His eyes burned red, piercing my soul. Here was the consort of the Huntress—to the Moon Mother. Here was the god that roamed the night, reminding people why they could never conquer nature.

Catching my breath, I pressed my hands to my eyes. "Lord of the Night . . . ," I whispered, bending over to touch my forehead to the ground.

Delilah let out a strangled cry and joined me. "He is . . . he is . . ."

"I am Herne, Lord of this land. And this is one of my sons, Tra. What have you been doing to him, Aeval? I thought I told you never to torment my children again, you devil."

I slowly glanced up at the god, a terror so deep in my heart I could scarcely form words. "Your Eminence . . . I am not . . . if it please . . . I'm not . . ."

But he stopped me, with a sudden laugh. "You are not Aeval! Who are you? And why are you so familiar?" And then, another pause, and he leaned down, looking at me like I might bend down to look at a bug. "You carry the mark and horn of the Black Beast. Who are you? And what are you doing in my realm? And why should I let you live?"

And I realized right then just how much trouble we were in.

Chapter 7

Crap. And I didn't usually use that term.

"We're in trouble," I whispered to Delilah. "We are in so much trouble . . ."

"Again, I ask you, girl: Why should I let you live?"

I forced myself to my feet even though I just wanted to cower at his.

"I am Camille, from Otherworld. I'm a priestess of the Moon Mother. I am the Chosen of the Black Beast. I am a slayer of demons." The gods tended to respect people who weren't shy about their exploits, so I decided to proceed on that premise and hope I wasn't barking up the wrong tree.

"Chosen of the . . ." Herne paused, and I felt him rifling around in my mind. The gods were good at that—getting inside your brain and worming around till they found what they wanted to find.

I hated the feeling—it reminded me of when Vanzir had been sucking at my energy, sliding into my thoughts just as he slid into my body. My mind, my magic, and my thoughts were my own. My body might be the temple, but my inner self, my *core* was the sacred flame.

But surprisingly, he didn't stay long, nor did he tarry over things not his business. After a moment, Herne withdrew from my thoughts and stared at me with a puzzled look.

"You may wander in my realm, but I will not protect you. You carry magic far too powerful for your own good, and because of it, you are in danger. Indeed, danger rides you like a steed, it clings to your back. You reek of Aeval's energy and yet . . . there is something beneath the stench of the Unseelie. And where you are going, young Fae, the Dark Queen will not be able to protect you."

After a moment, he let out a dismissive bark. "Half-breeds are irksome. I don't like puzzles." He motioned to Tra. "Run ahead. This is not Aeval. Leave these two alone and neither help nor hinder them."

"Wait—"

"Well, what is it? Hurry up." Huffing, his hands on his hips, he stared down at me, eyes flashing. Delilah looked at me like I was nuts.

At first I thought to ask him about Chase, but then I stopped myself. No use putting the detective in danger, in case Herne's bad mood extended to him as well. I quickly restructured my question.

"Have you heard of the Bog Eater? Do you know if he's near?" Might as well ask something that could help us.

Herne choked. "Now I understand why I don't trust you. Yes, that piece of filth is near. Anyone who cozies up with the likes of Stollen Kom Lightly deserves what she gets."

"I'm not—" I started to say, then stopped as Herne and Tra vanished in a swirl of frost-covered leaves. Both confused and relieved—we'd gotten off lightly—I turned to Delilah.

She broke into a nervous smirk. "You know the old proverb: *Foolish are those who summon the gods, for the gods might just answer.*"

"I didn't summon him. And Tra gives me the creeps. I hope he behaves and leaves us alone." Still shaking, I forced myself to calm down. "At least we know the Bog Eater is near."

"That doesn't make me feel any better." Delilah let out a

long sigh and shook her head. "I smell Chase." She pointed through a patch of waist-high ferns. "I think he's that way."

We plunged through the fronds, limp from winter's chill, and the rattle of dried leaves echoed with our passing. The overgrowth was dry from the winter, and leaves shattered with our touch, breaking into shards as we pushed our way through the tangle.

"Why would Chase have come this way? Maybe he ran off the path?" Delilah asked, but I could tell she already knew the answer.

"Easy one. Either he was carried, or he was running away from something and looking for a place to hide." I shook my head, gazing around in the unending sea of foliage. "How are we going to find him? I'm beginning to think we're nuts for coming in here on our own. We should have at least brought Smoky with us."

Delilah paused, then pointed ahead. "Look!"

I followed her gaze and there, in the tangle of a briar bush that bordered a glen, saw a jacket. It had to be Chase's.

We shoved our way through the last of the bushes over to the brambles, and I gingerly removed the jacket from the branch. It stuck on the thorns and I tugged, then tugged harder, and it ripped into my hands. I held it up to Delilah's nose, but even from here I could smell Chase on it. He'd come this way.

"He must have been in a big hurry if he had to leave this." I peeked through the pockets and took out his wallet, badge, checkbook, and anything else that looked like it might be important. As I did so, a card fell out. It was the business card of a local psychic—one I knew was legit and fairly accurate. I said nothing, but put it back into the wallet.

Delilah leaned over, and when she stood up again, she was holding a gun in her gloved fingers. "Chase's gun. And it's been fired. This is not a good sign." She looked around, her eyes brimming, but she didn't cry. She merely slid the gun's safety on and placed it into the bag containing the iron cuffs she carried.

"Should we continue?" I glanced around the glen. Ringed by tall oak and cedar, the glen was shaded and the ground dusted with a thick layer of white. Something caught my attention. At second look, I could see where something—or someone—had been dragged through the hoarfrost. "Look—there."

Delilah knelt by the tracks. She sniffed, holding the breath deep inside for a moment before slowly exhaling. "Chase. Chase was here. Something caught him and he fired at it, dropping his gun. Whatever it was, I think it overpowered him."

I followed the tracks with my eyes. "That looks like someone dragging dead weight—I don't see footprints indicating he was on his feet." If he'd been running after them, or resisting, it would have looked more like a scuffle.

"Come on." Delilah headed across the glen and I followed her, not wanting to go farther without additional help. But Chase had been captured, and who knew what had hold of him?

I fell in beside her and we followed the trail of trampled grass. When we came to the other side of the glen, there was a short path through a ring of cedar and oak, and we cautiously navigated through it, with Delilah's nose checking the air while I kept glancing over my shoulder to watch our backs.

And then, as we pushed through the trees, we found ourselves on the edge of a bog—long and wide—that stretched almost beyond eyesight. I caught the silhouette of land on the other side, but the marsh was covered with wisps of mist that lingered above the ground and it was hard to see much through the vapor. The smell of peat was strong, and the acrid scent of decaying vegetation rang sour through the air.

I gazed at the wide expanse of wetlands. Fens were treacherous. If we tried to work our way through there without the proper equipment, chances were we could get bogged down, no pun intended. There was no easy way to tell where the path was—the frost covered everything as it had back in the glen, but with the tangled foliage, it was impossible to follow any trail that Chase might have made.

Overhead, a mournful call echoed as a team of ducks came winging by.

Delilah turned to me, her face pale. "Want to make a bet the Bog Eater is out there, waiting? Do you think he has Chase?"

"If he does, then Chase might as well be dead." The words slipped out of my mouth before I could stop them. At her pained look, I bit my lip and then lightly laid my hand on her arm. "I hope not. Aeval didn't think so. Do you think he was dragged away into this strip of forest rather than the bog? Do you want to look?"

She gave a hopeless shrug. "Do you think we'll find anything? Or do you really think he's out there . . . dead?"

For the first time, even through all of the crap we'd been through, I saw defeat on her face as she held her breath, waiting for my answer. And that tore up my heart. Of all three of us, she was the eternal optimist, and though I was glad she'd grown up—she had desperately needed a dose of realism in order to be able to face what we were up against—the realization that my younger sister was no longer the happy-go-lucky kitten pained me.

I steeled myself and did something I rarely did. I lied.

"I don't think he's dead. No. If the Bog Eater had caught him, he would have eaten him up right there and we'd have found bloody remains. I think something else caught hold of him. Now, whether he's out in the bog or not, I'm not sure. We can't check on that without more help. But let's walk along the edge of the fen here, there's room enough—just be cautious for quicksand—and see if we can find any sign that whatever dragged him away took him into the forest instead."

Delilah began to breathe again. She flashed me a grateful look and leaned down to kiss my cheek. "Bless you. You've always known just the right thing to say. I know it's been hard, over the years—you've kept the family going and now, with what Father pulled on you—but . . . Menolly and I both owe you so much."

Averting my eyes so she could not read the truth of my thoughts, I gave her a soft smile. "That's what big sisters are for. Right? Now come on, let's have a look. Here—grab a wooden stick so we can test the ground as we go along."

Quicksand could easily hide in plain view, especially this close to a bog. A good walking stick could save your life.

We slowly moved forward, testing the ground every few feet. The path between the forest and the bog was narrow—a couple of yards at the most—and we tried to keep toward the trees. Even though I didn't really believe Chase had been dragged into the forest, I kept my eyes open. Maybe I was right; maybe we'd luck out and find a trace of him along the trail.

Delilah and I fell into an easy rhythm. The chill of the air kept us alert, as did the hum of whatever insects were able to brave the cold. I wasn't sure what they were, but it wasn't the lazy drone of bees or the sunset chirping of crickets. No, this was more a buzz, then a *pop, pop, pop.* I looked into the trees, searching for birds, and saw several—a hawk in one branch, unmoving but very aware.

In another tree, several starlings watched over the forest, along with the inevitable crows. Crows and ravens, symbols of Morgaine. Could she be nearby? But a little voice inside whispered: *There are more entities who have dealings with the black birds than just Morgaine. Be cautious. Stay alert.*

We picked our way along, tapping the ground, looking for signs of Chase. After fifteen minutes, I was almost ready to give up and turn back when something shiny on the ground caught my eye. It was in a tangle of huckleberry up ahead, lying partially beneath a dying fern.

"What's that?" I pointed to the object.

Delilah, using her stick to prod her way over to the bushes, knelt by the bush and gingerly reached to pick it up. From where I stood, it looked like a bracelet. She flipped it over to gaze at the backside, then looked up at me.

"Chase's watch. I bought it for him for his birthday this summer."

She'd had it inscribed. I'd been there when she asked them to engrave *From your favorite puddy-tat. Love, Delilah* on it. I swallowed a lump in my throat. Even though she was happy with Shade, Chase had given her something no one else ever would: her first chance at love.

I made my way over to her and we hunted around the

bush, finally discovering a small trail leading into the forest. It was covered by detritus—decaying leaves, fallen needles from the conifers, and other signs of winter—but it was there. And as we looked closer, we could see the indentations in the mulch. Again, it appeared as though someone had been dragged along through here.

"Come on," I said, feeling the first ray of hope I'd experienced since Chase disappeared.

We broke through the brush, stumbling along, following the trail until we came to a ring of toadstools.

A *faerie ring*. Magic emanated from them, old magic, trickster magic, and I sucked in a deep breath. As sure as I knew my own name, I knew that Chase had entered this ring, but not come out. Somebody had whisked him away.

"The Bog Eater?" Delilah's voice was thin.

I shook my head. "I don't think so. No, this *is* Fae energy—Elder Fae, most likely, but not the Bog Eater. And I'm sorry, but we can't go through that ring. We have no clue where it leads. It's even more dangerous than the bog."

She slumped to the ground, staring at the fungi. "I can't believe this. What the hell's happening? We should be chasing demons—*with* Chase. Not trying to find out what member of our extended family swept him off."

I hesitantly stuck my hand in the ring, holding tight to a branch of the bush next to me. My fingers instantly began to tingle, and the needle pricks raced up my arm. I yanked it out again, not wanting to tempt fate.

"We need more help. Let me see if I can find out anything else." This wasn't a good space in which to scry, but I pulled out the unicorn horn. Eriskel would probably bust my butt if he knew where I was with this, but it occurred to me that I might just be able to use the Elementals locked within the horn to find out more about Chase.

I took a quick look around, then settled myself against the trunk of a tree. "You keep your eyes open. When I'm communing with the horn, anything could sneak up on me and I wouldn't know it. I don't trust this place."

I held the horn in my hands, the cool crystal resonating through my body with a satisfying tingle. Here was magic

I understood, magic that I knew. Of course, at first it hadn't been that way—I'd been scared spitless when I realized that I was being given possession of the artifact. But now . . . *I guess we learn and grow and adapt.*

Closing my eyes, I took a long, slow breath and felt myself spiral inward, into the horn, into the energy, into the core. A dark chasm opened up and I fell, deep and long, diving inward. Down I tumbled, head over heels, spinning in a vortex of spiraling silver and gold. The winds raged around me as I aimed for the center star—a single shining point on the horizon. As it approached, I held my breath, hoping to land softly.

Thunk. I hit with a shudder that raced through me like thunder. And then, standing, I glanced around and found myself in the little room where I had first discovered the secret of the horn. A table and two chairs sat in the center, much like a garden patio set, and on each wall was fastened a large mirror, like a picture window.

On the south wall was a mirror reflecting a bronze desert, and there, in a flowing dress fashioned of molten lava, with hair burgeoning around her like hardened black pillow lava, stood a beautiful woman whose skin glowed with the color of sunset. She bowed.

I curtsied in return. "Mistress of Flames."

Against the west wall, the mirror showed a watery ocean rippled with cresting waves, and their roar echoed out of the picture as a merman rose out of the depths, leaping like a silver flash through the air, then back into the water. He rose again, shook his long mane of kelp-colored hair, then turned jet black eyes on me and inclined his head.

I nodded. "Lord of the Depths."

To the north wall, within the glass I could see a tangled forest with mountains rising in the distance. The Elemental who stepped forward was wearing a frosty cloak over a green robe beneath, and the faint scent of spring clung to the dryad look-alike.

"Lady of the Land." I nodded to her.

Lastly, I turned to the east and a ray of early-morning sunlight came shimmering through the glass as a stalwart man flew into the picture, astride the back of an eagle. They landed on the craggy mountaintop and he dismounted and fell to one knee, his leather armor brown against the flaxen strands of his hair.

"Master of the Winds, I am glad to see you again." I wasn't ever sure what to say, but the ritual didn't seem set in stone. And I truly was becoming fond of them. Even though I'd seen them only a few brief times, I could feel them with me whenever I carried the horn.

I turned to the center of the room and waited, and sure enough, within a few moments a man appeared. Tall— nearly seven feet; his skin was as brown as an oak, and his hair long and dark. He could play with his shape and form, however, and I had never ascertained what his true looks were. I smiled when I remembered the earrings he'd been wearing that I'd fallen in love with. He'd given me a pair just like them.

"Eriskel." I paused, wondering how to frame my request.

"You have need of our help? I assume we are not in the middle of battle or you would be calling on the powers of the horn from out there." He motioned to the table and slid into one of the chairs.

I hadn't yet figured out whether the jindasel liked me or just tolerated my presence, but whatever the case, he was bound by his nature to help me. He was part of the horn; he would not exist without it. When the Black Unicorn died every thousand or so years, his horn and hide were shed and made into ritual artifacts, and a small fragment of the Black Unicorn's spirit became trapped in the body of the horn, acting as the mentor for whoever ended up wielding the weapon.

Jindasels were formed by a number of creatures, off-shoots spinning out of the main spirit like an avatar. They took on an essence of their own—but the jindasels of the horn were unique in their ability to function autonomously, without the original creature that spawned them being near.

I leaned forward, elbows on the table, chin propped on my hands. "Can you or the Elementals of the horn sense into other realms or through portals?" I ran down what had happened and where we were.

Eriskel blinked, his eyes so wide they were surreal. He folded his arms across his chest and shook his head. "You need to get out of here. *Now.* This place is not safe. Not for you. Not for the horn. Do you know what would happen if one of the Elder Fae got hold of this artifact?"

"That thought has crossed my mind. Nothing good, I'm sure."

"Then go. Get your pretty ass out of here and protect the horn. If one of the Elder Fae gets hold of it, all hell will break loose. You think the Bog Eater's bad? You have no clue how ruthless and powerful some of these beings are. They may be your relatives in name, but you are like a dust mote compared to them. You could probably take one down in a fight if you brought all the powers of the horn to bear, but it would be dicey, and you—my lady—would not come out alive."

And with that, Eriskel ejected me from the horn. I blinked, the feel of his concern weighing heavy on my shoulders. Jumping up, I turned to Delilah.

"We have to get out of here. Now."

"But why?" She frowned, but one shake of my head spurred her into action. As we headed away from the mushroom ring, she looked around nervously. "What's going on?"

"Eriskel convinced me it's a very bad idea to have the horn here with me," I whispered. "I wish we could move faster—well, *me*. You can. I wish I could run faster. Now I'm going to fret until we're back out of the portal."

"I'll watch your back, never fear for that." Delilah didn't question, just held tighter to the iron blade. She winced. "I can feel the iron through the glove, but it's not too bad. Tingles in a really unpleasant way."

"Yeah, I know." We stumbled our way back through the forest toward the strip of shore between the bog and the woodland. As we stepped out onto the open strip of land, I stopped and looked around. "Notice anything odd?"

She paused, listening. "No birds."

"Yeah."

Not only had the birds stopped chirping and crowing, but everything else had gone silent and I could feel an undercurrent—something rumbling so low I could barely make it out. It was coming from across the bog in our direction.

I turned toward the fens. The marsh was quivering—or at least one line of reeds running through it was. My heart in my throat, I made sure my gloves were on and pulled out the iron flail from the bag I was carrying.

And then, the rumbling grew louder as an oh-so-tall creature erupted from the water, spraying peat and detritus and stinking fen water every which way. The man—was it a man?—rose up, a good eight or nine feet tall, and his eyes were spinning with the brilliance of sunlight bouncing off mirrors. He gave one long laugh, turned my way, and leaped from the bog.

Chapter 8

❧❧❧

"The Bog Eater?" Delilah jumped toward me, trying to intercept.

"No, I don't think this is him!" I scrambled to one side, managing to avoid the Elder Fae's long arms, but in my haste, I tripped over a root hidden under the leaf mould and went sprawling. Coming to my feet, I swung around, iron flail outstretched. "What the fuck are you?"

He said nothing but lunged again for me, and this time, he caught my ankle as he dragged himself onto land. My feet slipped out from under me as I went flying back to the ground. As I landed, I saw then that his legs were bound together with a finned tail. *Merman! A Meré—one of the Finfolk!* Oh fuck—even if he turned out not to be one of the Elder Fae, he was all too dangerous. But his energy spoke of ancient times and deeds.

Terrified—his grip was unrelenting—I sprang to a sitting position and brought the iron flail down across his arm.

With a screech that pierced my ears, he let go and jerked his arm away. Fae—definitely Fae. Before he could reach for me again, I scrambled away and, at that moment, felt Delilah grab one of my wrists. She dragged me out of his reach and to my feet.

Gasping for breath, I turned to gauge what he was doing. "We have to get out of here. He senses the horn."

The light in the creature's eyes was all too hungry, and he flopped forward some more, using those great, long, muscled arms to pull himself toward us. Delilah grabbed my hand and we ran, scurrying down the narrow strip of land back to the trail through which we'd first emerged on the bogs. I glanced back over my shoulder.

"Oh crap! He's transforming—his tail just became legs. Run!" I broke free from her and plunged through the overgrowth.

The merman/Fae/whatever-he-was had transformed to two-legged and was chasing behind us. And he knew how to run.

Delilah let out a garbled cry and once again passed me, grabbing my hand on the way and dragging me with her. We broke through the short path into the glen. I gasped, my lungs working overtime.

"We're going to have to fight. He's fresh and we can't keep running all the way back to the portal." I hopelessly turned to keep an eye on the entrance to the glen. "He'll be here any minute. Iron did affect him."

"Then iron it is. What about the horn?"

"I . . . I . . ." Truth was, I was afraid to use it, but then I yanked it out of my pocket. He was a water spirit; therefore, fire should work on him. I breathed deep, putting more distance between me and the entrance to the clearing. Sending my thoughts back into the horn, I whispered, "Mistress of Flames. Attend me."

As the energy of the horn began to well up, the creature appeared through the foliage and headed straight for me. I brought the horn up and aimed it straight at him, even as Delilah stabbed him in the side as he loped by her. He screamed, the iron blade of her dagger smoking as it met his flesh, but simply reached out to knock her off her feet and kept coming.

"Stop—stop or I'll be forced to kill you!" I wavered, hating to go up against such an ancient creature. Chances were he'd been around before the Great Divide. But his hunger, his thirst for the horn's power was glimmering in his eyes and he let out a guttural laugh.

"Mistress of Flames . . . take him!" A blast of pure fire burst forth from the horn and washed over him. He spent a moment staring at me, then leaned his head back, and I thought he was going to utter a long scream, but he just laughed.

Holy hell! The flames hadn't affected him. He began to move toward me again, this time each step deliberate. I stuffed the horn back in my pocket and held up the iron flail. This time, he did flinch. I noticed that his side was festering where Delilah had stabbed him.

Delilah was on her feet again, looking shaky. She raced forward, dagger at the ready, dodging as he reached back to ward her off. His gaze never left my face.

I sought the emotion behind his eyes. *Greed. Desire. Covetousness.* He wanted what I had. He wanted the horn. And he'd do whatever he could to possess it. Eriskel had been right.

I bit my lip. Flame had not worked. Perhaps . . . earth? And so I pulled out the horn again, and whispered, "Lady of the Land, please please help me."

The energy began to rise within the horn, running through my hand to circle through my body. I caught a whiff of sweetgrass and lavender, of oak moss and heavy soil . . . and then—as Delilah ducked his fist and swung low with the dagger, again slicing his side with a hissing gash—I whispered, "Let the hands of the earth rise up."

At that moment, the earth beneath our feet began to quake. It vibrated, shaking wildly as both Delilah and I went down. Out of the ground, reaching up through cracks forming on the hardened soil and frost, came dark hands formed of tree roots and old bones. They writhed, long fingers trembling, reaching, stretching to clasp hold of the creature's legs.

He let out a howl, trying to shake them off, but they held

him tight and began to slowly pull him down, began to draw him into the earth, inch by inch. Delilah scrambled up and ran to my side, helping me back to my feet.

I wasn't sure if the roots could hold him long—he was an Elder Fae, and they had some dominion over the world—so I gave one last look as more hands reached up to help drag him into the abyss.

"Come on," I said in a hoarse voice. "Let's get the fuck out of here. We have to leave." We turned and ran, but the creature's howls lingered long, until we neared the portal. I hurriedly whispered the password, twisting it at just the right point, and the aperture opened. We leaped out, back into the snow and ice of Seattle.

Aeval was there, much to my surprise. As we sprawled on the ground, gasping for breath, she knelt beside me.

"Best to put your weapon away," she whispered. "I would not touch it for the world, but there are many who would slice your throat to possess the Horn of the Black Beast."

I jerked my gaze up to hers. She knew, of course, that I had it, but I'd taken care to keep it out of the Triple Threat's presence. Out of sight, out of mind, out of potential disaster's way. Quickly stuffing it back in my pocket, I accepted the hand of her guard as he helped me up. Another gave a hand to Delilah. We dusted the snow off, but it clung to the mud and stickers we'd picked up on our journey.

Aeval gave me a soft smile, both magnetic and dangerous. "I am not the one you have to fear with your treasures, my girl. Now, did you find your friend?"

I bit my lip. The realization that we might actually have lost Chase for good was beginning to set in. I shook my head. "No. Well, yes, we found his trail. But we could not follow. Something took him through a faerie ring—toadstools—and we could not chance it. I don't think it was the Bog Eater. But there were other creatures . . . whatever came after us at the end there . . ."

Delilah and I described the creature to Aeval, and her eyes lit up, though not with fond thoughts, that much was obvious.

"You managed to cross Yannie Fin Diver. Best be cautious around all bodies of water now, girls." She swallowed hard and shook her head. "He's a bad enemy to make, and an even worse one to avoid."

"Is he Elder Fae? Does he stay within that realm?" I was sincerely hoping for a yes to my second question, but it seemed the universe was all about playing Fuck You.

"Yes and no. He can cross through the element of Water. He's Elder Fae, yes, but he might as well be a god to the mermen. And you know what the Finfolk are like." Aeval shuddered. Apparently she thought as much of the Meré as we did.

I nodded. "The Finfolk are terribly cruel, back home in Otherworld as well as here. They have long, long memories and will do whatever they can to avenge themselves."

"Killing Yannie Fin Diver isn't going to be easy, if even possible. The Elder Fae are not true Immortals like the Elemental Lords, but they . . . they are closer than even the Gods to life everlasting." Aeval looked worried, and when one of the Fae Queens was concerned, we'd better take it seriously.

"Then you don't think the Lady of the Land was able to kill him? He was being drawn beneath the ground. The same thing killed thieves back in Otherworld when I used the horn—"

"*Thieves?* What are thieves compared to the Elder Fae? Dust motes. No, girl. Those roots and bones were merely holding him back long enough for you to get away. Trust me, Yannie Fin Diver lives . . . and he will remember you."

"What do we do about Chase? Where do the faerie mushroom rings lead?"

Aeval frowned, her gossamer dress blowing in the breeze. But the cold didn't even seem to faze her. She shook her head. "Usually, they lead to a barrow and cross over into the realm of Fae. But you were already there . . . so this is an oddity. You find faerie mushroom rings here, quite often actually, but they are not common once you cross over. I'll do some research. Meanwhile, I think you are correct. I don't think the Bog Eater caught hold of your friend. I truthfully believe he still lives. As to how you will retrieve him . . . I'm sorry. I can help you no further."

She turned. "I am returning to Talamh Lonrach Oll now. I will see you within the week." And with that, the Queen of the Dark vanished into the swirling snow.

"What now?" Delilah asked, bleakly staring at Chase's watch. We were sitting in my Lexus.

"I wish I knew. I wish I knew someone who might help us. They have to be associated with the Fae. Let me think."

Damn it. Now, not only had we not found Chase, but we'd made yet another enemy. I frowned, fiddling with the receiver until I pulled in The End, a radio station that played cutting-edge alternative and grunge. As the music blared through the car, I ran through every idea I could think of.

Finally, I thought of something that might work, but it would mean more danger and more dealings with the Elder Fae. "Maybe Menolly can call on Ivana Krask again. She's Elder Fae and might be able to help us."

"Crap—the two words I did not want to hear. *Elder Fae*. What makes you think that Ivana Krask isn't playing footsie with Yannie Fin Diver?" Delilah shot me a look like I was halfway on the road to crazy.

"You're probably right, but that's the best I can think of for now. Come on, let's drop down to the Indigo Crescent and see how things are going, then head home. You can check out your new digs upstairs."

My bookstore—which had started out belonging to the Otherworld Intelligence Agency—had been partially destroyed in an explosion that killed one of my best customers and a dear FBH friend—Henry Jeffries.

I'd dedicated a plaque in the reading alcove to him, but it didn't feel like enough. He'd left me a surprising sum of money in his will, and with it, I'd expanded to a café next door, hiring others to run it. The Supes now had the Indigo Crescent Coffee Nook to hang out in. I was donating thirty percent of my profits above and beyond costs to the Supe Community Council to help various Supes in need.

We parked in the spot I'd reserved for my car. The Coffee Nook had its own little parking lot in back, which made it much easier for patrons to visit both my store and the restaurant.

We'd had an upswing in business lately, and the book-store was selling briskly compared to most booksellers in the area. Publishing had taken some hard hits, but we'd invested in setting up audiobook nooks, and Roz had thought of a cool promotion that appeared to be working. We offered a coupon club. When customers came in with proof that they'd bought the book in e-format, we'd sell them a print copy at a discount. In fact, if they bought ten books through the club, they got an eleventh in print for free.

Delilah and I headed inside, she vaulting up the stairs to her new offices, which had been renovated and cleaned up after the explosion, and I into my office. It had been quite a while since I'd spent more than a few minutes here, and even now, my eyes brimmed up. Every time I came to my store, I couldn't help but remember that Henry had died because he'd been working for me. Collateral damage. Too much, too much . . .

As I ran my hand over my new desk, still unused to the feel of the maple—my old desk had been oak—it hit me that life would never be the same. Too much had gone down, too much water under the bridge, too much death and carnage and too much uncertainty. But there were compensating fac-tors and life never stood still. It couldn't, or the stagnation would destroy us, slowly but surely.

"Hey boss!" Giselle peeked through the door, her voice hesitant. "I don't want to disturb you but . . ."

Giselle had been a gift from Vanzir. She was demon, but she could pass for a rather striking young woman with long wheat-colored hair and muscles to rival even the strongest woman I knew. She was athletic—stocky and tanned. Her eyes were brilliant blue, thanks to the contacts that covered her red irises. FBHs were used to eyes my color now, and topaz eyes, but the red demonic thing still wouldn't wash right and they'd think she was a vampire and begin question-ing too closely.

"Come in." I motioned for her to take a seat. "How are things going?"

She bit her lip. "Good, as far as the store goes. Deidre says that the restaurant is coming along nicely, too."

Deidre was a coyote shifter I'd hired to watch over the coffee shop. She was a cousin of Marion Vespa's—the shifter who ran the Supe-Urban Café—and Marion didn't have a job for her so I'd taken her on. Deidre and Giselle had become more than friends, and they made a volatile but interesting couple.

The look on Giselle's face told me something was up. "I know that look. Things may be fine here, but there's something bothering you. What is it?"

Giselle sucked in a deep breath. "Yeah . . . there is something. Twice now, someone has come in, asking about you. About when you're going to be here. The guy says he's Fae and from Otherworld, but boss, I know he's not. I know he's something else, but I can't pin him down."

A draft swept through and I was suddenly cold. "Who was it? What did he look like?"

"I don't know who he was. The first time, he tried to charm me, that much I can tell. I think he thought I was human and easily swayed. When that didn't work, he left. Today he came in, trying to bribe me by offering me a brilliant cut diamond. It was gorgeous, but I don't need diamonds. He seemed puzzled when I wouldn't take it."

I licked my lips. "Describe him?"

"He was around five nine, wiry but muscled. Bald with a single ponytail that was gathered from the center of his head. He looked . . . different, but I don't know how to describe it. Dressed in leather and fur. But I know this: He knows how to work magic. And he was intent on finding out when you were going to be down here, which is why I'm glad you came in through the back today."

"Yeah . . ." I hesitated. Coming in the back way was no guarantee to remaining anonymous. "I think I'd better get home. Delilah and I have a problem brewing, and I don't need another on top of it."

I called for Delilah and she came dashing down the stairs, carrying a sheaf of papers. "We've got to go. I shouldn't be here right now."

She gave me a quizzical look, then shrugged. "I'll meet you at the car. I want to grab a couple cookies from the coffee shop."

Smiling—Death Maiden or not, Delilah would forever be my younger sister—I nodded. "Just don't take too long."

I gathered up the books—it was time to go through them before sending them to the accountant—and then headed out the door, after thanking Giselle for keeping such a good watch on the shop. I climbed in the car and waited, watching the snow lazily fall on the ground. *Too much,* I whispered to myself. *Too much worry, too much to face, too much to lose.*

And then Delilah jumped in, warm cookies in her hands, and we took off for home, bathed in the wash of the fresh-fallen snow.

"Who do you think it was?" she asked on the way, handing me a cookie.

I waved away the sweet. For once, I didn't have much of an appetite. "I think . . . I think it was someone connected with Hyto. Remember, Trytian said he was traveling with a snow monkey."

"Fuck." Delilah leaned back in her seat, nibbling on the chocolate chip cookie. "They know where the shop is, then."

"Can you imagine what a dragon could do to my shop? To the restaurant? To all the people there?" Visions of screaming customers, caught afire from dragon's breath, raced through my head. Hyto wasn't *just* Smoky's father. He was a terrifying dragon—easily capable of destroying everything I'd worked to build up, along with any number of innocents. And he wouldn't care—FBHs were dust specks to him. And I was the thorn in his side.

"What are you going to do?" Delilah's voice dropped, and I realized she'd suddenly grasped the severity of what could happen.

"I don't know. Should I close the shop for now? Stacia killed Henry because of me. And she was leading a targeted campaign. What a crazed dragon might do . . . I can't even think about it."

I carefully navigated around a car stuck on the road. The streets were beginning to ice over with a thick layer of compacted snow beneath the glaze that was forming now that the temperature was dropping again. Though the traffic had melted off a layer of the snow during the day, now that it was afternoon the runoff would begin to freeze into black ice. Seattle drivers had no clue how to drive in the winter—and I was right there along with them. Except my reflexes were better than the average FBH's.

By the time we neared the house, we were reduced to twenty miles per hour to avoid sliding into a ditch. I finally turned into our drive with a sigh of relief. Home glistened like a welcome scene out of a Thomas Kinkade painting.

As we scurried toward the house, slogging through the snow to the porch—which someone had shoveled clean, though it was starting to pile up again—the chill of the air caught me. The temperature was dropping fast and would likely hit the low twenties tonight. That would make for a lovely commute tomorrow.

"If it's this cold now, I dread to see what it's going to be like tonight."

Delilah nodded. "I wish Menolly would skip driving her Jag and just go for a nice long walk to the Wayfarer—the cold wouldn't bother her."

"That might be a good idea. She wouldn't really hurt herself much in a crash—at least not most crashes—but she could hurt someone else without meaning to." As I opened the door, the bustle of the day hit us full force.

Trillian was setting the table for a late lunch. Iris and Rozurial were cooking up a huge pot of spaghetti and meatballs. Smoky was stomping in from the back porch, and I caught sight of the snow shovel as he hung it back up on its nail.

Shade was in the living room, coaxing a fire in the new woodstove we'd bought to help keep heating costs down. He blew lightly on the crumpled newspaper beneath the tinder, and it caught from the sparks that flew off his breath.

"Shamas at work?" I asked.

He nodded. "Yeah, he has the day shift this week, though he

may sleep there if the roads are too bad." As he stood, Delilah moved to him and he enfolded her in his arms, kissing
her deeply, rubbing his hand up and down her back. They
belonged together, as if they'd known each other all their
lives. Even from the outside, I could feel the bond that had
woven between the two.

The doorbell rang and I went to answer. It was Bruce,
Iris's boyfriend. He motioned for me to come out on the
porch. Shivering, I followed him.

"What's up? Why don't you come in?"

He smiled, then pulled out something from his pocket. He
looked like a young man barely in his thirties—right around
Iris's relative age. I wasn't sure how the aging process worked
among sprites and leprechauns, but I knew both were far, far
older than me in chronological years—hundreds of years
older. His tousled brunette hair was curly, reaching his shoulders, and his eyes sparkled with the purest blue—matching
Iris's own. He actually looked a lot like Roz, only without the
dangerous edge. Bruce and Iris made a striking couple.

"I wanted to ask your opinion about something," he said,
holding out a box. "Do you think she'll like this?"

I flipped it open. There, against the velvet cushion, rested
a platinum band with a sparkling mixed-cut blue sapphire
that had to be at least a full carat. On either side nestled half-
carat diamond baguettes.

Gasping, I shook my head. "Oh, Bruce. She'll love this.
This is . . . this is beautiful." I glanced at him. "So are you
going to officially ask her today?"

He blushed. "Aye, my sweet. It's time I did it proper. And
she is free now, to accept. She called me last night and we
talked long and deep. She told me what happened. I know
her dark secrets. She told me if I wanted to walk, she
wouldna blame me. She did kill her fiancé, after all. But the
gods work as they will, and I would expect my lass to follow
the will of her Lady and rid the world of evil. She did the
right thing."

I bit my lip. "Iris will want to stay here. Are you willing to
move onto our land? We can help you build a home all your
own—we have plenty of room here. Seven acres' worth."

"I would move to the moon, should that be where my Iris wanted to live." And when he smiled at me, I felt like the sun had come out. No wonder Iris was taken with him. Bruce O'Shea was like a welcome ray of sunshine and I could practically feel him tugging a rainbow along with him.

"Then come in. And Bruce, in advance, without jinxing it, welcome to the family." I leaned down and gave him a solid hug. And for one moment, I was able to block out the fear that had taken over my day.

Chapter 9

೪‿❀‿ꕥ

Lunch started out with a bang. We were gathered around the table when Bruce stood up and cleared his throat. Iris stared at him, her mouth full of spaghetti. I grabbed Smoky's hand under the table. He gave me an inscrutable look but smiled at me.

"Iris and I've been courting for a while now, and though I've been a fool at times, she's made me a better man." Bruce shifted from one foot to the other. "I know her secrets, she knows mine. And now, 'tis time to step up and be the man she's helped me become. I know you all consider Iris part of your family. Therefore it is only fitting that I beg your permission to ask for her hand in marriage. She is—and always will be—the girl of my dreams."

He was grinning like an idiot, but I could see fear masked behind his eyes—the fear of being rejected.

Iris gasped, but he looked at me and then Delilah. "You two might as well be her sisters . . . and Miss Menolly, too. Would you object to having me for a brother-in-law, should Iris accept my proposal?"

I broke into a smile a mile wide, wanting to cry. So often our meals were tempered with bad news, but this . . . "I have no objection, but know you this, Master Leprechaun: If you hurt our Iris, you'll have all of us to deal with."

Delilah laughed and clapped her hands. "I agree. I so agree. Oh, I wish Menolly were awake, but Iris, you can tell her first thing."

The men murmured, but I shut them up with a look. I turned back to Bruce. "Go on, then. If you want some privacy, the parlor is free."

"No," Iris said, slowly. "You are family. You've seen me through so much. It's only fitting you should share this." She stood and Bruce knelt at her feet, taking her hand in his.

"I am not of your race, I am not of your background. But I come to you, a son of the Rainbow Goddess. A son bound by the golden locks of both the goddess Iris, and my love, Iris." He clasped her hand to his lips and kissed it. "I promise you: I will honor you, give you shelter, give you children if it be the will of the gods, and love you as long as love shall last. Will you, Iris Kuusi, accept my offer of marriage and join me as my wife?"

Iris stared at him, her eyes glazing over like clouds in a blue sky. She sucked in a deep breath and let it out slowly. "Bruce O'Shea, I am not of your race. I am not of your background. I am the daughter of the goddess Undutar, priestess to the snow and mist. I am a child of the ice floes. I accept your offer to marry. I will honor you, make a home for you and our children, should the gods bless us. I will protect the household, and love you as long as love shall last."

And then she burst into tears, smiling, and fell into his arms, kissing his face, his eyes, even as he sought her lips.

After lunch, Smoky, Trillian, and I wandered into the living room. Delilah and Shade had volunteered to clean up so that Bruce and Iris could have the afternoon to themselves, and they were also taking care of Maggie.

Roz meandered in, looking bored. "Vanzir called. He'll be home in a few minutes." He gave me a short but meaningful look, and I gave him a quick nod. Crap. We'd have to be on guard. Again. Everybody but my husbands knew what had gone down.

I decided to fill the guys in on what Delilah and I had found. During lunch, Bruce's proposal had taken precedence and I didn't want to spoil it for Iris. Whether we discussed what next to do then or at dinner wouldn't matter.

"Come upstairs—you, too, Roz. I want to tell you all something, and I should tell Morio while I'm at it. Delilah will fill Shade in on matters." I dashed down the hall and stuck my head in the kitchen. "I sent the guys upstairs. I'm going to tell them about Chase. You run down the situation with Shade and come up after you're done with the dishes."

"No problem." Delilah waved me on. I'd started up the stairs to meet the guys when I heard the front door open. Must be Vanzir. And once again, we'd be walking on eggshells.

Smoky and Trillian sprawled on the sofa in Morio's room, while Roz sat on a nearby ottoman. Morio was propped up by a wall of pillows. He looked a little stronger today. I hurried to his side and planted a long kiss on his lips.

"How was your day?" He stroked my cheek, his nails black and sharp. He hadn't changed into either his fox or demonic form since he'd been hurt—he wouldn't have the energy to change back.

I pressed his hand to my lips and kissed each finger, licking the tips gently. He shuddered, closing his eyes. Morio had seldom talked about his heritage—he was Japanese and had come over when summoned by Grandmother Coyote, one of the Hags of Fate—but I suddenly wondered: What would his family think of me? He was married now. Had he told them? I'd never even thought to ask.

"Love, does your family know about your marriage to me?" I tilted my head, waiting.

He cupped my chin, lifting it slightly. "Yes, they know about you and your sisters. They know about us. Someday, you will meet them. They were . . . not entirely pleased, but neither were they against it. They reserve judgment. And they trust my instincts."

That was more than I'd hoped for. I nodded and didn't

bother to press the subject. As far as Trillian was concerned, I knew that he had long ago left his home and abandoned his family—or rather, they'd abandoned him. It wasn't even an issue with him.

Just then, Vanzir came creeping into the room. He was pale, which was normal—he looked a lot like David Bowie as the Goblin King in *Labyrinth*—but tonight he looked even more withdrawn. His eyes were luminous, swirling kaleidoscopes of a color to which we couldn't even put a name.

He slid onto a far chair and stared at me, his gaze focused on me. What the hell could have happened?

"Hey, where have you been?" Trillian asked him, staring at him a little too long for comfort. And then, without missing a beat, he turned his gaze to me, then back to Vanzir, and I saw understanding flash through his eyes.

Oh fucking hell. He *knew.* Somehow, he'd picked up on it. But when? Just now? Or had he known for a while? My stomach began to churn as Vanzir shrugged.

"I was hanging out in the Demon Underground for a while. Hey, dude . . . Smoky . . . have you heard the rumors about your father?" Vanzir was struggling to keep his voice neutral, but I could sense the fear beneath it.

Smoky gave him a short nod. "Yes. Unfortunately."

I broke in, trying to control *my* nerves. "We have further problems." I outlined what had happened to Delilah and me, first in the portal, and then what I'd learned down at the bookstore.

"So we've got to figure out what to do about Chase, and . . . I think the person looking for me at the shop was the snow monkey that Trytian mentioned."

My words died on my lips as I stared at the floor. The room was silent for a moment, and then before the testosterone could fly, I added, "I am thinking of selling the bookstore. I'm afraid for the people who come in. I'm afraid more innocent people will die because of the demons, or an irate dragon, or just because I'm a handy target for the Fae-haters."

Morio shook his head. "You can't let fear rule your life. If you do, you'll lose more than you know. Everyone on this planet takes a chance the moment they wake up in the morning and get out of bed. You've seen Earth's history—the wars in the Middle East, the world wars, the natural disasters . . . people dealt with them. Now, the biggest war is headed our way and you're doing everything you can to stop it. Closing the Indigo Crescent isn't going to prevent people from getting hurt."

"He's right," Trillian said, his voice surprisingly soft. "You have never been one to run in fear. That's one thing I've always loved about you. You said *the hell with it* and faced danger time and again. And now, my lovely wife, you need to stand up and face the facts of what's going down. *All the facts.*"

It was both a question and a demand. And I knew right then that Trillian would bring it up if I didn't. And Trillian didn't mince words. He didn't play fair, and he didn't side-step delicate issues.

I sucked in a deep breath. "Yeah. I'd better. Vanzir . . . will you please leave the room? In fact, you might want to go for a *long walk*. Roz, you, too. I've got something to talk over with my husbands."

Vanzir jerked around. He stared at me, then bit his lip, nodded, and left without a word, Roz following behind him.

Smoky looked puzzled, Morio perplexed. I walked over and locked the door. As if that could stop Smoky from breaking through the wall if he wanted, but hey, it was something. And it might give Vanzir an extra moment to make a break for it.

I turned, scarcely able to breathe. My loves stared back at me. Trillian nodded, and I realized that he was on my side. How he found out—and just how much he knew—I had no idea. But he wasn't going to go apeshit. Morio was still too wounded to throttle the demon. That left . . .

"I have something to tell you. You have to promise to remain calm. I need you to be calm for me. Before we left for the Northlands, something happened." I could barely whisper. "There was no way to avoid it. You *have* to understand this . . . *you have to understand* . . . Morio—remember how bad it was? Smoky, you were off helping your mother. And

Trillian wasn't there. We didn't have enough people in the tunnels when the ghosts attacked. It was bad . . . so bad . . ."

"Camille . . . what happened?" Smoky shifted, his hair coiling out to trail along my shoulder, but I pulled away, shaking my head.

"When Morio was hurt, Menolly and Chase were up top in the snow, trying to keep him alive till Sharah could get there."

"I don't even remember that," Morio said. "Just the pain and the feeling that my life force was draining away."

I pressed my hand to my stomach. "Yeah . . . I know. I *know* what that feels like. In the tunnels . . . Vanzir and I were left down there alone. We were fighting for our lives. I was throwing spells right and left. Vanzir was feeding so deeply from the ghosts that he was lost in the energy and couldn't break free."

Memories flashed through my mind, vivid, like a waking dream. It had been so surreal, and yet, all too real. "When we tried to get to the ladder, I couldn't find my gloves—and the rungs were iron."

Trillian nodded, and I could see he'd already forgiven me. He, of all three, would understand the most. He was my alpha, but he had the same Fae nature I did. Possessive? Yes. But to the point of stupidity? No.

Turning away, I walked over to the door and leaned against it, my head resting on the cool wood. Then I whirled around and pressed my back against it . . . eyeing the three men from whom I knew I could never keep secrets. They were my all. My everything. My loves.

I just hoped they'd feel the same about me after tonight.

Smoky started to stand, but I motioned for him to sit down.

"As I said, I threw some hefty energy bolts that night . . . the air was charged, drenched in energy. Vanzir was trying to feed on the ghosts, to keep them away from us. It was like being trapped in a horror movie with no one from the cavalry coming to save us. I got too close to Vanzir—he warned me not to, but I was trying to get his attention, to see if he knew where my gloves were."

I paused, waiting, searching Smoky's face. But Morio,

I couldn't look at Morio. How could I, when he'd been bleeding to death while I'd been down below, fucking a demon?

"What did he do?" Trillian asked, his voice even.

"His feelers were out, seeking energy, and right then we were attacked again. I cast another spell—a huge mother of an energy bolt. Vanzir latched onto me and began to feed."

Smoky stood, his eyes draining to cold, flat gray.

"Stop! Please stop. Wait. Let me finish," I begged him, still unable to leave the door. After a moment he sat back down, but his back was stiff, his expression unreadable.

"Vanzir didn't *want* to feed on me. He *tried* to stop himself, but his nature overtook him. He was draining me. It was horrible, but even through the pain and the invasiveness, I could feel his anguish. There was only one way I knew how to stop him. One way to make him break off from my mind."

I was crying now, both in fear and in sadness. So much had gone wrong. I held out my hands. "I gave myself to him. It stopped him from feeding on me."

Smoky slowly stood again, then stepped forward, staring at me with a look so harsh that I cringed. Trillian noticed and tried to intervene, but Smoky's hair thrashed, whipping him out of the way. Morio let out a cry.

"He *touched* you?" Every word punctuated by another step, Smoky reached my side. He grabbed my wrist and held it tight, shaking me as he drew me forward. His hair wrapped around my waist, lifting me up to face him at eye level. "I asked you if he touched you! Answer me!"

"Yes, he did. But he didn't have any choice—" My teeth were chattering now. Smoky caught my gaze and then, after a horrible moment in which I was truly afraid he might lose control, he very quietly put me down and gently pushed me away from the door. "Don't—don't go after him! He doesn't have his powers anymore! He can't defend himself."

Trillian and Smoky both turned to me. Morio was sitting forward as far as he could. I swallowed my fear.

"The Moon Mother came through me while he was . . . while we were . . . she stripped him of his powers and the soul binder. He might as well be mortal, except for his innate strength. She took away his ability to feed."

Smoky began to laugh then, but it was a horrible laugh, one filled with retribution and glee. "And so the Moon would wreak her justice before I have my chance. But I will have my say. Vanzir will know why even the gods fear a dragon." He turned and wrenched open the door so quickly that he tore it off its hinges. Tossing it aside, he made for the stairs with me running after him.

"Stop! Smoky! No." I put all the force I could muster in my voice.

He turned at the landing. "Why? Did you enjoy him so much? Are you so hungry for him that you would take a fourth?"

I let out a little cry. "How *dare* you? How dare you make light of what was one of the worst nights of my life? He fed on my mind—he didn't want to, but his nature pushed him over the edge. And just where the fucking hell were your ears when I was telling you about the attack? We were at *war* with a pack of hungry ghosts. They almost *killed* Morio— they would have killed both of us!"

Smoky let out a harsh cry. "I cannot stand that he touched you! That he violated not only your body but your mind!"

"He didn't rape me! I offered myself to him—"

"To get him out of your mind. Both attacks were violations— and in no way do I believe that he couldn't stop himself. He's probably been sniffing after your skirts since the beginning."

Smoky circled me, glaring.

"You're *my* wife—Trillian's wife. Morio's wife. I share you with them because it is what it is. But I refuse to share you with anyone else. I won't share you with some filthy stinking demon who worms his way into your magic and your mind. You are a priestess! He should have had *respect* for you. How can you defend him?"

Before I thought of what I was doing, I reached out to slap him across the face. A strand of his hair caught my wrist and held it taut. Smoky pulled me to him.

"You're my wife. No one gets away with harming you. *No one*. Do you understand?" His voice was thick, and he reeked of musk and anger. "You belong to me. We are paired.

Mated. I should carry you off to a dreyerie. I should keep you as a queen."

I could feel the energy of his dragon self rising around him. The thought that he might actually go through with it this time—he might carry me off along with Trillian and Morio—terrified me. Reasoning with men was bad enough, with all the testosterone, but Smoky was, beneath the gorgeous exterior, all dragon. And a thousand times more stubborn.

"Smoky. I love you. Please, believe me, I love you. But Vanzir . . . he got the short end of the stick. I'm okay. He's not. He has already been punished by my goddess. She did something far worse to him than kill him. She stripped him of his very nature."

Smoky trembled, nuzzling my neck. He pressed his lips to mine, savagely kissing me. And then he slowly put me down. When he spoke again, his voice was barely contained. "Go. Give me time. I can't think straight. If you stay here, I will find him and kill him. Once you are out of the way, I'll go to my barrow for the night. I can't look at you right now or all I want to do is hunt down the demon dog and destroy him."

I stumbled away from him, still afraid but clinging to the ray of hope he offered. Trillian didn't touch me as I walked by, but he whispered, "I'll try to talk to him. Best if you clear out for an hour or so."

"Morio—?"

"He'll be okay. Just go, my sweet." And as I hurried down the stairs, angry and afraid and in tears, Trillian turned to Smoky.

The minute I got downstairs, I hurried into the kitchen. "Did Vanzir get out of here?"

Delilah nodded, her eyes wide. Shade looked like he was ready to tackle something. I glanced at my sister, then her lover, shaking my head.

"I told them . . . about Vanzir . . ."

"I thought you might have," Shade said. "I could feel his

dragon rising from down here. In fact, I'm getting ready to leave for a little while. All it would take is one wrong word from me to set him off."

I nodded. "That's a good idea. I'm going to take a walk. I need to get out of here, but I don't want to drive anywhere." I hunted in the laundry room and pulled on my walking skirt—which Iris had washed—and one of Delilah's turtlenecks. It was too tight, especially around the bust, and I stretched it all out of proportion, but I'd buy her a new one. Throwing my cape over my shoulders, I let Shade walk me to the door.

Delilah gave me a kiss on the head. "Everything will be okay. Vanzir took off. He took the Chevy." We'd bought a couple of spare cars for the guys to use—not as pretty as ours, but serviceable.

"Good. But Smoky could trace him in a heartbeat. Okay, I'll be back in an hour or so. If I get too cold, I'll hang out at the studio." We'd turned a large shed on the property into a studio for Shamas, Roz, and Vanzir to sleep in. Occasionally, I sent my husbands down there to get them out of my hair when I wanted a night to myself.

As Shade walked me out into the snowy afternoon, the light was beginning to fade. Late afternoon might as well be dusk—the shortest day of the year was barely a week away. As we wandered into the twilight, I prayed to the Moon Mother that things would calm down. I'd never fully trusted Vanzir, but I knew he hadn't hurt me on purpose, and I wasn't one to hold grudges when I knew it had truly been circumstance and not premeditation at play.

Shade cocked his head to one side. "Give him time. His ego's been hurt."

"Ego—" I started to protest, but he held up one hand.

"You must understand the nature of dragons. He wasn't there to protect you. You were hurt. You didn't tell him about it immediately. Those three things came to a damning head. He might still have wanted to kill Vanzir, but he wouldn't have been so angry at you. He feels humiliated that he could not keep his family safe. Hell, I feel responsible for you, too, and you are not even my mate. You are my beloved's sister.

And if I feel this bad, can you imagine how much worse your husband feels?"

Shade and I reached the driveway. "Smoky absolutely worships the ground you walk on. The thought of anyone hurting you drives him into a frenzy. He is dragon . . . it is the way."

I nodded. "Yeah, I think I'm beginning to understand that. It's easy to forget I'm not dealing with just a man—a gorgeous, strong, stubborn man. But he *is* a dragon. He's not a human in a dragon suit. Not even a Fae in a dragon suit."

"Exactly. Now, would you like me to walk with you? I will if you want, but it might not be wise should he come to find you and discover another dragon at your side . . . even though I'm only half. Hell, I'm not even going to hug you, though I think you need a hug. My smell on you? It would be suicide." Shade laughed then, and I smiled for the first time in what seemed like forever.

"No, I'll be fine. We have the wards up. Delilah will come find me if something happens. I could use a little time to myself . . . to think."

"Then I'll pop out and go look for Vanzir. I'll try to help him sort out what to do now. Maybe we can pull everyone through this without a problem."

"Delilah sure found a keeper, that's for certain." I waved as he vanished into the shadows and popped out of sight. Thank gods for levelheaded men. Or at least as levelheaded as they were going to get. And on that note, I also sent a mental kiss toward Trillian. Maybe Smoky would listen to him. Maybe Trillian could calm him down.

After Shade left, I turned toward the trail leading to Birchwater Pond. Delilah had been right. A walk would do me good. I decided that, come rain or shine, I'd manage to get out every day for a quiet stroll. The snow had stopped falling and now a patch of sky was glimmering from between the clouds. Another hour and the stars would come creeping out.

The familiar footpath was welcoming, and my boots left soft impressions in the snow. I sucked in a deep breath, letting the chill fill my lungs as I strolled toward the pond. It had been a long time since I'd taken a walk by myself. Even during the full moons, I was in the sky, running with the Moon Mother on the Hunt, along with a passel of warriors and other witches who followed the Lady of the Hunt.

No, I needed more time by myself.

Up ahead was a bend in the trail, one fork leading deeper into the woods, the other leading to Birchwater Pond, where we often held rituals for the holidays. Where I'd married Smoky and Morio.

As I came closer, I saw a tall form in the trees, clad in a white cloak. His long hair floated on the breeze.

Smoky! Smoky had come to find me! I hurried to meet him. Trillian must have gotten through to him. Thank gods. Now we could get on with taking care of this and figuring out some compromise to keep Vanzir alive and my husband happy. My heart skipped a beat, and the worry and heartache began to ease.

As I rounded the fir tree standing between us, I held out my arms, wanting only to feel his embrace, his kiss. To beg his forgiveness for not trusting him enough to tell him when everything had first happened.

"Smoky, please, please don't be angry at me—"

But my words fell away as I stared at the man who towered over me. He gave me a slow, lecherous smile.

Taller than Smoky, his hair, almost as long as Smoky's, was pure white instead of spun silver—now that I was close enough, I could see the difference. He looked somewhat older, though it would be hard to place his age, but I knew he was ancient . . . dangerous and ruthless.

My heart began to race as I turned to run, but his hair reached out to grab me and he dragged me to him.

"No! No! Let me go, let me go . . . please, please let me go."

I wanted to wake up. To wake screaming to find it had all been a dream. But I was here, facing my worst nightmare.

Clenching his arm around my waist, he pulled me up to stare into his eyes, leaning his head against mine as I struggled to free myself. He pressed his mouth against mine, forcing his way between my lips. I choked as he deep-throated me. I tried to bite his tongue, but a strand of his hair caught me around the neck and squeezed until I stopped.

"What's the matter, Camille? You aren't being very friendly. That's no way to greet a relative, is it? After all, aren't you glad to see your *father-in-law*?"

And then, as Hyto laughed, I began to scream.

Chapter 10
❦

Hyto held tight, the strand of hair still around my throat. "At any moment, I could break your neck. Suffocate you. Rip your head off your shoulders. So I suggest you quit screaming."

I shut my mouth and waited for death—I knew that was why he was here. But instead, he reached up with another tendril of hair and caressed my cheek.

My stomach lurched. "The wards will have gone off. Smoky will be out here, searching for me." I struggled to talk against the restraint, my throat hurting.

"I don't think my son will be doing any such thing." He motioned, and out from behind a towering evergreen stepped the man Giselle had described. He bowed briefly to Hyto. "Meet Asheré, my snow monkey. He negated your wards with a blink of the eye. So nobody's going to know anything."

Panic set in. *Oh Great Mother, he's going to kill me here, and I'll never have a chance to say good-bye to my loved ones.*

I was about to beg him—*Just let me go and I won't say a word*—when the words died on my lips. Hyto was beyond reason. He wouldn't listen to me. He hated me. And I didn't beg. My sisters in danger? My friends' lives on the line? I'd be groveling on the floor. But I would never grovel for my own life.

"Nothing to say? No protestations? No begging for your life?" He looked at me quizzically, then let out a snort. "Well, no matter. But I can't go without leaving a calling card. Asheré—prepare the girl." He threw me to the ground and I stumbled.

Asheré grabbed me by my arms and I opened my mouth to scream again, but with a single word from the monk, my voice fell into silence and I could no longer speak. I struggled but another word from him and I couldn't move, standing still as night.

We stood there, watching Hyto as he moved to the side. I felt like I was in a dream—as frozen as one of the icicles on the house. Images of my sisters flashed through my mind—they would carry on, but I would miss them so much.

And Smoky, Trillian . . . Morio . . . who would find my remains? I prayed it wouldn't be one of them—or my sisters. Let it be someone who wouldn't hurt as bad. My cousin . . . Chase . . . anybody but my family.

Would they mourn for me? I thought of Maggie and tears began to roll down my cheeks. And Iris—at least I knew she would be happy now. Even in the midst of this war, she would have a glimmer of hope.

My thoughts leaped to my father. Would he regret cutting me off? Would he see my soul statue shatter? Would he hold the remains in his hands, wondering what had happened to his little girl? Or would he sweep them away, his heart still as hardened as it had become?

Moon Mother, I thought, *please, let my end be easy. Let me go quickly. Let me wander the night with your Hunt, let me find my way to the Land of the Silver Falls and reunite with my mother.*

And then Hyto caught my attention. He focused on one tree near the beginning of the trail and, with a loud roar that echoed from deep within his throat, he let forth a stream of flame from his mouth, setting one side of the fir on fire. As it lit up the night, he ripped my cape off my shoulders and tossed it on the ground near the tree.

What the hell? He could just leave my charred body here as a message to Smoky. That would do more than the cape.

Hyto caught the question in my eyes. A deep rumble echoed from his gut. His laugh was like a sledgehammer.

"A calling card, my dear. Simply a calling card. Because you are only half of the equation. I want my son to know I *own* you. I want to crush him with the knowledge that you belong to *me* now."

No . . . no . . . As I realized what Hyto was saying, I frantically tried to move, tried to break the spell, but I couldn't budge.

He leaned down to stare me in the eyes. "Remember? I promised you when we first met, *Anything my son owns is mine, to use or abuse as I see fit.* When Iampaatar comes to my dreyerie to rescue you, I will have shattered you so far, so hard, that there will be only little shards of your life left for him to pick up. And then, and only then, will I destroy him."

I began to shut my mind down as I realized that Hyto really *didn't* mean to kill me. Not yet. No, he meant to take me and break me and tear me to shreds. As the panic started to build, he gathered me in his arms and we began to turn, slowly at first, then faster and faster until the world became a blur and I lost consciousness.

I came to on a pallet. The first thing I felt was sharp hay poking into my side. The next, a scratchy blanket covering me. My clothes were still on—a good sign. I wasn't paralyzed anymore, but I forced myself to stay still. In the past, I'd learned that it was better to play dumb until I knew what was going on. Keeping my eyes closed, I strained to hear every sound I could.

The wind. I could hear the wind howling. It echoed, like it was outside blowing past an entrance. A building high on a mountain? A cave? The air felt thin, too—and that would back up my guess that we were at a higher elevation.

Shivering, I realized that I was cold, even beneath the

blanket. The chill was icy, far colder than it had been in my backyard. In fact, the scent of the air . . .

Oh no.

I knew where I was—at least the general region. I was somewhere in the Northlands. There was no mistaking that icy haze that hung in the air, filled with magic and the energy of the ice and mists. *Hell.* Hyto had meant it when he said he was going to carry me off.

I listened for any movement but couldn't sense anyone else near me, so I slowly opened my eyes and looked around. *Cavern.* I was in a cave, near a fire that burned brightly. I scooted over to it and rubbed my hands in the heat, then warmed my face near the flames, trying to avoid the stray sparks.

After a moment, I noticed a pot of liquid hanging over it and I found myself incredibly thirsty, but I knew better than to taste it without knowing what it was. For all I knew, it could be a death potion. Gingerly, I stood, pulling the scratchy blanket around my shoulders for warmth. My body hurt, and my head was foggy. I realized that we'd come through the Ionyc Seas. Hyto would be able to travel through them because he was a white dragon.

A ring of stones had been sheltering me from a larger part of the cavern and I hesitantly stepped beyond them, moving into the shadow near the cavern walls. Maybe I could get away. Maybe I'd luck out and there'd be an inn nearby? But I couldn't stay if there was one. Hyto would figure it out and burn the place to the ground. No, I had to manage to grab supplies and run. Run . . . *where* . . . ?

You've been in the Northlands one time, with Iris. And that was this past week. You have no clue as to where you are . . . at least not yet.

Irritated with my own logic, longing to run willy-nilly out of the cave, to put distance between myself and the freak-ass pervert waiting somewhere around here to pick his teeth with my rib bones, I crept through the shadows over to the mouth of the cave and peeked out.

Fuck. Just fuck me hard now.

Outside the entrance, a narrow ledge covered in ice and snow wound down the mountain. Narrow, as in so thin I'd be lucky not to topple over the edge the minute I tried to make a run for it. And we were at high altitude. I could see the peaks of other mountains.

I gazed over the panorama spreading out before me. If I weren't being held captive, it would be beautiful—a swath of white that linked glacier to glacier to . . . glacier . . . *Wait a minute. Could it be?* I squinted. In the far distance, I saw something against the side of the mountain that looked vaguely familiar.

Could that be the Skirts of Hel? We'd been there with Iris. Granted, if it was, it was still at least a day down the mountain, and then a good stretch of harsh walking from here. And no doubt, the path would be fraught with crevasses and avalanche danger. But if it was the glacial ice field, it was the one glimmer of hope I could cling to. Because near the Skirts of Hel Howl, the Great Winter Wolf Spirit, made his home. And he was an Elemental Lord. He could go up against a dragon, being one of the true Immortals.

A noise made me jump. Someone was coming. I hurried back to the fire, managing to lie back down before they entered the room. I had positioned myself so that I could see who it was through slitted eyes.

Hyto. Hell and double hell. From what he'd said, I had the feeling he was planning on leaving me alive until Smoky got here, but what shape I'd be in was up for debate. I wondered whether it would be best to continue playing asleep or prepare myself in advance in case he decided to kick me or something. I wouldn't put it past him. In the end, I chose to roll up into a squatting crouch from which I could either run or jump away.

He swept in, eyeing me with an impassive expression. It would have been hard to place his age, though if he were human I'd put him in his late forties. But he was lean and towering, like Smoky, and as much as I didn't want to, I could see a resemblance in the facial structure. There, the similarities ended.

His gaze never leaving my face, he slowly strolled over in my direction. The arrogant smirk on his lips would have been frightening enough, but the look in his eyes was as frozen as the ice. No mercy. No compassion.

I slowly stood, backing away as he entered the ring of stones and kept walking toward me. I wanted to say something, but what was there to say? *Please rethink this? You're going to die?* Oh yes, that would work on a dragon.

He stopped about a foot away from me, and his gaze traveled from my feet up my body, lingering over my hips and my breasts. The ice in his eyes melted just a little, replaced by a fiery lust.

Worse, far worse than the cold, aloof look.

"Still not going to beg for your life? Still not going to beg my indulgence? You are too insolent for a mortal—be you half-Fae or not." And he reached out with a tendril of hair. I thought he was going to use it to caress me again, but instead it coiled back like a serpent and then struck, slashing my cheek.

The sting of the blow caught me off guard and I gasped, bringing my hand to my face. A warm trickle of blood oiled my fingers and I began to shake. I took a step backward, but he caught my wrist with the same strands.

"Say it. Beg me for your life. I will not ask again." His eyes spun now, a whirl of mist and fog, and I could see the dragon rising behind him in his aura, so huge, so ancient that he'd probably watched mountains be born and die. He meant every word he said, and I didn't want to find out so soon just how far his temper could be pushed.

My knees began to give and I stuttered, "Please . . . please spare me." Ashamed, angry I'd given in so soon, I hung my head as my words came out in a whisper. But the blood on my cheek was running freely, and the man towering over me could splinter me like an axe splintering kindling.

"There, was that so hard?" He reached out with one hand and lifted my chin. "You will learn your manners, Mistress Camille. You will learn your place in my society. You will learn what it means to truly serve a dragon."

And then he pushed me away and I went sprawling to the floor. I didn't move—I didn't want to set him off again.

"I will have a woman come and prepare you. You are not properly attired to sit in my presence. You will do as she says." He turned and began to walk away. Over his shoulder, he added, "Oh, Camille? If you're thinking of trying to escape,

I give you this one warning: If you succeed, I will return to your house and destroy every single inch of your property. I will raze it to the ground. I will rape your sisters and that irksome sprite you keep around. And then, I will eat them."

And with that, he vanished back into the depths of the cavern.

I waited until he left, then scrambled to my feet. What the hell was I going to do? I couldn't escape—not without help or supplies. And if I did . . . would he truly carry through on his threats?

That is not the question, my gut echoed back at me. *You know he'll carry through. The question is, will they be able to stop him before he manages to destroy everything in sight?*

I huddled near the fire, waiting, until another set of footsteps warned me someone else was coming. It was a woman, as Hyto had said, and right away I could tell she was no dragon. She was one of the Northmen, from the looks of her. Sturdy build, with long, stringy, flaxen hair and muscles that told me she wouldn't put up with any shit from anybody. Which meant that unless I could take her out with a spell, I wouldn't be fighting my way past her.

She motioned for me to follow her, and, silently, I did.

We headed deeper into the cavern, and the persistent howl of the wind railed around us. The cave was so large and spacious that I could easily see Hyto changing form here. The walls were spare and worn smooth, and the supporting stalagmites and stalactites had grown up thick over the centuries. This cave had withstood time, and it felt old and hollow and deep.

I cleared my throat and eyed the woman. "May I speak?" I didn't want to be on the receiving end of *her* fists, either.

But she just nodded, seeming to understand me. I'd spoken in a variant of the Northern tongues—roughly, I wasn't that proficient, but I knew enough to get by. It would be useless to ask where we were, so I sucked in a deep breath and asked, "What are you going to do with me?"

"Prepare you for the Master. You are not dressed appropriately. I will bathe you and dress you and feed you." As she spoke, her face remained unchanging, but I caught a glimmer of pity in her eyes.

Hanging my head, turning on my glamour full force, I nodded slowly. "I did not choose to come here. He kidnapped me."

"No one chooses to attend him. At least none of the women." Her words were abrupt but clear.

"Why are you here, then? Why are you helping him?"

She stopped, turning to me. "I will tell you this once. Remember it. He has my son held captive. I help him to keep my son alive. Which means I will do anything he asks. Never forget that. I won't go out of my way to help the Master, but neither will I do anything to jeopardize my child. Do you understand?"

"Yeah . . . I understand." And I did. She was protecting her child; she would do what she had to. Hyto had a way with people, all right. He knew just what buttons to push.

"Good. Follow me and keep quiet."

We passed through several long chambers, each as vacant as the last. Either Hyto didn't share Smoky's love of fine living or all of his goodies were in his private chambers. Either way, the cavern was cold and barren and rough, and right now all I longed for was my bed at home and a soft cover and my loves by my side. I missed my husbands and sisters so much that I felt nauseated. But I kept my wits about me and tried to push fear to the back. I needed to remember the layout. If I had to hide, I needed to know where I could vanish.

We entered a smaller chamber to the left. Finally, here were living quarters—at least for mortals. Several beds were scattered around the chamber—I counted twelve—and a steaming pool of water sat in the middle of the room. A natural hot spring? Not likely. More likely melted snow heated by the huge fire burning in the fire pit. The room was still cold, but without the intense chill of the outer chambers, especially when the woman drew a curtain across the entrance.

"Sit and let me clean the wound on your face." She pushed me toward a narrow stone bench. I sat, fingering the raised gash that Hyto's hair had inflicted on me. It felt warm, and I wondered if dragon hair could cause an infection. I sucked in a deep breath as I heard a rattling coming from the far end of the chamber.

"What's that?" I jumped up, looking around.

"My son. Sit down." She pushed me back down and I slowly lowered myself onto the bench again. I squinted through the dim light of the lanterns scattered around the room. As my eyes adjusted, I finally saw it: a cage fashioned of iron and leather. It was situated a good six feet off the floor—hanging by straps from the ceiling of the cave—and was about the size of a linen closet turned on end.

Inside crouched a wild-eyed young man of around fifteen. He had long golden hair but it was matted into dreads, and so dirty it looked black. Shirtless, he wore a rough pair of trousers held up by a cord tied around his waist. He looked like he was wearing a mesh top, but as I squinted further, I realized the lines I thought were mesh were actually a grid pattern of welts. He'd been beaten, in patterns, enough to leave permanent scars.

Visions of Menolly's torture crept into my mind as I looked at the boy.

Hyto. It had to be Hyto. He would have no compunction about hurting a mortal—Northman or not. Child or not.

I looked up at the woman, who was watching me. "What's your name? What's his name? Did Hyto . . ."

"My name is Hanna. My son's name is Kjell. And yes, the Master punishes my son for my mistakes." Her lip twitched and she blinked, quickly, but I still saw her push back the tears.

"He threatened to kill the rest of your family, didn't he?" I didn't have to ask. I knew what kind of creature Hyto was. He would use every form of mental and physical torture in the book, and the threat of destroying family was a good way to make someone obey.

Hanna gently washed the wound on my cheek, then ran a thin line of some salve along it. "He killed my husband. I was able to smuggle my daughters away before he got hold of them. But he caught Kjell and me when we were trying to run." Another line of salve and she stood back. "There. Now remove your clothes. Don't even think about protesting. You must have a bath. The Master likes his . . . toys . . . to be clean."

Toys . . . and there it was. I swallowed hard.

"What about your son? He'll see me."

"He's locked in a cage. He's . . . Seeing a naked woman is the least of his worries. Obey."

I began to remove my skirt and the turtleneck, turning away from the cage. The strange boy rattled at the door, making guttural cries, but Hanna ignored him and I did the same. There was nothing else I could do but obey. If I struck down Hanna—and my ability to do so was a big *if*—I'd have no hope of escaping. I needed her. I needed to win her help, and to do that, we had to save her son, too.

As I stepped into the steaming pool, she poured a fragrant oil into the water. The scent was heavy, spice and amber and honey—much like the perfumes I used—and the warm heat of the water began to relax my muscles. I leaned back, as much as I didn't want to enjoy the feel of the water. I was tired. So tired. And the fear and cold had wormed its way through me.

I fought with myself for a moment, then decided if I relaxed, it would give me a little rest. I breathed in the steam, welcoming the warmth into my body.

Hanna handed me a cloth and bar of handmade soap, and I began to wash myself. As I gazed into the steam, I began to slide into a mild trance. And then it hit me like a ton of bricks. I might be able to use the Soul Symbiont ritual to contact Smoky, Morio, and Trillian. To at least let them know I was still alive.

I closed my eyes and inhaled slowly, then let out my breath in a long, steady stream, lowering myself deeper into the trance.

Down, down, deep into the abyss. Let myself slide. Where am I? In a place of swirling fog and mist. In a place of eternal snow. And there, there . . . are sparkles. Tracers. Follow the magic, follow the eye catchers, go racing through the mists. A whirl of whispers, a flutter of sparks, and . . . down farther, deeper within, follow the path to the spark that makes up my inner core, that most sacred of places kept safe from everyone and everything. And there . . . a pinpoint of light, the core of the magic . . .

Another breath, another whirl in the mists . . . go into the light, follow the trail . . . follow the path . . . and then—one more step and . . .

I was standing on the astral, knee deep in mist. The very air sparkled with energy, fluttering like a thousand electrical impulses. Or, what passed for air—on the astral I really didn't need to breathe, especially because I wasn't there fully in body but only in spirit. *Pink, green, yellow, blue . . .* the fluorescence reminded me of the bay at night when the algae flowed in on the tide.

Not sure where I was, I turned, scattering a stream of the sparkles. Where were they? Where were their signatures? I searched, focusing on their faces, holding them firmly in mind, and began to send out a call as I moved forward.

I might as well explore while trying to get through to them. The mist swirled around my legs, a welcoming presence. The astral made me feel safer—at least my spirit could escape, even if my body was trapped with a crazed dragon. And that promise seemed priceless right now.

Smoky, Morio, Trillian—I'm here! Can you hear me? Can you find your way to me? Help! I'm here! I'm alive! Smoky!

And then I heard a voice that I had never expected to hear. It came up from behind me, welcome and yet so out of the blue that I almost fell, whirling around to see if it was who I really thought it might be.

"Camille? What are you doing here?"

There, right in front of me, stood Chase.

Chapter 11

∽✦∾

"Chase! Oh Chase!" Overjoyed, I raced forward and threw my arms around him. Even though I was only on the astral in spirit, it still felt real and right now I needed a friendly face more than anything. I burst into tears, resting my head on his shoulder.

"Here now . . . it's okay. I'm alive. I'm just surprised you managed to find me. I've been out here wandering around for a while." He slowly disengaged me and smiled down at me. "How long have you been looking for me? How much time has passed? I haven't been gone for years, I hope?"

I shivered, slowly realizing that he had no clue as to what was going on. Of course he wouldn't—he was off in his own private hell.

"Chase . . . I'm sorry . . . I didn't come out here looking for you, though I'm overjoyed I found you. I'm trying to contact Smoky or Morio or Trillian. Listen—please, I may not have much time before they force me out of trance. Hyto caught me. He's holding me in the Northlands, setting a trap for Smoky. If you somehow find your way off the astral before they know where I am . . . please, tell them. And tell them . . . I love everybody."

Again, the waterworks hit and I burst into tears again. Chase stared at me for a moment, then pulled me into his arms and rested my head on his shoulder, patting my back.

"Ssh . . . it will be okay. I'll find my way out and we'll come rescue you. Has he hurt you? Are you . . ." He stopped, then shook his head. "You don't have to answer that."

I hung my head. "He's got something horrid in store for me. I know that. He's roughed me up a bit so far. But Chase—" My voice came low and raspy. "I don't think I'm going to get out of this one. Not without major damage. If at all. Promise me, if . . . if he kills me before I can get away, you will keep watch over my family?"

Chase nodded; I could feel his head bob. Feeling a little better, I cleared my throat and pushed away, drying my eyes. I wasn't the only one wandering lost right now. "What about you? Where are you? We followed you up to a mushroom ring, but we couldn't go through without knowing what was on the other side. Does the Bog Eater have you?"

He cocked his head, looking confused. "The Bog Eater? I don't like the sound of that . . . whatever he is. I'm not sure where I am, to be honest. Some old hag with more hands than I care to think about yanked me through the portal and raced off with me. She reminds me of a spider. I managed to get away; I got my gun out and fired, but by then I was lost and had no clue what was going on. She caught me again, reeling me in by a silken thread, and carried me through the mushroom ring. I was tucked away in a mound, tied up. She kept feeding me honey and bread, and poking me with one of her hands."

"We found your gun and your watch. Delilah has them." I grimaced. His adventure sounded about as pleasant as what I was going through. "Just how many hands does she have?"

He shrugged. "I don't know, but at least five or six. I was seriously afraid she was going to eat me, and I don't mean a blow job by that. I finally decided to try to use whatever powers I'm developing and . . . well . . . I ended up here. I'm not sure how . . . I don't even know if my body is here."

I focused on him, reaching out to trace the outline of his

aura. It was firm, solid . . . What the fuck? Chase had managed to propel himself onto the astral *in body*? How had he done that?

"Dude, I don't know how to tell you this, but you're here. Fully. In body. Listen—you be careful. There are a lot of nasty creatures out here on the astral, but if you're cautious you might be able to find someone to help you get home—"

Everything began to blur and I realized that I was phasing out. Hanna must be shaking me. "I've got to go. Please . . . be careful. Be safe. Find your way home." And then, without so much as a blink, I was back in the tub, and Hanna was taking the washcloth away from me and forcing me under the water.

I sputtered, clawing at her hands, trying to break the surface. After another moment, she let up and I broke out of the water, gasping.

"What the fuck are you doing? Trying to drown me?" I spit out a mouthful of the musky-tasting water and looked for something to wipe my eyes, which were burning.

She handed me a towel of a surprisingly soft weave and motioned for me to wipe my eyes. "I asked you to wash your hair and you did not listen." After taking the towel back, she handed me the soap. "Now lather up your locks and then rinse again. And be quick or I'll do it for you myself."

Glaring at her, but realizing it would be a mistake to point out that I'd been in trance and not paying attention, I rubbed the soap on my head and then rinsed the suds out of my hair. Hanna grunted, then motioned for me to stand up. Reluctantly, I came out of the warm water and the chill of the cavern struck me before she could wrap me in a fresh towel. I huddled beneath the drape, trying to stay warm, as she led me to the edge of a fire pit and bade me sit on a bench.

As I sat down, she took the towel and replaced it with a blanket, then took a rough comb and slowly began to brush the tangles out of my hair. After a moment, I heard what sounded like a choking sound, and when I turned, I saw tears in her eyes. She was biting back a frown.

"Hanna? What's wrong?"

She shook her head, but then after another moment said, "I used to brush my little girls' hair. I would brush and brush, then braid up their locks. They loved it. It was our special time each day, after all the chores were done. You remind me of one of them. She took after her father, with dark hair and pale skin."

That could be useful, I thought, then sighed at my own ruthlessness. But I was fighting for my life. I had to use anything I could.

"What was her name? How old was she?"

"She was a maid, old enough to marry but still young. Her name was Sifonar. She was . . . she was beautiful, and so many young men wanted to marry her. But she didn't want to wed—not yet. She wanted a life of adventure. Now . . . now I have no idea whether she lives or dies. I'll probably never see her or her sisters again," she said quietly, her brushstrokes becoming a bit more gentle.

I bit my lip, then inhaled slowly and let out my breath. "That feels good. Thank you."

"Hrmph." Hanna frowned as I glanced over my shoulder, but she continued the brushing and within ten minutes, my hair was drying and beginning to curl into its natural wave. I said nothing else, just crouched toward the flames, trying to stay warm.

"You are cold, girl?"

"My name is Camille," I said, slowly. "And yes, I'm cold."

"The Northlands are the heart of winter. It never warms up here. Oh, the snow recedes a bit, and a spare vegetation grows and flowers, but there's never really any warmth here."

"I know. I had just returned to my home from a journey here when Hyto captured me. While up here, I stayed with Howl's people, down near the Skirts of Hel." It was a calculated risk, mentioning the Great Winter Wolf Spirit, but I was willing to chance it.

Hanna dropped her comb. "Howl? You *know* the Elemental Lord?"

"Yes, I do." I stood and turned to her. "He was gracious in his hospitality. He is a powerful friend. A powerful ally. I believe he's near, isn't he?"

Her gaze darting frightened glances toward the cage with her son in it, she paused for a moment, then retrieved the comb. "Your hair is nearly dry. Now you must dress and then attend the Master in his chamber."

Crap. Not enough to push her into helping. I reached out, lightly touched her arm. *"Please, please, help me.* I can't stand the thought of going to him. He'll . . . I'm sure you've seen what he's done with other—toys—haven't you? How many survive? How many scream for help as he tears them apart? How many bones has he tossed to the side?"

Tears began to form in her eyes. "You look so much like my Sifonar. So much . . . but she is no longer here for me to protect. My son is, however." Then, with a final shake of the head, she added, "I cannot help you. I can't risk harm my own flesh and blood to help a stranger."

I dropped my hand. Of course she couldn't, and I knew it— knew it in my heart, in my gut. I didn't expect her to sacrifice her son for me. "Yeah. And that's exactly what I'm asking, isn't it? I'm sorry. Of course you can't help me. I wouldn't compromise my sisters for a stranger." Resigned, feeling numb, I shrugged out of the blanket. "Where are my clothes?"

"He wishes you to wear clothing of his choice." Hanna reached out, holding tight to my wrist. "Please, don't hate me," she said, a pleading look on her face.

"I don't." I shook my head, and meant every word. "I don't hate you, but you need to understand, I'm probably walking in to my death. And he's setting up my husband— his own son—to die. Don't you understand? Hyto is my *father-in-law.*"

A look washed across her face, a mixture of disgust and horror. "No. You are his family?"

"Apparently, to Hyto, family members don't get free passes." Hardening myself, I held out my arms. I'd have to be strong, have to cope with whatever was coming my way because right now I wasn't seeing any way out of this. "Dress me."

Hanna moved silently, avoiding my stare. She pulled out a silver thong. As I stepped into it, the silk of the material slid luxuriously against my skin, and my butt never felt quite so exposed, even when I was naked.

I felt like a prize cow, preparing to be paraded around the room before slaughter. Hanna then draped a sheer gown over my shoulders. It fastened in front with a jeweled clasp, so that my breasts rounded heavily over the top, exposed and full. I shivered as she dusted my nipples with a shimmering powder the color of ice.

As comfortable as I was in my body, the mere thought of Hyto seeing me naked made me sick to my stomach. I wanted to run and hide. Or maybe I should just jump off the edge of the world out on the ledge and go flying to my death. The thought gave me some comfort—if his torture was too painful, I could throw myself over the edge.

"You must eat before you go in." She led me to a table, where I sat and she brought me a slab of toasted bread with a soft cheese spread thickly across the top. It had the slight fragrance of honey in it, and even though my stomach protested, I forced myself to eat. I'd need all the strength I could get. Hanna offered me a pint of ale and I drank that, too, wincing at the heavy taste of yeast.

"I can't believe I'm here." I stared into my stein. Maybe I could do like Chase and project myself onto the astral—in body. I could find my way home from here that way. But I'd never done so before without the help of the Moon Mother, or without someone else's magic. It wasn't one of my talents and I wasn't sure how to go about it. But if Chase had managed . . . maybe I could, too?

Three bells rang, chiming through the cavern. Hanna frantically grabbed the stein away and pointed toward a hole in the corner. There were torn shreds of rough paper next to it. "Go to the bathroom, now. While you have the chance. The Master . . . rejoices in humiliation." Her words were low but the meaning clear. "*Hurry.* That is the signal to bring you to him."

I quickly used the rough outhouse and, shaking, washed my hands in the basin of cold water next to it.

Hoping against hope that a miracle would break through and save me, I stumbled behind Hanna as she led me through a maze of tunnels. It must have taken only minutes, but it felt like hours. Then, without warning, we were at the entrance to a gigantic chamber. A huge platform sat in the back of the room, and a smaller throne, sculpted from the very rock, sat in front of the dais. Instinctively, I knew that the platform was for Hyto when he was in dragon form.

As we stood in the entrance, a faint noise emanated from behind the platform. There, in the light of a fire that burned brightly to one side, stood Hyto in his flowing robes. His gaze caught mine from across the room and, never once looking away, he crossed the floor and settled on the throne. With a single motion, he gestured for me to move forward.

Hanna caught her breath and I heard a catch in her throat as she stroked my hair and whispered. "I'm sorry, Camille. I'm sorry. I hope . . . I'll be here when you . . . *if you* . . ."

"If I survive," I said slowly. And then, because there was nothing left for me to do, I moved forward, into the dragon's lair.

A low drumbeat seemed to follow my footsteps—perhaps it was the beating of my heart—as I slowly approached Hyto. I was shaking so hard my teeth chattered. I wanted to cover my breasts, to cover my body, to slink away, but I knew that he wanted me to feel that way. He wanted to humiliate me, to break me, so I forced my shoulders back and did not look away.

As I approached him, his gaze fastened on my body, and his hair wove around him, waving like the arms of some wild creature, sinuous and terrifying—totally unlike how Smoky's hair moved on its own.

"Ah, here she comes, with rosy cheeks and breasts so bare . . ." Hyto's voice was thick with sarcasm as he leaned forward. "If you were a dragon, you'd be an ugly duckling. As it is, for a mortal, you are attractive enough." He paused, and then suddenly one loop of hair shot forward and punched me in the stomach hard enough to knock me off my feet.

With a startled cry, I went stumbling against the rocks, feeling the backs of my thighs scrape on a sharp ledge. Hyto laughed.

"Stand up, *girl*. Now."

I scrambled to my feet, trying to ignore the sting from his lash.

"Rule number one: When I address you, you will reply, 'Yes, Master.' Do you understand?" There was no room for negotiation in the command, and I knew better than to piss him off. Much better to pick and choose my battles, and this one wasn't worth fighting.

"Yes, Master." I forced my quaking voice to form words.

"You learn quickly. Second rule: Whenever you enter my presence, you kneel until I command you to stand."

"Yes, Master."

The same strand of hair that had knocked me off my feet landed on my shoulder. I didn't wait for his prompting. I went down on my knees and this time avoided getting hit.

Hyto stood and moved forward. I could feel the shift in his mood.

Trained to keep my eyes on my opponents, it took everything I had to force my gaze to the floor. I'd met men like Hyto before—men who thrived on total power, total ownership. It was like staring a mad dog in the face—they'd kill for such affronts. I'd play the game, buy myself some time.

As little hope as I had for getting out of this in one piece, the more someone tried to humiliate me, the more I wanted revenge. And if Hyto took me out, I planned on doing as much damage as I could to him before the end. But I'd have to bite my tongue . . . wait for the right moment.

As his boots—white fur beneath the robe he wore—appeared in my line of sight, I struggled to keep myself calm. Or at least as calm as I could manage.

Tendrils of hair reached beneath my arms and lifted me off my feet so that they were holding me in front of him.

"Look at me, girl. Properly." The command was slow, sinuous.

"Yes, Master." I forced myself to meet his gaze without challenging him. I didn't want to see what I knew was there.

Desire. Lust. The will to hurt, to punish. The hunger for my pain. Oh yes, he was a sadist, just waiting to unleash himself on me.

"First, the collar."

And while his hair held me, he reached out and fastened a snow-white collar around my neck, with a silver loop in the front. When he snapped the buckle shut, I shuddered and realized that the collar had magic in it—what sort, I could not tell, but the energy flowed around my body and made me feel like I had an itch I couldn't scratch.

"Who am I, girl?"

"You are my Master." The words turned in my stomach, but there was nothing to do now but obey.

"That's right, and I can do anything I want with you. I could break your neck, or fry you up and eat you for breakfast. I could hang you over the cliff and watch you dangle there, freezing to death, left for the mountain vultures to pick clean."

"Yes, Master."

He chuckled, looking all too delighted. "Or . . . I could . . ."

The next moment, I felt another tendril of his hair curl up my body till it found my breasts. It coiled like a serpent, twisting around me like some rope out of a Japanese bondage scene. The pressure on my breasts was so tight I began to sweat, but then it eased off as the strands began to massage my nipples. I relaxed, grateful that the pain had stopped, when another strand—thicker this time—reached between my legs, caressing my thighs, caressing me between . . .

Oh fuck. No, please no. I closed my eyes, but the strands thrust my thighs apart and began to explore every crevice I had.

Hyto growled. "Look at me, I said. I want to see your face. I want to see your eyes."

"Yes, Master." Whispering, I opened my eyes again. He was grinning, feral and wild, dangerous as only a mad dragon could be.

"Oh, my pretty one. My son's *wife*. What a joke. You're not fit to be an entrée—you're *dessert*, you know that? Simply dessert. Whipped cream. Except that because you hold my son's heart, you are a crown jewel to me right now. My ace up the sleeve, so to speak. And that *excites me*."

And with another horrible laugh, he swiftly thrust a thick strand of hair into me, shoving the flimsy material of the thong aside. I struggled, but he held me tight with that horrible snakelike mane of his.

I let out a single scream, then bit my tongue as he suddenly pulled me to him, more of his hair holding my face to his as his mouth sought mine. His tongue deep between my lips, he kissed me, but he did not touch me with his hands.

And then the ravishment began in earnest; those crazed eyes pierced my heart as he toyed with me, never touching me with his hands, only with his hair. How much time passed, I couldn't tell, but I was raw and bleeding by the time he was done.

When he was finished, the strands abruptly withdrew, dropping me on the floor. I lay there, whimpering.

"Enough for now. I cannot have you expiring on me before Smoky finds his way here. We have plenty of time for more fun later on. I've business to address. The woman will attend to you. You will bathe and eat and sleep. I won't have a filthy toy in my presence. It's bad enough you are mortal."

As he paused, I realized he was waiting for my response. Fury and pain racking my body, I forced myself to my knees. Unsteady but managing to keep upright, I threw caution out the window and stared up at him, refusing to look away. I wanted to memorize his face, to memorize every crag and wrinkle, every scar. Because somehow, someday, I would watch him die—in pain, in anger, in absolute agony.

But for now, I knew I needed to survive. And so, as he waited, ready to slash me again for impudence, I merely said, "Yes, Master."

And then he was gone, like a thief in the night, and I was alone.

Hanna hurried in to get me, even as I curled in a ball on the floor. One look at her face and I knew she'd witnessed everything. She mutely offered me her arm and I leaned on it while she led me back into the chamber. I could barely walk, and blood trickled down my inner thighs, which were rubbed raw from the roughness of his hair.

"Get the collar off, please." I tugged at it, but she shook her head.

"The Master fixed it with magic. It won't come off. I'm sorry, Camille, I'm so sorry." She had drawn another hot bath.

"How long . . . how long was I with him?" It felt like forever.

"Half the night, my dear. Here—it will sting something fierce, but the water and herbs will help you heal. Get in the tub." She stripped away my clothes and tossed them in a corner.

I couldn't even manage to step over the edge of the tub, I hurt so bad. Hanna bit her lip and helped lift me into the water. I let out little whimpers of pain, but then a slow numbness began to seep through my legs and stomach, and I welcomed it in. Hanna must have put some sort of anesthetic in the water.

I stared mutely into the water, at the bruises and scrapes that covered my body, and all my resolve dissolved in a flurry of tears. My stomach twisted and I quickly turned to get on my knees as I leaned over the side of the tub. Hanna noticed my difficulty and brought me a basin. I vomited everything I'd eaten earlier. She held my head, stroking my hair, wiping my forehead and the back of my neck with a damp cloth.

When I was finished, she gave me a drink of water and I rinsed my mouth, and then she settled me back in the tub and handed me a mug of hot tea. The fragrant scent of berries rose to calm me.

"Thank you."

She bit her lip. "I want to do more. I want to do more . . ."

"Your son. I know."

"It's not right. I was born a warrior woman. Now I serve an evil dragon who blackmails me with my kin. I'm a coward." Her eyes were filled with shame as she fetched a washcloth and a soft soap. She motioned for me to lean forward. "I think I have some choices to make," she said softly, washing my back with the soap and cloth, taking care to go gently over the bruises and cuts.

"I will not ask anything of you. But if you decide to help me, babe, I can sure use it." Bleakly, I sipped the tea. It calmed my stomach and began to unknot some of the pain that Hyto had thrust onto me.

Smoky had never treated me this way. We played our bondage games, but they were love games—consensual, joyful, with pleasure rather than pain.

Hyto had invaded me, violated me in a way I'd never before experienced. In Otherworld, long ago, my boss—Lathe—had tried to blackmail me into fucking him, but I'd managed to squash that little game with Trillian's help. But this . . . this outright assault . . .

I thought of Menolly and what she'd endured at the hands of Dredge, and the thought made me stronger. Hyto had hurt me, yes, and he would probably kill me, but he wasn't going to turn me into a vampire. And so far, I'd been able to bear the humiliation he craved. I'd learned to be strong over the years.

Seeking comfort in the thoughts of home, of my loved ones, of everything we'd been through, I cemented my resolve. Hyto might kill me, but he wouldn't win. No matter what, he wouldn't win against me. And come what may, I'd at least make the cocksucker hurt like a house afire before he took me out.

Chapter 12

❧

After my bath, I was able to step out of the tub on my own, though I was bone weary and ready to crash. Hanna wasn't able to take off the collar, so I had to wear it. It reeked of Hyto, his musky scent filling my nostrils.

"Please, do you have anything to take away the odor?" I gestured to the leather. "It smells like him."

She quickly fetched a bottle and I rubbed a little of the ointment under my nose. It was almost like Vicks . . . and strong enough to block the smell of the dragon without angering him. Relieved and wrapped in a thick blanket, I let her lead me to the table, where I saw that she'd prepared a light meal of eggs, applesauce, bread, and honey.

"This should settle on your stomach without too much problem," she said, handing me a glass of wine to go with it. "You must eat to keep up your strength. But . . . before you do, I hate to embarrass you."

"What?" I asked, thinking there wasn't much she could do to further humiliate me beyond what Hyto had already done.

"I need to put a salve on your thighs and . . . your privates.

The Master roughed you up pretty badly, my dear. And we don't want the skin to get infected." She held up a jar.

Blushing, I nodded and leaned back, spreading my legs. She was quick, with a light touch, and she spread the salve on the injured parts of my body. She also spread some of it on the purple blossoms spreading across my back and stomach.

"It will work for the bruising, too. There now, eat and then you must sleep. We have no idea when he will call for you next." She fixed the blanket, tucking it around me again as she might tuck in a child.

"How long . . . how often . . . did he call for his other toys?" I glanced up at her, not wanting to know how many women had suffered over Hyto's lifetime.

She swallowed hard. "You are the first who's returned from his chamber."

I stared at her. "The others . . ."

"One night. The past few years, I've cleared away the bones of at least two dozen young women . . . the Master created this retreat some time back, before . . ." Hanna glanced around, then lowered her voice to a whisper. "Before his wife forced him out of the Reaches. I have been captive here for five years. In that time, all of the women brought here have died."

My stomach lurched again. So he'd had this chamber while still married to Smoky's mother. I wondered if she knew about it. And if so, what did she think? I couldn't imagine her being pleased. From what Iris had told me, silver dragons—like Smoky's mother—were at the top of the dragon food chain, and it would be an embarrassment to have a white dragon husband prone to behavior like this.

And then I realized what Hanna had said. "You've been here five years? And your son?" I glanced over at the cage where the silent boy lay sleeping.

"Kjell has been in that cage for five long years. He . . . it's been a while since he said anything to me. He can no longer talk. I don't even know if he understands me, though he likes it when I sing to him." Her voice low, she cocked her head to one side, and silent tears traced down her cheeks.

I wanted to cry with her. For Hanna. For Kjell. For the dozens of women Hyto had murdered. For myself. For my loves, so far away. For all of the wrongs of the world. But the enormity of what I'd been through hit me like a punching bag, and I slumped at the table. "I'm sorry. I can't take any more tonight. I need to sleep."

Hanna led me over to a pallet—much softer than the one I'd woken up on.

"Sleep. Here, drink this. Five drops of it will deepen your rest but won't make you groggy when you wake up." She handed me a little bottle. "The Master would beat me if he knew I had this, but . . . I use it when I can't stand being here, when I can't face myself or what I do for him."

I took the bottle and didn't even hesitate. I needed the rest. I swallowed five drops of the bitter liquid. "Did he ever . . . has he raped you?"

She shook her head. "He needs me too much to subject me to that. The women he has captured . . . Camille, he not only abuses them, but he eats them afterward, in dragon form. The first, he tried to molest in his natural form and it split her apart. He didn't try that again—he likes to play with his food before he eats. And it's no fun if his prey dies so quickly. I'm not saying this to frighten you, but to warn you."

"I know all about him," I said. "Remember? He's my husband's father. And I know that unless I escape, the minute my husband comes here to save me, Hyto will kill me in front of him. Anything he can do to intensify the pain, he'll do. I understand."

And with that, I slid under the thick quilt that Hanna tucked over me and closed my eyes. A moment later, I felt her lips on my forehead, and it was like my mother had suddenly returned to give me her blessing. I didn't say a word, but snuggled under the cover and immediately fell into a dark and deep slumber.

I was walking in a long, narrow tunnel that wound through the labyrinth for what seemed like forever. Somewhere, in the back of my mind, I knew I was wandering on the astral in my sleep, and that knowledge comforted me. I began to look for any sign of life—anybody who might be able to help me.

And then I was running. A shadow loomed behind me and, terrified it might be Hyto, I darted from side to side, looking for some cover, some place to hide. But the shadow stayed apace with me, and after a while, I turned to find that it was merely a reflection of myself.

"What do you want? Who are you? Why do you look like me?"

And then, I flashed—and was in the other body, staring at my bruised and aching self. "You know what I want," I found myself saying. "You know why you're running from me. Just admit it, because otherwise you're going to stand in your own way."

Blink, and back to myself. An ache stirred in my heart. "No, I don't want to think about it. I just want to get out of this dream."

My alter ego shrugged. "You can't, not until you reclaim the part of yourself you're rejecting. Not until you reclaim me. Think about it, Camille . . . think what the hell you're doing."

I hung my head. I knew, deep inside, what was going on. I didn't want to face it—didn't want to admit it.

"I . . . What do you want me to say?"

"The truth. Just fucking be honest with me—*with your-self.*"

I let out a shuddering breath. "Fine. You want honest? *This is all my fault.*"

"*How?* How the hell did you cause this?"

"If I hadn't let Vanzir fuck me, then I wouldn't have had the argument with Smoky, and Hyto wouldn't have caught hold of me." A bitter tang rose up in my mouth and my anger surprised me. "If I hadn't enjoyed Vanzir, this wouldn't have happened. Somehow—if I could have hated him for what happened . . . if I hadn't been agreeable . . ."

"You mean if Vanzir had raped you . . . or if you had killed him, then Hyto wouldn't have come looking for you?

Or maybe, if you had let Vanzir feed off your mind, none of this would have happened?"

Apparently, I was really good at needling myself.

"Yes—no! I don't know!" Frustrated, angry at myself—both sides of me—I leaned against a wall. "The argument over Vanzir led to my getting caught. This is all my fault."

"You fucking know that's not true—get it out of your head. Would you tell that to Delilah? Did Menolly deserve what she got because she couldn't hold her position and fell right into the midst of Dredge's lair? Did she?"

Angry now, furious that those words could even find their way into my voice—be it me, or an alternate me saying it—I lashed out.

"No! She didn't deserve it. Nobody deserves it. And those women Hyto killed didn't deserve it, either. And neither do I!"

"Then why are you harboring the secret fear that you *do* deserve it?" My alter ego was softer now, almost tearful.

I closed my eyes, hung my head. "I don't know. Maybe . . . maybe it's because I need somebody to be angry at, someone not out to kill me. I can't fight back against Hyto. If I can't scream at him . . . so who the hell *can* I scream at? Not at Hanna—she's my only hope for help. And it's not her fault, either. How can I deal with all this anger and fear and pain if I can't get it outside myself?"

"What about your magic? Don't ever forget you're a witch. You're a priestess for the Moon Mother. Doesn't that count for something?"

A cool wind rushed over me and I opened my eyes to find myself standing in a wide barren field. I was on the astral—in spirit, but above me was the Moon and she was peeking down at me, reaching down with her glittering touch to wrap me in moonbeams from the faint sliver that glistened in the sky. The promise of hope, of love, of finding my way in the darkness enveloped me, and I clung to the dream, clung to the strands of possibility.

I held on to her promise for all I was worth. My magic . . . what spells could I cast that might help me? Death magic wasn't going to do me any good—especially not without Morio—but perhaps . . .

Running through my repertoire of spells, I remembered the Summoning spell. I didn't have any physical components, but maybe I didn't need them. I was a priestess now—yes, untrained—but I had been chosen by the Moon Mother.

I closed my eyes and gathered all the energy I could from that faint sliver of light in the sky, and wove it between my fingers. *Please, please don't backfire on me now. Please help me. Please summon someone who can find me.*

I thought of my husbands, of Morio and Smoky and Trillian. Longing for them, I searched for their energy and felt the edges of it, but couldn't quite reach out enough. I looked for Chase, but he was gone and I silently wished him luck in getting off the astral, back home. And then—from a distance, I felt someone familiar.

Following the trail of energy, I started walking, then running at a pace only one of the Moon Mother's chosen can manage. The Moon had my back and she was giving me strength. I soaked it in, directed it toward my injuries, bade her be with me in spirit as well as body.

Moon Mother, my great Lady, you know I will bear whatever I must bear with honor, but I beg of you, help me. Help me escape, help me destroy my enemies, help me save my family. Help me topple the evil that seeks to tear me limb from limb. Guide me, Mother of the Night, Lady of the Hunt. Hear my heart, hear my soul, let me rest my head on your breast.

A great energy surged through my spirit, and my speed increased. I raced like the wind, like the hounds of Hel were following me. My hair streamed back, and with each step, each fall of my feet into the mists, my determination increased. *I would not let Hyto win. I would not blame myself for this.* Vanzir and I had done what we needed to do, and there were just some things you could never undo, never change, so you learned to live with them.

The energy up ahead was coming at me full tilt now, and, overjoyed, I flew toward it, stumbling to a stop before a figure that I now recognized.

Vanzir.

"Vanzir! What are you doing here?"

He looked as startled as I felt. "I don't know—I was out on guard duty and suddenly found myself here, running toward . . . I guess it was you." His eyes spun and he hung his head. "I'm so fucking sorry, Camille. I wish I could take this all away . . . take it all back. How did you get away? Are you okay?"

I stared at him. "I'm not here in body. Vanzir, I'm trapped in the Northlands. Hyto has me."

He nodded gravely. "I know he has you. We found the cloak and the mark on the tree. Smoky's already gone to OW, searching for you. Shade and Rozurial are getting ready to leave for the Northlands, so hang on. They're going to try to find you. Delilah and Menolly went to Grandmother Coyote—I'm not sure what happened because they just took off for there before I went out for a walk. Trillian and Shamas are staying home to protect the house and Morio and Iris and Maggie."

"Crap. Smoky's in Otherworld? Does he know I'm in the Northlands?"

Vanzir paled. "He's headed for the Dragon Reaches for help. He doesn't know exactly where you are, though. Smoky . . . oh Camille, he's terrifying."

"But you're alive?"

With a sad laugh, he inclined his head. "When Smoky realized that you'd been captured, he sent for me. Suggested a truce. He blames himself, Camille. He's in a terrible state— and that means he's highly dangerous. When he found the tree . . . and your cloak . . . he ripped several of the trees out of the ground and burned them to cinders. He changed into his natural shape and would have trampled the entire forest if Trillian and Iris hadn't stopped him."

I sank to the ground. "I want to come home. I need to come home. Vanzir, Hyto is . . ." Looking up mutely, I pulled up my skirts to show him the bruising on my thighs. Then I pointed to the collar around my neck. "I don't know how much longer he'll let me live. He's setting a trap for Smoky with me. You have to let Smoky know that it's a trap to catch him. I'm near the Skirts of Hel, to the north. In a cavern high up the mountain."

"You think the big lug doesn't *know* that Hyto's out to trap him? But that won't stop him from coming for you. And may the gods save whoever gets in his way. He'll kill anyone or anything to have you back."

After a moment, Vanzir began to flicker. "I feel like I'm being pulled back. I've got to go, Camille. I can't hold my place here. I don't have my powers, but something happened to me tonight—something to do with the Triple Threat. It happened out on their land—something . . . I don't know what—"

And then he vanished into the night, and I felt myself being drawn back to my body, but then before I reentered the labyrinth, I stopped, once again staring up at the sliver of the moon.

An ancient voice, resonating from the sky, showered down around me in a silver rain of whispers. "My daughter, I would save you if I could, but there is a destiny for all creatures, and this seems to be part of your fate. Your training, though—never forget your training. Remember you are my daughter, you are my child. I will always be with you, through the horrific and the joyful. I will always be watching, helping when I can, sending my love when I can't."

I began to cry—she was so sad, my Lady. I could hear it in her voice. I reached up toward the moon, wanting to go to her, wanting to ride the skies with the Hunt and forget everything and everyone in the lust of the chase.

But the moon disappeared, and I was once again walking back through the labyrinth. My alter ego waited, and I walked up to her and embraced her, and we became one. Feeling both stronger and terribly old, I continued walking till I came to my sleeping form.

It would be so much easier to cut the cord. But I knew now they were searching for me. The men who loved me, my family—they were doing everything they could. I couldn't give up on them. And so I slid into my body and closed my eyes, and fell into a deep, dark slumber.

* * *

Shortly before dawn—although I could not tell anymore what time of day it was—Hanna woke me.

"Camille, wake up, wake up."

I pushed myself to a sitting position, weary and aching but bolstered from the memory of what I'd found out. "What is it?"

"Hyto wants you. I'm to bathe you, feed you, and bring you to his chamber." Her brow was furrowed and she bit her lip as I groaned. Despite the salve, I hurt—there was no getting around it.

But then I remembered meeting Vanzir the night before and I steeled myself. They were hunting for me. I could do this. I could survive.

After another soak in the tub, which helped ease out my muscles, and another application of the salve to prevent infection, she handed me a thin, sheer skirt. No underwear—not even a thong, no top.

I looked at her mutely and she shrugged. "This is what he requested you wear."

"It's like a freakin' tutu. He's determined to humiliate me."

And the scary thought was, he still might be able to do it. I felt stronger now, even with the hell he'd put me through the day before, but another reaming like that, or worse . . . I couldn't guarantee I'd last through the pain.

My mind was strong, my will stronger. But torture had a way of driving the best person mad. And what Hyto was doing was torture. I slipped into the flimsy skirt and followed Hanna to the table, draping a blanket around my shoulder against the chill.

"I prepared food that might be easier on your stomach—soft bread and soup, and a baked apple."

I ate, quickly, then used the restroom—as it was—and turned to her. "Each time, my chances of returning lessen. Please, if I don't come back, hide my bones and give them to my loved ones. Because they *will* be here. They *will* rip that monster to shreds. And I want them to have what's left of me."

She pressed her lips together, but nodded, and mutely stood back, waiting for me to exit the chamber.

"I'm ready." I sucked in a deep breath and we headed back to the chamber of horrors, where Hyto was waiting for me.

This time, Hyto met us at the entrance to the chamber. The moment Hanna handed me over and left, there was no standing on ceremony. He caught me around the neck, his hair through the loop on my collar, yanked, hard, and I went down on my hands and knees.

"Good little bitch. Let's take a walk." And forward he strode, his hair still through the loop on my collar. He moved faster than I could keep up so that I half-crawled, was half-dragged along the rough, rocky floor. Before we'd gone five yards the abrasions were burning on my hands and knees and shins. The skirt was already ripped. Would I be punished for that, too?

As we reached the throne, he sat down and yanked me to kneel at his feet. He turned his booted foot up so that I was facing the bottom of it. "Lick."

"Yes, Master." Shaking, I leaned forward and grimaced as I pressed my tongue to the bottom of his boots.

Hyto gave me a quick, sharp tap to the forehead with his foot and I fell backward. He laughed, roughly. "I'm bored. Amuse me."

"What do you want me to do?" I couldn't help it—I almost snarled, but I caught myself before the surliness came through.

He eyed me for a moment, and then, his gaze never leaving mine, he reached down and parted his robe. From between the folds of material, his pale, thick cock sprang up. "Blow me."

I pressed my lips together, my stomach lurching. Of course he'd use sex against me—when throughout history *hadn't* men used sex as a weapon against the women of their enemies? Abuse the wife, hurt the husband. I wouldn't give him the satisfaction. Reaching inside, deep into my core, I sought for strength from the Moon Mother.

He'll never take my passion away from me. I'll give him what he wants on the surface, but he'll never have my heart. Never have my soul. Never have my joy or my desire. It's all a sham. All a play. All a nightmare and I'll wake up soon.

Close your eyes, my daughter. I am with you. The Moon Mother echoed deep in my heart, and a resigned sense of strength rose up within my soul.

"Yes, Master." I crawled forward, dreading the scent of his musk, hating the sight of his body, but the minute I leaned forward and placed my lips over the tip of his cock, the world began to swirl around me.

The wild moon, rising high, ripped me out of my body. I was racing with the Moon Mother, free over the early morn, and we were on the hunt. It was just she and I, and I let my head fall back as I let out a violent scream, reverberating through the air, ripping through my pain and anger and fury.

We raced then, chasing after the hounds.

I want to rip, to hunt, to tear to shreds, to kill . . .

Soon enough, you will have your chance. You are a daughter of the Hunt; you are one of my chosen. I cannot always protect you, but I can cushion some of the pain.

We raced over hill and dale, into the sky, my Lady and I. We rooted out animals hiding in the forest, we ripped trees from their roots and sent them flying like a tornado. We crossed the heavens and I let out my anger and aggression on the clouds, sending them spinning as I whirled through the sky, feeling like a shooting star. Dizzy with the chaos and mayhem, I let out a wild shriek and dove through cloud bank and star stream.

And then, when I'd spent my anger, my Lady held me in her arms, rocking me, letting me cry . . . and then . . . I spiraled down, down, a helix, a vortex, a ribbon of color, and reentered my body.

* * *

"No wonder Iampaatar claimed you." Hyto was staring down at me, his hands tangled in my hair as I opened my eyes and pulled away from him. A terrible taste filled my mouth, and I started to cough, swallowing quickly before I spit out his cum and got in trouble.

Breathing hard, he leaned forward. "I might keep you alive for a while, just for this. You know what you're doing."

"Yes, Master." I kept my voice flat. The exhilaration of the hunt still raced in my blood. The thrill of being with my Lady out on the astral. I begrudged the fact that he enjoyed it, but at least I wasn't left with the memory.

Hyto seemed to sense that he'd exposed too much emotion, because he pulled away and the intense aloofness returned. "Footstool. Now."

"Yes, Master." I frantically looked around for one, but there was none in sight.

"Don't be an idiot." He kicked me again, this time in the side, and I fell back, suddenly realizing what he'd meant.

Shuddering, I went down, on all fours, in front of him, and he propped his heavy boots across my back. "Now, don't move. Not an inch. Let's see how well you obey your father-in-law, girl."

I couldn't see him from the direction I was facing, could see nothing but stone and—out of the corner of my eye—the fire burning in the fire pit. How long would he keep me in this position? I knew he was punishing me for making him enjoy himself. He probably would have gone easier on me if I'd sucked at giving him a blow job.

After ten minutes, my back started to ache. I was a strong woman, but the combination of remaining on hands and knees while his feet—in those godawful boots—were digging into my back was starting to really hurt, especially against the abrasions he'd already put there. I winced but kept my mouth shut.

Fifteen minutes and I desperately wanted to shift, but I forced myself to remain in position. Twenty minutes, and he'd still made no move to let me up. By now, I had the backache from hell and wasn't sure how much longer I could stand this. It wasn't like playing horsey with Maggie while I was down on the floor, or even like sex play with my lovers. This was serious muscle-spasm time.

After a few more minutes, I decided to chance a glance up at him.

Hell. He was staring directly at me, lips curved in a half grin, half snarl, like a wolf waiting to attack. His eyes were glinting with a perverse joy and I realized he'd been waiting for me to break. I quickly looked away, but it was too late.

"So, you can't take an order." His feet hit the floor.

"I'm sorry, Master. I'm sorry." I broke out in a cold sweat. This wasn't going to be good, I knew it in my gut.

"You have a complaint? Maybe you don't like being related to me?" He leaned forward. Despite every inclination I had, I forced myself to stay in position. Run, and he might kill me.

"No complaints, Master."

His face inches from mine now, his eyes took on a cold, hard edge.

"The expression on your face tells me otherwise. So my hospitality is not to your liking, *my daughter-in-law*?" Suddenly he was standing, towering over me, all seven-plus feet of him. I instinctively scrambled away, but he caught me with that damned hair of his, holding me so tight I could barely breathe. After a moment, he used it to force me over a slab of rock, facedown, and brushed my hair from my back. Then, another long strand of his hair knotted into a harsh braided whip and, with a bone-jarring crack, he brought it sweeping across my lower back, right where the strain had been the worst.

My composure vanished. I screamed as the lashes fell, the bite of the braided hair stinging against my flesh. I could feel the welts rising.

"*You are not my equal!* Do you hear me? *You are not my equal!*" With each fall of the lash, Hyto grew more frenzied. After six strokes, he jerked away, panting, his hair coiling like snakes around his head.

I rolled over on my side, staring up at him, mute, unable

to do more than stifle the sobs that lurched up in my throat.
His eyes flashed and I knew we were at a pivotal point. I
could so easily die if I made one wrong move.

"I would kill you now . . . I would kill you . . . but it would
spoil my plans." In a ragged voice, he railed against me.
"How dare you lure my son away? How dare you set him up
to take my place? To strike me down in his mother's eyes?
How dare you come into my family and ruin my life! You
are a worthless lump of flesh. You are less than the worms of
the fields. Slut—cow! Filthy mortal!"

I said nothing. *Did* nothing. My life was hanging by a
thread.

Hyto caught me up, his hair so tight around my wrist that
it felt like the bones were going to break. He pulled me close,
eye level, and a sickly grin spread across his face. "Now, I
think you shall learn what it feels like to ride a real dragon
and not that weak son of mine."

Gritting my teeth, I began to disassociate. I heard the swish
of his robe as he pulled it back, and the next moment he was
inside me, ramrod hard and fierce. With every grunt, he reverberated through my body like another fist in my stomach.

*Menolly withstood this . . . she withstood worse . . . she
was strong. She made it through hell and back. I can make it
through this. I will survive this. I won't ever let him win—he
can violate my body but he cannot violate my soul.*

"You like this? Answer me, *slave*!" He yanked on my
hair, so hard I shrieked. "Remember who your master is,
Camille." The warning was so charged I had to respond.

"Yes . . . yes, Master . . ." The words echoed out of my
mouth, but they were hollow husks floating on the wind with
no power put into them. They meant nothing to me.

"I will kill you slowly, in front of him. My son will watch
you die in agony, and he will know he could do nothing to
stop me."

After a few moments he tore away, grabbing me by the
wrist and tossing me across the room, like a rag doll. I
landed on the floor with a bone-numbing thud. Sucking in a
deep breath, I glared at him through the tears and snot running down from my nose, no longer caring about his anger.

"Smoky loves me. He's my husband. *I will always know he loves me.* Do you understand that? You can beat me, you can kill me a thousand times over and I'll take that knowledge to my grave."

He stood there panting, staring at me, and then with a terrible cry he was at my side, kicking me square in the hip. I screamed as he yelled for Hanna.

She scurried in.

"Get her out of my sight. Now! Before I kill her."

Hanna hurriedly yanked me along, dragging me through the door and down the hall.

"Hurry, hurry! If we stay in his presence, we die." She bustled me back into the safety of the cave with the tub, pulling the curtain shut. Only then did she let me rest, pushing me onto the pallet as she huddled with me. After a while, she let out her breath.

"He is in a murderous rage. If we are lucky, he'll go out, to work off his anger. I know not what you did to him, girl, but I fear for you. I truly do."

I caught her gaze as she began to move around, looking for the ointments and salves to treat the welts and bruising. I knew what I'd done. He wanted me. And he *did not want* to desire me. I'd inadvertently challenged him by not kowtowing to him. I refused to beg him, to make him feel superior. But most of all, I simply existed. Smoky loved me and had taken my side over his father's. And there, right there, was the answer.

"All I have to do in order to anger him is exist. His son has turned on him. Hyto blames me." I shook my head. "That's the only thing."

Hanna nodded. "That would do the trick, all right. He's an arrogant beast—white dragons are the worst when it comes to their grasping ways. They crave power and they feed off fear. Any defiance is seen as an insult." She gently swept my hair to the side. "Let me attend to your wounds, girl. Then, sleep. Right now, it's the best you can do for your body."

As I leaned forward for her to examine my back, I realized that I'd hit on the core of Hyto's anger. My very existence had become an insult to him. He blamed me for his disgrace, for his fall from the Dragon Reaches. I had become his scapegoat, and he wouldn't rest until I—and Smoky—were punished for his madness. And somehow, I had a feeling no punishment was enough to make Hyto feel strong in himself again. He would never be able to terrorize us enough to mend his ego.

I was in the hands of a psycho. A psychotic *dragon*. Somehow, fighting Shadow Wing didn't seem quite so terrifying a prospect compared to this.

Chapter 13

❧❧❧

"Camille, Camille, wake up!"

I struggled out of slumber, still exhausted and hurting badly. My back burned, and I was sleeping on my stomach on the pallet, covered by extra blankets. I'd taken a fever by the time Hanna got me away from him.

She'd done all she could—used her strongest medicines and salves—but I'd been so strained by Hyto's abuse that I could barely move without crying out. Every place on my body hurt. And the fever, I suspected, came from my injuries.

When she brought me back to the cave, I told Hanna about my queasiness, and she helped me as I vomited as much as I could, then pressed a cup of tea into my hands. A few sips helped calm the knots in my stomach, and the fever began to subside.

"You're a skilled herbal woman."

She nodded, looking pale. Something had happened—I could sense it, but I couldn't pinpoint what. "I grew herbs and helped out my village as a midwife when . . . when I had a home." Then, she put me to bed and stroked my hair until I fell into an uneasy slumber.

Now, struggling out of bed, I coughed up a mass of phlegm into an old rag, and she pushed a waterskin into my hand.

"Drink deep."

I did, until I could speak. "What's going on? Does he want me again?" *Oh please, let it be something else,* I breathed softly.

Hanna sucked in a deep breath, kneeling by my side. "I think I may be able to get you out of here. Hyto flew off not an hour ago, hunting for his dinner. When he hunts, he's always gone for a good day, sometimes two. I will help you. You may not make it, but it's better than staying and letting him eat you up. He was so terribly angry. I don't think you'll survive another bout."

She shoved thick clothes into my arms, linen and fur, and a pair of fur-lined boots made out of leather. "I cannot allow myself to take my part in his crimes anymore. I'll never see Valhalla, but perhaps I can redeem myself in the eyes of the gods."

"What about your son?" I asked, but then something made me look over at the cage. Her son was there, but slumped over. I knew he wasn't sleeping.

"Oh, Hanna . . ."

"Hyto tortured him to torture me and keep me in line. I told you, my son's been locked up for five years—never once has he been allowed out of the cage. He turned into a wild child. Gone quite feral. I tried to keep him sane, tried to talk to him, but he had no release, no chance to stretch, to move his body. He was able to lie flat, but he hasn't had a chance to stand free since the Master brought us here."

She pressed her knuckles against her lips. "I've been selfish. When I brought you back tonight, I looked at my son and realized that he's no longer here. His life has been horrific. He . . . he lost his mind somewhere along the way. That's no way to live, and there's no chance to free him. I realize that now. So I finally decided to do the only thing I could. The only thing a good mother could." She caught my gaze, the pain in her face too much to witness.

"Couldn't we have broken the cage open?" The fact that

she'd killed her son shook me to the core, but then she put her arm on mine.

"Do not think I killed my son for you. The cage . . . it is magically enchanted. Over the years I've tried everything I could think of, but it won't open, it won't break. Dragon magic is tricky and dangerous. And my son . . . he was lost to me several years ago. I've made sure he's fed and I sing to him and talk to him . . . but he hears only the sound of my voice, not my words. He retreated into his mind. There was nothing left of the boy I gave birth to save for an empty shell. I gave him a sleeping draught that put him to sleep forever. And then, I sang him to sleep one last time." Tears clogged her throat and she let out a strangled cry and buried her head in her hands. I wrapped her in my arms, holding her until she forced herself to sit straight again.

She let out a shuddering breath. "It was too late for Kjell, but not for you. Whatever it takes to get you out of here, I will do. I don't care about myself. My son is beyond Hyto's reach, safe with his father."

There was no debate. Smoky and the others might be on the way, but it was only a matter of time before Hyto lost control and killed me. He was too angry. As much as he wanted to torture Smoky by ripping me apart in front of my husband, he didn't have as much self-control as he liked to believe. Most sociopaths lost it at some point, and he was a dragon on the edge.

My body protested, but I forced myself to my feet. "Let's go. You must come with me. I need your help and I can't leave you here."

She nodded. "My son no longer needs me to protect him. He has gone to his ancestors, I hope. And perhaps, I will redeem myself in the eyes of Thor and Frejya."

"May I say a few words for him?"

"I would be honored if you did, Priestess."

Putting her arm around my waist, she helped me over to the cage, and I stared at the slack body, tears running down my face. He'd never had a chance. He was of an age to take a wife now, but he'd never wed, never prove himself in battle, never grow into whatever he might have become. And the fault lay directly at Hyto's feet.

I reached into the cage, placed my hands on the cool body. Biting my lip, I breathed long and slow, trying to ignore my own pain. And then, lowering myself into trance, I felt for the Moon Mother, sought her presence. She swept over me, for a moment took away my discomfort as I whispered our prayer for the dead.

"What was life has crumbled. What was form, now falls away. Mortal chains unbind and the soul is lifted free. May you find your way to the ancestors. May you find your path to the gods. May your bravery and courage be remembered in song and story. May your parents be proud, and may your children carry your birthright. Sleep, and wander no more."

Making the sign that signified the Trail of the Dead, I let out another long breath and turned around. Hanna was crying, silently, but she managed a pained smile as she led me over to the table, where we both washed our hands.

She shoved a sturdy crust of bread into my hands, spread with cheese. A thick shard of jerky sat beside the plate, and a bowl of broth. I quickly ate and slurped down the soup while she slathered me in ointments again.

"Thank you," I said quietly, feeling numb inside.

"You'll need it. The weather outside is brutal."

"I know. I've been out there before. I also know that life around Hyto is far worse. I'd rather die in the snow. I don't trust him to keep me alive until his son gets here. He went apeshit on me, but he could have been far worse. And next time . . ."

"Here—put these on." She shook out the undergarments, trousers, shirt, and robe she'd shoved into my hands earlier. I slid into the clothes, wincing as the rough material brushed against all the bruises and abrasions covering my body.

While I was getting dressed, Hanna yanked out a couple of rucksacks she had filled with food and water and other things I could not see. I finished dressing and looked around for anything that might make a useful weapon. I had my magic, but it would be nice to have something sharp and pointy in my hands. She noticed what I was doing.

"You won't find any weapons." She shook her head. "Not here—except for the butchering knives. We'll take those. Hyto didn't consider them a threat in my hands, I suppose." She handed me a clean thick-bladed knife, wicked sharp and heavy. I slid it through the belt holding the fur vest I'd donned together in front.

"We should go. How long does he usually stay out to feed?"

"Sometimes all day; other times he returns faster. I think we've got about everything we can handle. Here—drape this around you." She wrapped a heavy white fur cloak around my shoulders, an animal hide with armholes slit in it. The warmth would help keep me alive. Hanna was similarly dressed.

"What about the collar? Can he track me through it?"

"Probably, but I can't take it off. His magic is too strong." She picked up a walking stick and handed it to me, then found another sturdy length of wood for herself. "I think we're ready. Let us get out of here."

With one last look at Hyto's secret lair, I followed her into the maze of tunnels. I'd never come back here alive—even if I had to kill myself to prevent it.

We wound through the stone passages until we came to an exit, which I was surprised to see was *not* the main entrance. The cave opening overlooked a steep path heading directly down the mountain. I glanced around and caught sight of what I was now positive were the Skirts of Hel—the glacial sheets near Howl's hideout.

"We have to make for there. I am friends with—"

"Yes, you told me. Lord Howl. If you are telling the truth, then we may actually have a chance, but we have to keep to the shadows as much as we can. The Master . . . Hyto . . ." Her tongue rolled over the name like an unfamiliar cavity, newly discovered and unwelcome. "Hyto will return from the air, flying, and if he should see us in the snow, he'll fry us to crisps."

"That's why the white fur? Camouflage?"

"Easier to hide in the snow, yes. So keep the hood over

your hair—it's dark and shows easily against the white. Dragon eyes are keen. Dragon sight is clear. Even when the dragon is mad. And there are other dangers—"

"Trolls, ice spiders . . . I know."

"So many creatures up here, and so little food." Hanna nodded, then stepped out into the snow, sinking to her ankles. "The snow has compacted through the winter, but the fresh fall is atop of it and so going will not be easy."

I followed her, my muscles protesting every move I made. But anything was better than waiting in that stinking cavern for Hyto to return. The fur boots she'd fashioned for me were actually quite warm, and I thought that if I should get out of this and ever have to return to the Northlands—something I wasn't planning on—I'd go native with my outfit.

We struggled down the path as fast as we could. Slipping and sliding, we barreled our way away from the cave, leaving a veil of fine powder in our wake. The snow had fallen again during the night and beneath the new inches was hardened crust, so we only sank up to our ankles.

Keeping to the cover of the scrub trees—high-altitude pines and firs that were windblown, growing at a slant—Hanna and I slowed. The grade was growing steeper as we made our way down the mountainside, and the air bonejarring. Every breath I took hurt my lungs and made my bruises ache, but now that we were out of the cave, I knew I couldn't go back.

An hour or so later, I motioned to Hanna to stop. As we'd gone along, I noticed that the mountain pines in the Northlands bore sharp needles, and they were strongly scented, reminding me of blue spruce. Strong scent was good—it would help to hide our own perfume. Being dragon, Hyto had a hypersensitivity toward fragrance, and anything we could do to confuse him, so much the better. I stripped off a handful of the spiny needles, broke them, then rubbed them over my face and hands, wincing as they pricked my skin. Hanna nodded, getting the idea, and did the same. The pitch stuck to my cheeks, but I didn't care. Anything to help keep Mr. Big Bad Dragon away.

A blast of icy wind came gusting down the slope, sending

snow everywhere. I gasped as the gust caught my breath and yanked it from my lungs. Leaning against the trunk of the pine, I forced myself to breathe deeply, slowly, until I felt able to continue.

Hanna led me off the main path, which seemed dangerous, but we didn't dare hike around in plain sight. Even in camouflage, we could easily be seen from the air. I was just amazed we'd managed to come this far without being caught or keeling over from the freezing temperatures.

Another half hour struggling through the snow and she motioned for me to crawl under one of the trees with her, where there was some protection from the wind. As I pushed my way under the low-hanging branches of the scrub, I happened to glance up the mountain. The cave entrance was still visible, but just a tiny speck against the vast sea of white.

Hanna and I huddled together for warmth as she fumbled around in the folds of her cape, pulling out a thick roll with a slab of cheese. She broke the sandwich in half and handed me my share.

"Thank you," I whispered, my throat raw from the air. The bread was dry and hard but I forced it down anyway, taking sips from my waterskin. I followed her lead. After drinking freely, I packed snow in the skin to melt for new water.

"No worry, Camille. We'll need a lot of food. We have a long way to go to reach any sort of safety, and I truly don't know if we'll make it, but we may be able to reach the Skirts of Hel by morning. We may have to bivouac for the night down lower. I'd stay under the trees, but there is one danger in that." She gave me a long look, as if deciding whether to spill bad news.

But I had far too good an imagination. "Let me guess: Hyto gets home, finds us gone, and decides we're hiding out in the trees, so he decides to burn every stand from the top of the mountain on down."

She blinked. "Yes, that was my fear. I didn't want to worry you, however."

I bit my lip, not wanting to say too much. "Back Earthside . . . where I'm staying . . . we are facing a danger far worse than

Hyto. Trust me, if it's big, bad, and possible, I've imagined it." I stared at the vast swath of sloping snow fields that spread out below us. "If he does decide to burn the woods, surely we'll know what's going on before he hits us. At worst, he catches us again. And frankly, considering what he could cook up for that, I'd rather die in a forest fire, I think."

Hanna bit her lip. "Yes, you are right about that. If he captures us, he'll just kill me, but you . . ."

"I know." I whispered. "I know." The pain he'd already inflicted had been bad, but even I knew it could be far worse.

"Come, finish your meal and let's be off again. The sooner we reach the glacial fields, the sooner we can make our way across to your Wolf Lord friend." She held out her hand and yanked me up. The bruises on my back and thighs screamed in protest, but I bit my lip. Hanna had given everything to help me escape. I wasn't about to bemoan my own state.

Over the rest of the day, we managed to elude any sign of Hyto, and the weather stood with us. We reached the bottom of the snow field where it evened out before heading into the Skirts of Hel by dusk, and I wanted nothing more than to keep going, but one wrong turn on the rocks and we'd have a broken leg, or worse. We found an outcropping of boulders and huddled behind them, trying to brave the winds the best we could.

Hanna suggested building up the snow on either side to block the wind, so we managed to find two boulders with enough room between them where we could stretch out. We packed snow around the entire fort, smoothing the sides to look like drifts. We couldn't do much about being seen from the sky, but with our cloaks and the darkness, there was a fair shot that Hyto wouldn't be able to spot us.

We took turns guarding each other as we stepped outside the snow fort to relieve ourselves, and then we spread out our cloaks and snuggled beneath them to generate as much warmth as we could. We didn't dare build a fire, but the snow packed around the sides sheltered us from the worst of the wind, and if we lay facing each other, we were warmed by each other's breath.

Sleep did not come easy and neither of us felt like talking, so we dozed, listening to the howl of wolves in the distance. Shortly after moonrise, I woke, sensing something was going on. I slowly peeked over the edges of the fort, up the slope toward Hyto's cave.

Fire. Fire was burning near the top of the mountain. I could vaguely make out where it was coming from—sparks were lighting up the sky near the cave. Hyto had returned and discovered we were gone.

I quickly woke Hanna and we scooted as far back in the shadow of the boulders as possible. My stomach lurched as we watched the pyrotechnics. I tried to keep my thoughts away from what might happen if he found us. A low rumble and we could hear the sound of a small avalanche racing down the slope, but I searched, reaching out, and could feel that it wasn't heading toward us, so we stayed put. Hyto must have set it off in his anger.

Another flare and the upper forests began to burn. A loud roar filled the air—this time Hyto rather than tumbling snow. It echoed all the way down the mountain to where we were, and it took everything I had to keep from screaming. I began to cry, silently, the tears freezing on my face. As my shoulders shook, Hanna drew me into her arms and I hid my face against her shoulder.

We clung to each other through the night, unable to sleep, as the show continued. Toward morning, before dawn hit, she leaned close and whispered, "We should go. Now, before first light. We may have a chance to cross the glacier in the mists . . . if we wait till they clear, he'll see us."

I nodded, staring out across the wide ice fields. The mist was thick; it would be dangerous, but we had no choice. My stomach lurched as she pressed another piece of bread and some jerky into my hands, but I knew we'd need the fuel and so I ate, chewing mindlessly, forcing it down my throat.

"Do you think he can find me from this collar?" I tugged on the fucking leash around my neck.

"I don't know," Hanna said. "I just know I don't want to chance cutting it off you and having some spell kill you or something."

When we finished, we packed up our rucksacks and headed out, cautiously creeping over the sides of our fort, trying to keep low to the ground. We skirted through the fields, from boulder to boulder, crouching as we went.

The rocks from the alluvial deposits were sharp and dangerous, and more than once, my ankle began to turn before I caught myself. The mist rose in swirls, like ghostly sentinels, and now and then I'd hear snuffles and movements in the fog, but we couldn't stop, couldn't chance finding out what they were. We had to reach Howl's cave before Hyto decided to fly lower.

The upper tier of forest was burning brightly, even in the new snow that had begun to fall, and I bit my lip, feeling a hollow sadness at the loss of the woodland. Hyto didn't give a fuck about the land, about the creatures who might be making their homes in the forest. All he cared about was his rage.

Another hour and we paused for a quick rest. The mist was starting to lift, even as the snowfall was growing deeper. With a ragged pant against the cold, I tried to gauge how long till we were near Howl's cave. It couldn't be that far away. And then I glanced up and saw the opening to Hel's Gate. Iris had confronted Vikkommin there and destroyed him for good. We were near.

"Hurry," I whispered. "We're almost there. We have to hurry."

We slid down the icy slope, crossing as fast as we dared. And then a roar filled the air again, and I glanced back at the mountain.

"Hyto! He's out and searching. Hurry!"

Hanna said nothing, just pushed ahead as we scrambled forward, trying to keep our footing on the slippery glacier. I fell once, but she yanked me back up, and even though the jarring pain in my wrist told me I'd broken my little finger, I ignored it, biting back the pain. My forehead had hit a sharp rock, but I'd only grazed myself and drops of blood were streaking down my cheek.

Hanna tripped next, and despite the pain in my finger, I helped her up as we scrabbled for footing. We were almost off the glacial field when a noise in front of us took us by surprise.

Out of the mists, a soft voice said, "Lady Camille. What are you doing here?"

I recognized the voice and—almost in tears—dropped to my knees. "Lord Howl, please, please help us. There's a dragon after us and we can't run any farther. Please, give us shelter."

Within seconds, a low whistle went out and we were surrounded by wolves. Howl, the Great Winter Wolf Spirit, stepped out of the mist, lean and muscled, in thick pelts of white, with a headdress of bone and silver adorning his head. He was dark and his hair long against his back, and a wild feral gleam filled his eyes.

"You are hurt." A statement, not a question. "Come, we will take you to safety. And then you can explain why you are out here at the ends of the world."

Several of the wolves transformed then, into dark warriors who gathered both of us up into their arms, and quick as the wind, we were racing back to Howl's lair, and to safety.

Chapter 14

Howl's lair was pretty much as I remembered it from just a few days back. A labyrinth of welcoming, warm caverns, with bathing pools and the smell of roasting meat filling the corridors. My stomach rumbled, but beneath the hunger I felt weary, beyond any movement or will to go on. I'd used up all the stamina and endurance I'd ever possessed.

I introduced Hanna to Howl, who had shed his outer pelts. With leather buckskin pants and a bare chest, he was pretty much dressed the same as last I'd seen him . . . except the headdress was different. He had long dark hair, gathered back in a ponytail, with eyes just as dark.

"Howl, please, meet Hanna. She saved my life." Even as I spoke, something gave way inside, and I slid to the floor, unable to stand.

One of the largest white wolves padded forward to press her nose against my side. I knew who it was. Sure enough, in the blink of an eye, she transformed. She was short, about five five, and sturdy; with eyes that glimmered ice blue, Kitää had hair as silver as Smoky's. Dressed in a white pair of soft leather pants and matching tunic, she knelt by my side and stroked my hair.

"You are hurt," she said, and I burst into tears as Kitää, Howl's wife, the Queen and Mother of the Katabas Wolf People, gathered me in her arms and rocked me gently.

I leaned into her soft body, wanting nothing more than to fall asleep, but one of the warriors raced in, kneeling at Howl's feet. Howl motioned for him to rise. "What news, Taj?"

"Lord Howl, the dragon at the top of the mountain has gone on a rampage. Fire is raging in the upper forests." Taj, who by the coloring of his hair I guessed was a gray wolf, was standing at alert. The rest of the pack picked up the scent of his worry off him and began to mill around, in both wolf and human form.

I let out a little cry. "Hyto. It's Hyto. He's made a dreyerie for himself up there. He's been there about five years, though—from what I understand."

Howl turned to me, slowly looking me up and down. "Indeed, the dragon has been living there five years. But you say it is *Hyto*? The *White Demon*?" And then he paled. "You have come from there. Is Iampaatar up there with him?"

I shook my head. "Hyto captured me." Stopping as a lump rose in my throat, I tried to keep my panic at bay and slowly showed him my collar. "He kidnapped me. This is his mark. He was trying to lure Smoky here, to destroy him."

Kitää gasped. "He caught you?" She looked into my eyes and I opened my heart to her, telling her everything that had happened with a single look. As her expression fell, she ducked her head, shaking it gently. "Oh my child, you are truly hurt."

Nodding, I forced the tears back. "Yes . . . But Hanna helped me escape, and Hyto is furious. We saw him raging early this morning, from the boulder field on the Skirts of Hel."

"We have to get you out of here," Howl said. "Before the dragon rains fire down on my people. That collar can lead him to you—once he comes out of his rage long enough to remember it."

"I don't want to put you in danger," I whispered. "But I

don't know if I can make it down to the portals on my own. I could barely make it here. I am hurt, bruised sore through."

"We don't have time to stand on ceremony." Howl motioned for Kitää to help me.

Hanna started to protest, but I shook my head at her. "It's okay. Howl won't harm me." I stripped out of the garments, now soaked with sweat and the scent of fear. As I winced, peeling off the underlayer of lighter clothing that had stuck to some of my open wounds, Kitää let out a sharp cry and Howl shouted.

"You poor child." Kitää hurried forward, examining my back. As she circled me, her gaze fell to the dark bruises and raw skin between my thighs and she raised her eyes to meet mine. "He has grievously injured you." She turned to Howl. "He has violated her, as well as beaten her."

Howl let out a low growl. "We will help you get safely home. I will not let him take you from our midst."

I inhaled a deep breath, shuddering, and as we stood there, a low shimmering caught my attention. "Someone is coming through from the astral—over there!"

The warriors of the tribe swiftly moved into position, weapons to the ready. As we waited with pent breath, three shapes flickered into view and I shouted with joy, as Rozurial, Shade, and Vanzir stepped in off the astral.

I stood there, staring at the three of them, naked except for Howl's collar. It didn't matter to me that I was naked—I'd been so exposed the past few days that it was beginning to feel normal.

And then I saw the expressions on their faces as they took in the bruises and welts on my body. Vanzir let out a sharp cry, as Shade began to rumble. Roz hurried toward me and gently draped his duster around me, but the inner pockets were full of weapons and I moaned as something sharp and pointy scraped a sore spot. He quickly pulled it away from my shoulders, but by then Kitää had found a luxurious fur drape and slid it around me.

All the adrenaline that had been keeping me going suddenly vanished, and once again I lost my balance and tumbled forward, into Roz's arms. He gathered me up and Kitää led him over to a soft pallet of fur pelts. As I tried to catch my breath, she motioned to a serving girl and soon I was holding a cup of hot broth, propped up by Roz, who was sitting behind me, with me leaning back against his chest. Vanzir and Shade knelt nearby.

"You're safe now, Camille." Shade took my hand, but I pulled away. Too much attention was making me feel weak. "What's this?" He fingered the collar, then let out a sharp hiss. "Evil! What evil do you wear?"

"Hyto's collar." I motioned Hanna over to sit beside me. "This woman saved my life. She's to thank for me escaping."

"We'll take you home as soon as you're ready to travel. And we'll get that collar off you." Roz stroked my hair back away from my face. I pressed my lips together.

"Where's Smoky?" I looked up at him, dreading yet needing to know the answer.

"Looking for you. He's on the rampage. He went to the Dragon Reaches to find out what he could about Hyto . . ."

I turned to Vanzir. "The other night . . . I don't know when—I've lost track of the time—you came to me . . ."

"I still don't know how I got out there, but when you told me you were in a cavern near the Skirts of Hel, I remembered what Iris had said about her journey and thought that maybe . . . just maybe . . . so Roz and Shade brought me along with them."

"We weren't quite sure where to look, so we have been looking as we came up the mountain from the portals," Roz said. "You told Vanzir near the Skirts of Hel, but we weren't sure in which direction. It took some doing to get our bearings, but it helped that I'd been here before."

"We have to get out of here." I struggled to sit up. "I can't let my presence put Howl's people in danger." The Elemental Lord would be able to handle Hyto, but his people weren't quite as powerful as he was.

"Lady Camille, it is true you are a threat here, but we will not ask you to leave until you are ready," Kitää said. She pressed a mug of soup into Hanna's hand and gave us soft bread and meat. We both gulped down the food, along with big steins of heady beer.

I wiped the crumbs off my mouth. "I need to get home. Hanna—you'd better come with me. If Hyto finds you, he'll kill you. I don't know if you can adjust to life over Earthside, but until we've somehow managed to destroy Smoky's father, you need protection."

"I'm not the one he's after," she said, softly brushing a stray strand of hair out of my face. "My dear, I've done what I set out to do—help you escape. I really haven't thought further than that. I thought I might search for my daughters . . . in hopes they still live."

I grabbed her hand. "You don't dare run off now. Hyto will seek you out, and he will kill you for your part in this. Do you want to chance your daughters' lives to him? At least come with me until we've found a way to deal with him."

She smiled softly, then knelt by my side. "You are a caring woman. I hope I can call you my friend." Then, after a pause, she added, "Yes, I will come with you. Warn me of things I need to be aware of. I've heard that Earthside has wonders unheard of in the Northlands and in Otherworld, but I will miss my home."

I pressed her hand against my lips and kissed it gently. "It does, my friend. And terrible troubles, as well." Forcing myself to stand, I turned to Shade. "We need to leave. I would not put Howl and Kitää's people in any further danger. How are we going to manage this? Can you carry two of us?"

He glanced over at Rozurial. "Let me take Vanzir. My travel is better suited toward those not of mortal stock. You . . . do you think you can take two of them at once?"

Rozurial bit his lip. "I don't know . . ."

Kitää stepped up. "I will go with you and carry one of the women. I can also travel through the Ionyc Seas. I will make the portal jumps with you to Elqaneve, where you can all travel through the portal back to Earthside. My husband, do you mind?" She turned to Howl, who nodded gruffly.

"Aye, woman, go ahead, but do not tarry on the way home, and be cautious. Dragons are wily, and dangerous, and too clever for their own good. Meanwhile, I will send a runner to the Dragon Reaches in search of Iampaatar, and bid him head homeward to his woman."

They found some clean clothes for Hanna and me and, with Kitää's and Hanna's help, I dressed. Then, after Hanna had changed into a clean outfit, we gathered in the main council chamber.

Shade slid his arm around Vanzir, Rozurial took me, and Kitää gathered Hanna to her. Without another word, we slid into the Ionyc Seas.

I was going home.

At the portal to the Northlands, we quickly jumped to Dahnsburg, then to Elqaneve. I was so dizzy from the change in altitude that I leaned against Roz most of the way. At the Elqaneve portal, I turned to Kitää.

"Bless you and your people, for giving us shelter. May the Moon Mother shine down on you in all her glory with all her blessings. I will not forget the debt I owe you."

She smiled gently. "You owe us no favor, save for to do your best to destroy the monster on the mountain. We knew a dragon had taken hold up there but weren't sure just who. That it is Iampaatar's father is a deathly knell. He is truly mad. And Camille—be cautious. If he catches you again, I dread to think what he'll do."

"I know what he's capable of," I whispered. "In the long run, I think I got off easy . . . but it wouldn't have been long before the real pain would have begun. I don't think I could withstand it."

"Just be careful, please. Remember the wolf people when you next go hunting with the Moon Mother." Then, before we could say another word, she ducked back inside the portal and vanished.

I turned to Roz. "Home. Let's get home. It will take Hyto some time to follow the signature in my collar, but we need to get it off as soon as we can."

And so we entered the portal, ignoring the stares of the elves filing in and out, and jumped back home, Earthside.

*   *   *

Grandmother Coyote was waiting for us. One of the Hags of
Fate, she watched over the worlds, as immortal as the Elemental Lords and the Harvestmen. I began to kneel before
her, but my aching joints wouldn't allow it, so I opted for
bowing slow and deep.

"Camille, you live. I thought you might when your
threads began to untangle from those of the white dragon."
She gazed at me, long and deep, from within the folds of her
hooded gray cloak. Grandmother Coyote's face was lined
with more rivers and valleys than a topographical map, and
her eyes were a streaming flow of whirling clouds and stars.
When she smiled, her teeth gleamed—sharp steel. She was
truly one of the ancients.

I thought about asking her help—there was always a
steep price to pay, but she leaned forward and took my hand,
upending it in her palm. She slowly shook out one finger
bone from the bag in her other hand, to land on my palm.

"Free advice, so listen well." She gazed at the bone in my
hand. "Do not stay in your home. Go instead to your husband's abode—the barrow. It will be safer. The dragon's fire is
seeking you out. He is not done with you yet, but you can live
through this if you are smart. As long as you wear his mark,
he will find you—and you cannot undo it until his death."

She removed the bone from my hand and dropped it back
in the bag.

"We have to kill a dragon . . . How can we do that? Only
Smoky stands a chance . . ." Feeling hopeless, I stared at the
old crone, wishing for all the world she might for once intervene. But the Hags of Fate seldom took sides in the way of
the world, letting events flow around them as they watched
and listened.

"There is another . . . there is help where you least expect
it." And then she turned to Vanzir. "Young demon, fret not.
You are not at the heart of this. And the gods can regift
where they've taken away . . . hold hope in your heart."

I turned to look at Vanzir. He shifted his gaze, but not
before I'd caught the distress in his eyes—which spiraled

like a vortex. I suddenly understood. He blamed himself for my condition. Any lingering anger I had toward him vanished and I moved forward, tears flooding my eyes.

"This wasn't your fault. It wasn't Smoky's fault. Or mine. The only one to blame here is Hyto. He's the one who hurt me."

"But if I hadn't . . . if . . . Smoky hadn't chased you out of the house, you wouldn't have been captured." The words came streaming out of his mouth, and for once I heard his voice crack with emotion.

"No . . . no . . . sometimes life just happens. Sometimes the universe plays horrid practical jokes on us. And sometimes, the world just sucks. Events snowball . . . shit happens, Vanzir. I don't blame you." And even as I said the words, I felt something within myself lighten and fly away, a secret resentment I'd been carrying around since that night in the tunnels.

Vanzir sucked in a deep breath and met my gaze. "You don't?"

"No, I don't."

Rozurial glanced around nervously. "I'm glad you two are all buddy-buddy, but we'd better get out to Smoky's barrow. I'll take you there through the Ionyc Seas, then come back for Hanna—"

"No." Vanzir's voice was so loud it sounded like a thunderclap. "We don't dare leave Camille alone out there. I'll bring Hanna in the car. You and Shade head out there with her. I'll stop at the house and let them know—Delilah and Menolly are probably at home."

"Menolly would have to be—we're into morning now." I shivered. The snow-covered wood was starting to get to me, and I was losing it fast. The next time I faltered, I'd probably pass out.

Roz and Shade agreed, and so, sheltered once again in Roz's arms, we leaped into the Ionyc Seas, and the maelstrom of traveling between worlds raged around me as I leaned into his shoulder.

I opened my eyes to find myself in a huge rock chamber, where Hyto loomed over me, a steel whip in his hand, holding me around the waist with that damned hair of his. I began to scream as he raised the whip high.

"How did you find me? Just kill me now . . . please, just kill me." I couldn't go through any more. I wasn't a rock, wasn't as strong as everybody thought. "I'm weak, I'm so weak. I can't be the anchor anymore. I can't hold up everybody's burdens . . . just let me slide into the darkness. Please."

"Oh, the darkness will swallow you deep and never let you go, girl. *When I'm done with you.* But we've just started, Camille. You and I have a long, dark road to walk together."

He laughed and the blows began to fall, one after another after another, white hot and searing into my flesh. As the skin began to peel back from muscle and bone, I cried out for Smoky, for Trillian, for Morio . . . for my sisters . . . not wanting to die alone at the hands of a madman.

"Camille! Camille, wake up!"

The voice cut through the pain, and I woke, screaming, to find myself in the mountainous four-poster bed that Smoky had in his bedroom, dressed in a filmy nightgown that floated away from my injuries. Slowly, groggy and feeling hungover, I pushed myself to a sitting position, wincing as I did so, trying to figure out what the hell was happening.

A blur of movement startled me, and I scrambled back against the pillows, dragging the comforter up to cover me. My heart raced and for a moment I couldn't focus, but then I saw that it was Vanzir who had woken me up. And Hanna was asleep in the rocking chair.

I tried to calm my breath and leaned forward into his arms as he wrapped them around me and held me quietly until the tears stopped flowing. He pushed me back then and offered me a handkerchief.

"I still have nightmares of my time with Karvanak," he said softly. "I never tell anybody—after all, I'm a demon; I've done worse to others. But his treatment . . . he was a sadist through and through."

"Like Hyto," I whispered, staring at the covers. The pale

blue-on-blue pattern was delicate, almost lacy. An odd choice, but Smoky had his elegant side that I'd always loved dearly.

"Like Hyto. I'm not sure all he did to you, but Camille . . . you're going to need some help to get through this, I think." Vanzir looked around, then picked up a bathrobe and wrapped it around my shoulders. "Can you walk? You should eat something."

I stopped him. "I'm glad Smoky called truce with you. I didn't want to tell him, but . . ."

"But you are married to him—and to Morio and Trillian, and they deserved to know. And you love them and wouldn't hurt them by letting them find out accidentally. I know. I get it. Believe me. Come, let me get you food."

I tugged at the collar. "I hate this. I hate this with a passion. And he can track me through it. I want it off; it feels like it's choking me."

"That was what the soul binder felt like, but that I went into voluntarily. This . . . you should never have had to wear this. I'm so sorry." And once again, his voice cracked. He shook his head, the spiked blond shag barely moving.

"Vanzir . . . what happened, happened. I forgive you. And I forgive myself. And that's all anybody will ever have to know. I won't let Smoky hurt you." As I stumbled out of bed, Hanna shifted. "Why isn't she in a bed of her own? She can't just sleep in the chair."

"She insisted on sleeping near you, to keep watch. I spiked her drink with a sleeping aid. The woman was worn out." He gazed down at her. "She's comely enough, but looks harsh . . ."

"She spent five years locked up with Hyto, doing his bidding, watching her son descend into madness because of the dragon. She has a right to be harsh." I motioned for Vanzir to gather her out of the rocking chair and put her in the bed. He did so, covering her gently with the blankets. Then, as I wrapped the bathrobe around my aching body, we headed out into the main living chamber.

The smell of my love was everywhere—dragon musk, but this was a soothing musk, a gentle, loving scent. Smoky could raze a town if he wanted, but he was my love and my heart. Hyto was a madman. As I sought to unentangle the two in my mind—Smoky took after his father in looks—I glanced around the barrow for the wind-up clock. Here, time slowed, and electronics ceased to work.

Smoky's barrow was located out near Mount Rainier, in a faerie mound—a barrow he'd co-opted from Titania for his own. Toward the back of the area he used for a living room, a dropoff led to a huge underground tunnel, through which he could fly in dragon form. To the right was the bedroom and bath, and to the left, a kitchen-dining area.

The furnishings were old, heavy wood, expensive antiques, and the scent of cigar smoke filled the air—Smoky was big on brandy and cigars in his own digs, though he abstained from smoking when around me because the smoke bothered both Delilah and me so much.

The scent of cigar was cut with the smell of sizzling sausage, and my stomach lurched. I realized I was famished. How I could be hungry after what I'd been through escaped me, but the fact was, my body craved food. As I achingly made my way toward the kitchen door, it opened and out came Delilah and Trillian.

"Camille!" Trillian dropped the plates he was carrying, and they shattered on the floor as he raced over to grab me up and spin me around. When I let out a shriek of pain, he immediately put me down. "Oh crap, I'm sorry. I'm so sorry. My beloved, forgive me." The look on his face was one I'd never before seen—a mixture of terror and joy.

Holding my sore ribs, I let him lead me over to the sofa and gently pull me down on his lap. "No . . . it's just . . . I hurt everywhere." And then, even as Delilah was rushing over, food in hand, I fell into his arms and kissed him deeply, trying to wash the memory of Hyto's touch out of my mind with Trillian's eager, loving embrace.

As I finally came up for air, he slid me off his lap and put a pillow behind my back. "Morio would be here if he could. Shade's at home, watching over him now, along with Rozurial."

I nodded, biting my lip. "Is Smoky back yet?"

"No, but he will be here soon, trust me, love. Now eat."

Delilah returned to the kitchen and brought out fresh plates, then fixed me a breakfast of sausage, eggs, and biscuits and a tumbler of orange juice as Vanzir swept up the broken glass. Her mouth was pursed, and she looked like she was about to cry, but I could tell she was trying to keep her composure.

As I forked the food into my mouth, I wasn't sure what to say. What *could* I say? Hyto had raped me, beaten me, humiliated me, and I still wore his collar, spelling out that I was his possession. Oh, I could just come out and say, *I'm fucked up . . . I can't get his image out of my mind.* Because it was true—no matter how much I wanted to, when I closed my eyes he was there, towering over me, his face a fury, his eyes gleaming with the darkness of insanity. But that wouldn't do any good except to make them feel worse.

"What . . . what do you need?" Delilah finally caught her breath and her words spilled out, sounding wan and hollow. She hung her head. "I'm sorry—I don't know what to say, what to ask. Menolly was here all night, pacing, but she had to go home this morning."

"How long was I out?" I jerked my head up.

"Close to twenty-four hours." She looked up as the front door opened and Shamas peeked inside. His eyes lit up when he saw me and he opened his mouth, then paused. After a moment, he let out a long sigh and held my gaze, offering me strength without pity, and I gratefully nodded to him.

"Delilah, your phone's ringing. I answered—it's Sharah." She glanced at me. "I guess I'd better . . ."

"Go take it. When you come back, I have something to tell you." In my scramble to get away, to find a hiding place where Hyto couldn't get me, I'd forgotten about Chase, but now the memory of meeting him on the astral flooded back. At least we might be able to rescue him, if nothing else.

As she headed outside, I turned to Trillian. "Is everyone okay? What happened while I was gone?"

"Absolute hell, my love. We were all in absolute hell. Smoky . . . you've never seen him angry. Pray you never do. I may be your alpha, but I think he's *all our alpha*. Dragons are not to be crossed lightly, and when you threaten their families . . ." He took my hands. "Seriously, I have never seen anyone so anxious to kill. Camille, I'm glad you love him, because now that you're back, he'll never, ever let you go."

I ducked my head. "I hope that he can stop Hyto . . . Trillian—he's insane. He hated me before; now I can only imagine the torture he has planned for me." And then I found myself blurting out, "I want to be strong. I don't want to be afraid of him! But I am—I am so terribly afraid of him. And he can find me . . . he can track me."

Trillian motioned to Vanzir. "I think she needs a drink. Brandy, please. For the both of us."

As Delilah came back in, she was smiling, though her lips were still pursed. "Smoky's back and on his way. He'll be here any minute. Camille, finish your breakfast. He's bringing Sharah with him to attend to your wounds."

Sharah . . . *Chase*!

"My mind is a little muddled. I was going to tell you a few minutes ago but spaced it again. That first night, I saw Chase. I went out of body onto the astral, after Hyto . . . was done with me." Biting my lip, I stopped, fighting back the memories. "Anyway, I was on the astral and I saw Chase out there—in body! We may be able to find him if we head out there looking. He can't get off the astral on his own, but he was alive and well."

"You saw Chase?" Delilah broke into a smile. "That is good news. And we need every bit we can get."

Just then, the door burst open and Smoky stood there, in all his glory, with Sharah standing a few steps behind him, looking shaken. Trillian gently backed away from me as my dragon strode toward me, pushing everything that impeded his progress out of the way. And when he reached me, I expected him to grab me up, steeling myself for the pain, but he fell to his knees in front of me and pressed my hands to his forehead.

His voice muted, he whispered, "Can you ever forgive me, my love? Can you ever, ever forgive me?"

Chapter 15

~&~

"Smoky, oh my Smoky!" And like that, I slid down to the floor, pressing against him, covering his face with kisses as his hair gently wound around me. For a moment, I flinched, memories of Hyto's cruel strands surging forth. But then I forced myself to relax as Smoky gently embraced me, pulling me to him. He covered my forehead with kisses, pressed his lips against the welts running across my cheeks, whispered my name against my mouth. Tears streamed down his face out of those glacial eyes, as he gathered me by the shoulders and held me back, drinking me in.

"Camille, my love, my only love. What did my father do to you? I wasn't there to protect you—how can you ever forgive me? How can I even ask you to forgive me?" And then he slowly stopped, his gaze fixating on the collar. "No . . . no . . . he did *not* . . ."

Jumping up, he stumbled back. "I will destroy him. I will carve him to shreds. I will wingstrap him until he screams for mercy, and then I'll tighten the screws! Hyto will die, painfully, in agony." He stood there, panting, and a musky, possessive odor rose off him like an aura made of ice. He was trembling, and I could sense the energy he was using to repress his rage.

The pain of his retreat was worse than anything Hyto had inflicted on me. I slowly forced my way to my feet and stood, staring at him. "Love, would you turn away from me because of what your father did to me?"

Smoky stopped, frowned, and then understanding crossed his face. "Oh my sweet. Oh, my love. I am not turning away from *you*—no, never think that." And he opened his arms. "I'm just so angry."

Painfully, I went to him, bit my lip as he enfolded me in his embrace, pressing against the bruises. I didn't have a clue how dragon society felt about abused women, but I was about to find out.

"You have to know . . . I have to tell you . . . and Trillian . . . what he did to me. And I have to get this collar off." I tugged on it. "I hate it—I hate the feel of it. I hate knowing he's still got hold of me."

Smoky examined it. "Damn him. He's used a cunning spell. I can't break this, but . . . maybe . . . I know someone who might be able to." And then he glanced down as my robe slipped off my shoulders. "Camille, what did he do to you?"

I stepped back and shrugged the sleeves up. "I'll tell you, but I need you to promise me you'll remain calm. I can't handle any more stress right now. I really can't. I feel like I'm walking a tightrope as it is. I can handle what happened to me, but only with your support."

Trillian motioned to Smoky, patting the seat next to him. "Dude, sit down."

Trillian would get it—during the civil war in my home city-state, he'd had been captured and raped by soldiers from the other side. He'd managed to both escape and eviscerate them. But his attackers had been Fae—mine, a dragon.

As Smoky headed for the sofa, the door to the bedroom opened and Hanna peeked out. She took one look at him and screamed, dropping to the ground and covering her head.

I rushed forward, cursing every painful step of the way. "It's okay—it's okay—it's not Hyto." Falling to my knees at her side, I gathered her in my arms. "Smoky . . . *it's Smoky*—Hyto's *son*. My *husband*. He won't hurt you."

As we rocked together on the ground, Smoky let out an impassioned groan, his expression racked in guilt.

"My father . . . that my father has caused such terror."

"Hyto captured Hanna and her son. He killed her husband and locked her boy up in a box for five years." I glanced up at him. "Over that time, Hyto killed at least two dozen women. Hanna had to clean up afterward . . . he forced her to bathe them for him and then take them to their deaths on the threat of torturing her son."

Smoky motioned for me to stand. "Tell us now. Tell me what he did to you. Show me what my father did to you." His gaze was deadly serious.

Delilah moved to help Hanna over to a chair as I slowly stood. Swallowing my shame, I dropped the robe in the middle of the floor, then slid the nightgown off my shoulders.

As it fell to the floor, Smoky and Trillian stared at me. I knew they were seeing the marks on my stomach, between my thighs—brilliant purples and black, deeply bruised, the skin raw and abraded. Slowly, I turned around, moving my hair to expose the long weals embedded deeply across my skin and the boot prints that had slammed into my side when he kicked me.

While my back was turned, while I was staring at the wall, I said, "Hyto raped me . . . as painfully as he could, wherever he could find an opening. He *meant* for it to hurt. He beat me, used me for furniture, forced me to blow him . . . had me on the floor like a worm, groveling, calling him Master. And he collared me like a dog."

I rattled his sins off like a grocery list. Keeping myself aloof from what had happened helped me cope with the memories that flashed through my mind like a revolving door. As I turned back to face them, I added, "Hyto taught me what it means to fear. *I want him dead.*"

Meeting their gazes, I forced myself to stand strong, even as a flood of emotions rushed through me. Delilah stared at me, tears streaking down her face, but I realized I couldn't cry anymore. I'd cried myself out. Now I just felt a core of white-hot rage beginning to build.

"I want him *dead*. And I want it to *hurt*. I want him to hurt as much as he hurt me. As he hurt Hanna. As he hurt his other victims."

Trillian slipped over to my left side, Smoky to my right. They did not touch me, but knelt at my side, each taking one of my hands.

"Oh, love, we will see to it," Trillian whispered. "I vow to you, I will not rest until your attacker is dead."

Smoky simply nodded. "Trillian's correct," he said abruptly. "I give you my word, my love. My father will pay for his sins with his life, and it will not be an easy out for him."

"We'd better get to planning then, because we also have to rescue Chase. I will not allow him wander alone on the astral while I can help. I refuse to let Hyto stop me from doing what I need to do. And if what you say is true, Hyto will be tracking me by this collar. I want it off. If it takes ripping his still-beating heart out in my hands to do so, then that's what I will do."

And my husbands—bless them—leaned in and kissed the palms of my hands gently. And I knew they would do everything in their power to see our enemy destroyed.

Sharah took me into the bedroom, along with Hanna, to examine us and tend to our wounds. As she examined my back, she said, "Do you know the one interesting thing about this?"

"I don't think any of it is *interesting*." I wasn't feeling particularly chatty.

"You'll want to know this. Your tattoos? They were right in line with several of the blows, but neither tattoo was touched. It's obvious the chain landed along them, but where your tattoos are, there is no mark—no wound."

I raised my head. "Really?"

"So help me, yes." She traced the lines crisscrossing my back. "These will heal. You will have scars, but I think I can minimize most of them. You'll need to rest, though—"

"I will rest when Hyto is dead and rotting. We have a

dragon to kill, and Chase to find." I then told her everything I could remember about seeing Chase on the astral. Even though she tried to remain professional, I could see the relief breaking in her eyes.

"I miss him so much. But Camille—you have to rest. I can dress these, but if you use them too much, they may tear open and scar—"

"Then color me marked. Menolly lives with her scars, and so can I. And if I *am* scarred, let it be a reminder that no man will ever touch me this way again. Be he dragon, demon, or devil. I have to get out there again. I *have* to see Hyto die. I can't hide at home or I'll never be able to go out again. Do you understand?"

I turned to her, grabbing her wrist and leaning forward. "Hyto taught me to fear in a way I've *never, ever* experienced. If I don't conquer this, I'll have nothing left. I don't have Menolly's strength, or Delilah's athletic ability. All I have are a handful of spells, some of which work when they have a whim to. I can't let this beat me. If I stay at home, cower in my room, Hyto will have won. I have to exorcise him from my mind. I have to get him out of my head."

Hanna stood up. "Let her do as she will. Camille is a brave young woman, and I thought sure Hyto would kill her the first night. But she withstood his treatment and even managed to drive him into a rage like no other I've seen. If she can come down off that mountain with the wounds she has, then she can withstand another battle."

She turned to me. "You would make the Northmen proud if you were one of us. You are a warrior woman in spirit, if not in body. And spirit is often far stronger than muscle and bone."

Sharah let out a long sigh. "You'll do as you wish, of course. You three always do. All right, but at least let me give you a painkiller. I have developed one that your system can withstand."

"Will it take me off my game?" I stared into her eyes, challenging her. Flanked by my family, by Trillian and Smoky, I found my courage returning, and I wanted to make them proud. I wanted to make *myself* proud. I wanted to prove that no pervert could cow me. The memory of groveling at Hyto's feet stung far more than the blows on my back or anything else he'd done to me. "I have to be alert."

Sharah nodded, and something told me she knew what I was thinking and understood. "You won't lose any speed with this one. But it will help you move around without as much pain, and so will the ointments I have for your wounds."

"Then I will gratefully accept it." I smiled then, and she leaned in and hugged me as a sister might. "Do you think Hyto might have given me a disease when he . . . when he . . ."

Sharah bit her lip. "You're pretty bruised up down there. I can give you a potion to dispel any disease he might have. I've never had the opportunity to treat a dragon for wounds, let alone an STD. So I don't really know."

"I hate asking Smoky about it—just another reminder of what Hyto did to me. *To us.* But I'd better take the potion, just in case." I kicked the ground, wincing as the blow ricocheted through my leg muscles. "Damned devil."

"We all have our devils . . . yours is just larger than most," she whispered as I downed the bottle of pink liquid she pressed into my hand. "Here, drink this for the pain. And if you need to talk, I'm here. You know that, don't you?"

"Yeah," I said softly. "If Hyto is my devil, then he's going to find himself on the wrong end of the pitchfork."

After she treated me, Sharah turned her attention to Hanna and I rejoined the others in the living room. Delilah motioned me toward the kitchen and, managing to convince Smoky and Trillian that I'd be all right without them joined to my hip, I followed her into the warm, cozy room.

As I slid into one of the distressed kitchen chairs, wincing, she pushed a sandwich in front of me. "You need to regain your strength. Eat more."

"Yes, ma'am." I pulled the sandwich to me—peanut butter and jelly? Since when did Smoky eat peanut butter?

As she sat down, staring at me, I felt my reserve slipping. "Camille . . . what do you need? You've always been here for us, and now it's our turn. Whatever you need, just ask."

She leaned forward and picked up a potato chip off the

plate, lifting it to my lips. I obediently opened my mouth and accepted the crisp, chewing slowly as I thought over her question. *What did I need?* My emotions were racing between heartbroken and furious.

I let out a sigh and put down the sandwich as she stood and poured me a glass of milk. "What do I need? What I need is for none of this to have happened. But it did, and now I need to figure out how to cope with it. My emotions are all over the board. I haven't had time to process what's happened. Hyto . . . he humiliated me, Delilah. I can withstand a lot of things, but that—no. He stripped me of my dignity, and he hurt me."

"How . . . how are you going to handle what he . . . the . . ."

I shrugged. "Rape isn't about sex—it's about wielding power. I know that much, and I refuse to let him destroy my passion. I won't let him take that away from me. But the pain . . . the beatings . . . I've never experienced pain like that before. And you know I've been hurt a lot since we came over Earthside. I'm not as quick or physically as strong as you and Menolly. The pain scared me."

Delilah bit her lip, then leaned forward. "You will get through this. It's your nature, Camille. But whenever you need to vent, just tell me—or Menolly—and we'll be there for you. If you need to scream in the woods, or beat up on some stupid troll, we'll find you what you need and let you whop ass on it."

I sucked in a long, deep breath and let it out with a shudder. "I thought I'd met evil before, but he is evil like . . . like Karvanak was—only less reasonable and far more dangerous. He's a sadist. He drinks deep from the pain of others. And he's jealous—he's so jealous of Smoky."

"It's sad when a father can't rejoice in the joys of his children." Delilah frowned. "At least Smoky didn't kill Vanzir. We thought he was going to, but when we found out you'd been captured, he went wild. He totally blames himself for it—if he hadn't yelled at you and told you to get out of his sight, you wouldn't have gone walking in the woods and been captured."

"I already had a talk with Vanzir about that. Smoky's going to have to get over it. I don't have the energy to soothe his fears. And whatever happened, there's nothing we can do about it now. The important thing is that we pull together. I notice they're in the same room out there and there's been no bloodshed. That's a good thing so far."

I finished my sandwich and flexed my hands, except for my finger held rigid by a splint. They were about the only part of me that didn't hurt, aside from the fractured bone. But Sharah's salve had worked wonders, and the pain was muted. As was the queasiness and my fatigue. Whatever was in that little vial was a wonder drug as far as I was concerned.

"We have to get over to the astral and find Chase. He seems to be able to home in on my energy field—we have similar sparks in our auras and I think he's going to end up wielding some interesting magic in the future."

"Are you sure you're up to it?" Delilah cocked her head, giving me a skeptical look.

"Keeping busy is the only thing that will save my sanity right now. I can't sit here forever, worried that Hyto is going to come barreling down on me. Come on, let's see if Smoky can take us over with him."

I pushed back from my chair, then stared down at my nightgown and robe. "I guess I'd better get dressed first, huh?"

She laughed, and her laughter felt good as it rang through the air. "Yeah, somehow I don't think those are fighting clothes."

"You said it, not me." I forced a smile to my lips and we headed into the other room. "I keep clothes out here for when we come to stay. Hold on and I'll be right out."

As I entered the bedroom, I saw that Hanna was back in bed, asleep. Sharah motioned me to the side. "She's malnourished and exhausted and has a nasty case of asthma. I've got her on meds, and she'll need to rest for a couple of weeks at least."

I nodded, quietly plundering the closet for a skirt, bustier, and jacket. I longed for my unicorn horn—until we killed

Hyto, it was the only thing that might stand between me and the dragon.

As I returned to the living room, the others were gathered together, discussing the best place to approach Hyto. I motioned for Delilah to lace me up.

"Are you sure that's wise? That corset is tight." She pulled on the laces and I let out a gasp of pain.

"It will help. I checked with Sharah. The support will ease my bruised ribs even though it makes the lacerations on my back hurt." I held up my hand. "Not much is going to help this little bugger but time, though."

Being back in my own clothes, among my family, I began to relax just a little. It would take time to heal, but as I glanced around from face to face, I knew that with their help I'd be back in control sooner than later.

"Chase was stronger than I've ever seen him. He had no clue how he'd gotten out on the astral, but the fact is he managed it."

Delilah let out a long sigh. "Smoky's the only one here who can reach the astral. He can't take all of us. If Roz were here, but he's not . . ."

"I can take three," Smoky said, "which means Delilah, Camille, and Trillian. Vanzir—" Here he stopped, again staring coldly at the demon.

Vanzir met his gaze, but did not challenge him. "Truce holds?"

Enough of this crap. I stood up.

"Both of you—listen to me. I don't want to have to say this again. I've had enough of feeling responsible for the hostility between you. So right now, it ends. No more. No more fighting. What happened between Vanzir and me happened. It shouldn't have, but it did. We were both injured by the aftereffects. It's over. Done. He's been drained of his powers, and I ended up as Hyto's plaything. We've both been hurt. So, Smoky, you have to stop. *You have to stop this.*"

Smoky sputtered, but I shook my head. "No. Just . . . *no.* I want you two to shake hands and apologize to each other."

Vanzir let out a long breath. "I don't do apologies easily, but I am sorry for this. I'm mostly sorry to Camille—it was she whom I hurt. But Smoky, my apologies to you, too. Whatever it takes to be on the same side again."

I turned to Smoky. "I'm waiting," I said, tapping my boot. I'd had enough of petty fights.

My dragon rolled his eyes. "Whatever you wish, my love. Vanzir, I remove my threats to dismember you. But remember this: Once was an accident. Twice—"

"Yeah, yeah, the big bad dragon will tear me to shreds." Vanzir waved him away, but then his gaze fell on me and he sobered. "I'm sorry. I just realized . . ."

I bit my lip. I had to make a choice. Either I could let this drag me down, or I could soldier on. And regardless of his feelings toward me now, I'd been born and raised a soldier's daughter and I still had that sense of honor. We didn't have time for me to wallow. I'd have to wait until downtime for revisit hell.

"Then let's get busy. Until we know what we're going to do about Hyto, we go on as usual, except I live out here because with this collar, once Smoky's father decides to come finish me off, I'll be a moving target and I won't put our house in danger."

"We can just transfer all the operations out here for now. Menolly can sleep in the barrow during the day—there's no chance for sunlight to reach some of the caverns here." Delilah leaned back in her chair. "We can leave a skeleton crew of Asteria's guards at the house. But we bring everybody else out here just in case Hyto decides to destroy our house out of spite."

I frowned. "If you think so . . ."

Smoky nodded. "There are labyrinths in the lower chambers—Menolly and Maggie can hide down there. I've actually got a well-lit living area down there, where the light of day never touches. You can't see it from up here."

"Then go outside and give Iris a call. Have them start moving things over." One worry off my list. "Meanwhile, Smoky, you, Trillian, Delilah, and I are going hunting for Chase on the astral. Vanzir and Roz, you take Shamas and go home. Do what you can to help Iris get ready."

As I stood up, I turned to Sharah. "Can you stay with

Hanna? I don't want her waking up and freaking out because we're gone."

"No problem," she said. "Duties at headquarters are pretty light right now." She paused, then whispered, "When you find Chase . . . tell him I'm . . . waiting for him."

Delilah let out a soft sigh. "I'll tell him, Sharah. I know he'll be happy to hear it."

And that was it. We were on the move again—me with a broken finger and a bruised and battered body. But it felt good to be in action again. I'd had my fill of being on the other end of the stick.

Chapter 16

As we sped toward Tangleroot Park, it occurred to me that I'd better let Aeval know I was back—if she even knew I'd been captured. But right now, I was determined to save Chase before he got in trouble. I couldn't bear the thought of him wandering alone forever, trying to find his way home. I knew what it felt like to be utterly alone.

We parked on the outskirts of the park and headed toward where we'd first entered the portal. I remembered what Aeval had taught me and was prepared to open it by myself. But to my surprise, we arrived to find the portal back again—unattended. Either it had sprung back up on its own within the past few hours, or nobody had been down this way to notice it for awhile. Given the time of year, the snow, and the obscurity of the park, I was betting on the latter.

As we neared the vortex, I stopped, sniffing the air. "Crap."

"What's wrong?" Delilah hurried to my side.

"I smell the Bog Eater—on *this* side of the portal. Damn it—he got through. He's loose somewhere, but the trail ends here and I can't track him."

One more thing on our worry list. Another of the Elder

Fae—a man-eating one, at that—had rejoined the world at large. And he wasn't terribly amenable to reason.

"Should we go after him now? Try to figure out where he went?"

I thought about it, then shook my head. "We won't find him today. He's passed by this way, but he's gone now. And I want to find Chase. Let's just go on—but we'll keep our eyes open. Pretty soon the Bog Eater's going to wreak havoc and we'll be here to track him down."

Smoky pulled me to one side.

"We have to speak. We have to discuss what happened." He put his arms around me, holding me gently against his chest. "I cannot bear to think you might blame me for my father's actions—though I understand why you might."

We hadn't had a chance to talk in private. Actually, that wasn't altogether true. The fact was, I'd avoided being alone with him and Trillian. I'd seen enough pain and worry in my life to understand that I'd have issues to work through, but I also knew that none of my husbands could have prevented what had happened, and that none of them were to blame. When it came down to it, we were all alone. There was no such thing as perfect safety. No such thing as invulnerability. One wrong move, one wrong slip, and any of us could be at the mercy of fate—or a psychotic dragon.

But once we were alone together, I'd have to let go. I'd have to have my breakdown and exorcise Hyto's ghost from my body and mind. Anyone being too kind to me right now threatened my ability to push back the rage and the fear. And Smoky's arms around me were too gentle, too caring, too loving for me to summon up my courage.

I pushed him back, my hand against his heart as I stared into those concerned glacial eyes. He looked so similar to his father—and yet he was not Hyto, and his nature took away the resemblance that could have come between us.

"I love you." Tears sprang to my eyes. "But we cannot talk about this here. I will need you—I will need you and Trillian and Morio, and my sisters, to get through this. But right now, I want to save Chase. If we can save Chase, I won't feel so helpless."

"I'm worried about you—your injuries are not mild, my love." A look of pain crossed his face. "I can't bear to think that my own flesh and blood did this to you. That I let him take you away."

"You didn't let him. It's not your fault, and I'll never blame you for what happened. *Hyto* is the one who hurt me. He's solely responsible for his actions, and we will make him pay. But right now, I have to keep busy. I have to keep from dwelling on the past few days. Do you understand?" I leaned up and kissed him gently on the cheek. "What is in your heart—that is what I love. Not how invulnerable you can make my life."

He covered my hand with his for a moment, then nodded. "As you wish. We will discuss it when you are ready. And I will do everything in my power to make sure you're never hurt again."

Uh-oh. That sounded a little too ivory-towerish for me, but I knew he needed to say it—needed to feel he could keep some control of the situation. Nodding, I motioned to Trillian and Delilah, who were waiting up ahead.

"Let's go get Chase." I sucked in a deep breath, wondering when life would ever return to normal. If that were even possible.

We approached the portal, and I turned to them. "I have to go first, but we form a chain. Once we're inside, we head toward the mushroom ring. Now that Smoky's with us, we can go through it and still get out of wherever we end up. And once we go through, I think from there, we head to the astral. That's where Chase managed to jump over."

They nodded. Delilah tossed me a bag, and I opened it up. "My iron! You brought me my handcuffs and flail!" For the first time since Hyto had caught me, I felt a smile truly break over my face.

She handed me a pair of gloves. "You'll need these, too. Now let's go get our detective."

We formed a line, with me in the front. Smoky insisted on being second, and neither Delilah nor Trillian countered him. Delilah went third, Trillian last. As we took aim toward the portal, I took a deep breath and led them through. The crackling energy was like a recharging burst of ocean air, and I sucked it in, holding it within my breath, within my very cells. I needed the charge. The surge of power felt like a glass of long, cold water to my parched body.

Through the portal and we were once again standing in the jungle of frosty foliage. Smoky and Trillian went on instant alert, Trillian drawing his serrated blade. Delilah and I glanced around. Neither Tra nor Herne was anywhere in sight, and I slowly let out my breath.

Now if we could just keep Yannie Fin Diver at bay, we might get through it without too much of a battle. But I didn't have my unicorn horn with me, so that should take care of the latter. He'd been after the horn, not so much me. With a little luck, if we hurried past the bog, he might not notice we were here.

I pulled my capelet closer around my shoulders and started forward, pushing past the guys. With Smoky at my side, I headed forward toward the other side of the frosted lea, in the direction of the rock-faced ravine leading into the glen. Trillian fell in beside Delilah.

Nothing stirred, save for a few crows watching us from the branches of the overhanging oaks. Silently, we passed through the magical realm, and with every step, the sense of heavy, old magic surrounded me. *Something* had been through here recently.

As we entered the ravine, I could feel the call of the rocks. There was quartz in the cliff face; that I'd bet my magic on. Quartz crystals sang to me, and ever since I'd been Earthside, I'd started noticing it more and more. For some reason, my connection to the mineral was more prominent over here, and I used it for the wards around the land.

Beside me, Smoky was keeping a close eye on the sides of the ravine, his gaze darting from side to side. We passed silently through the short passage and came to the thick foliage that separated the ravine from the bog.

"Be careful. Yannie Fin Diver is in that bog. At least we know the Bog Eater isn't around. Although the fact that he's prowling Tangleroot Park isn't any comfort, either. But Yannie is dangerous, and now he has a grudge against me because he couldn't get hold of the unicorn horn."

I pushed through to the open swath of ground that divided the forest from the peat bog. The sour tang rang in my nose, and as we passed by, I kept close watch for any sign of activity out on the surface. I didn't want to have to go into combat against one of the Elder Fae, but with Smoky, it would be a hell of a lot easier to take care of than with just Delilah and me. We crept along and had almost reached the area where we could cut into the bushes when a ripple on the surface of the marsh caught my eye.

Hell. Yannie Fin Diver rose out of the water. He spotted us and, a feral gleam in his eye, rose with a triumphant howl.

"It's him! Watch out!" I headed on a dead run for the woods, Delilah right after me.

Barely a beat later, Smoky turned into his dragon self. As he transformed, his long, snakelike body shimmering into sight, Smoky towered over the Elder Fae. He rose into the air, his front claws long and dangerously sharp, his wings whipping up a storm. The ripples on the bog water caused by Yannie's appearance turned into a flurry of waves, cresting against the path.

"Oh shit," Delilah said, turning to me. And then she flailed, her back heel sliding. Even as I tried to figure out what was going on, she fell backward into a quivering mass of sand and water and began to sink. Her head disappeared and I screamed, but then her head reappeared.

"Don't struggle—try to float on the surface as much as you can. Struggling will only drag you down quicker." Turning to find Trillian, who was watching the brewing confrontation between Smoky and Yannie, I yelled at him.

"Help me."

Trillian's gaze snapped to me, and when he realized what was going on, he raced over.

Yannie Fin Diver glanced up at the opalescent dragon and began to backpedal. Interesting; so even the Elder Fae could be cowed by dragons. I had been wondering if it came down to it, who would kick whose ass. But even though he was backtracking, Smoky didn't stop, but headed right for him.

I tore my attention away from them and fell flat on the ground, my walking stick out in front of me. I tried to push it across the sinkhole that was swallowing Delilah, so that she'd have something to grab on to.

Trillian leaped over the shifting quagmire in which Delilah was caught, barely landing on solid ground. He wavered, flailing his arms for a second, then regained his balance and immediately went down on his stomach like me, bracing the other end of my walking stick. We held it steady over Delilah, who was by now chest deep in the mire.

She grabbed the lifeline, dragging herself out of the sucking sand. As she clung to the staff, Trillian and I slowly edged it over the side of the sinkhole and she struggled to clamber out. I slipped one hand under her left arm, as Trillian reached across and slipped his hand under her right, and we pried her out as she scrambled onto the ground, covered in the wet slimy sand. She leaned her head on her knees, her short spiky haircut matted down by the gunk.

"Damn, that's more bog than quicksand. I hate that stuff. It's scary hard to get out of," she gasped, spitting out bits of sand that had gotten into her mouth.

A huge roar filled the air, and we all jerked around to see Smoky engage Yannie. The Elder Fae had grown terribly large, big enough to fight back. Crap. Maybe he wasn't so vulnerable after all. He raised his huge arms, and the kelp boas that flowed around his shoulders rose like stinging snakes and launched themselves at Smoky, catching him around the neck.

Smoky let out a loud rumble, blasting him with flame and smoke. I gasped, but the Fae managed to jump aside, merely singed. Smoky turned in midair, strafing at Yannie with his dragon fire, as the Elder Fae kept growing, reaching a good fifteen feet in the air.

He swiped at Smoky, hitting my dragon on the butt and knocking him off balance. Smoky caught himself and dove for Yannie, barely missing the top of his head with his talons. His wings gave one major shove and managed to beat up enough turbulence that Yannie went cartwheeling back into the bog.

Like a hawk diving after a fish, wings back, talons at the ready, Smoky barreled down toward the Elder Fae, who took one last look at his incoming opponent and splashed beneath the waters, churning a wake behind him as he headed out toward the marshy wastes. Smoky pulled up, skimming the surface of the water, chased him for a bit, then headed back to shore.

He transformed even as he settled to the ground, his hair whipping around him in a frenzy. I froze, staring at it, remembering what Hyto had done to me with his long locks, then slowly let out my breath, reminding myself that—at least for the present—I was safe from the freak.

Smoky wasn't even panting. And, as usual, clean as a whistle. I really had to find out how he did that, but so far, he wasn't telling anybody.

"He disappeared before I could kill him, but I doubt if he'll bother us now." He turned to Delilah. "Are you all right?" He sounded abrupt, but I knew that he cared about my sisters—even when he pretended not to.

"Yeah," she said, pushing herself up and wiping off what she could of the gunk that clung to her clothing. "I'm cold and wet, but I'll be all right." She shivered and Trillian offered her his duster, but she shook her head. "I move better without a long coat. I'll be fine for a bit."

I considered trying to dry her off with a spell, but the better part of wisdom prevailed, and I refrained.

"You cannot travel while chilled. Take off your clothes and lay them down on the ground." At her look, he shook his head. "Just do it."

Delilah obeyed as Smoky moved to the edge of the bog and, without another word, was in his dragon shape again. He swung his long neck toward her clothes and let out a great belch. Instead of fire, smoke came out, and soot. Even from where I was standing I could feel the intense heat behind the gust of air, and after two or three more puffs, he turned to her and blew a gentler gust over her.

"Thank you, Smoky." She grinned at him, and headed over to her clothes, which were dry, if still dirty. As she pulled on the stiff material, she caught my gaze and shook her head, trying not to laugh. I repressed a smile as Smoky shifted back and—looking pleased with himself—motioned for us to move on.

As we headed inland, toward the mushroom ring, my only regret was that Smoky hadn't managed to kill Yannie Fin Diver. Right now, I wasn't feeling very merciful toward my enemies.

We came to the mushroom ring before long, and once again a surge of trickster energy blasted out from it. Trillian blinked, shaking his head.

"Damn, whatever sort of gateway it is, it's strong. And cunning."

"Cunning is right. Remember—Chase was captured by what sounds like a spider-related Fae. Cunning and web-weavers go hand in hand. Spider creatures are smart." I pointed toward the edge of the ring. "I put my arm through there and it was kind of freaky. Okay, we ready for this?"

Smoky grunted and started to take the lead, but Trillian motioned him back. "This is Fae territory, dude. This is more my speed than yours. You stick close to Camille and Delilah." He stepped forward, and, reluctantly, Smoky moved back, a skeptical look on his face.

We tied up—portals like this weren't safe to travel through without having some connection to one another. Otherwise, who knew if we'd end up in the same place? Then, without another word, Trillian stepped through, me following, then Smoky and Delilah.

Most portals are disorienting; this was a freak show. The moment I passed through, a spiral of colors began to run around me as reality melted into a swirl of color and sound. I was still tied to Trillian, but the only thing I could see were brilliant blues and greens, rotating in on themselves, like the spiral on the old *Outer Limits* program.

My body felt like it was melting, it was so hot. Sweat trickled down my forehead, slowly forming rivulets along my cheeks. Droplets trickled down my nose, onto my tongue as I reached out to catch one. *Salty. Sweet.* I wanted to rip my clothes off—the heat was stifling. As I considered undoing my capelet, something in the back of my mind whispered, *Don't—it's the portal. It will pass. Don't fall for it.*

Keeping my wrap on, I shifted beneath it, the pain fading from my thighs, from my heart, from my back and bones. All I could feel was the heat—the mind-numbing heat, the heat rising in my body, spreading through my stomach, making me ache for someone strong to come along, to push me down on the ground and fill me full. I struggled not to strip bare at the thought that Trillian might be close enough to touch.

Music swept up—panpipes and drums, a tambourine, a lute—the dance called me in. To dance, to spin, to whirl under the stars, to leap into the great cosmic orgasm of the universe and never stop dancing . . . the swell of desire rose within my heart and I began to wander away from the path, but the rope around my waist stopped me.

Confused, I stared at the nylon coil wrapped around me, wondering how to get rid of it, when someone on the other end tugged—hard. Unprepared, I went sailing forward, stumbling through the swirls of color until the heat suddenly lessened and I tripped, finding myself lying prone in a snow-covered meadow, with Trillian waiting anxiously. Oddly, the snow didn't feel all that cold.

He knelt by me and took me by the shoulders. "Camille, are you all right?"

I looked around, perplexed. Smoky and Delilah were there already, but I'd been second. "How . . . what happened?"

"You got lost in there. The energy is magnetic and glommed onto you. We were trying our best to pull you out, but you were resisting. What was it?" My love searched my face, the dark gleaming skin of his hands stark against my skin. I kissed his fingers, reveling in the feel of them against my face. The seducing energy still held me in its grasp.

"I . . . I wanted to strip naked and run . . . to screw my brains out with somebody." I inhaled deeply and slowly let it out. After a moment, my head began to clear. "Whoever opened that portal is powerful and has a yen for magical energy. It's not quite the same as the portal through which we initially came, but there was the same seductive pull—the same sort of siren song."

"Hmm . . . perhaps a creature who feeds on magical energy?" Smoky extended his hand and I placed my left in it, my right in Trillian's, and allowed them to lift me to my feet.

"It wouldn't be the first we've met like that. Come on, let's see where we're at." As we began to look around, I realized that although we were in a frosty meadow, everything had an artificial look to it—as if it were two-dimensional. It was almost as though we were on a movie set.

"This feels . . . like somebody created this space. Tried to make it appear real but couldn't quite get the pattern down. The snow—it's not very cold. I noticed that when I was on the ground. Anybody else have any thoughts?"

Delilah leaned over a low-growing bush and inhaled deeply. "You're right—there aren't any smells to these bushes. Did you notice?"

I frowned, looking around. Closing my eyes, I lifted my nose and breathed slowly. She was right—there was no tang to the soil, no woodsy scent to the trees, no scent of ozone to signal that it had been snowing. It wasn't that the currents were free of fragrance, but I couldn't identify what it was.

"That's weird. I'm getting a little nervous now. What do you think it is?"

"I don't know." She glanced nervously around. "I'm beginning to wonder if this is a natural realm or not. It's not the astral, is it?"

Slowly, I shook my head. "Smoky, Trillian, what do you think?"

Smoky took a few steps forward, then stopped. He pointed past a small stand of small evergreens. "There's a cottage there."

"Cottage? Chase said something about being dragged to a cottage." I took a step toward it, cocking my head. "There's something odd about it. Do you notice anything weird?"

Delilah shaded her eyes with her hands and peered at it. "It looks almost as though the walls are moving."

As we started toward it, Smoky in the lead, I saw that

Delilah was right. The walls and roof of the cottage looked like they were in motion, like the very atoms of the house were dancing. Wondering what the hell it could be, we quietly descended the sloping path leading to it.

"I don't like the feel of this." Trillian shook his head as he drew his dagger. "There is danger here. All around. We are surrounded by it, as though we . . ."

His voice drifted off as I grabbed his arm. "Stop. Stop right here. Look closely—I see what's making the house move." I skidded to a halt, looking closely. "Oh, fuck."

"What?" Delilah squinted again, trying to see what it is. "I can't tell."

"I'm seeing the aura of the house. The movement isn't on an energetic level—it's on a physical level. The house is covered with spiders and bugs—they're swarming everywhere. The whole house is like one giant anthill, sans the ants."

And then, as I said it, everything came into perspective. The swirling mass became individual spiders and beetles, scurrying in swarms all over the house. In the narrow slits between the layer of bugs, I could see what looked like white strands—a cocoon! The house was a giant cocoon.

"Oh Great Bast, do you think Chase is in there?" Delilah's voice spiraled, slightly hysterical.

Shaking my head, I started to back away, my teeth chattering. I could take many things, but swarms . . . not so much. "No . . . he was in body on the astral. And if we're smart, we'll jump over there now!"

"But we have to know if he's in there. We have to be sure. I'm sorry, I can't rely on just your dreams that you had while that freak of a dragon held you captive. It might have been a fever—"

I wanted to slap her, but I knew she was right. I'd been accurate about Vanzir, but that didn't mean I was right about Chase.

Smoky glanced from Delilah to me, waiting for some sort of direction. "I could just burn down the house—"

"No! What if Chase is in there?" Delilah let out a small mew, like she usually did when she was going to transform into a tabby cat, but I could tell that Panther was just below the surface. She squeezed her nails into her fists. "I can't afford to transform, not yet. But we have to do something."

"I think the decision has been made for us," Trillian said, pointing toward the cottage.

Out of the house came a scrabbling figure, moving from side to side at first, then heading our way. She looked like an old woman wrapped in a red and black robe, almost like one of the Hags of Fate, but she had six arms, and in no way did she have a human look about her. Her hair was knotted into a tight little bun on the top of her head, and her beady little eyes held a grasping expression. I caught a flash of hunger that swirled through the air. She was ravenous. Whether for blood or flesh, I wasn't sure, but she wanted it *now*.

"If she's that hungry, then she hasn't fed for a while. Chase isn't in the house." I said it softly, but the others caught my words and nodded. Before she could reach us, I reached up and called down the power of the Moon Mother. This was one of the Elder Fae, and we were going to need all the help we could get.

"Moon Mother, don't fail me now," I whispered, sending a bolt of energy toward the creature. The lightning wrapped itself around her, forking into a web. But instead of stopping, she merely smiled an unholy smile and the energy began to absorb into her body.

"Oh crap, she's the creature who eats *magical energy*— that's why she captured Chase and that's why the portal was singing to me." I stepped back as Smoky, Delilah, and Trillian moved forward. I couldn't use my magic—not only would it be useless, but it would strengthen her.

As I fumbled for my iron flail, she was suddenly in front of Smoky, and then vanished. I looked around, frantic, and the next thing I knew, the creature was standing beside me, her arms out, ready to wrap me in her deadly grasp.

Chapter 17
❧❧❧

"Cripes!" I jumped as she lay her barbed hands on me and, with a strength far beyond my own, yanked me to her chest. As I struggled to get free, she started wrapping me in something—a silken thread. She was spinning a cocoon around me. "Fucking hell, get me out of here!"

Smoky grabbed her by one of her upper arms and started to pull, but her head swiveled around, her jaws opened, and a pair of nasty-looking fangs came down on his hand. He yelled, pulling his hand away, and I could see blood on the skin. He let out an angry rumble and his hair came out, separating into six sections, each one wrapping around one of her arms.

The Elder Fae gave a long screech and twisted back to me, intent on her spinning. I couldn't see where the thread was coming from, but knowing the way of spiders, I really wasn't sure I wanted to.

Trillian launched himself at her, bringing his serrated knife down on one of her arms. The blade reverberated off and he stared at her, confused.

"Exoskeleton," I yelled. "Her appearance must be an illusion! She's got an exoskeleton."

He nodded, darting back as she flailed at him with one of her arms. Even though Smoky's hair had a good hold on her, she seemed to be strong enough to resist his trying to pull her off me.

Delilah ran around behind me, and a sudden prick on my back sent me into a world of pain—it was just for a second, but I screamed. "What the fuck are you doing?"

"I'm sorry—I'm trying to cut these webs off you, and all I've got with me is the iron knife. I must have poked through your cape." She continued to saw away at the threads and I sucked in my gut, hoping to avoid another confrontation with her blade.

Smoky's talons came out, and even though the wound on his hand appeared to be festering a little, he brought his nails around to rake against her side. They skidded off, once again thanks to her outer hull. Whatever she looked like under that jacket of skin must be shiny and hard.

"Enough," he said, launching himself onto her, his hair straining to pull her arms away. One finally let go of me, and—with a popping sound—he dragged it off her body, out of her arm socket, and whipped it across the meadow, tossing it a good twenty yards.

The Elder Fae shrieked as an ugly brew of liquids and blood came rushing out of the socket. I struggled to keep out of its path—she might have venomous or acidic blood or a whole bunch of nasty things in the stew that made up her bodily fluids.

The attack shifted her attention. While she was still holding tight to me, she was also trying to attend to her wound, and she let go of me with one of her right arms, using it to reach across in order to probe her wound.

As she did, Trillian brought his knife down across the jointed part of her elbow and sawed quickly. The forearm fell off, again streaming what I could only think of as bug juice onto the ground.

I closed my eyes, tired of the whole thing. Focusing on an inner flicker of light, I nurtured it brighter and realized I was touching the core of the death magic that Morio and I used. Struggling to remember his part along with mine, I clumsily

fashioned it into a purple globe, stroking it with my mind.
The energy swelled until the globe was flaming, burning with
the flame of karmic retribution. I called upon the power of the
Netherworld to fuel me, to channel through my body. A sinuous
thread began to pulse, swirling around, catching me up in it.

Oh, I missed this—this practice. And I missed my connection with Morio. We'd been away from our magic for
only about three weeks, but it was too long. He was my
priest, he was my mage, and I was his witch.

As I worked the power, I sensed him on the outskirts. He
was sleeping, but he'd found his way to me, in a slow, encircling way.

Do not extend your energy, my love.

I can help you without hurting myself, came his reply.

*You are still wounded. The ghosts siphoned much of your
energy away. You must replenish it before tackling battles,
even from the dream state.*

*Shut up, my beautiful wench, and let me help you. I am
healing faster than you think.*

And I quieted down, even through my concern, and let
him work with me to fine-tune the flame.

*You are ready. Aim for her third eye. Aim for her psychic
center, especially since she's one of the Elder Fae. She won't
be able to feed off this spell.* And then Morio withdrew.

I sucked in a deep breath, still trying to avoid her snapping
fangs, and then I pushed the flame outside of me, aiming
directly for her third eye. There was a huge flash and she
screamed. The next moment, her grip loosened and Smoky
pulled me away from her, and we all backed off as she began
to shake, surrounded by a violet lightning, and then—with a
loud crack that split the air—she dropped to the ground.

Panting, I stared at the still form, but Delilah's warning
shook me out of my thoughts. "Hurry! The house—they're
coming for us!"

A glance at the house showed that the mass of swirling
spiders and beetles were sweeping off the house in a moving
shroud across the ground, headed our way. I let out a squeak.

"That's our cue to make tracks! It's time to shift over to
the astral."

Smoky swept open his long white trench and I snuggled on one side, Trillian holding tight to me, and Delilah snuggled on the other. As he enfolded us in the voluminous coat, the familiar shifting lurched beneath our feet as we flickered out . . . and then onto the astral.

The mist rolled thick here, and I caught my breath before I remembered I didn't have to breathe. The astral realm was one of those places that you couldn't think too hard about because the conundrums would drive you crazy if you tried to reason them out.

The mist rolled ankle deep along the ground, covering everything in sight, but I could see barren tree stumps—or what passed for trees here—and the air was a shimmering silver, darker toward the horizon and lighter toward the zenith of the sky. Boulders littered the path, although here on the astral they could just as easily be a creature as a rock.

That was one of the things to remember: Though the surroundings took on a look similar to what we saw on the physical, you could never count on things to be the same. In other words: *A rock is a rock isn't necessarily a rock.*

My body began to tingle. I always felt alive and vibrant on the astral—ever since I first learned how to navigate it back in Otherworld. That was one of the few magical tasks with which I'd actually impressed my teachers. I'd taken to astral travel like a duck takes to water.

Now I glanced around and tried to get my bearings. Chase was still over here, I could feel it in my bones. And my bones were proving to be a good premonitionary tool, if that was a word.

Closing my eyes, I let myself drift. The others stood back, waiting. After a moment, I sensed a far-distant spark that felt terribly familiar, and I locked my sights on it.

"I've got him, I think. But it's a ways." I looked at Smoky. "My love, can three of us ride on your back as I direct you where to go?" I quickly gave him directions.

I could run faster on the astral than just about anybody I knew, except for Rozurial, but it made sense to conserve our energy in case we found ourselves in battle. And though I could run faster out here than Smoky could fly, he could fly faster than Trillian and Delilah could run. This way, we wouldn't chance getting separated. Also, a side benefit: There were beasties on the astral that were mean as sin, and some, it would take all our efforts to destroy. If they saw a dragon on the move, they might think twice about attacking us.

Smoky nodded and motioned for us to move back. Within seconds, he shimmered into dragon form and snaked his neck down for us to climb on. I sat at the front at the base of where his neck met his shoulders. I was used to riding on his back when we went out for nighttime flights up near his barrow where we wouldn't chance being seen.

Delilah gave Trillian a little boost—she was taller than he was, though he was stronger, and then she hopped up herself. They clung behind me. I pressed my knees to Smoky's side and leaned forward, holding tight to the loose hairs that roped off his neck. They whipped around my waist, and around Trillian and Delilah, as he launched himself into the air.

We soared up and once again, my heart lifted. Hyto might be out to kill me, but his son was my husband and flying on Smoky's back had become one of my greatest joys. As he tipped a wing to the left, turning so we were heading in the direction in which I'd sensed the familiar energy, I heard a laugh from behind me.

"I can't believe I've never done this before! This is fun! I'm surprised you aren't scared, though," Delilah said. "I know you're afraid of heights."

I grinned, even though she couldn't see my face. "I'm not afraid of much when I'm on Smoky's back."

Trillian let out a *hrmph*, but then I felt his arm snake around my waist and he kissed me on the shoulder. Whispering in my ear, he said, "We were so afraid we'd lost you forever, my love. All three of us—we couldn't bear the thought. Without you . . . Fox-Boy, Dragon-Dude, and I . . . we are less than we should be. Than we *have to be* when you're around." Tears sprang to my eyes and I ducked my head. What Hyto had done to me had scarred me forever, and yet—and yet—I knew that scar tissue could be stronger than the original flesh.

I just had to learn how to use what had happened to empower me, rather than to tear me down.

"I love you—all of you. I love that you are all willing to be part of my life. I love that you work together to make our lives happier. And I love . . . that you all want to be with me. I'm going to need your help to overcome this, but I refuse to let Hyto win. I refuse to let his abuse of me rule my life. I refuse to let him ruin *our lives.*"

Trillian pressed his lips against the back of my neck, gently, without insistence, just a gentle reminder that he had my back, and I began to cry, softly, grateful that I was back among those who loved me. Even though we had a fight ahead of us—for Hyto would not let it rest, and neither could we—for now, we were as we should be.

"We don't blame Vanzir anymore. . . . After you vanished, he came back and read us the riot act. Made us realize that we were blaming the two of you for what couldn't be helped. He chanced the lizard killing him to defend your honor. He's not part of our triad, but . . ."

I shook my head. "What happened, happened. It was *nothing* like what Hyto did to me. Vanzir . . . is not one of my heart-mates. I have no desire to take him for a partner, although now I understand him a lot better than I did, and I no longer distrust him. But I don't blame him. All I want is to let it go and know that you guys aren't going to break his neck."

Trillian let out a long breath. "As you wish, my love."

Smoky must have caught our conversation because he did a sudden spiral in the air, coiling up and then down in a playful twist. I laughed, holding tight to him, as Trillian held on to my waist, and Delilah to Trillian.

And then, a straight shot on toward the energy that was building as we grew near it. The mist raced past, occasional thin strips of it rising to our level, and below the ground was covered with the rolling fog as far as we could see. Most of the astral plane was covered in boiling mists—it was simply part of the makeup of the realm. There were other planes of existence, most bound together by the Ionyc Seas, but for the most part, I tried to stay off them. The etheric realm was less physical than the astral, and others—still even less so.

We flew straight as the dragon flies, as the saying goes, for what seemed like an hour, though in reality time didn't exist over here. But for humans—for any mortals, however long lived—there would always be an internal sense of translation to a time-based system.

After a while I tugged on Smoky's hair. We headed down toward the ground, spiraling in for a landing. As he gently settled, I slid off, bracing my foot on his wing to help me descend. Trillian and Delilah joined me. As I looked around to gauge my bearings, I felt a distinct leap in the source of the energy signature we were following.

"This way," I said, motioning for them to follow me. Heading toward what would be the east, if we were back in our realm, I set off, letting the energy guide me. As we made our way through a large field of what reminded me of ferns and overgrown rhododendrons, we came to a central pond. The water wasn't real water, of course, but it glistened and rippled, and as I leaned forward, I realized it was alive. It rose and I jumped back with a start.

As it stood there, transforming in shape to vaguely mimic a bipedal form, I felt a sparkle of magic from it and, with a hesitant hand, reached out my index finger. A thin tendril spread out from the mitten-shaped hand, and it quietly touched my finger.

A rush of energy flooded me, like a waterfall of sparkling droplets. I had a flash of rainbows and prisms, of shattering glass and gleaming spires, and then a gentle wash of peace followed.

Gently, I disengaged and watched as the creature once again took its original form, melting back into its watery self.

"How beautiful," I whispered. "Pure joy, transcendent peace." And then I realized that my heart's aching had lessened. I closed my eyes and the intense feeling of being violated had faded—just a little but enough for me to function easier. "It may not be the bluebird of happiness, but this creature . . . offers a rare gift."

"What is it?" Delilah asked, staring at the glistening pool.

"A water Chirp. I've heard tales of them, but this is the first time I've ever seen one." Silently wishing it well, I skirted the pond and we headed toward the other side of the field.

We had barely reached another thick stand of astral ferns when a rustle on the other side stopped us. Out of the bushes stepped Chase—a look of relief spreading across his face.

"Thank God it's you guys! I felt your energy, Camille. I felt you aiming straight for me." He looked half-crazed, but then being stuck alone on the astral for several days would be enough to drive any FBH nuts. Especially one in the middle of a major life transformation.

Delilah rushed forward, giving him a long hug. He pressed his eyes closed as she squeezed him tight, then stepped back. "Camille—are you okay? I thought . . . we talked, I was sure of it, and you were not in good shape . . ."

I nodded, stepping forward. "We did, but I escaped. We have to get you home, though. Off the astral. It's not good to stay here in body when you are still alive. At least not for as long as you've been out here. Come."

Turning to Smoky, I said, "How are we going to do this? You can only take three at a time. And we need to return to the mushroom ring first. If we jump off the astral here, there's a good chance we'll end up in the Northlands, and trust me, I'm not ready to go back."

"Then we fly back and I return you two by two into the . . . well . . . wherever that realm is. But we'll have to be cautious— the house was swarming with spiders and beetles and we don't know what they're doing now. They may be waiting for us." He frowned. "I almost would rather jump back into the Northlands."

I knew he wanted to hunt down Hyto, but I put a soft hand on his arm. "We can't take him on without all of us there."

Smoky pursed his lips, but just nodded his acquiescence. "Come then, let's return and see what mayhem the others have been up to at my barrow."

He shifted into dragon form and—with Chase in our midst—we climbed back aboard, straddling that great white neck, and set a course for our starting point. Once there, Smoky resumed his human form so he could transport us off of the astral realm. First, he took Chase and Delilah over, leaving Trillian to protect me. Then he hurried back for us.

Once we were all near the spider Fae's house, I glanced at where we'd left her body. Whatever remnants had been left were gone. No sign of her. And the swirling of the house had resumed.

"I don't like the looks of that—could she have survived?"

Delilah frowned, shaking her head slowly. "Dealing with the Elder Fae is tricky. There's a lot we don't know about them. Let's just get out of here while we can. I have no desire to hike on down to see if she's still alive. Or if something else has taken up residence."

We set off, hoofing it back through the mushroom ring. On the shore, we avoided the spot of quicksand. Out on the peat bogs, I could see the distant form of Yannie Fin Diver. He stared at us but made no move to come closer, and I had a vindictive sense of delight as I flipped him off. Tough shit if it made him mad. I was with my dragon and I'd reached my limit of taking crap from jerks, pervs, and freakazoids.

We came through the ravine back into the main glen. Still no sign of Tra or Herne, but I sent out a brief hello to both of them, wishing them well. Tra wasn't on my favorites list, but hell, he was the son of a god. That alone was a good reason to be a strange duck. And Herne . . . he was just incredibly powerful. He'd stopped his kid from picking on us, so much the better.

As we headed toward the portal, Chase looking infinitely relieved, I whispered the words Aeval had taught me and the aperture opened. Through the vortex we went . . . back home. Back to Earthside. Back to figure out what the fuck to do about Hyto.

The minute we came through the portal, Yugi was there, waiting. I blinked, surprised to see him, but he tipped his hat and, shivering, said, "Sharah called. She wanted me to come out here and wait for you, to give you your cell phones and a message."

"What now?" I felt the color drain from my face. If she

had a message that couldn't wait, what the hell had happened now?

The police officer, Chase's second-in-command, clasped Chase's hand and pulled him in for a pat on the back. "I wasn't sure we'd see you again. Good to have you back." As if he realized he'd just hugged his superior officer, Yugi held up his arms in a no-harm, no-foul gesture, blushing, and fumbled to salute.

Chase let out a short bark of laughter. "Don't sweat it, Yugi. I'm glad my men miss me when I'm gone. Better than you guys talking about me behind my back." He rubbed his hand across his eyes. A glimmer of sparkles filled the dark brown irises, and he crossed to me, lifting my chin up, his face solemn. "Camille, bless you for coming to rescue me. I was so worried that when I finally did get out—if I did, you'd be . . ." Here he paused, as if the words had gone cold on his tongue.

"Dead?" I whispered back. "I thought I would be."

"Life's taken some interesting turns, hasn't it?" He cleared his throat and then, aware everybody was looking at us, backed away.

I turned to Yugi. "What's Sharah's message?"

"Everybody's moved over to the barrow except for Menolly. She'll go at sunset, of course. But there's someone at the house waiting to talk to you. You need to stop there before going back to Smoky's barrow." He turned to Chase. "And Sharah said that if they found you . . . please call her the minute you get the chance." He handed the detective a cell phone.

I accepted mine, flipping it open. A call to the house got hold of Iris. "What are you doing there? Is anybody with you? I know you want to wait until Menolly wakes up, but—"

"Sharah's out at the barrow with Morio. I'm in Menolly's lair. No worries that way—I'm safe enough. But up top, there's somebody waiting to talk to you. He tried to swear me to secrecy, but Camille, you are my family. He . . . well . . . I don't know if he is or isn't."

"Who is it?" I was beginning to hate waiting games and secrets, wanting all the information up top, front and center.

"Your father. Sephreh ob Tanu. He's sitting up in the

parlor, waiting for you right now, and I have no clue what he wants, before you ask. He just showed up today and demanded to see you. I told him to go out to the barrow and wait but he refuses." Iris *tsked* a couple of times and then snorted. "He's a stubborn man. You two are so much alike."

"Alike, my ass. He disowned me. I have nothing to say to him." But then I stopped. What could he want? Had he finally seen his way past Tanaquar's grasping need for control? Or was it something more mundane? "Fine, I'll stop there on the way home. But I'm not holding hope. And don't you dare fix him any tea—not until I know what he wants."

As I flipped my phone shut, I looked up at Delilah. "Father is at the house. He wants to talk to me." At the sudden look of joy in her eyes, I held up my hand. "I don't trust this conciliatory gesture. And maybe he just came to deliver the rest of my stuff. Who knows what he wants? I'm not getting my hopes up because the last thing I need is another fucking jerk dragging me through the mud. Emotionally or physically."

She nodded, wisely biting her tongue, and we piled back into the cars, heading for our home. As the streets sped by, Hyto's collar chaffed against my neck. I had the feeling he could sense me—wherever he was—and he was just biding his time until he was ready to come destroy my world.

Chapter 18

The house came into view and my heart thudded like a loco-
motive picking up steam. My father had disowned me
around the equinox. He'd cut off ties with me. My sisters had
quit the OIA—the Otherworld Intelligence Agency—in protest of my being fired.

As I got out of the car, one look down toward the trail
leading to Birchwater Pond told me that Smoky had, indeed,
been more than a little upset. Near the mouth of the path,
trees had been uprooted and tossed around like a dog might
toss a branch. Scorch marks blackened the ground. I swallowed hard, trying to not remember when I'd realized it was
Hyto and not Smoky waiting for me.

Smoky stood at my shoulder and gently put his arm around
me, glancing into the sky. "Come, let us go in. And whatever
you want, just tell us and we'll make it happen, my love."

I nodded, slowly, following them up the stairs to the
porch. As we entered the house, Trillian and Delilah immediately spread out, searching for any unwanted guests. Iris
peeked in from the kitchen and motioned toward the living

room. I blew her a kiss, touched by the tears in her eyes when she saw me standing there.

Motioning for the others to remain behind, I silently walked into the living room, afraid to look at my father. Afraid to see that he might be here on business only. It had torn me up to lose his love and support, but he'd forced a choice I couldn't make in his favor. He'd given me an ultimatum, and I'd responded the only way I could—the only way my conscience would allow.

He was sitting there, his hair a braided mirror of my own, his eyes the same misty lilac color as my own. He glanced up. I couldn't read his expression. As I approached the sofa where he sat, he stood, holding my gaze.

I nodded. Let him be the first to speak. Let him take the reins so I'd know what I was dealing with.

"Camille . . ." His voice was edgy, unsure.

"Welcome to our home, Ambassador. What can I do for you? Or would you rather speak to Delilah? I know just what you think of me." My voice took on a raw edge as the words spilled out, unbidden, unplanned.

Father stared at me. First came the challenge—but he'd taught me well, and I said nothing more. Just waited, unwilling to look away or blink. Would he reach out? Would he open his arms to me? Or would he be cold and professional and say what he had to say?

After a moment, he quietly reached inside his pocket and pulled out a folded paper. "I bring you a letter from your Aunt Rythwar. She bade me deliver it—in fact, she insisted. I also make one last plea: You have not yet joined Aeval's Court. Turn away and you will be welcomed back into Tanaquar's presence again. And . . . into mine."

So . . . it was the latter. I slowly picked up the letter and stared at it, then set it back down on the table. With a long look at Father, I walked over to the window and stared out at the snow that was piling up.

"Do you know where I spent the last few days?" When he didn't answer, I shrugged. "No, of course you wouldn't. And you wouldn't care." Turning around, I touched the collar locked around my throat. "You see this? A dragon captured me. He raped me, he beat me senseless. My body is covered with his bruises and the feel of his hands. His collar is locked on until we can kill him. He's out there, now, looking for me."

Sephreh let out a little cry, but I ignored it. I continued on, my voice as hard and cold as I could make it.

"But I *escaped*. I climbed down a snow-covered mountain, terrified and exhausted. My *family* was searching for me. I kept hope . . . because, you see, *they* love me. They stand behind me. I kept hope because I know there's a demonic war brewing and we're waiting for Shadow Wing's next move."

"Please, stop—"

"No! *I will have my say and you will listen.* This is *my house*, not yours. I kept up hope because my goddess offered me strength when the darkness threatened to engulf me. When I was bleeding from the beatings. When Hyto held my head down, forcing me to suck his cock. When my *father-in-law* kicked me across the rock floor like an abused dog . . . I escaped because I knew what I needed to do. Because people who love me were looking for me. *Because I was raised to be the daughter of a soldier, to never give up.*"

"Camille—" My father let out a strangled cry, his expression stricken. "Please understand . . ."

"Not anymore. No more. I took over for Mother when she died. I kept my sisters going. You put that responsibility on my shoulders, and I willingly accepted it. But I'm no longer your obedient servant." I shook my head at him. "I don't exist to you, do I? I'm no longer your daughter. I'm *dead* to you. Why should I have expected you to give a fuck? Why did I hope you'd care?"

"You don't understand! My duty to the Court and Crown—"

"You *chose* the Court and Crown over your family. I hope that Tanaquar keeps you warm in the winter, that she doesn't toss you out if you lose your usefulness to her. Because you've made it clear you no longer need us."

"Camille—" My father's voice cracked. He looked both angry and yet heartbroken.

Picking up my aunt's letter, I headed for the foyer. "Thank you for this . . . but I've got a lot to do before my initiation into Aeval's Court. I've got a dragon I'm thirsting for vengeance

against. And I'm a priestess of the Moon Mother . . . and my
Lady comes before anyone and anything. *She* was there for
me. *You* weren't. Tanaquar wasn't. *Go home, Sephreh.* Unless
you want to be my father again, on *my* terms, go home."

As I left the room, I could hear him whisper behind me.
"Camille, my little girl . . ." But he didn't try to stop me.

I passed Delilah in the hall. "He's in there. If you have
anything to say to him, do so. I'm going to grab a few clothes
before we head back out to the barrow. I'm done with him."

She took one look at my expression and her face fell. "I
gotcha. Oh, say, I need my litter box out there."

"Oh delightful. Just make sure you keep it clean or
Smoky's going to have a fit." I grinned at her then, grateful
for the chance to laugh at something.

What Delilah said to our father, I didn't know—I didn't
want to know, actually. Instead, I sat on my bed and opened
the letter from Aunt Rythwar.

Dear Camille:

*Your father finally told me what happened between the two
of you—or at least, his version. I can readily believe yours
differs. I want you to listen to me, and listen good: When
your father brought your mother back from Earthside, it
took most of the family years to accept the alliance. But I
saw in Maria a beauty, and a kindness that so many of our
own people do not have. And for that alone, I loved her.*

*You and your sisters grew up strong. You had to, in order
to withstand the slings and arrows headed your way. And
you've become admirable women, strong and doing always
what you feel is right. Despite your father's interference. I
love your father, he is my brother, but sometimes I want to
shake him one. He's a fool, too beholden to the duty he feels
he owes the Crown. It makes him look past the wrongs
committed in the name of the Court and Crown, and only
the strongest of sins can make him move out of his rut.*

*I know he has disowned you. This was not easy on him,
but he's a fool for believing that Tanaquar will be any better
than Lethesanar was.*

What I'm trying to tell you is this: You have me. You can always come to me if you need help, or a place to stay, or a home. You, Delilah, even Menolly—I do not fear her vampyr nature. You are my nieces and I love you all. I miss you and send you my love. Please give Shamas a hug from me, too. I'm the only mother he has now.

Aunt Rythwar

I folded the page and slipped it into my purse, then went about throwing a few more pieces of clothing in a bag. At the last moment, I stopped, opening my jewelry box. There lay all three of my wedding rings. I usually didn't wear them for fear of losing them, but right now, the only thing I could think of was how much I wanted them on my fingers. I slid them on—two on the left hand, the third on the right.

"Are you ready?" Delilah popped her head in. I nodded, threw my backpack over my shoulder, and followed her down the stairs, wondering if Father was gone but unwilling to ask.

"He left," she said quietly, reading my thoughts. Or most likely, she just knew me well enough. A glance out the window showed that dusk was almost here. Though I longed for the safety of Smoky's barrow, I motioned her into the kitchen and put my bag on the table.

"Let's have a bite to eat before we head back out. We'll wait for Menolly. Having her with us will make me feel safer, too."

Iris rushed over to me, threw her arms around me, and hugged me tight. "I'm so grateful you're safe. I'm so glad you came back to us."

As we eased into chairs at the table, she put a tray of sandwiches in front of us. "Eat up. I'll heat up some soup, too—it won't take but a moment."

Hungry, and sore as hell—today had taxed my bruises—I bit into a roast beef sandwich and chewed thoughtfully. The bustier was rubbing against my back, and I glanced over my shoulder. "While we're waiting, can you put something on my back to help me stop hurting? Sharah did earlier, but it's worn off."

As I undid the hooks and eyes on the front of the bustier, Delilah moved around behind me to help take it off. I winced as it peeled away from the wounds crossing my back. It helped with my ribs, but the lashes were a pain in the ass to deal with. Delilah let out a choked sound as Iris came back with a bottle of salve, and then I turned to find both of them in tears.

Just then, the secret door behind the bookshelf opened—our biggest running joke now in the household, since most everybody had figured out where the door to Menolly's lair was—and there stood Menolly. She started to say something, then fell silent. Striding over, she shoved Delilah out of the way and made me stand.

"What he did to you . . ." Her voice was soft, but I'd long learned that a soft-spoken Menolly was a dangerous Menolly. After a moment I sat back down and she knelt beside me, taking my hand. "Did he . . . or do I have to ask?"

"Yes, he did." I gazed down at her. "You were my strength. You were my inspiration. I remembered what Dredge did to you and kept thinking, *If she could resist that . . . I can resist this. If Menolly could withstand the torture she underwent, I can handle a beating or a kicking. Or being raped."*

Menolly let out a snarl as she traced the lashes on my back and the bruises on my ribs. "He'll die. Hyto will die. None of us will rest until he's taken down. You helped me with payback to Dredge. I will be at your side until Hyto goes down."

Delilah knelt at my other side. "That goes for me. Nothing can withstand our bond. *Nothing* is stronger than our connection."

Iris watched us closely, then motioned for them to move. "Let me tend to her wounds. Sharah's good, but I've had far more experience." As she slowly slathered the bruises with the salve, the pain began to subside again. "The collar . . ."

"Won't come off till he's dead," I said flatly. "Now I understand how Vanzir felt—to an extent. His was voluntarily yoked. Mine wasn't. But the result is the same. Hyto can find me, Hyto can trace me, Hyto lays claim to me until we get this fucking thing off."

We gathered our things and headed out of the house to where the guys were waiting. Trillian, Smoky, and Chase were there. I looked at the detective. I'd expected him to go back to the station, but he shook his head.

"I told Yugi that until we take care of Hyto, I'm on leave. Officially, I'm on sick leave." As we climbed in the cars to head back to the barrow, I realized just how grateful I was for my family and friends. They were everything to me.

The drive back toward Mount Rainier and the Puyallup Valley was fraught with cars swerving on the ice. Highway 167 was insane, but we finally managed to get away from the mishmash of rush-hour traffic—and rush hour was about three hours long around here—and drive through the back roads to the turnoff leading to Smoky's land.

We were nearly to the barrow when Smoky asked me to turn up the drive instead. Over the past months, he'd created a rough road leading closer to the barrow so we didn't have to park at the house.

But now we stopped in front of the house where Tom Lane—Tam Lin—used to live when Titania had hung out on the land, bothering Smoky, deep in her cups. Things had changed so much, in a little over a year—so much so it was hard to remember what life had been like before we'd taken on Bad-Ass Luke and first found ourselves thrust into a demonic war.

As we got out, Smoky motioned for just Delilah and me to join him. We headed up the steps, toward the glowing lights that emanated from within the house. Smoky knocked lightly, and within seconds, the door opened.

Estelle Dugan stood there, eyeing us with a half smile. "He's practicing his swordsmanship today."

Smoky nodded. "Any better?"

She shook her head. "I'd invite you in, but I'm trying to keep him calm. He fades in and out, but yes, for now he has some semblance of . . . where he is. But I think Georgio is long gone. It's just St. George left." She smiled then, fully, looking like a mother glowing over her child.

St. George. Georgio Profeta. We'd first met last year, when he was prowling around our windows. Don Quixote, jousting at windmills. Lancelot, trying to win fair Guinevere. Georgio was every wounded hero who'd found a real live dragon to slay. With his plastic armor and his toy sword, he'd struck at Smoky. And Smoky—being who he was—let the poor man live. Even took him in, set him up with a nurse. No one mentioned it much—Smoky wasn't one for praise—but we all knew that he felt sorry for the man. That somehow, Georgio had touched his dragon's heart.

"I want you to be careful. I have guards out in the forests, but I tell you now: My father is on the loose and he's out for blood. Keep St. George inside. My father doesn't care for humans." Smoky stared at Estelle for a moment. "Are you okay? Do you need anything?"

She shook her head. "No, Lord Smoky. We are well taken care of. I will watch over Georgio. He's . . . I'm all he's got, you know. As far as humans go."

Smoky nodded. "I know. That's why I check on you every few days. If you should see anyone strange lurking around—especially someone who looks like me—be sure to call the guards the way I told you to. Tell them to come get me immediately. If I send for you, come immediately to the barrow."

And then we turned and, without another word, descended the stairs. I glanced up at the moon, needing her strength. Needing her comfort. "I need to be outside when we return to the barrow. I need to meditate beneath the Moon Mother."

Smoky swept me into his arms. "Then I will stand by you and keep watch. I will never leave you alone again—not until Hyto is dead. I will not let him touch you again, if I have to fly with you to the farthest heights of the Dragon Reaches. I will not let you down again."

His forehead touched mine again, and I reached up and kissed his lips. Gently at first, then as he held me, I wrapped my arms around his neck and kissed him deeply, hungry for his touch. I needed them all—my men, to wipe away the memory of Hyto's fingers on me, to wipe away the memory of his taste, of him inside me.

"I need you tonight. Trillian, too . . . and Morio. If he can possibly join us. I need you all. I need you to reaffirm that I'm yours. That you're mine. That we are bound and that nothing can break those bonds."

Smoky bit his lip, looking uncertain. "You are still hurt, Camille."

"I may be hurt, but I'm hurting worse inside. And you . . . the three of you can heal what's in my heart. Bruises on the body will fade. The memory is what haunts me."

He shook his head. "Not yet. Trust me, you aren't ready yet. I know—don't ask me how, but I know. But we will be with you tonight, and sleep by your side, and guard you. We will be there when you fall asleep, and there when you wake." And then he carried me to the car and slid me into the driver's seat.

As I put the car in gear, I took one last look at Georgio's house, and thought that if such a fragile man could manage to have so much courage, how could I do any different?

When I entered the barrow, the first thing I did was make a run for the bedroom where Morio was, in a bed that Shade and Roz had specially set up for him. I raced over the side and jumped on the mattress beside him.

Morio gave out a cry. "Camille! Babe! They told me the truth. You're . . ." He stopped, eyeing me up and down. "You're not okay. I can see it in your aura. But you will be. Trust me, you will be. We'll see to it."

He leaned up, and I covered his face with kisses, not caring that it might tire him. "I missed you so much. How are you feeling?" The last thing I wanted to talk about right now was Hyto, and I prayed that somebody had already covered what had happened with him.

Morio gathered me into his arms, gently encircling my waist in a way that told me he knew how damaged my body had been. He held me at arm's length after a moment.

"By now, you've heard how crazy Smoky went when you were kidnapped." A statement. "What you may not know is that Vanzir went down to the Triple Threat to beg for their help."

"Vanzir? Went to Aeval?" I vaguely remembered him

saying something about it but had for the most part forgotten. I blinked.

"Yes, and they're the ones who empowered him to travel through the astral realm. He has no clue they were the ones who did it, but I can tell. He's wearing Fae energy in his aura now, and I'm not quite sure what the hell went on with him. Howl sent the word to Smoky while he was still in the Dragon Reaches."

"A lot went on I wasn't aware of." I paused. "Do you know . . . what happened to me?"

He gave me a long look, then nodded. "I do. Camille, I love you, to the ends of the Earth. I am not angry about Vanzir, not in the least. I understand the gray areas in life and you know I'm not the possessive type. I will be at your back forever, in whatever you need. I can share you and be content . . . but only when you want to be touched."

I nodded. Sometimes I thought Morio understood me better than just about anybody. We had a connection that broke through *shoulds* and *shouldn'ts* . . . Perhaps it was brought about by our magic together, perhaps by some other free force that rang deep inside us.

Leaning my head against his shoulder, I let out a long sigh. "I wanted Smoky and Trillian and you . . . tonight. I want to wipe the memory of Hyto off my body, but Smoky won't. I think he's afraid it's too soon, that you'd hurt me. But nothing can hurt me worse than what Hyto did to me. I want a good memory to replace the vile ones."

Morio smiled gently. He leaned me back on the bed beside him. "I'm still weak, but there are things I can do . . . to help?"

Shuddering, I nodded, and slid out of my skirt and panties, then unfastened my bustier. He winced when he saw the bruises running the length of my body, but motioned me back into bed.

"Lie back in my arms. If you need me to stop, then just say the word." With one hand he stroked down the side of my body, gently playing my skin with his fingertips. His darkened nails—sharp and black—became the bow on the violin as he deftly stroked my breasts, lowering his mouth to my nipple, tugging it very gently with his teeth before lightly sucking.

I caught my breath, a wave of desire and fear racing through me. I wanted him, but I was afraid to give in to the feeling. I still hurt—was this a bad idea? But then his fingers slid down my stomach, fluttering over the bruised skin so lightly I barely felt them except for the sudden flurry of hunger from deep in my body. He reached my clit and softly stroked the embers, coaxing them to ignite, as he whispered in my ear.

"Camille, give yourself up to me. Let me guide you, take you down. That's right, breathe deep and surrender to the feel of my fingers." As he swirled against me, his fingers dancing lightly over my body, my breath caught in my chest and I felt the weight of the collar on my neck. Maybe this was a mistake—maybe Hyto could feel me? Could he sense what I was sensing?

"Spread your legs, my love, let me fully explore you." Morio's voice brought me back into myself as a sob caught in my throat. I did as he asked, spread my legs, and he slid two fingers inside me, cajoling me, caressing me, tickling me into a delicious froth of hunger.

But there he was—Hyto's face, smirking down at me. Hyto's body, ramming itself into me. I fought for control, fought to shove him out of my mind. Fought to take control of my body back from my attacker.

"Camille, breathe deep . . . once, twice . . . tell me where you are."

The words lurched out of me. "Caught between heaven and hell, my love," I whispered, my throat thick with phlegm. "I need to release, need to let go, but what if he feels me? What if he's watching through the fucking collar? What if he uses me?"

"Let go of him. There's nothing you can do about the collar right now. And if he is? Then let's give him a show to know what he's missing—to know what he will never, ever have. What he took from you wasn't sex, it was strength, and what I give to you is strength."

Morio's voice was smooth, satin on skin, and it pulled me

down into a haze of sexual hunger. I inhaled deeply on his command, then slowly let it go as he began to stroke me faster. I heard myself crying, sharp jagged little pants as my fear fought the growing heat, but then she was there, with me, the Moon Mother.

This is who you are, Camille—you are a priestess of the Hunt, a witch, a sexually charged being. You cannot hide from yourself in fear that others may see it and desire you. You have to be who you are. Don't be afraid of your passion. Hyto will feel you through the collar, or he won't. Either way, it doesn't take away from what you and Morio are doing, and it doesn't let the evil into you.

I struggled, trying to move beyond the fear, trying to get beyond the roadblock with Hyto's face on it. His leer bothered me most, the grasping leer. But then I felt—rather than saw—another pair of hands stroking my legs, and yet a third sliding across my arms. The circle was complete—all my men were with me, surrounding me, helping me, protecting me. Trillian leaned forward and kissed me deep, and I felt the dark charming swirl of his sensuality run through me like a waterfall. I shuddered, wanting more.

Smoky's hair lightly played on my body, but in such gentle swirls that I could no longer see Hyto—instead, there was my dragon, my love, staring down at me. Morio kept up the gentle stroking, insistent, not letting up, pushing me higher and higher.

And then, suddenly, the lightning inside broke, thunder crashing through me, reverberating from head to toe, and with a giant shudder I screamed, one long cry, and all the anger and tears and frustration broke through, flooding me with a wave of cleansing tears as I came long, sharp, and hard.

Gasping, swirling in the haze of passion, I opened my eyes to see the three of them staring down. Still crying, I gathered them in, realizing they'd never turn their backs on me even in the darkest of times.

Chapter 19
❧

I let out a long breath, my body still aching but no longer feeling like it was under a ton of pressure. As they helped me sit up, I shivered and Morio wrapped me in his blanket.

"Thank you," I whispered, feeling suddenly shy. "I . . . I . . ."

"You need to heal, and whatever it takes, we are here for you." Trillian chucked me under the chin. "But for now, I think you need food and sleep."

I nodded. "I can't sleep alone tonight. Smoky, will you allow Trillian to share the bed with us? I know this is your barrow, but . . ."

Smoky let out a soft rumble. "Always, as you wish. But Morio is right. We all need dinner." He handed me my bathrobe and I slid into it, tying the belt firmly around my waist. The soft silk felt smooth against my back and, with a swish of material, I headed for the living room. Morio eased himself into a wheelchair and wheeled himself behind me, as they brought up the rear.

Iris had managed to somehow turn the small kitchen into a full food factory, and now a gleaming platter of stew sat on the table, while Rozurial and Vanzir set out paper plates and plastic utensils. Trillian hurried to take a bowl of dinner rolls from her, and as soon as everything was on the table, we dug in. Trillian brought a plate to Morio, and Delilah brought one to me. As I was sitting there, I saw Menolly over in the corner, her gaze fastened on Morio. He was looking at her, too, and my stomach thudded.

One more thing to deal with—the blood she'd given to him in order to heal him had created a sexual bond between the two, and now they had the hots for one another. I wasn't too concerned. Though I really preferred that my husband not fuck my sisters, if he had to, at least Menolly would do her best to keep from hurting him. But right now, I didn't want to be worrying about walking in on them, along with everything else.

I sauntered over to Menolly. "The pull still there, huh?"

I swear she blushed, though vampires don't. She shrugged. "Yeah, but we've got it under control. And with what's going on, I'm not about to do anything to make your burden heavier."

"If it happens . . ." I turned to her and looked her straight in the eyes. "If it happens, I won't blame either of you. I prefer that it doesn't, but I'm not going to throw fits. We've seen the result of that . . ."

This whole mess had driven home the fact that there were some things not worth throwing tantrums over.

Menolly nodded, then hung her head. "Though the connection is compelling, to be honest, I normally wouldn't find him all that attractive. Roman—yes. But he's a vampire, and when it comes to the boys, I want someone I can toss around. I fully understand this is an unnatural bond. But you . . . how are you doing?"

I slid into a chair by her side, quietly enjoying the stew. "Honestly? Angry. More angry than anything. The pain makes me angry, the bruises make me angry . . . the knowledge that he's been inside me without my consent—makes me angry. I've never felt so much anger. Not since you showed up at home and we realized what Dredge had done to you."

Menolly laid her hand on mine. "You helped save me from what he had planned. Nobody could save me from him, but you stopped his plans for me. I'll never forget that. And I intend to repay you."

Chase meandered over, a strange look on his face. He'd put down his plate, and now he rubbed one temple. "I feel rather strange," he said. "Does anybody have any aspirin?"

I shook my head. "I'm sorry, we can't take aspirin. Maybe Sharah is carrying some—" But as I spoke, he started to crumple and hit the floor with a thud. I jumped up, looking around wildly for Sharah, who was over in the corner with Delilah. "Sharah! Stat—*now*. Chase just fainted."

She raced over and knelt down by his side, feeling his pulse. "Thready, fast . . . weak." A hand on his forehead, and she wiped it on her jeans. "He's sweating up a storm. Could be from him being out on the astral so long, and not used to the magic it took to get him there. I need to get him back to the FH-CSI for some tests. What's the quickest way to get him there?"

Smoky stepped forward. "I can take the two of you through the Ionyc Seas. I'm not sure how it will affect him, but if you want him there without a ninety-minute drive, especially in this weather, then you'd better let me take you."

She nodded. "Help me get him up."

Smoky swept Chase up in his arms. "Climb inside my coat and put your arms around me. I'll carry him. It will be safer." To me, he said, "I'll be back shortly. Don't let anyone in until I get back." Before I could say a word, the three of them vanished, as if they'd never been there.

"What do you think is wrong?" Delilah crowded close to my elbow.

I shook my head. "I have no idea. But I don't even want to think about what might be wrong. He was out on the astral for a long time. We should have made sure Sharah looked him over. Too much has been going on."

Vanzir sidled over. "I have news," he whispered. "But we have to go outside. Need to make a phone call."

I bit my lip. "Shade's going with us."

"Sure. I'd welcome the big guy. The fact is, I can no longer be counted on to protect you, not without my powers. I'll get him."

As Vanzir moved back through our ever-expanding household, I slid my cape around my shoulders, then wandered over to the door and opened it, staring out into the darkening evening. Snow drifted down, softly kissing the ground, and the chill of the night embraced me like a silken shroud. I put on a pair of slippers and stepped outside, turning my face up to the flakes that whispered past.

So much had happened. So much was still happening. I longed for the comfort of our own home. For the familiar pattern we'd built over the months. For Maggie to be playing in her playpen near the stove, while Iris searched through catalogs for goodies she might want for the kitchen, and Delilah read computer magazines and watched trash TV.

As I leaned against the doorjamb of the barrow, staring into the darkness, I tried to wrap my mind around where we were. Chase was in trouble, and I had the feeling it was tied to his time in the spider freak's house. But there wasn't a damned thing we could do to help.

We were waiting on Hyto—and he'd find us, not the other way around, was my guess. And until he did, I was stuck with this fucking collar. Would it interfere with my initiation? Speaking of which, if I didn't take care of this matter, would I even dare undergo an initiation at this time? What if Hyto came in charging, leveling Talamh Lonrach Oll?

At that moment, Vanzir and Shade appeared and we wandered out away from the barrow so Vanzir could put in his call.

"Carter left me a message and I didn't have a chance to return his call till now." He punched in the number to our main contact for the Demon Underground. I moved away, giving him privacy, and Shade followed.

"Do you know your dragon relatives?" I asked Shade. "Would they object to your relationship with my sister? It might be good to know up front if we're only dealing with one set of insane in-laws." I didn't mean to sound snide, but I couldn't help it. I was getting damned tired of bigotry. My own father refused to tolerate Trillian because he was

Svartan. Smoky's father hated me to the point of madness. The Rainier Puma Pride disapproved of Nerissa's relationship with Menolly. We couldn't seem to please anybody.

Shade held up one finger, then vanished back inside. Within seconds he'd returned, carrying a chair. "Sit down. I know you're still pretty banged up."

Grateful, I sat. "Thanks. You're a sweetheart."

He grinned. "I try to be." Then, kneeling down by the side of my chair, the gorgeous man with the craggy scars leaned on one of the arms. "My family . . . my mother is dragon. My father was Stradolan. Not a common mix but one of the few you'll see come out of the Netherworld. Black dragons live in the shadows; they run similar energy to the Stradolan and often pair up for working magic. My mother and father were one such pair. They fell in love during their work, and I am the result."

"I knew you didn't live in the Dragon Reaches."

"No, shadow dragons do not put as much stock in the hierarchy that, say, silver or white dragons do. They exist in a slightly different plane than the rest of the Dragonkin. And Stradolan . . . how to explain—the Stradolan are solitary beings. We know and recognize our family, but seldom do we meet after we are grown and away from our parents. So my mother and father would not be averse to meeting Delilah or her sisters. They would be aloof, but no more than is their nature."

I frowned, trying to wrap my head around the thought of an energy being falling in love with a dragon but then just stopped. It was no different than Smoky falling in love with me, or Morio and me.

"What about you? You don't seem so aloof."

He grinned then, and his teeth flashed brilliant white. "I was taken from my family very young and fostered in the Autumn Lord's realm. He made me hang around the Death Maidens a lot. I learned very quickly how to interact. Especially when they used to play tricks on me."

"So you grew up out of your natural element."

Shade gave a little shrug. "Not so much. After all, Haseofon is a temple of the dead. The Autumn Lord is one of the Harvestmen, as well as being an Elemental Lord. But look,

Vanzir appears to have finished his phone call." He nodded at Vanzir, who was headed our way.

"I talked to Carter. He's worried. He's heard rumors of a rogue portal—roughly opened but usable—set up to the Subterranean Realms. It needs to be shut down, but first we have to find it. Someone mentioned they thought it was up in Shoreline, but there are also rumors that it's over in the Lynnwood area. Nobody really knows for sure."

I stared up at him. "Crap. Has anybody been using it, do you know?"

"Yeah, Carter says that someone in particular slipped through who we're going to want to know about." He glanced around to make sure we were alone, then leaned close enough to whisper without being overheard. "Telazhar."

My stomach flipped. A necromancer from the Scorching Wars down in the deserts of Otherworld—Telazhar had long ago been sent to the Subterranean Realms and there, he'd trained demons, including Stacia Bonecrusher.

"Is Carter sure? Telazhar, loosed on the general populace . . ." Suddenly Hyto didn't seem like our biggest enemy. I looked up into Vanzir's whirling eyes. "We're in trouble. Big trouble."

He nodded. "Yeah. I wish to hell I had my powers back."

"I wish you did, too." I hung my head. The Moon Mother had done as she saw fit, but I couldn't figure out how taking away Vanzir's powers—ones he was already conflicted about—had done anything to help us.

"I don't blame you," he said. "Trust me, Camille—I don't blame you for anything. I'd give anything to take back what happened. But I can't. I'll do whatever I can to help, though. I'm still working on your side, powers or not, soul binder or not. I just hope Smoky decides to let me stick around." He bit his lip. "I'll never touch you again. I promise."

I licked my lips, feeling awkward. "Vanzir . . . if the circumstances were different . . . I guess what I'm saying is that although I would undo what happened if possible, it's not because of *you*. You were incredible. Never doubt yourself. Never worry about . . ."

He laughed, a little too harshly, but he was nodding.

"Same to you, woman. Just don't tell your fire-breathing husband I said that."

I nodded, then turned to Shade, who had moved back to give us some privacy. "We'd better get back inside to tell the others the news." Telazhar was a necromancer so powerful he'd make Morio and me look like dabblers.

As we headed inside, we were just in time to see Smoky appear. He held up his hand as Delilah started in with a flurry of questions about how Chase was doing.

"I stayed for a few moments to find out what I could. But Sharah has no clue. She said it will be morning before she's able to finish a battery of tests. Meanwhile, he's stabilized and not in immediate danger." He took off his trench coat and hung it over a knob on the coatrack near the door. Turning to me, he held out his arm and I slid beneath the shelter of his embrace.

"Sharah hopes to have some news by tomorrow morning, Delilah—she suggested you call her around nine A.M." He paused, then looked over at dinner. "I'm still hungry; if you'll excuse me, I'll finish eating."

I realized that I'd skipped most of my dinner, too, and joined him at the table, filling up another plate. Iris volunteered to heat it up, but I shook my head.

"This is fine. But I have some news for everybody." I looked around. "Where's Hanna? I haven't seen her since earlier."

Menolly spoke up. "She was feeling punky, so we fixed up a bed for her in a little cubbyhole the first level down. She doesn't mind—she said she was used to being stuck in a cave."

"Yeah, well, that needs to end soon enough." I let out a short breath. "She suffered at Hyto's hands for five years, though not in the same way I did. But she lost more than me." I thoughtfully chewed a mouthful of potato.

"What was it you had to tell us?" Delilah asked. She looked worn out. We all did. Living in Smoky's barrow was going to crowd us, but we didn't dare go home.

"Vanzir has something to tell us, actually. News. Not good. Bad, in fact. Real bad. Hang-on-to-your-hats bad." I decided, why get their hopes up? We were already facing a world of hurt, might as well Band-Aid it and just yank it off fast.

Vanzir cleared his throat and told them what Carter had told him. When he finished, everyone sat there, staring at him. Then at me. Then all hell broke loose and the barrow was awash with voices.

After a moment, I slowly, painfully climbed on top of one of the chairs and let out a whistle. Delilah winced—her hearing always gave her trouble with shrill noises.

"Shut up. Everyone just shut up. There isn't much we can do about it now. There isn't much we can even discuss doing about it. Tomorrow, we put out feelers. Hunt around, see what we can find. We do our best to trace the rogue portal—but I guarantee you, Telazhar isn't going to be hanging around waiting for us. I have no doubt he'll make himself known, however."

"Do you think he's working for Shadow Wing?" Roz began to carry plates into the kitchen for Iris.

"I don't know. Stacia was working to edge Shadow Wing out of his position. Telazhar trained her. Chances are he's on a rogue mission, but then again—we can't be sure."

I tried to run through all the permutations. Telazhar could be working on his own, or for Shadow Wing. For all we knew, Trytian could have coaxed him to come over. No matter which way you cut it, it added up to a very dangerous sorcerer hanging around Seattle, and that just wasn't going to fly.

"All we know is that he's trouble and we can't let him stay over Earthside. If he tries to make it back to Otherworld, they can deal with him—and will. He'll be put to death if he tries to reenter OW."

A knock on the door interrupted me. Smoky answered it, cautiously peering out into the night. Almost immediately, he pulled back and opened up the door, allowing Estelle and St. George to enter. Georgio looked up at Smoky and began to sputter, mingled wonder and fear spreading across his face. He'd recognized Smoky as a dragon from the first time he saw him. Sometimes those who walked with one foot in another world—whether it was the world trapped inside their own minds, or another realm—could see beyond the superficial.

"What brings you to my barrow?" Smoky asked.

Estelle shook her head, tears streaking down her cheeks.

"Someone came to the house. Someone I did not recognize. He was average height, bald—except for a long ponytail hanging from the center of the back of his head—"

"Asheré! It's Hyto's snow monkey!" I turned to Estelle, panic rising. "What did he say? What did he want?"

"He indicated we'd better get out of the house if we didn't want to be . . . how did he put it? Cannon fodder. He told us to bring you a message, Lord Smoky."

Smoky looked seconds away from losing his cool. I took his hand in mine and held it tightly. He glanced down at me and I stepped closer to him, the barrow suddenly feeling all too exposed.

"He said to tell you that your sire is coming, and if you don't want to see the surrounding area razed, you are to meet him in the clearing yonder—with Camille—tomorrow morning at dawn. If you don't show up, then Hyto will begin to systematically destroy all the houses and humans around the area. And then he vanished."

My breath caught in my chest, and the collar around my neck began to pulse. I reached for it, trying to yank it off, but it just throbbed, slow and steady, and I couldn't breathe. I fell to my knees, gasping for air, the room spinning.

"Move, move and give her space," someone said.

"Get out of the way!"

"Let me in there."

The words became a whirl as I fought for control, fought for consciousness. Hands lifted me and I wasn't sure where they were taking me, but I found myself in a dark hall, staring down a long corridor. Behind me, Smoky and Trillian begged me to open my eyes, but something from the darkness beckoned and I felt that I had to go ahead, follow the trail of twinkling lights that spread out in front of me.

I teetered on the edge of a black, vast abyss, and then went spiraling into it, head first, swan-diving into dark sparkling night.

The sparkles floated, dancing through the darkness, whispering my name. They dove and whirled, spun in a vortex of delight, shivered around me and through me as they swept me into their midst.

Come, come ... follow our trail ... follow us into the grove ...

I hesitated, then—feeling no sense of Hyto nearby—decided to do as they asked. I'd reached the point where I had to run on instinct because I was certainly not in control of my life anymore. Everyone else was taking a bite out of me; maybe if I just gave in and did what they wanted, everything would be okay. Hell, the damned collar around my neck was proof that I no longer could count my life my own—not until it was off.

Allowing the sparkles to drag me along, I found myself almost giddy. I finally wasn't fighting. I was giving in—letting the universe do what it would. Even though I was afraid, whatever happened would happen and I could only react. There was no control here to fight for.

The sparkles led me through the dark until I could see a ring of trees ahead. Were we outside? Inside? I didn't know, but I followed the lights and suddenly found myself outside under the night sky.

The moon was still waning, a shadow in the night. She turned her face to me and smiled down onto the snow, through the icy chill. The sparkling mantle of white stretched through the silhouette of a woodland, mirroring the glittering stars that shone overhead. I could hear the beat of the land, the pulse of the magic that filled the area, and a whisper of elements swirled around me, a cacophony on the wind, weaving a dance as I approached the center of this mysterious glade.

I caught up my breath, squinting, curious as to where I'd been led. But then my questions were answered, for out of the towering trees stepped a figure tall as the sky, tall as a building. He stood astride two cloven hooves, his cock and balls enormous pendulums between his furry legs. His torso, gleaming under what light there was, led to a high and noble bearded chin, and atop a head of cascading locks, two spiraling horns rose high into the night.

"Herne," I whispered, going down on one knee. *When in the presence of a god—kneel.*

His son, Tra, danced around him, piping a melody that ricocheted through my core, hitting my blood like silver wine, and I longed to follow it into the forest. I laughed, feeling awash in sight and sound and the touch of velvet magic on my skin.

"My daughter." Out from behind one of the trees stepped my Lady, clad in a white gown that barely covered her thighs. Her breasts were full and ripe, heavy under her gown, her nipples raised with arousal. Herne held out his arm and she slid into his embrace. I caught my breath, the scent of their desire making me ache to join them.

"My Lady . . ." What could I say? What was I supposed to say? I greedily soaked in the energy, basking in their presence. I could become a living statue, stay here forever, root deep into the forest and let the ivy grow wild over me.

"You need our strength, my child." The Moon Mother stepped over to me and gazed down, her eyes filled with sorrow. "I did what I could to help while you were in the dragon's grasp. He is crafty, that one, and old, and treacherous."

I nodded, tugging at my collar. "Can you release this for me?"

She pressed her lips together, shaking her head. "I would, but I cannot. Freeing yourself from his slavery is woven in the hands of your personal destiny, and not even the gods can challenge the Hags of Fate. There is a reason this has all happened to you, my dear, even if you do not see it now. Walk through the fire, and you will be far stronger than those who have tried to subjugate you."

Nodding, I let her words ripple through me. No one—not the gods, not mighty heroes, and certainly not mortals—could win against the Hags of Fate. And the Hags of Fate worked within the balance of the realms, of the worlds.

They were the law of the universe, bringing chaos when order reigned too strong, enforcing law when chaos reigned supreme. I accepted the natural balance of life. Shadow and light, both had their place. Even when it hurt.

"What can you do for me, if anything?" I did my best not to sound expectant. Unlike many, I didn't expect the gods to help me out of rough situations. That wasn't their job. But I would happily accept all the help they could give if it meant getting even with the Big Bads. Especially Hyto.

The Moon Mother reached down and stroked my face, and the welts on my cheek vanished. She motioned for me to disrobe, and I did. A stroke from her hands and—though the bruises remained—they weren't nearly so painful. A gentle palm between my legs, fingers rippling over the raw skin and abrasions Hyto had left me with, and their pain, too, faded, and I began to breathe easier. She then kissed my forehead and a river of silver began to run through me, filling me like summer rain. I reveled in the healing waters of her magic, soaking it in, bathing in the glimmering mist that foamed up around me.

"My daughter, listen to me. Sometimes when you give up control, you actually take control. Sometimes letting go means taking the lead. And sometimes fear is the only control someone has over us. Whatever happens, you are my child, and I am deep in your heart. You are my priestess. Kneeling in body can be a shallow gesture—kneel in your heart before those who deserve it. The Hytos of this world don't need to know the difference—let them be damned."

As she turned me toward the path, she leaned down and whispered, "Sex is my passion. Herne is one of my mates. Never let anybody take that passion away from you. They may abuse your body, but they cannot own your soul. Because I have first claim on it. *And I yield my priestesses to no one.*"

I found myself, cleansed and recharged, back on the path, following the trail of sparkles, down the tunnel.

A few moments later, I began to lose consciousness, and when I opened my eyes, I was on the bed, surrounded by my loved ones. The collar still chafed, but I knew—even though I still wore Hyto's mark—he would never own me again.

Chapter 20

❧❧❧

"Camille—are you okay?"

I was getting a little tired of that question. "Yes, I'm fine. I just had a panic attack and then an out-of-body experience, and quite frankly, please, just give it a rest. I need more food. I need sugar. Caffeine."

As I mulled over what had happened, I realized that the panic had disappeared. I was still terrified of Hyto, but now the fear was based on the battle we were facing, not what he had already done to me.

"There is no help for it—Smoky, we have to face him. We can't let him decimate the area." I pushed away hands that would keep me in bed and stood, the pain in my body substantially less than it had been a few minutes ago. "I'm tired of hiding. I'm tired of being afraid. I'm tired of feeling like my life is out of control. I am going to face him, and I'll be carrying the horn of the Black Beast when I do. Your father doesn't know I possess it."

The cloak made out of the Black Beast's hide would go a long way toward protecting me, too. I straightened my shoulders. "It's time to end this."

Delilah stood beside me. "I'll be there."

Smoky frowned. "I don't want my wife in any more danger from—"

"You idiot. Still you spout off about this?" I hit him lovingly on the arm. "I'm in danger as long as Hyto is alive. I'm in far worse danger if you get yourself killed and I'm still alive. We stand together. We're husband and wife."

"And husband." Trillian stepped forward.

Morio started to pipe up, but I stared him down. "Not you. Shut up. You have every reason for staying in bed, and stay there, you will."

"I can be of use—"

"Yeah, you'll be of use all right. I'll be so worried about you that I won't be able to concentrate. You stay here, guard Maggie and Iris—"

"Oh no, girl." Iris slipped through the pack. "I'll be there with you. My powers are far stronger than they were before we went back to the Northlands. Long have you helped me and protected me. I owe you one, Camille. I owe all of you a great deal. I'll be there."

I held up my hand as they all started to chime in. "I got it, I got it. All for one, one for all. But somebody has to stay behind to guard Menolly while she's asleep, and Maggie, Morio, and Hanna. And Georgio and Estelle." I looked over at the pair, and they both smiled shyly.

"Fair maiden, what sort of treachery could you possibly worry your beautiful head over?" Georgio said, sweeping into a low bow. "I would be glad to put asunder your worries."

I quietly walked over to him. "St. George, my stalwart hero. Do not worry yourself over this matter. You stay here and help to guard those who must stay behind, and you will assuage my worries. Will you do that for me?"

He smiled then, his face lighting up. "I will do that and more for you." With a look over at Smoky, he shook his head. "I still find it odd that you would unite yourself with the dragon—you know I must slay him—but until that day, we stand a truce between us if there is a common enemy come to call."

Feeling my heart warm, I leaned forward and kissed Georgio on the head. "Brave knight. Stand tall."

Turning to the others, I shrugged. "Well, then. Trillian, Vanzir, Roz—you three stay here tomorrow. Shade, Delilah, Iris, Smoky, and I will march out to meet . . ." I paused, my gaze flickering over to Georgio. Best he not know another dragon was coming into the mix. He hadn't figured out Shade yet, which was a good thing. "To meet Hyto."

Smoky let out a long sigh. "I wish . . . I have to make a quick trip. Stay inside, all of you. I'll be back as soon as I can. Do *not* let Camille out of your sight. I implore you." He slipped on his ankle-length trench and took off out of the door.

"Where's he going?" Vanzir asked.

"I have no idea," I said. "Not a clue."

By the time Smoky got home, Trillian, Morio, and I were the last ones up. We waited in the bedroom, me sitting cross-legged on the bed while Morio sat fidgeting in his wheelchair and Trillian paced the room. As Smoky burst through the doors, I let out a long sigh of relief.

"I was afraid you might have gone to meet Hyto by yourself—to hunt him down." I blurted out the words before thinking them through.

Smoky scowled. "No, but that doesn't mean the thought didn't occur to me. But no, I had other matters to attend to. Come. We should get some sleep before tomorrow. We'll need all our energy."

I bit my lip, staring at the floor. "This may be the last night we all have together. Hyto is ruthless." Lifting my head, I gazed at each of them, exhausted. "I'm tired." Part of me felt like we should have sex—celebrate life even in the midst of what we were facing, but the truth was, I was just exhausted. "Sleep with me. Surround me with your love."

And so they pulled Morio's bed close to Smoky's four-poster, and then Smoky, Trillian, and I crawled into the billowy folds of the comforter, and together, pressed warm against each other. I trailed my hand over Trillian's side to hold Morio's as we slept.

*   *   *

Sometime before dawn, we woke and dressed. I wore my spidersilk skirt, a matching tunic, the cloak of the Black Unicorn, and sturdy granny boots. As I slid the horn into my side pocket, relieved that it still had power in it, I wondered what would work against a dragon—which element? White dragons used mist and snow and ice . . . but they also breathed fire. Would wind or earth work best? They flew, so they were adept in the air. But earth . . . earth might actually do some harm.

Breakfast was a silent affair, with Delilah serving fried-egg sandwiches, and Trillian silently fuming. He wanted to come with us, but he knew that we needed him there to protect the others.

Iris had changed clothes, too—she was in her priestess robes, and her hair was done up in a wrap of braids around her head. She carried her wand of Aqualine crystal with her, and as I sat playing with my food, she slipped over to my side.

"Don't fret. We'll take care of him." She lightly touched the collar around my neck. "Something feels different about this."

I nodded. "I can't lose it just yet, but the Moon Mother came to me last night, and some of its power has been stripped away. I can't tell you quite why, but I feel stronger. Ready to face him." Inside, I was a quivering ball of fear-jelly, but I tried to own the fear and let it go.

Iris smoothed my hair back and braided it. "No sense giving him any advantage," she said. "I think you're learning a hard lesson, one that you've never been able to accept. You're learning that you can't always be the rock, you can't always be the one who makes things better."

"I'm not in control of this situation. Only of my reaction to it?" I smiled at her, drinking in her winning smile and brilliant blue gaze. Iris had far more common sense than most people I knew, but she wasn't soft. She was the epitome of tough love—and she had that rare gift of making you love her for scolding you.

"Ah yes . . . then you are learning." She stood back, eyeing my hair. "There, done for now. Finish your sandwich and we'll go."

"Thank you," I mumbled, taking another bite. I shoved the last bit of sandwich into my mouth and drank down a huge glass of milk.

Delilah dusted her hands on her jeans. "I can't believe we're going to fight a dragon. Smoky, Shade, I just hope that you guys can take care of him, because I'm damned if I know what to do."

Shade jerked his chin at her, smiling. "You and your sisters need to have higher opinions of yourselves. Come now. Let's be off and get this done so we can attend to other business."

His almost laissez-faire attitude went a long way into helping me calm down. Smoky said little, merely pulled me onto his lap and wrapped a gentle arm around my waist. I leaned into him, forehead against forehead, and kissed him lightly.

"We can do this, my husband."

"We can, my wife." His voice was calm, but his eyes were flashing with lightning and I knew he would not rest until Hyto was lying in a million little pieces strung out over the forest. Sometimes he loved me so much—they all did—that it scared me. I never wanted to endanger that love, but I was so far from perfect that I wondered if I was worthy of their devotion. Just then Trillian leaned in over my other shoulder and kissed me. I walked over to Morio for another kiss. Finally we were ready, and—with one last glance at the barrow—we headed out to meet Hyto.

The path leading to our designated meeting place was winding and steep. Smoky insisted on lifting me over every tree and boulder—to save my strength, he said—and Shade helped Iris. Delilah was able to clamber over the trees without a problem; she was tall enough and strong enough.

"You made Trillian and Roz stay home because they are more vulnerable to Hyto, didn't you? Vanzir, too?" Delilah caught up to me, blowing on her hands. The early-morning air was damp and moist, filled with the taste of snow.

I nodded. "Yes, but that's not the only reason. We really do need someone to watch over Maggie and the others. What if Hyto breaks through us? Smoky's got it set up that if he falls, a warning will go off in the barrow. That will give them enough time to run."

"I didn't know that," Delilah said, suddenly grim. "This is really it, isn't it? We're fighting a dragon?"

None of us had ever been on the receiving end of a dragon's fury except Roz—once when he pinched my butt in front of Smoky—and me, at the mercy of Hyto. I hated to think about what waited in store for us when the battle was to the death.

"I didn't know it, either, but he told me shortly before we left the barrow. He also told Trillian, so they know what's going down. Menolly—she's safe enough, we figure, tucked away in the lower levels. I doubt Hyto would go to much bother trying to find her. But the others . . ."

As we crossed a clearing, a deer came out of the undergrowth, standing near entwined buses of huckleberry and bracken. She stared at us, not moving but poised to run, and I gazed into her eyes as we passed by. She couldn't control what we were doing, but her reaction was one of caution, wariness. I raised a hand, slowly, greeting her as we passed by.

The snow grew thicker, heavy and wet, as the grade of the path increased. I tried to tune in to the land here—if I was going to use the Earth Elemental to counter Hyto, it might help if I could make a connection with the land. I'd have to start paying more attention to my surroundings once I was part of Aeval's Court, so I might as well do it now.

Suddenly, I realized I was thinking of the future as if there really was one. The thought *We might actually have a chance* . . . ran through my head, and I wondered where it had come from.

As we continued, I began to have an odd feeling we were being followed. I glanced behind us but could see nothing. When I mentioned it to Smoky, he listened, then shook his head. The hush of snow falling on snow muted sounds, and the world took on the same surreal white glow that the Northlands had held.

"I can hardly wait for spring," I muttered under my breath. "I've had enough snow to last me a lifetime."

"You and me both," Iris said, now riding along on Smoky's shoulders. "I am dreaming of planting flowers and vegetables. Last night, a pansy chased me down the path in my dreams, threatening me if I didn't make it stop snowing."

The sudden break in mood made me laugh. Even though I was trying to keep quiet, my voice rang out down the slope behind us, and I bent over, stifling myself. I managed to quickly sober up, but it took everything I had not to giggle.

Smoky and Shade said nothing, but Delilah gave me a sideways look that told me she was either very annoyed or very much in agreement with me.

We came to a level area on the slope, before the grade of the hill started up in earnest. Another half-hour's hike, it looked like, before we reached the rendezvous point. The treeline was still dense. We weren't even into the real foothills of the Cascades yet, though it wasn't that hard to get an up-close-and-personal view of Mount Rainier from the road. But here the vegetation was thick, the snow deep, and the going problematic.

"At least he doesn't want to meet us up on the top of the glaciers. I don't fancy a climb up Mount Rainier to fight a dragon." Even as the words left my lips, there was a noise to the right and a bolt of lightning came shooting out at us. It missed Delilah and me but caught Shade on the arm. He shouted and dodged to the right as the glaring fork disappeared.

"Crap! Is that Hyto?" I turned, quickly seeking out any form that might tell us he was in the area. But the area from where the attack had come was thick with fern and bracken, covered in large drifts of snow. A hole had melted through it—the spell had to have come from there, but it was low to the ground and somehow I didn't think that Hyto could keep himself hidden that well. He was too arrogant; he'd want us to know it was him.

Shade motioned for us to stay on the path and hurried over to the area, kicking the plants askew. "Nobody here. But there was, and they wore . . . some form of sandal, would be my guess."

"Sandals? Hyto doesn't wear sandals." I frowned. "He

wears boots and they're damned hard and heavy. I know, my
ribs show the damage." Smoky let out a low bark and I
turned to him. "Keep hold of yourself, my love. Not once
while I was there did he wear anything but those damned
boots."

"Should we follow the tracks?" Delilah asked.

Shade gazed at the direction in which they'd gone. "I don't
know if that will do us any good. That was powerful magic.
Anyone who can command a strong lightning bolt . . ."

"My father cannot." Smoky set Iris on the ground and she
shook her self out. "He can control mist and fog and snow,
better than I can, but he can't control the lightning. Unless he
was using a scroll, there's no way he could have cast a spell
like that."

"Then who . . ." I paused. "I know who." And I did—as
sure as I knew my name. "Asheré. The snow monkey—he's a
rogue monk from the Northlands. Trust me, it's got to
be him."

"Are you sure?"

"Makes sense to me." I took a deep breath and looked
around, expecting to see him at every turn, but there was
simply nothing there. "He's playing cat and mouse with us.
That has to be it. Keep your eyes open—he'll probably try to
dishearten us before we ever come into sight of Hyto. Reason tells me that much. Hyto likes to torture his toys. Anything that can demoralize us, he'll do."

"His ego won't allow the snow monkey to make the kill,
however." Smoky let out a long breath. "My father is the
epitome of arrogance."

"Yeah, I know that too well." I chewed on my bottom
lip. "When he was beating me, he was screaming that I
was not his equal. He blames me for setting you against him,
and consequently for getting him thrown out of the Dragon
Reaches."

"He would have been thrown out eventually, regardless of
what I did or did not do. My mother was reaching the end of
her patience. When I went to help her not long ago, she told
me that she'd already decided to deny him in Council, and

that his behavior toward me—and you—was just the final straw." Scowling, he shook his head. "Hyto was never a good husband, but she married him because of civil obligation."

I had never heard Smoky talk so much about his family. Most of what I knew about them came from Iris's knowledge of dragons. "You mean it was a marriage of convenience?"

He picked up Iris again and settled her on his shoulder, holding her tight with his hair. I smiled, watching how carefully he made sure she was comfortable. We took off again, up the slope.

"Not exactly. My grandfather—Relae, my mother's father— had promised his friend Layr, Hyto's father, that he would grant a marriage between one of his daughters and Layr's son. Hyto was the ninth son of a ninth son but had not been able to find a wife. At the time, my grandfather didn't know that Hyto was unbalanced."

"You mean, even as a youth he was deranged?"

"I think so, yes. Mother says the signs were there, but . . . she accepted her father's request and married down in class. It did not affect her status, being a silver dragon, and she loved her father very much and wanted to honor his request. By the time they figured out Hyto was disturbed, Mother had already had several children. She decided to wait, hoping things would get better. Denying a partner in the Dragon Reaches has long-reaching consequences, if you can prove they've behaved badly. Hyto would have been shunned."

Another thought cropped up—one I'd been wondering about for awhile. "Smoky, when we first . . . when I first came to your barrow, you told me *you* were the ninth son of a ninth son. But not long ago, you told me you were the eldest son?" Might as well get things out in the open. I decided that from here out, if we survived, it would behoove me to learn as much as I could about my husbands' families and cultures.

Smoky shuddered. One strand of his hair whipped out, striking a tree as we passed. I shrank back, remembering Hyto's attacks.

"It is complicated. For one thing, mortality rates among

dragonets are extremely high. Not many live to adulthood, which is why dragons have such large family records but such small actual families. I was the ninth son to hatch—"

"*Hatch?* You were . . . you came out of an *egg*?" I stared at him now, wondering just what else I was clueless about. Smoky's life was becoming stranger to me as the minutes wore on.

He broke into a little smirk. "What? I'm a dragon. If we were to have a child—and I do believe that is possible—it would be a live birth because you are not of dragon heritage, but . . . Shade—he was hatched. His mother was dragon."

Shade cleared his throat but merely nodded. Delilah stared at him, then at me. I shrugged. So our lovers had crept out of eggs. So had we; the eggs had just stayed inside our mother and turned into us.

"Anyway, there were fifteen eggs in the first batch of eggs my mother gave birth to. All hatched. Nine boys, six girls. I was the ninth son. We all lived past the first year, so we were all counted as actual children and listed in the Hall of Records. Shortly thereafter, the weaker ones began to die. Out of that first clutch, three sons and two daughters survived."

"So you were the ninth son on record, even though at that point there were only two brothers older than you?"

He nodded. "And one older sister. Dragons typically have two to three clutches. Mother had two. Out of her second clutch, only one son and two daughters survived to be entered into the records. Only a total of ten sons and eight daughters made it to their first year. And out of the ten sons, only three of us made it to puberty. The rest died. Four of the girls made it. By the time I left home, Hyto had engineered the death of my two older brothers. My eldest sister had died in a fall from the dreyerie. So I am now the eldest. I have one sister from my clutch still alive—younger than me. The children from the second clutch are alive as well, but if Hyto had stayed around much longer, I guarantee they wouldn't be. My clutch sister married and left, out of his reach."

Speechless, I stared at him, a gaggle of questions racing through my mind, but I wasn't sure just how to phrase any of them.

Delilah broke through my whirling thoughts. "Why did your father kill your siblings? I thought being the ninth son of a ninth son is important. Surely he couldn't be insecure about his place?"

Smoky stomped over a fallen tree, barely noticing it. His voice was rough as he said, "It is important. I have greater powers than my brothers. Just as Hyto has greater powers than the others in his clutch."

That explained a little more—so there *was* a birthright involved in dragon powers. I wondered if the girls had an equitable match.

"As for why he attacked his own children—Hyto saw them as threats for Mother's attention and her treasure. White dragons are greedy. They are arrogant." He stopped to help me over another downed tree.

As we started up again, Smoky let out a long sigh. "I have those traits, to a degree. But I honor my mother and chose to cultivate her legacy instead. Not all white dragons are vicious and evil—my grandfather isn't. He fought next to the Northmen in the wars. But Hyto . . . he is the worst type of white dragon. I choose not to let his heritage corrupt me, though I admit I have his quickness to temper and his impulsive nature."

At that point, we rounded a bend and Smoky stopped. He set Iris down, bidding her to stand next to Delilah. We were near a huge fir, one so tall I could barely see the top of it. The undergrowth around it was thick, covered with snow, and I nervously looked around. This would be the perfect place for the snow monkey to show up.

"Should we stop here? There's too much cover and we could be in danger." Delilah must have been reading my mind. Even Shade looked nervous.

"We've been in danger since we started out this morning." Smoky let out a long breath. "We're meeting help here. When I left last night, it was to ask someone to accompany us. She agreed to meet us this morning."

She? Wondering whether he'd made a trip to Talamh Lonrach Oll to ask a favor from Aeval or Titania—I knew he'd never ask Morgaine—I glanced around, looking for any sign of the Fae Queens.

But then, out from behind the fir, stepped a woman as tall as Hyto, but far more stately. She was pale, with eyes the color of gunmetal, and her hair flowed down to her butt, a sparkling array of silver strands with a pale ice blue cast to them. The tendrils moved and twisted and I caught my breath.

Dressed in a filmy robe the color of early dawn, she glided forward, graceful as a dancer. Her aura sparkled with magic and I let out a little gasp. Smoky was powerful. Hyto was strong. But here—here was the true nobility of Dragon-kin. It permeated her every movement, her eyes, her stance. And I suddenly understood why the silver dragons were the Emperors of their kind.

The woman's gaze met mine and she held me fast. At first, the energy rolling off her was aloof, but after a few moments, a sparkle filled her eyes, and for some reason I had the feeling that I'd passed a test.

"Iampaatar, I taught you better manners than this. You *will* introduce us." Her voice was the sound of wind chimes tinkling in a thin breeze.

Smoky bowed low, pressing her hand to his lips. Then, standing, he motioned for me to come forward. "May I have permission to use your public name, my Lady?"

"Of course. What would you have her call me otherwise? *Hey you?*" The corners of her lips turned ever so slightly upward, and I met her gaze with a weak smile. I knew where this was leading, but no way, nohow was I taking the lead. *So* not my place to interrupt a dragon.

"Yes, Mother." Looking contrite in a way that I'd only ever seen him look around Iris, Smoky cleared his throat. "Honorable Lady Vishana, it would please me if you were to greet my wife, Camille te Maria D'Artigo, priestess of the Moon Mother. Camille, this is my mother, Lady Vishana. Your mother-in-law."

I waited, wondering what she'd do. Would she strike out, as Hyto had? Or would she ignore me? But the next moment, she reached out and took my hands in hers. As she held them, she gazed down with those steel eyes and then a smile spread across her face. Oh, she was still aloof, but the smile was genuine, and as she spoke, a note of sincerity filled her words.

"Camille, I have been waiting to meet you since Iampaatar first told me of his marriage. So you are the one who has stolen my son's heart? Welcome to the family." And then she leaned down and kissed me briefly on the cheek.

Chapter 21

As she stood back, still holding my hands, I breathed a slow sigh of relief. Then her gaze fell on my neck and she reached out to finger the collar. I swallowed. What the hell was she going to think of me, wearing Hyto's symbol? Would she resent me? Would she despise me for being weak?

But as she searched my face, I felt myself opening up to her. There was something regal yet just about her energy, and I leaned closer, silently pleading for her to understand that I had not *chosen* to allow Hyto into my life.

"I am so sorry that my ex-husband found his way to you." She read my expression thoroughly, and when she'd finished, she turned toward Smoky and her words came out with a catch. "I should have denied him sooner. This would not have happened if I'd paid attention when I first began to notice his behavior. Shortly after you and your siblings were born, I should have cast him out. But I wasn't sure . . . I thought perhaps he was still young and rash."

Smoky shook his head. "He's gone over the edge. Hyto is lost."

Finding my courage, I spoke up. "He's furious at Smoky

and at me. He means to destroy us. He kidnapped me and was going to use me as bait to lure Smoky in, but with a little help, I escaped."

Vishana listened, then crossed her arms. "Surviving Hyto's perversions takes a strong spirit. We have to be cautious. He's wily and will not give any quarter." With a glance past us, she pointed to Iris, Shade, and Delilah. "Introductions, my Iampaatar. You are not bred from coarse society. You *will* be civil."

As I tried to stifle a laugh, Vishana flashed me a sly grin. "I'm sure you've found my son a chore to tame. I understand you have two other husbands, as well."

Startled that Smoky had given her that much information, I nodded. "Yes . . . actually. I hope you don't—"

With a harried gesture, she cut me off. "It is of no concern. In the Dragon Reaches, we, on occasion, allow plural marriage, and taking a lover is common. But I am surprised at my son. He was always the most headstrong." Then, after a beat, she added, "For him to share you means that his love is stronger than life. Remember that, Camille. You are blessed. But so is he—for you to come with him on this hunting expedition tells me you have a brave heart, and the conviction to stand by your husband is honorable."

I had a feeling that *honorable* was an important word in Vishana's household. Turning to my sister, I started to introduce the rest of them, but my mother-in-law held up her hand.

"Ah, ah, ah! I asked my son to do the honors. It is his task, and I will not have him turning into a boor. Mind you, keep control of your household, Camille. Just because he is dragon, there is no reason for my son to ride roughshod over everyone. Do you understand? The household rules are set by the wife and to be obeyed."

Smoky fumed but said nothing while I let out a laugh. I'd just been given permission to scold my husband by his mother.

"If you're quite done talking about me, please allow me to introduce my sister-in-law, Delilah Maria te Maria D'Artigo. And this is Lady Iris Kuusi, priestess of Undutar. And this is Delilah's lover, Shade. He is—"

"Half shadow dragon. I can sense it, my son. And . . . half Stradolan." Smoky's mother looked Shade up one side and down the other. "Fascinating. I've never met a half-breed shadow dragon before. Your kind seldom mate outside the ranks." There was nothing inherently rude about the comment, but somehow it felt like she'd given us a valuable tidbit of information there.

Shade bowed. "Honorable Lady Vishana, I am pleased to make your acquaintance. Please accept my services."

"You are soft spoken and well mannered. Teach my son a lesson or two, if you would. I fear that living alone for so many centuries has made him pigheaded. But he is a good man, and I'm proud of him." Vishana glanced at the top of the slope. "Well, then. Shall we find Hyto and take him down? I don't have all day to dawdle, and I'm in no mood to prolong this battle."

I stared at her. "You're coming with us, then?" I hadn't been entirely sure what she was here for. I'd been *hoping*, but hope doesn't always spring true.

"Oh, yes, my dear. I'm here for a fight, and I won't leave while Hyto still stands. Come then. Iampaatar, lead us to the battle. Camille, protect yourself. I will not lose a daughter-in-law the day I meet her."

And so, with Smoky carrying Iris in the front, we headed up the mountain to the crest of the slope, as the snow fell silently around us.

Delilah fell in beside me, with Shade bringing up the rear. She leaned close. "I never thought about the fact that my future mother-in-law might be a dragon also." She seemed thoughtful.

I nodded. "From what Shade says, though, you may never meet her."

"What should we watch out for with Hyto?" Delilah fingered Lysanthra—her silver dagger. No use using an old iron knife on Hyto. Dragons weren't vulnerable to the metal. I didn't want to tell her that no matter what side you came in from, he was dangerous, but that was simply the fact.

"Whatever you do, keep away from his hair. Which means distance attacks, which you don't have." I bit my lip, thinking maybe we should have brought Rozurial. He had all sorts of tricks up his sleeve.

But then Delilah surprised me. She pulled a handful of little round red balls out of her pocket. I recognized them immediately.

"Roz's fireballs! When did he give you those?" I loved Roz's gear—coveted some of it, actually. But he never gave me any of his baubles, probably because of my predilection for making the wrong things go *boom*.

"This morning, before we left. Nobody wanted to be left behind." She bit her lip, the tip of one of her fangs piercing the skin. A drop of blood oozed out and she licked it up.

"I know. But we can't focus on our job if we're trying to protect the others." And there it was: If everybody came, then we'd be not only leaving two unprotected members of our family at home—along with Hanna, Georgio, and Estelle—but we'd be so busy trying to make sure that Hyto didn't hurt them, we'd all end up dead.

Smoky stopped and held up his hand. We were near the top of the hill. We paused, then started again. The woods here were silent, and a pall fell over me. The tension of the forest rose; it was as if some silent intruder had taken root. The elephant in the room that nobody wanted to talk about.

My breath came in puffs as we ascended the last fifty feet of the trail, which led to a plateau. Cresting the top, I stopped cold. There, about fifty yards away in the clearing, stood Hyto and Asheré. They weren't alone. In front of them stood a mountain troll and several hungry-looking wolves.

As we approached, Hyto stared at Vishana, his expression shifting. "What are you doing here? This is not your fight. Get out of my sight, *sclah*."

I looked up at Smoky. He was scowling, barely holding himself back. "He just called my mother the equivalent of a cunt." His nails sprang into talons and he began to tremble.

Grabbing his arm, I shook my head. "We have to get rid of the riffraff first. Cannon fodder—to weaken us."

Hyto sauntered forward. "My son, how does it feel to know

what I did to your wife? She loved every minute of it. When I was fucking her, she screamed out my name—not yours. And then begged me for more."

I caught my breath. "He lies."

"I know," Smoky said, cautioning me as I brought out the horn. "Save it for him, after we take care of the others."

Turning to the troll and wolves, Hyto said, "Save the dark-haired girl and my son for me. The others you may destroy at will."

The wolves trembled, and I realized they were no ordinary wolves, but goblin steeds. Trained to destroy, with glowing red eyes and snarling muzzles that showed long, razor-sharp teeth. Delilah let out a cry and I sensed her beginning to shift. Within seconds, a black panther stood next to me, and next to her I saw a ghostly leopard. Our sister Arial had come to join in the fight.

Smoky pushed me behind him as Iris moved in by his side, her wand at the ready. She had a look on her face I'd never before seen—dead anger. And I'd seen Iris pissed off before, but this look . . . I stepped back.

Shade moved forward and held up his hands—I couldn't tell what he was doing, but it was death magic of some sort. That I could feel into my bones.

And then the wolves leaped forward, and the troll moved in.

I shoved the unicorn horn back in my pocket—no use wasting the energy on creatures we could take care of in other ways. One of the wolves leaped toward Delilah, and she engaged it, tumbling into the snow, grappling it with her front paws. The wolf snarled, its long teeth flashing dangerously near her throat.

Iris didn't wait—she sent a wave of frost forward toward the rest of the wolves. Even though they were used to the cold, the temperature around us suddenly dropped a good fifty degrees and the wolves slowed.

Shade whispered a charm, and a veil of smoke began to drift out of his fingers, aimed at the troll. It caught several of the wolves in its wake and they yipped, painfully, and backed away, whining.

The troll began to lumber forward, howling as the smoke hit him. Sparks flickered against his skin, and I suddenly recognized the spell. It was far too advanced for my Moon magic, and Morio had no clue on how to use it. Called Sparking Smoke, the cloud carried a bevy of painfully hot sparks forward to engage the enemy.

Smoky moved forward, toward the troll, and the troll roared to life, swatting him hard with the side of his hand. Smoky whirled, his trench flying behind him as he lashed out with both talons and hair, slicing across the troll's body. The troll screamed again as blood foamed onto the ground, melting the snow.

I turned toward Vishana, who had not moved. Her gaze was fastened on Hyto. But nothing was attacking her at the moment. Delilah let out a loud yowl as she bit the neck of the wolf. From my stance, I could see the vague outline of Arial on the other side, ripping at the wolf's belly from the astral realm.

A low growl caught me by surprise, and I turned to find that one of the wolves had somehow managed to get behind me. It launched itself at me as I called on the Moon Mother for strength.

The creature caught me between its paws and I hit the ground backward, sprawling in the snow and losing my concentration. Its jaws came snapping toward my face, but before it could bite, Hyto shouted and it stopped, holding me there. Another blink of the eye and the wolf went flying to the side, with one shrill whimper.

I stared up to find Vishana's hand stretched out. Grasping it, I let her pull me to my feet. I'd barely stammered out a thank-you when another wolf came in from the side. She held out her hand and out of her palm a spear of ice appeared and sailed through the center of the wolf's forehead. It dropped without a sound.

Smoky grunted. He had fully engaged the troll, leaving long bloody streaks along its belly. Another moment and a length of his hair rose to encircle the creature's neck. The troll grabbed hold of the strands, yanking on them, but he was no match for an angry dragon, even in human form, and Smoky's rage seemed to build as he throttled it dead.

"Got you, you bastard!" Shade's cry made me whirl around. He had just caught another wolf on the wing, his blade deftly slicing its throat. Delilah and Arial had taken down the last wolf and we turned toward Hyto and Asheré.

Hyto nodded to his snow monkey, and the rogue monk held out his staff. A wave of pale mist began to emanate from it, and I found myself backing away and pulling out the horn.

"Poison! I can smell it from here. Poison gas!" I held up the horn and called on the Master of Winds.

Master of Winds, heed my call. Bring the winds to save us now!

As I thrust the horn into the air, a gale sprang up and raced through my body, sending me to my knees. Still I held steady, even though Delilah and Iris went tumbling to the ground. They rolled to the side, though Shade, Vishana, and Smoky managed to keep on their feet.

The winds howled forth from the horn, raging along the crest of the hill toward Hyto and the monk. It caught the cloud of poison in its wake and dispersed it, pushing it back. Hyto just laughed, but Asheré looked to be in trouble as the gas backfired on him, swelling around him. He dropped the staff and clutched at his throat. Hyto stared at him, not moving to help him.

Asheré reached a hand toward his master, but Hyto just let out a snort.

"Weakling. You fool, you never thought of this potential consequence and so you pay the price." He kicked the gasping monk out of the way with a single swift foot to the stomach and headed toward us, his robes fluttering against the snow. "The poison won't work on me, girl. I advise you to spare your sister and that pint-sized sprite by sending them away. *Now.*"

My stomach lurched. He was right. They were no match for Hyto. Even with Smoky, Vishana, and Shade, Delilah and Iris weren't equipped to take him on. I turned to them.

"He's right. Get out of the way. Now."

"We aren't leaving you." Iris held firmly to her wand.

"This isn't a question of loyalty. It's a question of self-preservation. Move, now. And if things go wrong, run as hard as you can and hope to hell you can reach the barrow before Hyto does." Pale as night, I turned away.

Delilah took Iris's hand. I could feel her watching me but didn't turn around. "Come on, Iris. Let's move back a little. She's right."

Hyto stopped about twenty yards from us, and there was a sudden shifting as he began to transform. Out of a cloud of mist and snow, a white dragon—twice as large as Smoky—rose up before us. He looked like Smoky, only his skin was more white than opalescent, and his horns were far longer; the mane on his back whipped back and forth. He crouched on all fours, staring at us, and split the air with a violent chuckle.

Terror struck me through and I stood rooted to the ground. I'd thought Smoky huge when he was in dragon form, but now I realized he was still young—he wasn't nearly the stature of his father.

Holy crap. This wasn't going to end well. I could feel it in my bones.

Vishana turned to me. "Back away. Now. Let us have room."

I realized she and Smoky were getting ready to change. Shade grabbed my hand and moved to drag me out of the way, but before he could, there was a rustle in the woods behind us. I heard Delilah let out a long cry. Iris, too.

Turning, I saw someone rushing forward. Someone I recognized.

Oh, no. Please, no. Please, don't let this happen.

There, in full battle armor, with sword held high, raced Georgio. St. George, come to battle the dragon. He stared up at Hyto, his eyes wide with wonder and anger.

"You will not pass, serpent! You will not pass! Leave the winsome Lady Camille alone."

"No! Shade, help him." I pushed Shade away from me and simultaneously yanked the unicorn horn out of my pocket, aiming it at Hyto. The winds had not worked, but he was on the ground now.

Hyto was eyeing St. George with the look of a kid eyeing a Popsicle. His long neck coiled and—

Lady of the Land, take him down!

There was a roar as the ground began to shake and the snow fell from the branches of the trees to land with a plop on the ground. A low rumble filled the area as an earthquake echoed through the valley. The ground shifted in tortuous bends, like the waves off the ocean whipped up by a gale.

Below us, on the slope, I could hear the roar of an avalanche, and I prayed no one else had been coming up the mountain. Hyto shifted from side to side, dancing as nimbly as a dragon could dance, to keep his balance as the ground rocked back and forth.

Shade raced forward, grabbing Georgio before he could take on the dragon of his dreams, and practically flew with him to where Delilah and Iris waited. I glanced back, making sure that Georgio was safe. He seemed to have fainted, which was probably for the best. The last thing we needed was his interference.

I turned back to find Smoky and Vishana holding hands. Then mother nodded to son and they began to transform. As I scrambled out of the way—I knew better than to be in the way of three angry dragons—they rose up.

Vishana was as large as Hyto—even larger. But her skin shimmered with silver and her eyes were steely and hard. She flattened several trees and bushes as she backed up to get her bearings.

Smoky was smaller than both, by far, but when I saw him from this vantage point, it seemed incredible that I'd ever been astride his back.

Hyto dipped and coiled, his neck winding as he rolled his head back, and then a hailstorm came roiling by, chilling the air and dropping the temperature further still. The pellets of ice spread out over the area, catching Smoky and his mother and moving beyond in my direction. Before I could cloak up, the stinging ice bullets began to lodge into my skin and I gritted my teeth, turning away so that they hit against my back. The cloak of the Black Beast absorbed much of their impact, but the reverb was like being hit over and over by thumbnail-sized BBs.

Vishana let out a low roar as she sprang into the sky, followed by Smoky. They circled overhead, and I had the distinct feeling they were challenging Hyto. He gave one long look in my direction, then joined them. As I watched, they spiraled in a circle.

And then came the flames, belching from Smoky's stomach, to scorch along Hyto's side. Hyto raised his head and let out a terrible shriek as the blast blackened the skin. I could hear Smoky's laughter from where I cowered, waiting.

Hyto whipped around, his tail slamming against Smoky, sending my love reeling back head over heels through the air. I gasped as he fell, through the sky, plummeting down toward the ground. But shortly before he reached the tops of the tallest firs, he pulled up short and went shooting back toward the pair of circling dragons.

Vishana charged forward, aiming directly for Hyto, her neck waving from one side to the other. As Hyto swung to meet her, she skidded in the air, whirling around, so that her tail whipped into his face. Knocked back, Hyto went spinning. He caught himself and turned in time to catch her before she could rake his side with her claws. She managed to catch one of his wings, and I saw a smear of red against the white, droplets raining down like snowflakes.

Smoky joined the fray, another belch of fire scorching Hyto's other side. Hyto returned fire and Smoky dodged the first ball of exploding flames, but the second caught him by surprise and he careened away.

The next moment, Vishana swooped over the top of Hyto, her claws trailing down and catching him along his back. He screamed, his call sending another avalanche down the slope of the mountain.

"Fuck!"

Delilah's scream caught my attention and I whirled. She was fighting Asheré, who had apparently recovered enough to grab his staff and make his way over to them. They were fighting hand-to-hand, and for a wounded monk, he was doing pretty good. Shade launched himself out of the bushes, but before he could reach them, Delilah raised Lysanthra and brought it whistling down on the rogue monk. It pierced his shoulder and drove through the bone—I could hear the splintering from where I stood.

Asheré shouted, grabbing his arm, and Iris took that moment to whisper some charm. As we watched, the monk began to shift, and I realized he was turning inside out—Iris had her powers back, all right. As his flesh split, his organs spilling to the ground, I stared at her, and she grinned and gave me a thumbs-up. A gruesome high-five before collapsing with obvious exhaustion. But it was a high-five, nonetheless, because we no longer had our mad monk to cope with.

I turned back to watch the fireworks going on in the sky. Hyto had taken a couple of direct hits and dove into a cloud bank. Where was he? Could Smoky and Vishana have dispatched him? But then I heard something behind me, and a shadow fell across me from the back. Frowning, I turned. There, barreling down out of the clouds, talons out, was Hyto, dive-bombing me.

"Motherfucking pus-bucket!" First came the anger. When would the fucking creep leave me alone? But then fear settled over the fury and I began to run, slogging through the snow. I could hear Delilah and Iris screaming, and from the side, I saw Shade heading my way.

Vishana and Smoky had flown a wide circle, searching for him, and only now were winging back, combing the thick blanket of clouds into which Hyto had vanished. I could tell by the way they were circling.

"Going somewhere?" The rough voice echoed with laughter as Hyto's talons came sweeping down to close around my waist. I screamed again, shrilly as I could to catch Smoky's attention, and struggled, pushing against the talons grasping me tight.

Hyto let out a loud bellow. "This time, you won't get away. And this time, my pretty little bitch, you're going to die. Slowly, painfully, one limb at a time."

As he launched us off the ground, I stopped trying to get him to let go. We were in the air, sailing up above the ground.

As I looked down, Shade stood there, looking helpless. He'd just reached where I'd been. Delilah and Iris were struggling forward and Asheré was a bloody blot on the ground.

I held on for dear life, clutching Hyto's leg, wondering what the fuck was going to happen now. If Smoky or Vishana attacked us, Hyto could easily cut me in half. But even as I tried to figure out a way out of this mess, I noticed that Shade had vanished. I knew he couldn't transform into his dragon shape during the day, but he'd gone into the shadows. Maybe there was something he could do from there to help.

"Are you ready for me, wench? I told you, *you belong to me*. That collar around your neck proves it. And now you're my means to an end. I know my son. And I know my wife." Hyto's voice rumbled down to me, and we spiraled higher into the sky as the snow began to fall in earnest.

Chapter 22

꧁ ❧ ꧂

Hyto kept hold of me as we sailed into the sky. I could hear Delilah and Shade screaming from the ground below, and I looked down to see them staring at us, horrified. The ground sped away at a dizzying speed, and my fear of heights began to kick in. Everything was spinning, and the only thing between me and a plummeting death was someone who hated my guts. Delightful.

As I tried to think about what I could do from my position, I heard another shriek echoing from our left. I did my best to look around and saw that Smoky was staring directly at us. He knew that Hyto had hold of me. Vishana came circling around, her great wings giving her position, even as her long, snakelike body coiled to give her purchase in the air.

Hyto hovered, his wings gently beating the air. "What are you going to do now? Going to strike me with your fire? Send me spinning to the ground? She'll be dead before you touch me."

"What do you want?" Smoky's voice echoed across the expanse.

Hyto laughed, then said. "Your life, my son. Your life. If

you choose to follow, meet me on the Cusp." And then, the world began to spin, and everything vanished in a cloud of smoke and vapor.

We were in a different realm, but it wasn't the astral, that I could tell. And it wasn't Hyto's private dreyerie. He was still in dragon form, but as we soared over tall timber, toward a misty ledge on the cliff face, I saw a cavern mouth. Great, *more caves*. I was mildly claustrophobic and with all the caves and barrows lately, all I wanted was to spend a week out under the open sky.

Hyto hovered over the ledge and let go of me about four feet off the ground. I dropped to the narrow outcropping and scrambled to catch my balance. As he was transforming, I quickly looked around for a place to run, but there was none. Unlike his other dreyerie, this place had no path leading down. The cliff was straight with granite beneath the snow. I'd never be able to climb down the rock face. I decided to chance the unknown and raced into the cave before he could lay hands on me again.

"Camille? Where the fuck did you go, girl? Get your ass back here or I guarantee, you'll be begging me for mercy when I find you!" His voice was harsh and he was panting. He must have been hurt by the attacks while in dragon form.

I glanced around, wondering where the hell I could hide. I couldn't see—coming into the darkness after the blinding light of the snow-covered mountain had the same effect as if someone had snapped a flash camera in my eyes. I stumbled ahead, holding my hands out to feel for the walls. After a moment, I made contact and I pressed against the rock, praying he wouldn't notice me until I'd found a place to hide.

"I said, get the fuck out here." And there he was—standing not ten feet away. I could see the glimmer of his robes.

Hell, what was I going to do now?

He swung around and then stopped, staring in my direction. A low, throaty chuckle told me the jig was up. "Well, well. There she is." He started for me and I backed up, fumbling in my robe for the unicorn horn. It still had some energy left in it—probably enough for one big blast. If I had to, I could bring down the cavern on both of us, and I was considering doing just that. The thought of being buried under tons of rubble wasn't all that appealing, but the thought of Hyto putting his hands on me again was even less savory.

"Leave her alone!" Smoky's voice came from the front of the cavern and then I could see him—my eyes were adjusting. "You wanted me. You have me. Let her go and I'll stay."

"No!" I shouted at him, realizing he was getting ready to make a trade. "Don't you dare! He'll kill me after he kills you. It's both of us or neither."

Hyto let out a loud snort. "She's smart for her kind. I'll give her that. She's also sweet. Her meat will be tender and delicate . . . or maybe I'll keep her around to be my toy for a while. She's very amusing when she's in pain." And then he lashed out. A jagged spear of ice came reaming out of his palms, aimed directly for my husband.

I screamed and thrust the horn in the air. Maybe none of us would come out of this alive, but Hyto would die. "Lady of the Land, hear me!"

The cavern shook violently and the spell Hyto had cast slid off target by a mere inch, but it was enough to give Smoky time to dodge it. Hyto let out a string of curses in what I could only imagine was dragonese. I grabbed for the wall as a low rumble began to shift through the cavern. There was a roar behind me, and I screamed again as rocks and rubble began to fall.

"Camille!" Smoky shouted at me, and I tried to make my way around Hyto, but the damned dragon caught hold of me with his hair and drew me toward him.

"You decide to play for keeps, then you take the consequences, girl." He wrapped his hair tight around me and I screamed as he squeezed until I could barely breathe.

The shaking went on and on, and the ceiling began to cave in, stalactites crumbling to the floor from where they had hung for a thousand years. A cloud of dust began to rise and I started to cough. I could hear Smoky shouting my name, and Hyto's horrible laughter as the world started to spin.

The roar became thunder, and the thunder a cascade of

sound and movement. I closed my eyes, trying to protect them from the debris, and held tight the unicorn horn. I just wanted everything to stop. Regardless of the consequences, I wanted it all over. I was tired of fighting Hyto, of being afraid every time I turned around. I was tired of the pain and threats, and the knowledge of how ready he was to make good on every one of his ugly promises.

"Enough," I whispered. "Moon Mother, enough. If you want me to come home to you, take me now. But please, spare Smoky and his mother. And send Hyto to the depths of the abyss."

There was another loud roar, and then the dust suddenly began to clear and I felt myself fall to the ground. I opened my eyes and saw that Hyto was screaming—I couldn't hear him through the cacophony of the falling rocks, but the long tendril of his hair that had held me up was on the ground, cut off from near his head. As I stared, droplets of blood began to flow out of the severed ends. Next to him stood Vishana, her nails long talons, dripping with blood.

I whispered to the horn, "Calm, please . . . calm the earth." And the shaking slowed to a halt. As I stood up, bruised and covered with cuts from the flying debris, Smoky struggled out of another pile of rubble. He raced over to me and pulled me into his arms, but I pushed him away.

"We aren't done yet," I said, nodding to Hyto.

Vishana turned to the white dragon, who was struggling to stand. She lifted one delicate arm and backhanded him so hard that she tore a long gash in his face. He let out a curse but fell back, leaning back against the rocks. A large stalactite that had been delicately propped against a pile of rubble shifted and fell across his legs. He was trapped by a ton of rock, and there wasn't room for him to transform into his dragon self.

Smoky stepped forward, but his mother held up her hand. "Your father's life is forfeit. But since I am here, I have the final say. This shall be done in the Dragon Reaches. Gather your wife, and I will take Hyto. Meet us in the Council chamber. Camille has first right of punishment."

First right of punishment? What did that mean? I was about to ask when Smoky merely inclined his head.

"As you wish, my Lady." He tenderly lifted me in his arms as Vishana grabbed hold of Hyto's arm and, the bedraggled dragon in hand, vanished.

I wrapped my arms around his neck. "I don't understand—what's going on? Where are we going?"

"You are going to meet my people, my love. We're going *home*. To the Dragon Reaches." And then, before I could say a word, the world again began to turn, and we spun around and around through the Ionyc Seas, just me in the arms of my beloved Smoky.

The hall was larger than I could have imagined. Picture an amphitheater large enough to seat row after row of dragons—in their natural form. Add to that a central pavilion from where Smoky told me the Wing-Liege and the Council presided. The ledges for the dragons were fashioned of a stone that reminded me of marble. One entire wall was open, missing, facing the sky, and I realized that the dragons flew in from there, landing on the spacious deck that stretched the entire front of the pavilion. The skies here were pale blue, with billowing clouds rolling across the sky. The temperature was chilly, but not icy cold like in the Northlands, and I wondered to just what realm the Dragon Reaches belonged.

As we appeared in the center of the room, there was a bustle and a number of dragons—some in their human form, others in their natural form—stopped to stare at us.

Vishana strode into the room. "Your father is being wing-strapped for now. But I have spoken to the Wing-Liege and he has already agreed: Hyto must die. The question is, who gets the first right of punishment. We will meet within two hours. You have time to rest and relax. Camille, I imagine you would like to bathe—the dust in the cavern was thick and your people do not have our natural abilities."

I stared at her, realizing she was as clean as a whistle. Same as Smoky. "What is with you dragons? How do you *do* that?"

Vishana laughed. "Iampaatar told me that you and your sisters continually badger him about his secrets. I'm afraid this one is not to be found in a detergent bottle or a washing powder. Now, Iampaatar—take your wife to my chambers. Bid my chambermaids to wait on her—whatever she needs."

"Excuse me, but the collar . . ." I left the question unfinished, merely brushing the yoke I still wore around my neck.

"That will be removed soon enough. You will never need fear wearing it again after we are done today." And then, with a gracious nod, Vishana left us, gliding over to talk to a group of other dragons, who I assumed were silvers. They had the same coloring and feel that she did.

Smoky insisted on carrying me, and I didn't object. After the past few days, being pampered was a blessing. I wrapped my arms around his neck and covered him with kisses as we headed out of the Council chamber.

The Dragon Reaches were huge—as befitted dragon-sized inhabitants. As we entered the main complex, I realized that most of the dragons were walking in human form through the corridors, but the chambers themselves were large enough in which to change shape.

Smoky carried me down one marblesque corridor, and as I gazed at the walls, I realized that as ornate as the chamber was, it was far from pretentious. The engravings on the walls were muted, tone on tone, but as I looked closer, they proved to be meticulous and I began to get the impression that they were history in motion—a pictorial history of the Dragonkin.

The light in the chambers came from open windows along the walls—huge slits that looked out onto the sky. How far up we were, I could not fathom. I felt a little giddy, but whether it was from altitude or from just the knowledge that Hyto was locked away, I didn't know.

"I hope Delilah's not too worried," I said, suddenly realizing that my sister had no clue what had happened to me. The last she saw, I'd been carried off by Hyto, and Smoky and Vishana had disappeared along with us. "I wish I could let them know I'm alive."

"They'll know soon enough. I know it's hard, my love, but we cannot leave yet. We must finish matters with Hyto." Smoky buried his face in my hair and gently kissed my

cheek. "I am so proud of you, Camille. You've been brave—
and you've kept a calmer head than I."

Saying nothing, I tightened my grip around his neck, reveling in the feel of his arms, his presence. We came to a turnoff to the left and Smoky opened the ten-foot door leading
into the chamber. As he carried me over the threshold, I let
out a little gasp.

Smoky set me down. "Welcome to my family home in the
Dragon Reaches. Your home, too—I told you on returning
from my last trip that the Council put the seal of approval on
our marriage. You are welcome here, as much as any dragon."

The room sparkled. Voluminous lengths of silver and
blue material draped across the walls, sparkling with metal-
lic threads. The same crest I remembered seeing on a shield
in Smoky's bedroom adorned the wall—a huge bas-relief
sculpture set in lapis lazuli and silver. A dragon, glancing
over his shoulder, was engraved on the front with nine silver
stars shooting out of his mouth into the sky.

Stretching over the dragon—two silver foils crossing
blades shimmered, set in silver. Beneath the dragon, nine silver snowflakes drifting down from the sky. The borders of
the crest were set in silver, with two vertical lines of knot-
work to the left of the dragon.

I slowly walked over to the crest. "Tell me. This is the one
in your barrow. You said that belonged to your father and
your grandfather . . . is this, then, Hyto's symbology?"

Smoky nodded. "It is my paternal crest, yes. But I count it
as my grandfather's more than Hyto's. Hyto did not deserve
it—he carried the shield out of obligation rather than honor.
Over there, on the other wall, is my mother's crest."

On the opposite wall, the crest was set in silver and onyx.
In the center, a dragon coiled, etched in the onyx. To the left,
five sparkling silver stars. To the right, four stars faceted from
diamonds. I gasped at the size of the diamonds—they were as
big as my fist. Overhead, nine lines of silver arched over the
dragon. Below, something had been written in silver, but I
could not read it. Instinctively, I could tell that this crest out-
weighed the other in importance—by a long, long ways.

"What does this say?" I asked, kneeling down to look at the writing.

Smoky knelt beside me and made a sign of genuflection toward the crest. His voice was low. "It says, *Dreams into action, life into death, take honor to heart, bring honor to breath*. It means . . . my mother's family is one of the oldest in the Dragon Reaches. I am truly a lord among my people. We are looked to for role models. My mother is very big on honor—which is why she married Hyto in the first place. Her father had promised . . . she could not break his promise."

I nodded. "I think I like your mother."

He smiled, then. "She is an amazing dragon, a woman who values truth over treasure. She does what needs to be done and does not flinch from duty. Come though, you should bathe and prepare yourself for the Council."

A shiver of fear ran through me. "What should I expect? What am I getting into?"

Smoky paused, then shook his head. "You will be fine. I cannot prepare you because it is expected that you come to Council as who you truly are. If I coach you and you act according to what I say, the elders will know."

Oh yeah, that made me feel better. I swatted him. "Fine, then. Give me soap and water and if you can find something that will fit me, clean clothes?"

Smoky led me to a bathing chamber with a huge marble tub that was filled with bubbling, steaming water. I stripped and he ogled me as I crawled into the dragon Jacuzzi, enjoying the whirl of froth that immediately began to ease my muscles. I leaned back against the marble, nearly falling asleep, letting the tension soak out of my body. After a moment, I noticed that Smoky had taken off his clothing and was crawling into the tub with me, a lecherous look on his face.

His long, muscled body was magnificent and I couldn't help but run my gaze over the six-foot-four icy drink of water. His hair coiled and curled, sure signs that he was ready for playtime, and one glance at his cock told me the same thing. He was standing at attention, engorged and rigid. A swell of desire broke through my weariness.

"Oh, you think you're getting some?" I couldn't help but laugh. My wounds weren't hurting as much, thanks to the Moon Mother, and the knowledge that we had Hyto strapped down and preparing to face trial made me ever so giddy. I leaned forward, crossing my arms over my breasts. "What makes you think you can crawl into my bath unasked, sir?"

"Because, you are my chosen mate, and my wife, and I know you too well—you've got that look on your face that says you're hungry for sex. I'm sorry the others aren't here. Well, I'm not, to be honest, but I know you like to play with all of us. I'll just have to be enough this time." But his eyes were twinkling and I knew he was teasing.

"You think so? What if I say I have a headache?" But at the sight of his puppy-dog face and pleading eyes, I relented. Truth was, they were all enough, at any one time. But for keeps, I did need all three of my husbands. I loved them all, and my love for them just kept growing as we were together. I couldn't imagine any other combination that would make me this happy.

I pulled him to me, and he knelt between my legs in the spacious tub, as I leaned back against the warm marble. He fastened his lips to mine, as his tongue entered my mouth, playing against my own. We kissed for a long moment, him lying atop me, my breasts pressed to his chest.

And then I pushed him back, just a little, my hands on his shoulders. "We need to talk first. We really need to talk."

He looked a little hurt and his expression stabbed into me. "Did I do something wrong? Are you not ready yet? I know Hyto's attack . . ." His voice drifted off and he stroked my face. "Do you want to wait until the collar is gone?"

"No, no, my love. It's not you, and I do want you. But we need to discuss a couple of things first. I want there to be no secrets between us." I slid up to a sitting position and took his hands in mine as he sat cross-legged in front of me.

"All right. Then what?"

As I gazed into his eyes, I couldn't help but smile. "I love you so much. I love you . . . And Trillian and Morio. You are my chosen mates, as you would say. I am a better woman because of your influences on me. Please, though, know that what happened with Vanzir . . . there was no choice. It wasn't his fault. It wasn't mine. Don't blame him—he was trying to protect me and the energy blew up in our faces. I don't want you angry at him. I would never have let him touch me like that if there had been a choice."

Smoky pressed my hand to his lips, kissing my fingers. "I realize that, now. I wanted to kill him at first . . . but then you disappeared and Trillian and Morio convinced me I was being stupid. They wanted Vanzir to help find you. And he did. I won't hurt him, my love. I'll even be nice to the demon. Just don't think badly of me."

"I could never think badly of you. You are not your father, Smoky. You are a good man—a great dragon." I stroked his face, feeling the smooth skin under my fingers. "Don't you ever have to shave?"

He shook his head. "I seldom have more than a five o'clock shadow. Green dragons tend to have facial hair—but silvers and whites, rarely. Is there anything else on your mind?"

I nodded. "Yes, love. Your father and what he did to me. Smoky, it's going to take me a long time to get rid of the memories, but the Moon Mother helped me understand my reactions to some degree—and I know that I'll come to grips with his attacks eventually. What humiliated me most was groveling at his feet—I will never bow to any man's foot again, unless it be a king or sovereign where custom dictates. And when he beat me . . ."

I paused. But he read me as if I were ink on the page.

"I will never touch you that way. I will never lay hands on you—I will not hurt you, Camille. I'm sorry . . . I wish I could wipe away what he did, but at least I can help mend the scars."

The catch in his voice broke my heart. I was not the only one who'd been hurt. Hyto had done his best to destroy both me and his son. He'd made Smoky feel helpless, feel like he could not protect his family. He'd ripped at Smoky's very sense of self. We would have to mend each other's wounds.

"My love, kiss me." I pulled him in then, hungry for his touch. He hesitated, but I pressed my lips to his.

And then his weight was against me and we were leaning

back in the bath, with him stretched out against my body. The mood shifted—we needed one another, hungry and desperate to reconnect.

"Camille . . ." He covered my face with kisses, his hair gently dipping into the water to gather me up. I wrapped my legs around his waist, not wanting to dally, wanting him to reclaim me, to leave his mark on me that I was his, not Hyto's. My nipples were taut, stiff against his chest, and he lifted both of us out of the tub.

My legs still wrapped around his waist, he carried me, with both of us dripping and wet, into a chamber off the bath. There, a bed with blue coverings waited. I scarcely glanced at the room, but on the nightstand, I saw a picture of me in a silver frame, and on the other nightstand I caught sight of a picture of me with all three of my loves on the day we brought Trillian into the marriage. Our wedding picture.

"Smoky, don't ever leave me," I whispered into his neck, as we stood by the bed.

"You're mine. Forever mine." He lay down, reaching for me. "Ride me, my love. Take control—it must be at your own pace." And then, his hair gently—ever so gently—lifted me by the waist and brought me down astride his hips.

"Hold my arms," I whispered, and two more strands rose to take hold of my wrists, stretching them wide so my back arched. Held firm, but by my own will, I could feel him waiting below me, pressing against me, making me wet I could barely stand it.

I lifted up and found his eager cock and then, with a wanton cry, slid down on him, the friction driving me wild as he thrust himself into me. I was so slick and he was deliciously thick and wide that I let out a little shriek, squirming against him as his heat began to pulsate through my body. I moaned, my head dropping back as we began to move, synchronizing rhythms.

His hair stroked my back, my sides, my face as he reached up and cupped one of my breasts, squeezing the nipple. With his other hand, he reached around, fingering my ass, slowly working his way in with his index finger. A white-hot flame shot through my body and I let out a low groan as I rode him, rocking against his hips, feeling him drive into me again and again.

We were flying. I opened my eyes to see the clouds building outside the window as we rocked. And all the pain, all the anger, all the fear dropped away as we soared. As we reached the zenith, it started to snow.

"Smoky, love me." And then I burst into tears, coming hard and fast—my entire body caught up in one giant orgasm of release.

Chapter 23

~~~

By the time I finished my bath, this time uninterrupted except by Smoky washing my back, he had found me a long silver dress to wear. It was his mother's and it dragged on the ground, but her chambermaid tried to pin it up enough so that it looked halfway presentable. I was also bustier than Vishana, and as I glanced in the mirror, I couldn't help but feel that I looked like a wanton love goddess in a makeshift toga.

"I can't wear this! What if Hotlips is at the Council?" I turned to Smoky, frowning. Hotlips had been his fiancée from an arranged marriage until he'd managed to buy her off.

He smirked. "Is her opinion really of any importance to you? It's not to me. But as you wish." He motioned to the maid—who I suspected, from the color of her eyes, was a green dragon. "Find something that *truly* fits her, please."

"Yes, Lord." The maid vanished out of the room.

"She doesn't talk much, does she?" The woman had barely said a word to me since she'd come in and found us in our second bath of the day. Her eyes had glimmered with a smile, but she'd said nothing other than to curtsey and greet me as Smoky introduced me.

"She's an indentured servant. Long ago, her father accosted my mother. The Council sentenced his family to serve my mother until the day she dies. Mother chose to train a handful of maids from the sons and daughters and leave it at that. She could have the whole damned family at her beck and call, but she doesn't abuse privileges."

"Life in the Dragon Reaches isn't easy, is it?"

"No." Smoky was dressed again by the time the maid— I never did catch her name; maybe she didn't have a public one—returned. She carried a dress similar to the one I'd tried on, but it was shorter and fit better. I slid into it, marveling at the weave of the fabric. It was warm, while appearing to almost float like silk around my body.

"This is lovely. Thank you." I gave her a warm smile and she returned it before fleeing from the room, only to return with a large platter filled with meats, cheese, and bread. We ate silently.

We were just finishing up the last of the loaf when a soft chime rang through the chamber. Smoky stood, motioning for me to join him. "Time to go. That's the sound that means the Council will convene shortly."

As we headed out the door, I wondered what was going to happen. And how. Images tumbled through my mind, broken bits of Hyto's sneering face, his grasping hands . . . but then it was all moot as we came to the Council chamber and entered.

There, in the center of the floor, lay Hyto, in dragon form. His wings were strapped back, in a rigid framework that looked like a combination of steel and wood and rope. The frame held them in what had to be a painful position. A ball gagged his mouth, strapped over his muzzle, and he could do nothing but thrash on the floor. For all of his sins, I was horrified as I realized just how much humiliation and pain the setup provided. But at a flash of memory of groveling at his feet . . . my horror vanished and I breathed out a long sigh.

Atop the podium were a group of five silver dragons, the center one being the largest dragon in the entire place. He had to be the Wing-Liege. The others gave the air of nobility and I figured they must make up the presiding Council members. The Emperor was nowhere in sight.

As I looked around the stadium, the ledges were filling with dragons, most in their natural form. Vishana was standing to the side, in her dragon form, and as Smoky saw her, he, too, stepped back, and within seconds my husband had transformed into his natural bent.

I was beginning to feel conspicuous.

After a few minutes, the Wing-Liege let out a loud roar and chimes rang through the amphitheater. Everyone quieted down. Then came a spate of words in a language I did not understand. Shortly after that, a flash of shimmers and the entire Council, Smoky, and his mother shifted into human form. The Wing-Liege spoke again, and Hyto shifted, the wingstrap contraption now pinning him to the ground with its weight. What appeared to be a set of guards moved forward to remove it and to hold him in check. Hyto gave me a long look, but he said nothing, did nothing. Simply challenged me with his gaze.

The Wing-Liege spoke again.

"We will stand in this form today because the complainant's daughter-in-law is involved in the proceedings, and she is not of Dragonkin blood. She is, however, sealed into our society by marriage, and therefore has the right to attend this Council."

I wanted to thank him but decided to keep my mouth shut. It was too easy to stick my foot in and turn up the temperature.

As the Wing-Liege began to read off something that had been imprinted on a scroll, I phased out. It sounded like an exceedingly boring list of rules and regulations, and although I wanted to pay attention, I had no energy left. I was tired. I was still hurting, and I was worried about the others. Did they think I was dead? Were my sisters trying to track me down?

An hour later the Wing-Liege turned to me and I snapped back to attention. Compared to Hyto, he looked positively old. I was ready to drop—I was exhausted and could barely think. He smiled, his lips pulling back in a feral grin.

"You bear our lengthy discourse with grace, Camille, wife of Iampaatar. We thank you for this—I know you must be weary. But the formalities are done and I would now read the charges against Hyto. If you have any to add, please, feel free after I am finished." And then he stood and I forced myself to shake out of it and pay attention.

The Wing-Liege moved around the dais till he was standing in front of Hyto, who was being held upright by two guards.

"Hyto, you were cast out of the Dragon Reaches on pain of death. You were sent forth to mend your ways. You were recently caught attempting to murder Vishana, she who denied you, but we gave you one last chance and allowed you your life. For that breach alone, we should have put you to death. But your sins are long and numerous."

Hyto started to speak, but the Wing-Liege raised his hand and a crackle of lightning played over his lips. Hyto let out a shriek and closed his mouth.

"You kidnapped the wife of Lord Iampaatar. You abused her, raped her, beat her, and forced your collar around her neck. The penalties for those crimes: death. You attacked your son and would have killed him if you could. The penalty for that crime: death. You have lost any lenience we might have given you. You have lost the right to speak in your own behalf."

He turned back to the Council. "Lady Vishana has given the first right of punishment to her daughter-in-law. Does this meet with your approval?"

The other dragons whispered among themselves. One stood, pushing his chair back. "It does, Your Lordship."

The Wing-Liege turned to me. "Lady Camille Sepharial te Maria D'Artigo, wife of Lord Iampaatar, you have the first right of punishment. Name Hyto's method of death, or if you wish to strike the final blow yourself, that is within your right."

I gulped. They were giving me the choice of how Hyto would die? Even offering me the chance to kill him myself?

Feeling awkward and thrust into the spotlight, I walked up to my enemy and stared him in the face. I'd killed before, and been glad to see some of them die. But this was Smoky's father, and I'd be ordering his death in cold blood.

Hyto gazed down at me, the sneer still on his face. "Do you have the courage to order my death? You'd better, girl, because if you don't, I'll be back. I'll be after you until the day I die. I'll kill everyone you love. I'll destroy everything you hold dear. I'll rip you to bits, first through your emotions and then by your body. You are my she-devil and I will not rest until I've driven you so far into oblivion that you can never reach daylight."

He meant what he said. If they locked him up, he'd find a way out. His hatred would sustain him. There was no choice—Hyto had to die. And my responsibility included ordering his death. Vishana would, if I couldn't bring myself to, or Smoky, but this was *my* battle. Hyto had injured *me* and it was *my* duty to claim punishment.

I turned to the waiting dragons—now my people as much as the Fae or the humans. I had married into a powerful clan, and they weren't squeamish. I couldn't afford to be weak in their eyes . . . nor in my own.

I turned back to Hyto. "I will not raise my own hand to you—I will never sully myself by touching you again. But I claim your death—for Lady Vishana, for Lord Iampaatar, and for myself. I claim your death through a quick, clean bolt of lightning." I would not lower myself to his level. As much as I'd wanted to torture him—to make him scream the way he'd made me scream, I would not become what he had become—a sadist.

The Wing-Liege motioned for me to look at him. "Is this your will? That Hyto die by lightning?"

"It is." I glanced over at Smoky and Vishana, and they both gave me long smiles, nodding their approval. Apparently, I'd passed yet another test.

"Then I pronounce sentence. Hyto, you will die by lightning. Now, here, before another day passes." Apparently dragons didn't wait around once they'd made decisions.

Two poles were brought to the center of the pavilion and placed in holes in the floor to hold them upright. Hyto's arms and legs were fastened with manacles, spreading them wide.

His hair moved wildly, but where Vishana had severed the long thick strand, blood had crusted over. I suddenly understood—their hair was part of their bodies. It had a life of its own because it wasn't just dead keratin.

Hyto said nothing—not another word. He simply grinned his sickly smile, watching me the entire time as they lashed him to the poles. The dragons on the tiers were murmuring, but I got no sense that they were enjoying this. It wasn't some Roman arena, or goblin death match. This was justice, and they were witnesses to it being carried out.

I looked up to find Smoky and his mother standing by my side. Smoky took my hand and I suddenly felt horrible. I'd just sentenced his father to die. But he gazed down at me and squeezed my fingers.

"It's all right," he leaned down to whisper. "This was long coming, and not your fault. You simply got caught in the crossfire."

"My son is correct." Vishana leaned down on my other side. "Blame not yourself, Camille. Hyto brought this on himself. He taught me a lot about what not to do—how not to be." She smiled gently and reached out to cup my chin. "You are lovely . . . granted, at first, I would have rather Iampaatar married a dragon—but that matters no longer. You are family. You will bring your sisters here to meet my children."

I swallowed. That was going to be one hell of a dinner party. "You know my sister Delilah is in love with a half shadow dragon." I blurted it out before I realized what I was saying.

Vishana laughed. "Yes, remember? We met. And he seems a refined gentleman. The coming years should prove interesting."

And then the chimes rang. The Wing-Liege motioned for us to stand quiet. He turned to Hyto and held out his hands, palms up. A hush descended on the hall.

"To walk freely in the halls of the Dragon Reaches means to abide by its rules. You have broken your vows. You have dishonored the halls. You have dishonored your race. You have dishonored your name. You have cast yourself out by your actions. You are cursed to wander the abyss, barred from the Shining Stars forever. You will walk in limbo, your spirit forever bound to wander between the worlds. Your name will be stricken from the Halls of Records and you will be expunged from the History, placed among the exiles. Hyto, you are no more the son of your father. You are no more the father of your sons and daughters. You are denied on all sides. You are no longer of the hive. You are alone. You were pronounced pariah. Now you are pronounced cast to oblivion."

And then, with a single gesture, a bolt of lightning struck out from his palm, forking over Hyto like a net, sparking and glowing as it seared into his body. Hyto began to scream as smoke rose from his robes and his hair caught fire. Still the lightning played across him, until his pale skin was black with crust. And then the wind gusted through, as the lightning stopped, and he crumpled to ashes, and the wild breeze caught him up and swept him away, out of the Dragon Reaches, into the softly falling snow.

At that moment, my collar loosened and fell to the floor. I was free.

After that, it was a blur of voices and meetings, of the Wing-Liege declaring that everything from Smoky's grandfather would pass to him. And then of Smoky speaking up, convincing them we needed to go home, and of Vishana handing me a wrapped gift, whispering that it was a temporary wedding gift and a better one would follow.

"One more thing," the Wing-Liege said, holding up his hand. "Lady Camille, you have the right to claim damages for what happened to you. We should not have let him go free when he tried to kill Vishana and are we indirectly responsible for his assault on you. We owe you reparations. What would you ask? Jewels? Gold? A home of your own here in the Dragon Reaches?"

I stared at the man, at his stance, at the emblems he wore denoting his rank. He'd just offered me the key to the kingdom. Then glanced over at my mother-in-law. She believed in honor. She'd been just and fair with me.

"Sir, Lady . . . gold and gems are lovely, but they do not

bring lasting joy. I have a home back Earthside. And one here—my husband's home is enough for me. But what I would ask . . . You know of our war against the demons? Smo—Lord Iampaatar told me that much."

"We do."

"Then I ask a boon. I ask that when—*if*—we need your help to fight against the demons, the dragons will come to our aid. That you will be on our side in the demonic war we're fighting."

The Wing-Liege sucked in a deep breath, but then he smiled, full lipped and sensuous. "Lady Camille, such a request is greater by far than our most brilliant gems. But it is also one we cannot—and will not—refuse. Consider us your allies."

And then we were surrounded again, by dragons on all sides in their human forms, wanting to meet me, wanting to congratulate us on surviving Hyto's attacks.

After another half hour, we were able to slip away.

"I need to get home. They must be frantic with worry."

"Patience, love. We can go now. But sometime, we'll come back and explore, and you can truly get a feel for how grand this place is."

I already had a feel for it but decided to play along. Smoky was proud of his home, and well he should be. I wrapped my arms around his neck, holding the wedding present between us, as he swept me up and we whirled our way into the Ionyc Seas and returned to the barrow.

As soon as we came out of it, I just wanted to sleep. The Ionyc Seas always made me tired, but I couldn't let it stop me—I had to get inside and—

"Camille! It's Camille and Smoky! They're alive!" Iris was standing outside the door, and she screamed to the others inside when she saw us. A little unsteady on my feet, I made my way over to her and caught her in my arms and she reached for me, holding her tight. The next moment a teary-eyed Delilah came bounding out, followed by everyone else. We stood in the freezing snow, hugging, all talking at once.

"We thought you were dead. I was getting ready to go to Y'Elestrial to see if your soul statue was still unbroken. We thought . . . we thought . . ." Delilah burst into huge sobs and Shade pulled her into his arms.

"Enough!" Smoky's voice thundered over the mayhem. "Everyone inside so we can tell you what happened."

As we entered the barrow, I saw that Hanna was up, a haunted look on her face. And there were Georgio and Estelle. Thank gods for Shade. He'd saved our poor friend, and I would forever love him for that. I was tired of collateral damage. Hurt me? Fine. Hurt my friends? Not so much.

Everybody settled down, and I realized that we were near sunset. "Give it ten minutes until Menolly is up—I don't want to have to repeat this."

"Nice dress," Trillian said, his eyes shining at me. "You are so beautiful. I was so worried, my love."

"Make that two of us," Morio said, forcing his way out of the wheelchair. "I don't know what I'd do without you."

I kissed him first, then pushed him back into the chair. "Sharah says you need another two weeks in that, buster. So sit down. And this dress"—I turned to Trillian—"was a gift from my mother-in-law." Then, after kissing *him*, I turned around to see Menolly standing at the edge of the chasm behind the living room, holding a very playful Maggie.

"What happened while I was asleep? Something, obviously."

I let out a laugh, and then, with Smoky's help, told them everything that happened. Well, almost everything. We left our lovemaking out of it. Trillian and Morio could know, but not everybody wanted or needed to hear that much detail. Sometimes TMI *was* TMI.

"So, he's dead." Delilah glanced up at me. "Are you going to be okay?"

"Yeah, I am. I will. It may take some time, but Hyto can't hurt us again."

"Unless his ghost makes a visit," Morio mumbled. "He's been cursed to limbo. We'd better put up wards. I don't want any more angry ghosts or hungry ghosts popping in to say hi. Especially a dragon's spirit."

Choosing to push *that* thought out of my mind, I sucked in a deep breath. "Tomorrow night is the Solstice. I enter Aeval's Court. After what I went through with Hyto, I think I'm ready. And I'm ready to start hunting down Telazhar. Give me demons and spirit seals any day over an angry dragon."

Smoky pulled me onto his lap as we sat at the table. "Speaking of dragons, my mother likes you. Open your wedding present. She is sending us something else later on—this is just to tide you over."

I stared at the box he held out, wondering what it was. As I untied the ribbon and unfolded the silk wrapped around the box, I thought about what family meant. The dragons were now our allies. And they were part of my family. Smoky wanted to have a child, to cement our bonds. Though I wasn't the mothering type, I was beginning to see the wisdom of this, the politics of it, and . . . it would make him happy.

Perhaps when the war was over . . . when things were safer . . . but then, I'd have to have Trillian's child first if I had one from Smoky, and then Morio's. It would mean a lot of trouble and nannies because, although I knew I'd make a good mother emotionally, I wasn't the type to be a stay-at-home mom. Minivans and soccer practice and picket fences weren't my speed.

But for now the whole question was moot. We were a long way from winning the war. And we were a long way from knowing we'd even survive the next battle.

I shook thoughts of the future out of my head and opened the box. Inside, I found a silver-framed plaque. It was Vishana's family crest, and imprinted beneath the crest, written in silver, was my name. She had truly accepted me. I was part of her clan.

Chapter 24
❦❧

The next night, I drove out to Talamh Lonrach Oll and parked in the parking lot. A horse-drawn carriage waited for me, and I climbed inside, dressed in the robe of the Black Beast, beneath which I wore nothing but the perfumes and lotions with which I'd oiled my skin. The spent horn rested in the robe's pocket, and I carried the silver-knobbed staff that Aeval had given me.

The cart wound its way, not to the palace, but out into the land itself, through the snow to a trellised archway that led to a modest cottage. I thanked the driver and stepped out, a shiver of anticipation running through me.

The moon was a shimmering quarter, waxing as she smiled down onto the snow. The sparkling mantle of white stretched through the woodland, mirroring the stars that shone over the blackened night. In my heart, I could hear the beat of the land, the pulse of the magic that filled the Court of the Queens. The whisper of the elements swirled around me, a cacophony on the wind, weaving a dance as I skirted the cottage and followed the path beyond it toward the steaming pool in the center of Faerie.

Everything shimmered here—from the woodland to the ground, to the very air. And my magic hummed, alive and vibrant. The Moon Mother surrounded me, my heart and soul. This night—the Winter Solstice—I would take my place as her priestess.

Tears flowed down my cheeks as I remembered my first initiation, when I'd entered the Grove of the Moon Mother over in Otherworld, bound by silver chains, not knowing whether my Lady would accept me into her service as a Moon Witch.

Now, I was growing, changing. I would become the first Earthside High Priestess of the Moon Mother in thousands of years. I would train under the Earthside Fae Queens—in Aeval's Dark Court, under Morgaine's watchful eye.

Tears flecked my eyes. I was about to assume a mantle both heavy and brilliant, one of which I hoped I was worthy. Thank gods and Earthside technology for waterproof mascara and lip lacquer. I dashed the tears away and stepped forward, crunching in the frozen snow, pins and needles shooting through my bare feet. I would come to my Lady with both body and feet bare as the day I was born.

How many years since I'd walked this path—back home in Otherworld—the path to my initiation as a witch for the Moon Mother? Too many to count, but now I was ready to take the next step on my journey, a thousand miles from where I'd begun, a world away from where I'd come.

The hush of the forest rested around me, the snow muffling all sound as I came to the edge of the hot springs, dropped my cape, and stepped into the steaming pool. Here, the water was brilliant, glowing a deep sea green. How they managed to heat it, I didn't know, but magic permeated the glade.

As the warmth began to seep into my frozen limbs, a sense of purification and cleansing raced through me, and as the water hit my knees, it washed away the lingering pain of my bruises, of Hyto's abuse, of the fear that had held me in its grips. His abuse fell away in the magic of the night.

Another step, and another.

The water hit my waist and my heart lurched. After this night, I'd forever be pariah in my home city-state, but some things were greater than blood, some oaths more binding than family. I mentally sent my father a kiss, wishing him well, tears pouring as I relinquished his birthright, his legacy, and his love for a greater passion and allegiance.

Another step, two more . . . and I spread my arms for balance, my shoulders shimmering beneath the glistening surface.

The water splashed against my breasts, and images of Smoky and Morio and Trillian filled my thoughts. Bowing my head with gratitude for the loves of my life, I reached out for them, but even a link as strong as ours could not penetrate the magic of the Fae Queens. I thought of Delilah and Menolly, and Iris . . . and began to cry in earnest. They could not be here tonight—this was a journey I had to make on my own—but I knew they were with me in spirit.

One more step and I was at the center of the pool. The water lapped at my chin, and I sucked in a deep breath and ducked under, letting it stream through my hair. As I came up, gasping for breath, I saw *them*, standing there on the other side of the pond, waiting for me.

Aeval—my new Mistress. I would belong to the Court of Darkness and Shadow from here on out. I would be under her will and walk with her under the Dark Moon. And beside her—her opposite. Titania, Queen of the Light. To her left, Morgaine—my half-Fae, half-human ancient cousin, Queen of the Dusk, who was now my teacher.

And, a little ways away, in full riding outfit and crop, stood Derisa, the High Priestess of the Moon Mother from Otherworld. She had taken my oath so many years ago. And she would take my new oath—the one binding me as a member of the Priestesshood.

They waited, these four, and as I made my way to them, a flash of snow lightning crashed behind them and there, in their midst, stood the Black Unicorn and Raven Mother for just a second, before they faded out of sight.

The Queens of Fae began to laugh, wild and free, and I swallowed my fear. There was no going back. There would be no chance to return from here.

And then I saw *him*—hiding in the shadows. My heart

skipped a beat as he raised one hand in salute, his spiky platinum hair shining under the pale moon.

What was he doing here? But there was no time for questions. I had to trust in the ritual. I had to trust that Aeval knew what she was doing. I had to trust Derisa, and most of all, I had to trust the Moon Mother.

Sucking in another long breath, I steadily began my journey out of the pool, toward a ritual so secret I would never be able to tell anyone what went on. I began my journey into the arms of the dark . . . into the shadow of the unknown.

We were gathered around the Yule tree, the room lit only by the sparkling lights that glittered on the tree and around the windows. I glanced around, thinking that our living room, once spacious, was now crowded with our family. Crowded with chaos and love. In the corner, Nerissa and Menolly curled in the oversized chair, whispering together.

Shouts echoed from the coffee table—Delilah, Shade, Rozurial, and Vanzir were sitting cross-legged around it, playing some card game that seemed to require slapping the table every minute or so. Vanzir raised his gaze to meet mine and a smile played at the corners of his lips before he turned his attention back to the game.

Iris and Maggie played beneath the tree, the lights glowing like a halo around them. Maggie was enjoying her new doll. G.I. Joe and Yobie were apparently kissing cousins. I snorted, wondering what the hell the good ol' boys' brigade would think of that mashup.

A noise from the kitchen made us all look toward the archway, where Trillian and Bruce appeared, carrying trays filled with sugar cookies and hot cocoa and fudge. Delilah's eyes lit up like she hadn't seen food for days.

"Bring me some of that, please," Morio said. He was feeling strong enough to sit in the rocking chair, and though I saw the glances darting between him and Menolly, I took a deep breath and let it go. Life happened. My sister had saved my husband and it had created a bond that we still didn't understand. But he was alive, thanks to her.

As Bruce handed Morio a mug of hot cocoa, I turned to Smoky. I was sitting on his lap on the sofa, his hand on my thigh beneath my skirt. His hair played lightly around my shoulders, touching me as if he were reassuring himself I was there.

The snow was falling gently outside; we could see it drifting lazily to the ground, and I was about to suggest a moonlight walk when Delilah jumped up.

"I want to give Camille her present now," she said.

I grinned. "But we already exchanged gifts . . . granted, a day later than the Solstice, but you gave me a M.A.C. gift certificate."

She shook her head, grinning. "That wasn't your real present. I needed Shade's help to get you this one. And I'm so glad I did, considering what you gave me. Thank you, Camille. I never would have bought this for myself." With a sideways glance at the bottle of Chanel No. 5—our mother's perfume—that I'd given her, she smiled shyly.

Curious, now, wondering what could require Shade's help to purchase, I slid off Smoky's lap and leaned forward. "What is it?"

Delilah nodded to Shade, who sucked in a deep breath and held out his hands. A shadow slowly filtered out of his fingers to settle in front of me, and out of the shadow walked . . . a cat? But it looked different—ever so slightly ghostly, caught between the physical and the astral.

At my look of confusion, Shade said, "There are many creatures wandering the Netherworld who don't realize they're dead. We help some of them cross over, but others, like this little girl, prefer to just remain in between."

The shadow cat, a long-haired gray girl, leaped up on my lap. I could feel her energy, almost as if she really had weight, and she leaned against me, purring. Hesitantly, I ran my hand along her side. She was just corporeal enough for me to feel a faint wash of silk under my hands. When she rubbed her chin against my boobs, I knew I was lost.

"She's beautiful . . . and loving."

"She isn't ready to move on—but she misses people. She was looking for a person, and when I told Delilah about her, she thought you might just be the one. For one thing, with you working death magic, you can sense spirits easier, so she can manifest for you." Shade smiled as I broke into a wide grin.

"And for another thing, she doesn't set off my territorial instincts. And I knew you wanted a kitty so bad." Delilah beamed at me and leaned forward.

I took her hands and kissed her, the cat between us.

"What are you going to name her? And thank goodness I won't have another litter box to look after," Iris said.

We all laughed, as I stroked the shadow cat, wondering what to call her. But then it was obvious. "I'm going to call her Misty. I just hope she sticks around . . ." I was already in love with the little creature, and the fact that she was spirit and not flesh didn't bother me. The spirit world was just as real as ours. We'd all found that out in one way or another.

As Misty ran over to Morio and jumped on his lap, I took a deep breath. This—family and their love—this was the best medicine I could have to heal me up. I prayed we'd be able to make it last.

THREE WEEKS LATER . . .

I was packing a bag, getting ready for a brief weekend away with my husbands. Morio was on his feet again, and we were ready for a quiet break. We were only going over to Bainbridge Island to stay in a condo for the weekend and walk on the beach, but it sounded like heaven to me.

Iris came in and sat on the bed next to me. Misty snuggled up on her lap. The little cat had manifested enough so everybody in the house could see her. Maggie played great games of chase with her but never could lay a finger on her, so there was no worry there.

I glanced over at Iris, smiling. "How's Hanna adjusting?"

"She's doing great. She's decided to stay for a while and is quickly learning the ways of this world. I think she's afraid to go home, afraid she'll never find her daughters again. Or worse, that she'll find out they died. She keeps saying she's used to far harder work than this, and I tell you, I'm grateful for the help. With as many people as we have living here now, it's been getting unwieldy."

"I know; I'm glad she's agreed to stay." I paused, brushing the smooth weave of the skirt I'd just packed. "I'm so looking forward to this vacation."

"I know, and I'm glad you're taking it. The four of you need some time together, without the rest of us around." She paused, then added, "I've something to tell you." Iris flashed me a fair grin. She looked radiant, and I attributed it to having that monkey of a curse off her back.

"What's up?" I prayed it wasn't something that would keep us from going on our trip.

"Nothing major . . . don't worry. You will have your fun on the beach with no interference, even if it is cold." She sighed. "Perhaps we'll catch a break this weekend while you're gone, and find a lead to Telazhar."

So far, all our searching for Telazhar and the Bog Eater had come to a big fat zero, though Vanzir thought he might be on the trail of one of the spirit seals. We'd been looking high and low for signs of the sorcerer the past few weeks, and the rogue portal, and the Bog Eater, but had struck out on all three counts.

I folded another skirt into the suitcase, then tucked in perfume, bath oil, body wash, and whatever else I could fit.

"We need to find something soon. I don't trust this lull. So, what is it you wanted to tell me?" I zipped up the case and lowered it to the floor. My bruises were almost gone, and although my back had scarred, it wasn't terribly noticeable unless I was under harsh light.

She broke a little smile. "Oh, just that it's a good thing Hanna decided to stay, because we're going to need her more than ever soon enough. Also, that we'll be needing to build the house for Bruce and me sooner than we thought. We're getting married on Valentine's Day. I want you to officiate at the wedding, if you would. Be our priestess?"

"*Valentine's Day?* That soon? Of course I'll be your priestess! But why the rush, if I might ask? And I know you need a house—we're really outgrowing ours with all the additions to the family . . . but there's room for Bruce until we get yours built." I grinned at her. "You really love him, don't you?"

The Talon-haltija broke out into that milkmaid smile that lit up her face and she ducked her head, her golden hair shimmering in the light. "Yes, I do. Though there might be room for Bruce here, well . . . the reason we're getting married early, and going to need our own cottage right away, is that . . . well . . . I'm going to have a baby."

Baby? I straightened up, and then I understood why she looked so radiant. "You're pregnant?"

She nodded. "I've known for a week. It happened so quickly. I thought it might take quite some time after the curse was lifted—but apparently the gods had other plans. The first time after we came back, I guess . . . well . . . *bingo.* Oh Camille, *I'm going to be a mother* and I wanted you to be the first to know, after Bruce! You were there for me when I broke the curse, when I needed help. You've always been there for me."

And then she started to cry. And I started to cry. I pulled her into my arms and held her tight, kissing her cheeks, joining her as she let out a peal of laughter.

"We have to tell the others. You come now, come downstairs with me and let me make you some tea. From now on, little mother, you get special treatment. Hanna—that's why you're so glad Hanna's here!"

Iris nodded. "Yes, she can help with Maggie and the cooking and cleaning. I love our little gargoyle, but I won't be able to let her near the baby. Not until they both grow up a bit."

As we headed down the stairs, I thought about what this meant. Even in the midst of darkness and snow, in the midst of demons and men who were so full of hate they had to torture others to make themselves feel better, life could spring forth and bring a ray of joy into the world. As long as there was love, there was hope. And where there was hope . . . there was possibility.

We gathered everyone around the table. Smoky was holding Maggie, who was playing cat's cradle—or her own particular form of it—with his hair.

As Iris told the others her news, I stood back, watching my family. Watching my lovers, my sisters, my brothers-by-choice. We were a community. We were connected even though we all had our separate lives.

Delilah and Menolly slipped over to my side and took my hands, and I leaned my head on Delilah's shoulder. We were truly all forking out onto our own paths. Delilah had Shade and the Autumn Lord and her training as a Death Maiden. Menolly was getting ready to pledge herself to Nerissa, and she and Roman had been going to a lot of vampire events lately. And I—I had Smoky, Morio, and Trillian, and the Court of the Three Queens. Add on top of that, we were *all* fighting a war, with all the skirmishes in between.

But come what may, we were forever together.

We would always be sisters.

CAST OF MAJOR CHARACTERS

The D'Artigo Family

Sephreh ob Tanu: The D'Artigo Sisters' father. Full Fae.

Maria D'Artigo: The D'Artigo Sisters' mother. Human.

Camille Sepharial te Maria, aka Camille D'Artigo: The oldest sister; a Moon Witch. Half-Fae, half-human.

Delilah Maria te Maria, aka Delilah D'Artigo: The middle sister; a werecat.

Arial Lianan te Maria: Delilah's twin who died at birth. Half-Fae, half-human.

Menolly Rosabelle te Maria, aka Menolly D'Artigo: The youngest sister; a vampire and *jian-tu*: extraordinary acrobat. Half-Fae, half-human.

Shamas ob Olanda: The D'Artigo girls' cousin. Full Fae.

The D'Artigo Sisters' Lovers and Close Friends

Bruce O'Shea: Iris's fiancé. Leprechaun.

Carter: Leader of the Demonica Vacana Society, a group that watches and records the interactions of Demonkin and human through the ages. Carter is half demon and half Titan-his father was Hyperion, one of the Greek Titans.

Chase Garden Johnson: Detective, director of the Faerie-Human Crime Scene Investigation (FH-CSI) team. Human who has taken the Nectar of Life, which extends his life span beyond any ordinary mortal and has opened up his psychic abilities.

Chrysandra: Waitress at the Wayfarer Bar & Grill. Human.

Derrick Means: Bartender at the Wayfarer Bar & Grill. Werebadger.

Erin Mathews: Former president of the Faerie Watchers Club and owner of the Scarlet Harlot Boutique. Turned into a vampire by Menolly, her sire, moments before her death. Human.

Greta: Leader of the Death Maidens; Delilah's tutor.

Hanna: One of the Northmen. She was held captive by Hyto for five years and helped Camille escape, returning Earthside with her.

Iris Kuusi: Friend and companion of the girls. Priestess of Undutar. Talon-haltija (Finnish house sprite).

Lindsey Katharine Cartridge: Director of the Green Goddess Women's Shelter. Pagan and witch. Human.

Marion: Coyote shifter; owner of the Supe-Urban Café.

Morio Kuroyama: One of Camille's lovers and husbands. Essentially the grandson of Grandmother Coyote. Youkai-kitsune (roughly translated: Japanese fox demon).

Nerissa Shale: Menolly's lover. Worked for DSHS. Now working for Chase Johnson as a victims-rights counselor for the FH-CSI. Werepuma and member of the Rainier Puma Pride.

Roman: Ancient vampire; son of Blood Wyne, Queen of the Crimson Veil.

Rozurial, aka Roz: Mercenary. Menolly's secondary lover. Incubus who used to be Fae before Zeus and Hera destroyed his marriage.

Shade: New ally. Delilah's lover. Part Stradolan, part black (shadow) dragon.

Sharah: Elfin medic; Chase's new girlfriend.

Siobhan Morgan: One of the girls' friends. Selkie (wereseal); member of the Puget Sound Harbor Seal Pod.

Smoky: One of Camille's lovers and husbands. Half-white, half-silver dragon.

Tavah: Guardian of the portal at the Wayfarer Bar & Grill. Vampire (Full Fae).

Tim Winthrop, aka Cleo Blanco: Computer student/genius, female impersonator. Human.

Trillian: Mercenary. Camille's alpha lover. Svartan (one of the Charming Fae).

Vanzir: Indentured slave to the Sisters, by his own choice. Dream-chaser demon.

Venus the Moon Child: Shaman of the Rainier Puma Pride.
  Werepuma. One of the Keraastar Knights.
Wade Stevens: President of Vampires Anonymous. Vampire
  (human).
Zachary Lyonnesse: Junior member of the Rainier Puma
  Pride Council of Elders. Werepuma.

GLOSSARY

Black Unicorn/Black Beast: Father of the Dahns unicorns, a magical unicorn that is reborn like the phoenix and lives in Darkynwyrd and Thistlewyd Deep. Raven Mother is his consort, and he is more a force of nature than a unicorn.

Calouk: The rough, common dialect used by a number of Otherworld inhabitants.

Court and Crown: "Crown" refers to the queen of Y'Elestrial. "Court" refers to the nobility and military personnel that surround the Queen. "Court and Crown" together refer to the entire government of Y'Elestrial.

Court of the Three Queens: The newly risen Court of the three Earthside Fae Queens: Titania, the Fae Queen of Light and Morning; Morgaine, the half-Fae Queen of Dusk and Twilight; and Aeval, the Fae Queen of Shadow and Night.

Crypto: One of the Cryptozoid races. Cryptos include creatures out of legend that are not technically of the Fae races: gargoyles, unicorns, gryphons, chimeras, and so on. Most primarily inhabit Otherworld, but some have Earthside cousins.

Demon Gate: A gate through which demons may be summoned by a powerful sorcerer or necromancer.

Dreyerie: A dragon lair.

Earthside: Everything that exists on the Earth side of the portals.

Elqaneve: The Elfin lands in Otherworld.

Elemental Lords: The elemental beings—both male and female—who, along with the Hags of Fate and the Harvestmen, are the only true Immortals. They are avatars of various elements and energies, and they inhabit all realms. They do as they will and seldom concern themselves with humankind or Fae unless summoned. If asked for help, they often exact steep prices in return. The Elemental Lords are not concerned with balance like the Hags of Fate.

FBH: Full-Blooded Human (usually refers to Earthside humans).

FH-CSI: The Faerie-Human Crime Scene Investigation team. The brainchild of Detective Chase Johnson, it was first formed as a collaboration between the OIA and the Seattle police department. Other FH-CSI units have been created around the country, based on the Seattle prototype. The FH-CSI takes care of both medical and criminal emergencies involving visitors from Otherworld.

Great Divide: A time of immense turmoil when the Elemental Lords and some of the High Court of Fae decided to rip apart the worlds. Until then, the Fae existed primarily on Earth, their lives and worlds mingling with those of humans. The Great Divide tore everything asunder, splitting off another dimension, which became Otherworld. At that time, the Twin Courts of Fae were disbanded and their queens stripped of power. This was the time during which the Spirit Seal was formed and broken in order to seal off the realms from each other. Some Fae chose to stay Earthside, others moved to the realm of Otherworld, and the demons were—for the most part—sealed in the Subterranean Realms.

Guard Des'Estar: The military of Y'Elestrial.

Hags of Fates: The women of destiny who keep the balance righted. Neither good nor evil, they observe the flow of destiny. When events get too far out of balance, they step in and take action, usually using humans, Fae, Supes, and other creatures as pawns to bring the path of destiny back into line.

Harvestmen: The lords of death—a few cross over and are also Elemental Lords. The Harvestmen, along with their followers (the Valkyries and the Death Maidens, for example) reap the souls of the dead.

Haseofon: The abode of the Death Maidens—where they stay and where they train.

Ionyc Lands: The astral, etheric, and spirit realms, along with several other lesser-known noncorporeal dimensions, form the Ionyc Lands. These realms are separated by the Ionyc Seas, a current of energy that prevents the Ionyc Lands from colliding, thereby sparking off an explosion of universal proportions.

Ionyc Seas: The current of energy that separates the Ionyc Lands. Certain creatures, especially those connected with the elemental energies of ice, snow, and wind, can travel through the Ionyc Seas without protection.

Koyanni: The coyote shifters who took an evil path away from the Great Coyote; followers of Nukpana.

Melosealfôr: A rare Crypto dialect learned by powerful Cryptos and all Moon Witches.

The Nectar of Life: An elixir that can extend the life span of humans to nearly the length of a Fae's years. Highly prized and cautiously used. Can drive someone insane if he or she doesn't have the emotional capacity to handle the changes incurred.

OIA: The Otherworld Intelligence Agency; the "brains" behind the Guard Des'Estar.

Otherworld/OW: The human term for the "United Nations" of Faerie Land. A dimension apart from ours that contains creatures from legend and lore, pathways to the gods, and various other places, such as Olympus. Otherworld's actual name varies among the differing dialects of the many races of Cryptos and Fae.

Portal, Portals: The interdimensional gates that connect the different realms. Some were created during the Great Divide; others open up randomly.

Seelie Court: The Earthside Fae Court of Light and Summer, disbanded during the Great Divide. Titania was the Seelie Queen.

Soul Statues: In Otherworld, small figurines created for the Fae of certain races and magically linked with the baby. These figurines reside in family shrines and when one of the Fae dies, their soul statue shatters. In Menolly's case, when she was reborn as a vampire, her soul statue re-formed, although twisted. If a family member disappears, his or her family can always tell if their loved one is alive or dead if they have access to the soul statue.

Spirit Seals: A magical crystal artifact, the Spirit Seal was created during the Great Divide. When the portals were sealed, the Spirit Seal was broken into nine gems and each piece was given to an Elemental Lord or Lady. These gems each have varying powers. Even possessing one of the spirit seals can allow the wielder to weaken the portals that divide Otherworld, Earthside, and the Subterranean Realms. If the all of the seals are joined together again, then all of the portals will open.

Stradolan: A being who can walk between worlds, who can walk through the shadows, using them as a method of transportation.

Supe/Supes: Short for Supernaturals. Refers to Earthside supernatural beings who are not of Fae nature. Refers to Weres, especially.

Talamh Lonrach Oll: The name for the Earthside Sovereign Fae Nation.

Triple Threat: Camille's nickname for the newly risen three Earthside Queens of Fae.

Unseelie Court: The Earthside Fae Court of Shadow and Winter, disbanded during the Great Divide. Aeval was the Unseelie Queen.

VA/Vampires Anonymous: The Earthside group started by Wade Stevens, a vampire who was a psychiatrist during life. The group is focused on helping newly born vampires adjust to their new state of existence, and to encourage vampires to avoid harming the innocent as much as possible. The VA is vying for control. Their goal is to rule the vampires of the United States and to set up an internal policing agency.

Whispering Mirror: A magical communications device that links Otherworld and Earth. Think magical video phone.

Y'Eírialiastar: The Sidhe/Fae name for Otherworld.

Y'Elestrial: The city-state in Otherworld where the D'Artigo girls were born and raised. A Fae city, recently embroiled in a civil war between the drug-crazed tyrannical Queen Lethesanar and her more level-headed sister Tanaquar, who managed to claim the throne for herself. The civil war has ended and Tanaquar is restoring order to the land.

Youkai: Loosely (very loosely) translated as Japanese demon/nature spirit. For the purposes of this series, the youkai have three shapes: the animal, the human form, and the true demon form. Unlike the demons of the Subterranean Realms, youkai are not necessarily evil by nature.

PLAYLIST FOR *COURTING DARKNESS*

I listen to a lot of music when I write, and when I talk about it online, my readers always want to know what I'm listening to for each book. So, in addition to adding the playlists to my website, I thought I'd add them in the back of each book so you can create your own if you want to hear my "soundtrack" for the books.

Aerosmith: "Sweet Emotion"

Air: "Napalm Love," "Clouds Up"

Alan Parsons Project: "Breakdown"

Alice Cooper: "Some Folks"

Alice in Chains: "Man in the Box"

Bon Jovi: "Wanted Dead or Alive"

Bravery: "Believe"

Buffalo Springfield: "For What It's Worth"

CCR: "Born on the Bayou"

Chester Bennington: "System"

Chris Isaak: "Wicked Game"

Clannad: "Newgrange," "Banba Oir," "I See Red"

Cobra Verde: "Play with Fire"

David Bowie: "Fame," "Sister Midnight"

Death Cab For Cutie: "I Will Possess Your Heart"

Deftones: "Change (In the House of Flies)"

Depeche Mode: "Dream On," "Personal Jesus"

Disturbed: "Down with the Sickness"

Everlast: "What It's Like"

Faun: "Ne Aludj El," "Deva," "Punagra," "Konigin," "Iyansa," "Rad," "Sieben"

Gabrielle Roth: "Mother Night," "Rest Your Tears Here"

Gary Numan: "Hybrid," "Cars (Hybrid Remix)," "Down in the Park," "Melt," "Halo," "Soul Protection," "Walking with Shadows," "Survival," "Sleep by Windows," "My Breathing"

Godhead: "Penetrate"

Godsmack: "Voodoo"

Gorillaz: "Stylo"

Hedningarna: "Gorrlaus," "Juopolle Joutunut," "Chicago," "Ukkonen"

Hugo: "99 Problems"

Jay Gordon: "Slept So Long"

Lady Gaga: "I Like It Rough"

Ladytron: "Mu-Tron," "Black Cat," "Ghosts," "Burning Up"

Lenny Kravitz: "American Woman"

Lindstrom and Christabelle: "Lovesick"

Little Big Town: "Bones"

Loreena McKennitt: "The Mummer's Dance," "All Soul's Night"

Low: "Half Light"

Madonna: "Four Minutes (To Save the World)"

Marilyn Manson: "Godeatgod," "Arma-Goddamn-Motherfucking-Geddon," "Tainted Love," "Sweet Dreams"

NIN: "Closer," "Sin," "Get Down Make Love," "I Do Not Want This," "Down in It," "Deep"

Nirvana: "Heart-Shaped Box," "You Know You're Right," "Come As You Are"

Notwist: "Hands on Us"

Orgy: "Blue Monday," "Social Enemies"

PCD: "Don't Cha," "Buttons"

Radiohead: "Creep," "Climbing Up the Walls"

REM: "Drive"

Rob Zombie: "Never Gonna Stop"

Rolling Stones: "Gimme Shelter"

Saliva: "Ladies and Gentlemen," "Broken Sunday"

Seether: "Remedy"

Simple Minds: "Don't You (Forget about Me)"

Sully Erna: "Avalon," "My Light," "The Rise"

Tears for Fears: "Mad World"

Thompson Twins: "The Gap"

Tina Turner: "One of the Living"

Tool: "Sober," "Schism"

Tori Amos: "Professional Widow," "Caught a Lite Sneeze," "Muhammad My Friend"

Transplants: "Diamonds and Guns"

Vartinna: "Riena (Anathema)," "Maaria, Miero (Outcast)," "Mierontie (Path of the Outcast)"

Warchild: "Ash"

Woodland: "Rose Red," "Lady and the Unicorn," "Blood of the Moon," "The Grove," "The Dragon," "I Remember," "Morgana Moon," "Gates of Twilight"

Wumpscut: "The March of the Dead"

Zero 7: "In the Waiting Line"

Dear Reader:

I hope that you enjoyed Courting Darkness, *the tenth book in the Otherworld series, as much as I enjoyed writing it. The book was dark, but it had to be, given the nature of Hyto and his anger. And I'm very happy with the way it ended.*

To clarify the time frame: Iris's story was told in Ice Shards, *which came out in the* Hexed *anthology in June 2011. So* Blood Wyne *took place in early December, immediately followed by the events in* Ice Shards. *Then* Courting Darkness *takes place. The three stories are boom, boom, boom, one after the other—all within about a three-week timeline.*

I hope you're looking forward to reading Shaded Vision, *book eleven of the Otherworld Series, available in February 2012.*

For those of you new to my books, I wanted to take this opportunity to welcome you into my worlds. For those of you who've been reading my books for a while, I wanted to thank you for revisiting the D'Artigo Sisters' world. I loved writing Courting Darkness, *and though it was a dark book, it lays the path for so many adventures to come. As the series continues to branch out, I look forward to seeing just where the sisters and their friends end up next. Which is why I'm giving you a taste of* Shaded Vision *by including the first chapter in the back of* Courting Darkness.

But if you're one of my Indigo Court readers, don't fear—book three in that series, Night Seeker, *will be out in July 2012.*

So, without taking more of your time, I'd like to present the beginning of Shaded Vision, *and I hope it whets your appetite for the next book!*

Bright Blessings,
~The Painted Panther~
Yasmine Galenorn

"I'm going to be sick! Move!" Iris shoved past me and ran to the bathroom. I could hear her retching and then, after a moment, the toilet flushed and the sound of water ran in the sink.

Grimacing, I decided she could manage on her own and busied myself by putting the finishing touches on my outfit. *Please, oh please, let me be dressed up enough for tonight.* My jeans were new, for a change, with no rips, and dark black, and I was wearing a bright fuchsia tank top with a rhinestone kitty on the front. I'd traded my utilitarian leather belt for a white leather one with a silver buckle, and I'd grudgingly changed my shit-kicker boots for a pair of suede ankle boots with three-inch heels, which put me at an even six four.

My spiky hairdo was back to the golden shade it normally ran, although I'd waffled and finally asked Iris to add in some chunky platinum highlights and a few thin black ones, and now I had tiger-striped spikes. Camille had helped me with my makeup, and I looked reasonably ready for clubbing, even though my usual night was spent hanging around in front of the TV with Shade, curled up eating junk food and trading kisses.

I slipped into my black leather jacket and patiently sat on the edge of the bed, playing with one of my kitty toys. The squeaky mouse had become a favorite of mine and—even in human form—it made me grin.

Iris poked her head out of the bathroom.

"Will you stop that damn noise? You've been obsessed with that mouse night and day for the past two weeks." She'd fixed her makeup and, with a look that told me she wasn't at all sure about our plans, she edged out of the tiled room and shouldered a smile. "Do I look okay?"

Grumpy notwithstanding, I could tell she was anxious. Six weeks pregnant, even though she wasn't showing yet; her hormones were playing her like Jimi Hendrix played his guitar. Add to that, tomorrow she was getting married, and our Talon-haltija sprite was as jumpy as a cat in a thunderstorm.

"You look beautiful," I said.

Iris looked radiant, for all she was going through. Her ankle-length hair shone like spun gold, and her face was smooth and flawless—pregnancy agreed with her in the skin department. Her eyes were luminous, round and blue as the early morning. And she still had her figure—she was curvy and buxom and for all her size, at three ten, she put me to shame.

She stared at me for a moment. As she cautiously dashed at her tears, trying to keep from messing up her mascara, she gave me a blissful smile. "You're so sweet. Can you braid my hair for me? I sure wish I had Smoky's abilities and could order it to fix itself."

"I think a lot of people want a taste of Smoky's talents." I sat her down and divided her hair into three sections. "I know I'd love to come out looking peachy clean every time we fight a battle."

After I wove one section over the other and finished it off with an elastic-coated rubber band, Iris coiled it around her head in an intricate pattern, leaving the tail end of it hanging down to her midback like a tidy, intricate ponytail.

"I wish you could, too. Then I wouldn't have so much laundry to do."

She laughed and smoothed her skirt—a gorgeous cobalt blue number she'd paired with a pale gray button-down shirt and a pair of white pumps. The Finnish house sprite looked like a pretty secretary rather than the high priestess she was. Talon-haltijas were good at blending in. Even when they could whip your butt in a battle.

"Ready?" I stood, reaching for my purse.

She closed her eyes and pressed one hand against her stomach. "My stomach feels like it won't ever be ready for anything again, but let's get a move on." As we left my room, she glanced up at me. "By this time tomorrow, I'll be Iris O'Shea. Bruce's wife. What the hell am I doing?"

I laughed at her panicked expression. "You're marrying the leprechaun you love, Iris. And you're going to have his baby, so you might as well get used to it. Life's changing." Cocking my head, I added, "So you're taking his last name?"

She nodded. "If Kuusi was my family name, I'd hyphenate. But . . . as much as I loved the Kuusis, they weren't . . . I worked for them. I tended to them but when it comes down to it, they were my employers. So I figure, I'm starting over yet again, I might as well start with another new name. Only this time it's just the last name, not both. You're right. Life is changing. And I'm embracing it."

As we headed downstairs, I realized that was so true for all of us. Life was changing all around us. Some things for the better, some things not. And there was no way to stop the ride now that we'd all gotten on board.

The guys were sitting around the living room looking guilty. Not sure what they were up to, I gave them a sideways glance as we passed into the foyer and then the kitchen where my two sisters—Camille and Menolly—were waiting with Menolly's lover, Nerissa. A trail of wolf whistles followed, and Iris gave me a look and shook her head.

"They'll be out like a light by the time we get home, want to make a bet?"

"I kind of hope so." I really didn't want to think about what kind of trouble they could get up to without us there to supervise.

Menolly's coppery cornrows shimmered under the lights,

and she was dressed in blue—tight jeans and a denim jacket over a rust-colored turtleneck. Her boots were even made of denim, and they sported thin stiletto spikes, almost as high as Camille's.

Camille, on the other hand, was fully decked out in her usual fetish noir. Chiffon skirt, a green underbust long-line waist cincher with black boning and silver hooks and eyes, beneath which she wore a shiny black spaghetti-strap top that left nothing to the imagination with regard to her DD breasts. She balanced on a pair of sky-high stilettos that I couldn't even imagine wearing and was carrying a sparkly black wrap.

And Nerissa, who was munching on a bread stick she'd found in the cupboard, wore a flirty tiered powder pink skirt that barely covered her butt, and a glitzy tank top. An Amazon of a woman, she was a werepuma who wasn't afraid to tackle life with my sister the vampire—and she was always ready to party.

Camille lit up as we entered the room. "You both look great. Sharah's meeting us at the club. Come on, let's get this show on the road and leave the house to the guys. Trillian told me they've got a fully stocked bar, but he didn't say anything about a stripper . . . I'd be surprised if they don't just end up playing that damned Xbox all evening."

Supes or not, some of our lovers and cohorts had developed an addiction to video games. It seemed odd to watch two grown demons battling it out over Super Mario or whatever was the latest Xbox rage.

"What about Maggie? Who's looking after her?"

"Don't you worry about our baby gargoyle. Hanna's watching her." Iris picked up her purse. "I'm ready."

"Then we're ready." Camille arranged her shawl. "Bruce gave us the use of his limo and driver. Ladies, our chariot awaits."

"At least we aren't headed out to get our butts kicked."

I peeked back in the living room at the guys. They looked innocent enough, but the amount of trouble an incubus, a demon, a leprechaun, a dragon, an FBH (full-blooded human), one of the dark Fae, and a half dragon, half shadow

walker could get into boggled my mind. I had a bad feeling
that without us to watch over them, they'd wreck the house.

Iris must have been reading my mind because as we clat-
tered down the porch steps, she muttered, "Here's praying
Hanna can keep those men in line."

"We're praying right along with you." Camille nodded to
the limo. "Bruce's driver is named Tony; tip him big tonight.
Okay, let's go, ladies. Iris, this is your last night as a free
woman, we're going to live it up."

"Just so long as my supper stays where it's supposed to,"
Iris countered.

As we maneuvered through the melting snow—spring
was finally on the way and though it was still cold, most of
the harsh winter snows were standing puddles of slush and
mud now—Tony got out of the car to open all the doors for
us. The limo was lush; roomy enough for six in the backseat.
I decided to push my worries away for the evening. Nothing
would go wrong. It was the night before Valentine's Day—
and the night before Iris's wedding. The gods had to be kind
to us at least once, didn't they?

The Demented Zombie lived up to all the hype except for its
name. Though not a high-class club, the disco seriously
rocked. Run by a Fae couple from Otherworld, they had
named it after a drink they served. I was determined to find
out if the drink was as good as rumor had it.

We slid through the crowd. "Do you think we'll be able to
find a table?" I asked, looking at the crowd on the dance
floor. Most of them were women, and I had a sudden feeling
Menolly and Nerissa had brought us to a lesbian bar. "Hey,
this a gay bar? Not that it matters, but . . ."

"Not so much. And we've got reservations for the big
table in back they keep for parties, so chill." Menolly shouldered her way ahead, and after a moment we caught sight of
the bar. She winked at the bartender—who looked like your
average hunky guy, except I could tell he was Were—and
motioned us over to the big table that had balloons surrounding it. Oops, dangling ribbons. I stared at them for a moment

and my tabby wanted to come out and play, but I forced the instincts back long enough to turn to Camille.

"Balloons—ribbons? You think it's such a good idea around me?"

She snorted. "Can't you control yourself for one night? Sometimes I think you use the fact that you're a werecat as an excuse to do what you want. Now, be a good Kitten, Delilah, and behave yourself."

As we slid around the table, I heard a familiar voice and looked up to see Sharah hurrying up, carrying a large pale silver box wrapped in a pink ribbon. Her blond hair caught back in a sleek ponytail, the elf looked good. Very waiflike in her go-go dress and white knee-high boots. She made retro work.

Sharah was Chase's girlfriend. Chase used to be my boyfriend, but we broke up and now were good buddies. Sharah had slipped in to fill the void and they seemed to get along together. Whatever the case, I knew enough to keep my nose out of it.

She handed me her present for Iris, and I put it with the others on a side table as the waitress came up to take our orders. We quickly went around the table. Iris couldn't drink, of course, so she ordered a glass of orange juice. Camille ordered a rum and Coke, Nerissa asked for a mai tai, Sharah and I ordered Demented Zombies, and Menolly ordered a bloody vamp—which was actually just blood, but it sounded better that way.

"Here—you have to wear this tonight." Camille pulled out a rhinestone tiara with a miniature veil attached and plunked it on top of Iris's head.

"Only if you guys are wearing party hats, too." Iris shook her finger at us, at which Nerissa pulled out a pack of sparkling princess crowns. We all slid the cardboard hats on as Iris grinned and adjusted her tiara.

The music started—Lady Gaga's "Born This Way"—and Menolly and Nerissa excused themselves to the dance floor. A stunning pair, their dancing got dirtier, and they began to pull in looks from both sides of the fence. I stifled a snort— some of the women looked jealous; others looked at them

like they were the best thing since sliced bread. Not a gay
bar, my ass. The few men around didn't look interested in
anybody but each other.

A rather tall biker chick tapped Camille on the arm.
"Dance?"

Camille blinked, but then grinned and excused herself to
work the floor as the music turned to "Weapon of Choice."
After a few seconds, Biker Chick was looking mighty impressed. Camille had lost herself to the music and they went
spinning around the floor, Biker Chick's arm hooked around
Camille's waist.

"I'm glad to see her smile," Iris whispered to me.

"Yeah, after Hyto's attack, I wasn't sure how she'd come
through." I leaned down so Iris could hear me. The noise in
the place was almost deafening.

"It will take some time for her to fully move on, but I
think she'll be okay. Eventually. Her men help a lot, especially Smoky, though it can't be easy, him looking so much
like his father."

Sharah leaned across the table. "Nerissa's counseling will
go a long way to helping, and at least Hyto didn't infect her
with any disease."

"My sister's doing a remarkable job. She always pulls
through."

I couldn't forgive our father, though, for not standing up for
her after he knew what had happened. That he'd sat in our living room, listening as she told him what horrors the crazed
dragon had put her through, and then chosen to leave had hardened my heart to him. His own daughter, kidnapped and raped,
and he walked away. Our cousin Shamas had threatened to go
home and confront him about it. We persuaded him to hold off,
but he was pissed enough to do it without our consent.

Iris tapped her fingers on the table in time to the music as
the others returned from the dance floor.

"Did you want to dance?" Menolly asked.

She shook her head. "Not the best idea. Stomach's still a
bit queasy."

Sharah handed her a packet of saltines. "Here, these will
help."

Iris munched on them. "I see presents—and they're un-opened." She grinned, motioning to the stack of boxes on the side table. We'd brought gifts from the guys, too.

"Not just yet," I said, glancing at Camille and Menolly. I'd been in charge of the party, much to their dismay, and one of the first things I'd decided was we were going to entertain Iris to the max. "Up, you two."

Camille grimaced. "Oh please, do we *have* to?"

"Yes, as excruciating as Delilah's yowls can be. We have to." Menolly's eyes were pale as frost but she smiled a toothy grin. "Come on."

A path opened in front of our table to reveal the stage and a karaoke machine. I snickered.

"You just wait. I'll get you back for this." Camille shook her head, leaping lightly up on the stage.

"Hey, Menolly's not complaining."

"*She* can *sing*! You and I are pathetic . . . well . . . mostly."

We clambered up on the stage and Menolly swung around in front of us, striking a pose with legs spread and both hands around the microphone. Camille and I took up our stations as her backup singers. The music swept in, and, with a deep breath, we dove into our rendition of "We Are Family."

We turned on the glamour, dropping our masks so our charm shone through, and the crowd went wild, laughing with us and clapping along. We spun and twisted to the music, throwing our hearts into it. Even though Camille and I weren't that great in the vocal department, we warbled away while Menolly carried the song. We'd been practicing in secret for over a week now, and though we weren't polished, we were doing a pretty good job keeping a beat to the music.

Menolly leaped off the stage, carrying the microphone with her, and danced her way over to Iris. Gently lifting the sprite onto her shoulder, with another leap she made her way back onto the stage, where she set Iris down and we sur-rounded her, singing as she clapped and swayed to the music.

People started throwing dollars on the stage, "for the bride," and by the time we finished, jazz hands and all, we'd collected seventy-five bucks and several rounds of free drinks, which put an end to Camille's and my being able to sing anything.

"You guys are great," Iris said as we headed back to the table. "And thank you. Presents now?"

I laughed, a little too loud, and burped. How many drinks had I managed to put away? I counted—there were only three glasses in front of me, but the Demented Zombie was one hell of a drink and packed more than a punch. I wasn't sure what was in it, but it was better than catnip.

I glanced around. I'd arranged for some special entertainment for the evening and—and . . . *there he was*. The guy was fine, gorgeous, with dark hair to his shoulders. Even beneath his policeman's outfit, it was obvious that he was ripped. I motioned to him and he sidled over to the table. The music dimmed and everyone around us turned to watch.

"Are you Iris Kuusi?" His voice was smooth—so smooth it made me want to slide up against him.

She blushed bright red and her eyes glistened. "Yes . . . ?"

"Iris Kuusi, you have the right to *scream as loud as you want*. You have the right to *get aroused*—" And with that, he motioned to someone at the counter, and Amanda Blank blared out from the speakers as his hips began to move.

He was a great dancer, keeping up to the beat in perfect rhythm with the rapper even as he—woo-hoo! There went the jacket, tossed on the ground near him. As he slid his hands to the cuffs of his shirt, he jerked and the shirt ripped off and landed in Iris's lap. Gleaming muscles flexed as he wrapped his arms behind his head and swiveled his hips in a move that put Elvis the Pelvis to shame.

"Wow," Sharah said, breathing softly. "Just . . . Wow . . ."

"Wow is right." I felt a little glassy-eyed myself. He looked far better than I thought he would and his dance was just . . . well . . . the way he moved his hips had me thinking about a different kind of bump and grind. Oh yeah.

Camille was looking at him suspiciously, and Menolly was staring at the crowd, but Nerissa, Sharah, and Iris were all fixated on the dancer. He slid his hips from side to side and caught my attention once again, as he grabbed hold of the waistband and—just like that—the pants flew off and over to the side.

Now in a tight G-string leaving nothing to the imagination, with fringe shimmering down the sides and in front, he began to gyrate toward Iris, whose eyes had gone immensely wide as she stared at what was coming toward her.

I was staring, too, but suddenly realized that my attention was no longer on the stripper, but on his fringe. Boy, that fringe looked like it would be fun to play with—to bat around, to yank on, to chew on . . . to. . . .

Before I could stop myself, I was shifting right at the table. A few screams echoed around me, but mostly, I heard a lot of laughter. None of it mattered as I pounced on the object of my lust. Those strings—those glorious strings, all dangling and fluttering, calling my name—and all I wanted to do was reach out and grab one and have my way with it.

"Delilah! No!" Camille's voice echoed from across the table, but the fringe was too pretty and too dangly. The next thing I knew, I'd sideswiped Stripper-Boy's thigh and was hanging from his G-string, several of the pieces of fringe in my mouth, tugging on it.

"What the fuck? Where'd the cat come from?" The guy suddenly didn't seem quite so chipper anymore. As he tried to pull away, I yanked harder.

Menolly put her arms around my tummy and tried to pry me away. Determined that the fringe was going to come with me—it was *my toy*, damn it—I held on for dear life.

Riiiippppppp. . . .and the G-string gave way. Triumphant, I held the fringed banana hammock in my mouth and started to purr, glancing up at Menolly, waiting for my praise. The least she could do was tell me what a good girl I was.

The stripper, in trying to get away from my claws, fell toward Iris in the process but managed to catch himself on the edge of the table. Iris stared at the dangling penis that now hung, free as a bird, flapping inches away from her face. She looked fascinated at first—or so I thought from my cat's fuzzy brain—but then as she opened her mouth to speak, she started to cough and, the next moment, vomited all over the stripper's goodies.

* * *

From there, it was all downhill. There was no way to salvage the evening after that. As the stripper disgustedly wiped down with a towel the barkeep gave him, I managed to gain enough control to shift back. Still tipsy, and with the taste of sweat-soaked G-string in my mouth, I blushed and cleared my throat, trying to stay steady on my feet.

Iris was wiping her mouth, totally embarrassed. Sharah and Menolly were taking care of the stripper—I saw a few extra twenties pass hands. Camille had moved over to their side.

"Dude, you've got some sort of glamour going on. Don't deny it—I can sense it a mile away. You're an FBH—full-blooded human. So what gives?" Her voice was low, but loud enough for me to catch.

He jerked his head up and stared at her. "Babe, I dunno what you're talking about."

"Don't even try with me, dude. You have no clue who you're dealing with. I just want to know where you got the potion. There'll be an extra fifty in it if you tell me the truth. And I'll know if you lie." She pulled out her purse and waved a fifty-dollar bill under his nose.

He paused, then cleared his throat. I tried to focus on what he was saying, but it was hard because the drinks and shifting and the promise of those dangling fringe pieces had all clouded my mind.

After a moment, the stripper shrugged. "What the hell. Why not? I got it from a little shop in south Seattle. Name's Alchemy for Lovers, and they said that if I put three drops on my dick before a performance, it would increase my profits. Boy, were they right." He gave a sideways glance to Iris, then me. "Well, until tonight, that is. Damn stuff burns a bit, but hey, it makes sex better, too."

He sounded vaguely hopeful, but Camille motioned for him to leave.

The bartender was giving us dirty looks, so Menolly gathered up the presents. With Nerissa carrying the cake and Camille helping to guide me, we stumbled out to the car.

Tony was waiting right where he'd parked. He opened the door and we crawled in.

Nerissa sat up front with him, holding the cake in her lap, while Camille and Iris sat on one side. Menolly, Sharah, and I sat on the other side of the back seat, and we set off for home to finish partying where we wouldn't chance ruining anybody else's evening.

We pulled in the driveway and slid out of the limo just in time to see Vanzir and Roz tossing each other around the yard. They were both stripped to their waists and were involved in what looked like some sort of Greco-Roman wrestling match.

"What the hell . . . ?" Camille stared at them, then shook her head.

"I'm not *even* going to ask." My head was pounding. Apparently the Demented Zombies weren't agreeing with me. As I squinted, I saw Bruce stumbling around, chasing a dog that looked suspiciously like Speedo, the neighbor's basset hound. "Holy crap, how much have *they* had to drink?"

"I dunno, but we've got a pair of dragons on the roof." She pointed to where Smoky and Shade were sitting on top of the roof, dangling their legs over the side. Neither looked too cozy, but they were talking and not arguing for once. A pile of rocks near the cars told us they'd been having a rock-throwing contest. At least they hadn't broken any windshields, as far as I could tell.

As we stumbled our way into the house, we found Cousin Shamas, Morio, and Chase in the living room, playing poker. The table was covered with change and dollar bills, and it looked like Chase was wiping the floor with both of them. Empty bottles of Nebelvuourian brandy and Elqaneve wine were strewn about, along with a couple empties of Irish whiskey. The smell of cigars made me want to hurl, and I glanced at Camille, who was also wrinkling her nose.

"Honey, you're home!" Morio glanced up at Camille. As he stood up, he tripped and went sprawling at her feet, where he stayed down, just reaching out to play with her strappy shoes.

"You're drunk." She moved her feet just out of reach.

"Ya think?" Morio burped and promptly dragged himself to his feet, where he threw one arm around her shoulders and one arm around Menolly's. Camille's eyes narrowed and she glanced at Menolly, who quickly sidestepped out of Morio's embrace. He still wasn't quite over the bond that had developed when some of her blood went into his veins, but Menolly seemed to have shaken it . . . or most of it.

"You're *all* drunk." I glanced around as Shade and Smoky followed us in, clutching Bruce between them. "Well, maybe not those two, but geez . . ."

The pair seemed relatively sober, but then again, they were dragons and it probably required a whole keg of hard liquor to even begin to get a dragon bombed.

Smoky took the cake from Sharah and carried it to the kitchen, returning with Trillian, who had his nose in a book. One look at Iris's pained face and Trillian set down the book and slipped back into the kitchen, returning a moment later with a package of saltines. She gave him a soft smile and began to eat.

As the guys sprawled out in the living room and we joined them, Iris made the mistake of telling them about the stripper.

Smoky leaned forward, his eyes whirling. "You watched another man remove his clothing for entertainment?" He glared at Camille.

"Chill out, Iris threw up on him and that killed the mood."

"I can't help it if I have morning sickness all the damned day!" Iris looked hurt and Camille slipped over to give her a hug, then plopped down on Smoky's lap. His hair reached up to stroke her shoulders and entwine around her waist.

"I'll bet the gentleman wasn't expecting *that* response." As Shade began to laugh, the phone rang and I picked it up.

"Delilah?" Yugi was Chase's second in command at the FH-CSI—the Faerie-Human Crime Scene Investigation unit. And he sounded so frantic I could barely understand him. "Please, we need you over here *now*. Sharah especially. It's an emergency."

"What's up?" A tingling in my gut told me that whatever it was, we were in no shape to deal with it.

"There's been a bombing at the Supe Community Council. Four confirmed deaths so far, and two people are in intensive care. We don't know how many others were in the building. Rescue teams are heading in as soon as the bomb squad confirms no more danger. Get over here. *Now.*"

As I hung up, staring helplessly at the phone and wondering if any of my friends were among the dead, I realized that regardless of the celebrations going on in our private lives, we were always on call. There would never be another moment when we could fully relax—not until we'd pushed back the demons and stopped Shadow Wing and his cronies. And even then . . . there were other horrors in the world waiting for us to stop them.

"Sober up any way you can," I said, setting the receiver back in the cradle. "We've got work to do. And it can't wait till tomorrow."

YASMINE GALENORN
Blood Wyne

AN OTHERWORLD NOVEL

We're the D'Artigo sisters: half-human, half-Fae. We're sexy, we're savvy, and we just turned in our badges to the Otherworld Intelligence Agency. My sister Camille is a wicked good witch. Deliliah's a werecat and blossoming Death Maiden. And as for me? I'm Menolly, acrobat extraordinaire turned vampire. But being a vamp isn't all it's cracked up to be, especially when the Godfather of all vampires decides to play Prince Charming . . .

It's the holiday season and a vampire serial killer is on the loose. Hungry ghosts are tearing up the town and people are running scared. I strike a deal with Ivana Krask—one of the Elder Fae—and, too late, discover strings are attached. But when I turn to Roman, one of the oldest, most powerful vampires around, for help, he offers me more than I ever bargained for.

YASMINE GALENORN

Night Veil

AN INDIGO COURT NOVEL

Cicely Waters grew up believing she was simply one of the magic-born—a witch who can control the wind—but when she returned home to New Forest, Washington, she discovered she was also one of the shifting Fae. Now she must perfect her gift. For Myst has captured Grieve, the Fae prince who holds Cicely's heart. To save both her beloved Grieve and her friend Kaylin—whose demon is waking—Cicely must journey into the depths of the Indigo Court.

But even as Cicely gathers strength, old alliances are breaking faith. And new allies, like the hedonistic vampire Lannan Altos, promise to take Cicely down a far darker path than she's ever traveled before.

"The magick [Galenorn] weaves with the written word is irresistible."
—Maggie Shayne, *New York Times* bestselling author

M829T0511

Don't miss a word from the "erotic and darkly bewitching"* series featuring the D'Artigo sisters, half-human, half-Fae supernatural agents.

By *New York Times* Bestselling Author

Yasmine Galenorn

WITCHLING
CHANGELING
DARKLING
DRAGON WYTCH
NIGHT HUNTRESS
DEMON MISTRESS
BONE MAGIC
HARVEST HUNTING
BLOOD WYNE
COURTING DARKNESS

Praise for the Otherworld series:

"Pure delight."
—MaryJanice Davidson, *New York Times*
bestselling author

"Vivid, sexy, and mesmerizing."
—*Romantic Times*

penguin.com/projectparanormal

*Jeaniene Frost, *New York Times* bestselling author

Can't get enough paranormal romance?

Looking for a place to get the latest information and connect with fellow fans?

"Like" Project Paranormal on Facebook!

- Participate in author chats
- Enter book giveaways
- Learn about the latest releases
- Get book recommendations
- Send paranormal-themed gifts to friends and more!

facebook.com/ProjectParanormalBooks